S

ON
SUPER HEROES
4

By William D. Arand

Copyright © 2022 William D. Arand
All rights reserved.

Dedicated:

To my wife, Kristin, who encouraged me in all things.

To my son, Harrison, who is always an optimist.

To my daughter, Amelia, who always offers a smile and a laugh whenever she sees me.

To my family, who always told me I could write a book if I sat down and tried.

Special Thanks to:
Bill Brush
Sarinia Phelps
Travis Ledlow
Nyx Wylder
Niusha Gutierrez

SOVEREIGN VERSE NOVELS(In Suggested Reading Order):

The Selfless Hero Trilogy(Arand):

Otherlife Dreams
Otherlife Nightmares
Otherlife Awakenings
Omnibus Edition(All Three)

Dungeon Deposed Trilogy(Arand):

Dungeon Deposed
Dungeon Deposed 2
Dungeon Deposed 3
Omnibus Edition(All Three)

Fostering Faust Trilogy(Darren):

Fostering Faust
Fostering Faust 2
Fostering Faust 3
Omnibus Edition(All Three)

Super Sales on Super Heroes Trilogy(Arand):

Super Sales on Super Heroes 1
Super Sales on Super Heroes 2
Super Sales on Super Heroes 3
Omnibus Edition(All Three)

Wild Wastes Trilogy(Darren):

Wild Wastes
Wild Wastes: Eastern Expansion
Wild Wastes: Southern Storm

Omnibus Edition(All Three)

Remnant Trilogy(Darren):

Remnant
Remnant 2
Remnant 3
Omnibus Edition(All Three)

Monster's Mercy Trilogy(Arand):

Monster's Mercy 1
Monster's Mercy 2
Monster's Mercy 3
Omnibus Edition(All Three)

Incubus Inc. Trilogy(Darren):

Incubus Inc
Incubus Inc 2
Incubus Inc 3
Omnibus Edition(All Three)

Swing Shift Trilogy(Arand):

Swing Shift
Swing Shift 2
Swing Shift 3
Omnibus Edition(All Three)

Right of Retribution Trilogy(Arand):

Right of Retribution
Right of Retribution 2
Right of Retribution 3

CULTIVATING CHAOS NOVELS:

Cultivating Chaos(Arand):

Cultivating Chaos

Cultivating Chaos 2
Cultivating Chaos 3

* * *

Chapter 1 - Root Cause Analysis -

Felix blinked, lifted a hand, and rubbed at his eyes with his wrist.

It didn't seem to really do him any good.

Sighing, he leaned back in the chair, moving away from his desk and the work he'd been doing. The light terminal in front of him held a very detailed report on everything that'd gone wrong with Legion as a company.

From the beginning start-up with him and just a handful of Heroes, using their points to make gold, and buy a pawnshop.

It hadn't been any of his actions originally that'd caused them problems.

At least, not any of the actions he'd taken as a CEO.

What'd caused them the biggest headache during the early days of Legion had been owning Kit Carrington. The Telepath known as Augur.

The Heroes' Guild had been desperate to free her and use her to fight Skipper. They had gone so far as to attack Legion constantly and even blow up a school.

Hmph. Though to be fair, if it wasn't for all that they did to stop us, I wouldn't have had all the opportunities I did.

Or the chance to really bond with Eva the way I did.

So... definitely was an oversight on my part, but it wasn't the real problem. At least, not in the end. That was correctable.

Looking at the screen, he found it was right where he left it. In the dead center of the monthly profits and losses back during that period of time.

There were incredible gains that they had made. Pushing themselves ever higher at almost every turn.

"That was when we did the best," he muttered to himself.

"Dear?" asked Andrea.

"Darling?" Adriana said at the same time.

"Love?" Myriad prompted.

Turning his head, he looked toward the couch that sat in his personal office.

The Powered mercenary who he'd picked up during that time frame was seated there in all three versions of herself. Or more accurately, the three Elex sisters.

They all shared a similar look between them.

Three sets of blue and green mismatched eyes that always held a love of life in them gazed back at him.

Even Myriad had put whatever demons she'd had to rest since returning to the fold.

Andrea reached up and tucked some of her dirty-blond hair behind an ear and tilted her head to the side. Adrianna's brown hair and Myriad's black hair were just as short, and actually cut in the exact same hairstyle.

"Oh, just… going over the final report I had put together," Felix murmured, swiveling in his chair to face them. "Felicity did most of the heavy lifting for the data and analytics and put in her own thoughts.

"It's my turn to review it and add whatever I see fit. Didn't mean to say anything aloud."

All three Elex women gave him a broad smile at that.

"Nn!" said Andrea, nodding her head quickly. "Work later, come pet us. Pregnant Seconds deserve petting. More petting than any Other or Prime."

Adriana and Myriad didn't respond to her words, though both of them just stared at Felix. Adriana had a flirty smile on her face, while Myriad had raised an eyebrow.

He still found it rather surprising that Myriad had snuck back into the city after they lost the HQ in Wal. The servers going down had brought her around to find out what'd happened.

Or more accurately, to find out why Felix had stopped writing to her.

Which he hadn't, there'd just been an issue with his email settings.

"You know, it's good to have you all with me," Felix murmured rather than responding to Andrea's request. "Any Others we need to retrieve? Are there any more of you running around out there that I need to get back? Call me selfish, but I want all of the Elex girls."

All three women looked thoughtful, looked at one another, and then back to him. He was certain they had some type of ability to talk to one another that they'd never let on about.

"No," they said in unison. "We're all here."

Nodding at that, Felix turned back to his desk.

Standing beyond it was Felicity.

At some point, she'd snuck out of his bedroom that was joined to his personal office and had joined him.

She was dressed in a t-shirt and jeans. She looked incredibly casually dressed and quite comfortable with herself.

Not to mention, she was beautiful and well-suited to such clothes.

It seemed to him that her pearl-gray skin tone made her clothes all the brighter in contrast. Her dark eyes and pitch-black hair certainly added to that belief.

Raising his gaze, he found her smiling at him.

"Good morning," she murmured to him. Then she leaned over and pressed a kiss to his lips, her hand coming up to gingerly caress his cheek. "You snuck out without even waking me."

"An Other took his place! We thought you'd sleep longer if someone was in the bed!" Andrea cheerfully provided from where she sat. "You were so cuddly and warm. We didn't really know what to do."

"I realized that after I got a handful of you, Andie," Felicity said in a dry tone, turning her head to look toward the Elex girls. Then Felicity gave Felix a wink and stood up.

"Huh? Oh. Oh! Is that why you got all handsy with us like Felix does? You were a bit rougher than him. Be softer next time," Andrea asked.

Felicity looked somewhat surprised at the words and grinned.

"What?" Adriana asked, turning to look at Andrea before the Elf could say anything.

"Here!" replied Andrea in a loud whisper that everyone could hear. "Take seven. She has the memories of it and what Felix did to her yesterday morning on the couch!"

Adriana nodded her head quickly as an Andrea materialized out of the Andrea on the couch.

She stood up, turned, and then vanished into Adriana.

A few seconds later an Adriana Other stood up off the couch, stepping away from Adriana, then moved into Myriad.

Another couple seconds passed before a Myriad Other bounced off the couch and returned to Andrea.

"I… okay then," murmured Felix and then went back to the report. In the years since knowing the Elex women, he'd learned one thing.

Don't try to understand it, just move with it.

He did wonder for a moment about the fact that they were sharing an Other between the pregnant Seconds, considering that they were being so paranoid about that only a month ago.

"Oh, you're just being soft, Andie. It wasn't that rough, Fell," Myriad said, reaching up to touch her own breasts experimentally.

"Maybe some pinching next time, Fell. Just a bit," Adriana finished, leaning back against the couch and crossing her legs.

Felicity nodded her head, then gave it a shake, before finally looking back to Felix.

"I thought I wanted some of the Elex fun, but I'm not sure I have the patience," she remarked in a concerned tone. "Or… the stamina, maybe."

"They're a lot of trouble. Especially Adriana when the mood strikes her, I've found. But they're all worth it," Felix answered conversationally as his eyes started to flick through the report again. "Faith is definitely needed to make sure they're all taken care of."

"You do get a little Miu-y sometimes," Myriad murmured, turning to look at Adriana, though there didn't seem to be any judgement in her words.

"Don't lie, Ria. We all know you like when I share those Others with you," Adriana said defensively. Then she looked at Andrea as if daring her to say anything.

Andrea only nodded and didn't look up. She was busily working away at what appeared to be troubleshooting an issue with a pistol. Pulling back the slide while pointing the gun down toward the floor, she peered into the ejector.

"I… I'm going to have to really think about my previous statement," Felicity said in a whisper, then went and got a chair. Dragging it over to where Felix sat, she set it next to him. Sitting in it, she rested her left hand on his thigh and looked at the display.

Felix smirked as he kept reading through the financial results.

Then he sighed and flicked to the next section. It was one he didn't actually want to get into because he knew this was where he'd started to make mistakes.

"I wouldn't blame yourself," reassured Felicity from beside him. "There was no way of knowing that running for government in Tilen would do that. There's no way anyone could have known about that kind of result.

"Skipper was too off the rails. Too random. No one ever managed to pin her down on an expectation."

With a grunt, Felix read through what was written.

It was more or less what he expected.

The period of time when they moved to Tilen, took over and hired through high schools, and finally became somewhat of a government functionary.

This time, he was able to note several points where profits dipped and almost became non-existent. As well as periods when there was a clear lack of funding in their bank accounts.

"It's like… looking at every single instance when I decided to get involved in the government, or politics," Felix grumbled and pointed out a few points. "It just… every time I stepped up to a stage, it got worse.

"Whenever we kept a low profile, behind the scenes, we were fine. I just kept pushing it all up to the top though. Making a target out of myself. Then Legion by proxy.

"It was never Legion that was the issue. Just me."

Felicity let out a slow breath that sounded like a balloon being deflated. She didn't argue with his statement, she just squeezed his thigh in response.

"Even when Skipper invaded and I got ripped into Tilen with Eva, it was all because I'd painted a giant target on me," Felix continued, his voice rough and angry. Then he flicked the report further along. "And this whole period is all because of me. Almost no profits. Constant losses of people. Bleeding out reserves almost as fast as we replenish it.

"If it hadn't been for Vince and everything he gave me, I'd have lost it all right there. Without everything that came from Yosemite, from the Dragons, Elves, Dryads, to you, Legion would have been ground down to nothing."

Shaking his head, he sighed and closed the report completely. He couldn't look at it anymore. There was too much frustration and far too many issues to realistically sort through without him getting emotional about it.

"Is that so?" asked Felicity while leaning forward. It forced her out of his periphery and more into his view. Her gaze was hard and her eyes were fixed on his.

"I mean... yeah? Kit was deeper into her own head than she'd ever been inside anyone else's. Lily was doing what she could for me, but I'd already locked her out.

"Same goes for my poor Beastkin over yonder. All locked out.

"You had to forcefully break your way in, then break me open, until I finally... until I finally stopped breathing my own farts."

Felicity grinned at that and wrinkled her nose. She reached up with her right hand and cupped his jaw, then gently patted him. The hand on his thigh squeezed again.

"You say the best things in the worst ways. You really are a turd, dear. It's a good thing that you're worth the effort and I love you as deeply as I do.

"Also, I'm pleased that you feel that way and think of it so," whispered Felicity, her eyes moving back and forth across his face. "It's wonderful to know you view me so highly, my sweet little Ixy."

Blushing at the pet name, Felix did his best to pretend he hadn't heard it. Instead, he cleared his throat.

"Well. Anyway, I kept pushing. More

politics, laying waste to our enemies, and forcing Legion to be a target by my own actions," continued Felix. "To the point that deities were acting against me, until I got locked on a different plane. Right up to causing an enemy to rip apart an entire government and use me as the tool to do it.

"Wal wouldn't have fallen if it weren't for me always pushing everything to the front. It's like... like watching everything falling apart and realizing I was the one who caused it all."

"You were also the one who built it all," Felicity reminded him, her hand still on his cheek. She hadn't moved away from him at all. "May I remind you that Legion is growing again? We're also bringing in fresh recruits here and there who we can scavenge from the old world.

"Those missions to bring back resources aren't just material in nature. There are people, as well. They almost immediately accept as soon as Legion is mentioned. Your Legion.

"Your Legionnaires. You built all of it. So much so that Vince—that aggressive and chaotic warlord—wanted nothing more than to heave all of the government onto you.

"He's quite happy now as a military resource. Very happy to simply lead his own forces and let everything else be handled by you or Elysia. Where the military arm of the Legion of Yosemite rolls to him, in which he passes it to Petra. Which of course all of it is still just called... Legion.

"Could just anyone have done that? I know I couldn't have done it. I know how to manage what you've built, but I couldn't have gotten it to where you did."

Felix couldn't help himself and felt his mouth curl into a small smile. His eyes dropped down to the desk in front of himself as he considered her words.

"She's right, of course," stated Miu. She'd been in the corner this entire time. Simply staying in his presence.

Ever since her death, zombification, then return to the living, she'd become less insane.

Or at least Felix thought so. No one else seemed to agree with him though.

Maybe I've just fully accepted my pet monster. My little psycho.

Looking to the corner where he knew she was—despite there being nothing to indicate she was there—Felix smiled. His eyes didn't move from the corner and he waited.

Felicity had been forced to drop her hand from his face, but she still had a hand on his leg. She was now looking in the same direction as Felix.

It wouldn't take Miu long to become overstimulated from his gaze. Even if he couldn't see her, he knew it would have an effect.

In fact, he imagined it would only take ten or twelve seconds. Counting them off in his head he waited.

Six, five, four, three—

"Fes, help me. Ask… ask him to look away," pleaded Miu. Not yet appearing, though she was clearly having an issue. "He… he can't look at me… like that. I'm… I'm on duty. I'm not his Miu right now. I'm Legion Miu."

"Fes?" questioned Felix, actually turning to look at Felicity again. He knew that word given his relationship with Vince.

Fes what was Vince's people called the woman in charge of a marriage. The "First Wife."

"Fell is Fes," Myriad answered for him.

"Our Fes is the best!" cheered Andrea a second before she pulled off the slide from the pistol. "She always smells kinda like Felix now, so I'm a little interested. Lily told me that Fell would probably let me join her and Felix in bed."

"I mean… our Fes did say she wanted some of us. She wouldn't have gone all gropey if she wasn't interested, after all," Adriana offered as an answer. "Maybe we should join her the next time she's with Felix. We could just drown her in Others like we do Felix. He always gives up and lets us do what we want. We could just pile on both of them."

"Oh, yes, yes. That could be fun. Fell is very pretty after all," Andrea blurted out. Then she leaned forward and held out the slide to Myriad. "Ria, I don't think this is fixable. Opinion?"

"Hm? Lemmie see, Andie. Back up, Ana. Your boobs are in the way," Myriad murmured, looking at the piece held out in front of her while manhandling Adriana's chest to push her backward.

"Sorry," Adriana said with a shrug as she was moved. "And that does look pretty mangled.

The hell did you do to it, pistol whip someone with the barrel?"

"Twenty-seven did it back when we left Wal and hid it from us until a week ago. It was eight's favorite pistol," grumbled Andrea.

Myriad, Adriana, and Andrea fell into their own conversation about the gun, leaving Felix to look back at Felicity in a private silence.

Felix stared at the Elf, wondering about the title she'd been given.

"I... well... Kit and Lily aren't here," Felicity said with some hesitation. Then she winced and looked down to his desk. "Someone has to lead your wives. Andie is... Andie. Miu is Miu. That really just... leaves... me, I guess.

"I'm not Kit or Lily, but I'll do my best. My absolute best for you as Fes."

Felicity lifted her face and her eyes locked on his. There was a steely determination in them that left no room for any other answer for her.

He knew her motto and what she believed in. She'd told him in no uncertain terms.

"Felix first," Felicity said in a breathless whisper. "Legion second."

"Felix first," answered Miu as if it were a call to action.

"Felix first," replied the Elex girls.

"Pancakes, a close second. Very close," added Andrea.

"Waffles," proclaimed Adriana.

"French toast, actually. Superior to both and I

can add as much powdered sugar as I want. A lot easier to make in the field, too," Myriad countered, resulting in a sudden and profound silence from Andrea and Adriana.

"Heathen," hissed Andrea. "At least a waffle is just a pancake with abs."

"Betrayer," Adriana growled, both of them now looking at Myriad.

"Well, how can I not join in? Though I'm pretty sure he doesn't swing that way at all," chimed in Felix's benefactor. An Overgod by the name of Runner Norwood. "Felix first?

"Oh, who am I kidding? I'm not handsome enough to pull off something like that. Now… if I had a name like Sameerixis. Or maybe Alexander. Then maybe I could make something happen.

"Also, if I had to pick from those three, I'm afraid I'd throw down just for bacon. Nothing else. Just bacon, with bacon, and a side of bacon. Maybe with a little extra bacon."

Runner appeared in the seat near the wall of his office.

He looked incredibly normal, as he always did. He was dressed in clothes that would fit in almost any modern-day setting.

His bright-blue eyes were directed at the ceiling rather than anywhere else and his black hair hung back behind his head without any styling to it. He didn't give off the feeling of an all-powerful Overgod.

Even though he really was one.

"So… how's it going… see you've got three very pretty Beastkin ladies," Runner said and then looked over to the Elex women. He gave them a finger-gun point. "Beautiful and pregnant. The Elex sisters. Your litters… will be amazing. You know that?"

As soon as they saw Runner, all three Wolf girls had bristled. Their ears flattened and their tails rose up.

Now they all looked as if they weren't sure whether to smile and thank him and then talk about the weather, or draw weapons.

"Nn! Why thank you!" Andrea said and clapped her hands together, before twisting to one side. "We've really been thinking of names, Mr. Overgod. Can you tell me what'd be best in the future?"

Runner blinked at the question, then laughed.

"Wouldn't that spoil the fun?" he asked instead as Adriana and Myriad slowly grew less tense. Apparently, Andrea's words had hit the right switch in them as well. "You'll do fine, Miss Andrea. Just fine. Keep to the beliefs in your head and never change that.

"Your Prime always tells you the same, does she not? You wouldn't be wearing the silver earring otherwise."

Each Second Other wore a silver earring. The Primes wore a gold one. The Thirds wore bronze. It was an easy way to tell the important Andreas, Adrianas, and Myriads apart from the others.

All three of their Primes were currently visiting the children of Vince in Yosemite. Something they did often.

"Oh! You're so very right, Mr. Overgod. Can… can you tell me how many of my litter… will make it? There's always a few that don't make it. That's what Mother told me," asked the Beastkin in a far more worried and nervous tone.

"Consider it a late baby shower gift, but your litter will survive in its entirety. All three of your litters. Right, then," Runner said and then looked back at Felix as the Elex women squealed and chattered to each other. "I've come to make you an offer. One that I think you'll like."

"Listening," said Felix, meeting his benefactor's stare.

Silence works even on gods. Doesn't it?

"Yes… it does," muttered Runner, then he sighed and sat up. "I want you to go take over a world for me. Do exactly what you did with Legion on your own home plane, but this time taking into account all the lessons you learned previously.

"And before you say no, I, of course, do have a carrot to offer as well for this. One I think you'll take and not hesitate about. A motivation and a reward all at the same time."

Felix shook his head. He didn't want to go through what he'd already gone through once. His leadership had led to a stunning defeat.

"If you complete this task, it will open the way to get Lily and Kit out. They'd be a single day away after you finished. Literally," clarified Runner, who then went absolutely silent.

He just stared at Felix.

Waiting.

Unable to help himself and feeling the weight of the silence, Felix felt the question coming up from deep inside him.

A question he couldn't stop, regardless of how much he knew the silence was working against him this time.

"When do I start?" he finally asked a second before a wolf-like smile spread out over his face.

Chapter 2 - First Pick -

"Well, let's talk details first. I know I've got your attention and that you're eager. It wouldn't do for me to take advantage of you since you're more akin to a partner to me," explained Runner with a shake of his head. "Let's take this somewhere else first. We won't be gone long, maybe an hour while we chat. You can decide what to do from there.

"And yes, before you ask, you could return here afterwards to consider what to do or say goodbye. While there's a time limit involved in the mission, it isn't exactly immediate, either. We've got a day or so before I'd need an answer."

"No need to give me such considerations," Felix stated firmly with a shake of his head. Gesturing with his hand, he made a chopping motion. He'd miss everyone and would regret not being here for a few important events, but he needed Kit and Lily back. There was no time to delay. "I accept, send me with written instructions. Now."

Runner looked unsure as he considered Felix's words. Then he shook his head and sighed.

"No. We'll talk it out first. Come on, let's go. We'll hash it out, then you can make your choice. It won't take long, but it's worth it for you to hear me out first," disagreed Runner. Then he stood up and made a small hand gesture to get up. "Well? Shall we go?"

"Yes. Can I take anyone with me?" Felix

asked, already knowing that everyone in the room would literally demand to be with him wherever he went.

In fact, he knew for certain that the Elex women were likely already contacting their Primes and Thirds to let them know what was going on.

"No. We'll only be gone for a single second to them for this chat. It'll be as if we never left and you can discuss it all with them, then. Now… shall we?" prompted Runner.

"Yes."

Felix stood up with a nod of his head.

Then was suddenly somewhere else.

It looked a lot like a living room of sorts. One that appeared quite lived in with even children's toys spread out and discarded.

A lot like what he'd seen from his nephews and nieces, in fact. Where things would just tumble out of their hands whenever something else caught their attention.

"Sorry, sorry," Runner apologized and waved a hand at the room. "I… well… once you have kids, you'll understand. I swear I cleaned up this morning when I started the day."

Runner gestured to a couch off to one side and then walked over to it. He picked up what looked a lot like an action figure and tossed it onto the nearby coffee table. Then he sat down and gestured to a recliner in front of him.

Taking the seat, Felix folded his hands into one another and then leaned forward.

"Just send me," he repeated. He really didn't care.

All he wanted was Kit and Lily back.

There would be regrets and worries aplenty, but he simply wanted them back.

"Stop. I get it," pleaded Runner with a heavy sigh. "I get it. I'd be doing the same thing you are if I had a similar chance. I'd say the same thing you are.

"But I need you to listen to me. This'll be a bit different and also the same. My request is probably the simplest answer I can give you. I need you to take over the government in the country I'm planning on dropping you in."

"Take over... as in, be a king?" asked Felix, his interest suddenly resurrected.

Resurrected and now clamoring for information.

A chance to rebuild Legion into what I had wanted. Not what I did with it, but what it should have been.

What it should have been without me shoving it into a place it never should have been.

"In whatever fashion you feel is best. So long as you could reasonably say that your choices, your decrees, would be law," elaborated Runner. "King, CEO, emperor, god, prime minister, whatever you like. So long as you are in charge.

"That's the request. How you do it, is entirely up to you. Though... based on what I can see from here, it feels like you've been recently contemplating how you'd do it again if you had the chance."

Felix was doing his best to wrestle his mind to focus on the conversation. He really needed to be paying attention to what he was being told.

"Okay," Felix managed to get out with a modicum of control. He'd already been beyond willing at the mention of getting Kit and Lily back. Now with what his benefactor had offered, the situation had only become more of a need to Felix. "What're my limitations? Last time I had deities pushing on my points in a way I felt was entirely unfair."

Runner nodded his head, winced, and then shook it.

"No limitations. There's no gods at all. They're all long dead. Killed by their own worshipers. Summoned, slaughtered, and doled out as artifacts. There's a few spirits, but they won't trouble you," answered Runner. "Your power will be in full swing. Nothing to hold it back but your own imagination.

"Though, I can tell you right now, the world won't present you with the same options it did previously. Your upgrade power will still certainly be there, but it won't be exactly the same."

"How so?" asked Felix, hoping to get some clarification.

"I'm not entirely sure, but from what I can gather, you might need extra bits and bobs to complete an upgrade. I think.

"Kinda guessing here, but I'm pretty sure that's the change. Everything else should function the same."

Extra bits and bobs? Hm.

That could be problematic depending on what exactly it is.

"Do you mean—"

"I don't know," interrupted Runner with a shrug of his shoulders. "Sorry, just trying to save you the hassle of not getting an answer. I really don't know more than what I said. I'm admitting ignorance."

Frowning, Felix stared at Runner for several seconds before finally nodding his head. If that was really all he knew, then so be it.

"What else do you know then? What other limitations would I be hitting? Any roadblocks I'd need to plan for?" asked Felix. He'd turned the corner from simply wanting to accept to wanting to know everything.

"You can only take three people with you when you go. You really will be starting over for the most part," warned Runner. "You'll be able to come back when you're done, of course. Once you're in control and at the right time, you'll be able to direct the flow of events. Make it so a portal could be built very quickly.

"Oh, and anyone you bring with you might end up changed. This world is and isn't similar to your original one."

"Changed. Changed how?" prompted Felix

when Runner leaned backed in the couch and stopped talking.

"Uh... oh, an example then. So if Felicity went with you, she'd be permanently turned into a Human, lose all her magical powers, and become quite ordinary.

"Though someone like Miu wouldn't be as bad off. She'd lose the superpowers that weren't hers at birth, like all those shadow assassin things, and return to how she was when you first met her.

"Or at least, that superpower. She'll still be Miu and... well... insane. Though I won't deny, I've always had a soft spot for the ones that are a bit cracked. You should meet my wife, Minxy."

Processing what he'd been told, Felix really didn't like what he'd heard.

"Can I get a list of what would happen to everyone I could bring with me?" inquired Felix. "I wouldn't want to bring someone just to have them irrevocably changed. And it'd be permanent, right?"

"Yeah, it'd be permanent. Any change made to get you all there, couldn't be undone. Just as you ended up changing when you stepped onto Legion planet, by the way. You just didn't notice the changes since there were so many points of congruence.

"The world I'm sending you to has a lot less of those. A lot fewer things that it can simply adapt to. It has far more variables that'll simply be forced on you.

"So yes, Felicity would permanently become

a Human. Miu would lose her wraith-like powers. You could theoretically change them with your own power once you got there, but… that'd be very expensive to do so. Prohibitively so.

"And before you ask, I don't get to change what things will cost to you. That was assigned by the world and… and the… and the guardian spirit who guides it. I can do many, many things. Act in many ways. But the worlds you're inhabiting are not… ones I can truly meddle in. Not freely."

"Could you move me and my people to a world you could actually meddle in?" asked Felix in a sudden fit of curiosity.

Runner's face clouded up in thought as he considered the question.

"After I kill Zeus, that man you met made of static, yeah. I could," admitted Runner. "Could fix anyone you brought with you to the new world as well. Wouldn't be an issue.

"Assuming… well, assuming we won. If we didn't, then… there ya go. It's a war of Overgods, I suppose you could say."

Hm.

It's a lot to risk.

Would Felicity even be the same after that? Is part of who she is mentally part of her Elven heritage?

"List?" Felix requested for the second time.

"Ah, yeah. Sorry, here. There will probably be a few changes that don't appear on that paper, but they're minor and hold no consequence to you," mumbled Runner, flicking his finger toward the table. A piece of paper appeared there.

Picking it up, Felix began reading through it quickly.

Adriana Elex	Power Limit: Five same Others until **DATE**
Andrea Elex	Power Limit: Five same Others until **DATE**
Berenga Campbell	Race change to Human, Prosthetics Failure
Blue	Limited magic until **DATE**
Caroline Campbell	Race change to Human, No magic until **DATE**
Daphne Campbell	Limited magic until **DATE**
Edith Torres	None
Erica Newberg	None
Eva Campbell	Power Limit: All powers removed
Faith	Limited magic until **DATE**
Felicia Illiescu	Race change to Human
Felicity	Race change to Human, No magic until **DATE**
Green	Limited magic until **DATE**
Goldie	None
Ioana Illiescu	None
Jessica	None
Karya Campbell	Limited magic until **DATE**

Kris	None
Leila Campbell	Race change to Human
Mouth	Limited magic until **DATE**
Miu Mikki	Power Limit: Original powers only
Myriad Elex	Power Limit: Five same Others until **DATE**
Petra Campbell	Race change to Human
Ramona Campbell	Race change to Human
Red Campbell	Race change to Human
Talia Waas	Race change to Human
Taylor Campbell	None
Thera Campbell	Race change to Human
Victoria Volante	Power Limit: Original powers only

Reading over the list several times, Felix felt like he got the gist of it and set it down. Looking at Runner, he couldn't help but smirk.

"So many Campbells. Seems like Vince is trying to repopulate a city by himself," he remarked with a shake of his head.

"Your brother is very in touch with his desires," Runner laughingly said. "I rather like his approach. But yes, he has a much higher… body count… than you do.

"Nothing wrong with that by the way. I keep trying to keep my own down but events conspire against me.

"Now… questions?"

"Dragons, Humans, and Beastkin aren't changed. Not really, at least," murmured Felix with a gesture of his hand to the paper.

"Yes. Dragons died out with the dinosaurs, but they existed," admitted Runner with a shrug. "The Beastkin didn't actually exist in this world, but there was a reasonable precursor race that had a few very similar genetic offshoots. It'll work well enough to modify them. Dryads exist but are more on the 'Nymph' side of their heritage here. Won't change much for them.

"As for Elves… there's never been Elves there. Not a one. Or Dwarves. Honestly, this world is very mundane. Extremely so.

"No magic of any type whatsoever. Well, a few faith-based magics. A Dryad could do a couple of things, but nothing huge. No Powereds, really. No mythical creatures outside of a few one-offs.

"It's all science. All technology. Big on physics and natural laws. Not so much on the theoretical stuff. I wouldn't expect to be fielding energy weapons any time soon.

"At least… until after the day of awakening. When supers start to show up."

"I figured that's what this… date… was. Something akin to a world-altering event that would shift everything."

"Yup. Awakening. The day people start to develop powers and abilities. Some of them get magic, like… ah… magic-like powers."

You were going to say Lily.

Weren't you?

Runner coughed into his hand, then looked around as if he were trying to figure out something. Apparently, he didn't want to admit he was reading Felix's mind right now.

"It's alright. I'm not upset about it at the moment. I can get her back. You said that this would lead to her. Didn't you?" pressed Felix.

"I did," confirmed Runner, now meeting Felix's eyes. "And it will. This will directly lead to getting Kit and Lily back. Ryker… err… Uncle… set it up that way.

"Once the Guardian Trials are activated, a bunch of other things will trigger across the planes and worlds. It'd be much more difficult without it going live."

"Right… so my job is to take over the government of wherever I end up and I need to do it… by a certain date?" asked Felix and lifted up his hand. He'd lifted two fingers already.

"Not by that date, no. You'll probably want to already have influence by that point, though. It'd help. As for the Awakening itself, it's about two years and twenty-two days off. You have some time to work with for that alone."

"Yeah… need to have influence by a certain date. Is there a date I actually need to get this done by though?" Felix asked.

"Ah… about six years from where you start.

Give or take several months. Like I said, this isn't a sprint. More of a marathon."

Felix held up a third finger. Then a fourth before he'd even gotten to the next point.

"Six years is my time frame. I can only take three people. Those I take could be, and would be, irreversibly changed."

"Yeah, that's about right. Those are the salient points you've got there."

"No going back and forth, right? Nor can I take anything with me?" asked Felix.

"It's... yeah. One-way trip until completion. I might be able to make some changes on the Awakening day, but it'd be really limited in scope and size. It'd cost me too much to let people go back and forth or send a fourth person with you.

"And no, nothing with you. Just your bodies. Even your clothes won't be going with you. You'll literally appear without anything. Even any dental work you had would be reverted to normal."

Felix stared into the middle space between himself and Runner as he thought on that. He needed to be incredibly picky about who he brought with him.

He needed power. Needed survivors.

Those who had enough willpower to push through things that would drive weaker people to their knees.

"Eliminate everyone from Vince's side from the list. I wouldn't feel right taking one of them," murmured Felix, still staring into nothing. "Then...

get rid of the Elves."

He really didn't want to leave Felicity behind. Having her with him would make his life infinitely easier.

Except he wasn't sure of that. There was no guarantee that the change in race wouldn't mess with her. On top of losing her magic, as well.

Not to mention... I think I'd need her to stay behind and act as my proxy. I'll be gone for years and... well... she's the only one I'd trust.

She can act in my stead and carry out what I'd do. She was already doing a great deal of the heavy lifting for me.

"Done and done," reported Runner.

"Check off Ioana and Felicia. I couldn't bear to take one and not the other. Those two are way too happy with one another for me to separate them. I'd feel like a tool bag."

"Also done. By the way, I should make one point very clear in this, if you take Andrea, and either Adriana or Myriad, they'll all be combined. By five same Others, that includes the different iterations of the original Andrea Elex. So if you take an Elex, only take one. It'd be a waste of a slot otherwise and they'd be forcefully combined. Even if they were a Prime."

With a grunt, Felix shook his head.

He couldn't deny he'd considered taking all three Primes and all of their Others with him. In a way, they were most certainly his ace in the hole.

He could have easily started banking things

up and expanding her ability to make more Others.

"Any other last-minute points of note?" grumbled Felix.

"Slavery is completely outlawed here. On top of that, with no actual magic to back-up contracts, there's no way for you to legally own someone there," Runner offered up helpfully. "You'll have to earn your points through other means rather than owning people.

"Oh, and I completely forgot one detail. Your power doesn't reset at midnight. It's more like a bank account rather than a daily limit. Your daily amounts become deposits to that account if unused."

Several ideas flipped through Felix's head as he considered that. He didn't think it'd be too much of an issue.

In fact he thought it'd be rather helpful.

"Well… own anyone outside of the three you bring with you. You'd own them, of course. For everyone and everything else, you'd have to obey the laws of the land," finished Runner.

"I'd own… them? Hm," mused Felix, instantly thinking about the Dragons. "Remove Adriana and Myriad. As well as Eva, Edith, Erica, and Jessica as well."

"Okay. That leaves you with Andrea, Faith, Goldie, Kris, Miu, and Victoria. Not to mention the other Dryads and Dragons in your bodyguard team," summarized Runner. "And yes, you could take all Dragons with you. Though they can't really hide their horns or… well… scales. No magic for them to truly use, remember?

"They'd look as they always do in their Human version of themselves, in a Human-only world. You'd have to get up some points to modify them a bit before you could really go into public with them. I like the direction though. They can shape change into their Dragon form as they like, of course."

"Fine… fine. Okay. Andrea and Goldie then to start with," finalized Felix with a nod. With those two at his side, he'd have a great deal to work with.

While Andrea could do many things simply because of her others, she also had a massive amount of generalized knowledge. After having done so much through so many Others, her ability and experience were incredibly high.

Goldie could be his powerhouse. Kris would likely be far too "Dragon-like" in her personality. It was entirely possible she could go off into a rage and he couldn't stop her.

On the other side of the argument, there was no way he could forget walking in on Goldie happily altering his clothes as if it were the most normal thing in the world.

He also distinctly remembered her taking on modern military weaponry, including tanks and helicopters, and actually coming out the other side mostly intact. Or at least intact enough that she could regenerate the rest.

"Amongst those left then are… Faith, Miu, and Victoria. Not sure what I'd do, to be honest," confessed Runner.

Felix could only agree with that sentiment for a few seconds before he realized that wasn't quite true. Miu and Victoria were mostly interchangeable.

If Miu was being reduced down to her original power set, then she'd be on parity with Victoria.

"Faith… or Miu slash Victoria," murmured Felix.

He knew he'd already have some issues with Goldie as she tended to be somewhat of a walking sex-dream. Doubly so when she decided to get cuddly or warm-hearted with him.

If he added Faith into that mix, he'd have to really work at keeping himself on track. On track and not stuck in a rut.

A rut of rutting Faith and Goldie, that was.

"I mean maybe I'm just the horn dog in the room, but I'd take Faith. She's lovely. Very lovely. Would definitely help with what magic she has to keep Goldie and Andrea going," interjected Runner. "Not to mention… well… she's almost just as good as Miu. Since she'll be reverted back to where she originally was with her powers."

As soon as Runner mentioned Miu being given her original powers, Felix had a stray thought. One he knew would work, but he needed to smother it.

To not make it prominent in his mind.

He began to think earnestly and hard about Faith. All the things he'd done to her, and what she'd done to him. Over and over in his mind, running it around repeatedly

"Yep, Faith it is," Felix said aloud with a nod of his head. "No need to send me back to talk to the others or think it over. You can just put me, Goldie, Andrea, and Faith on that planet.

"Well, after you make sure they're willing to go with me. I wouldn't want to just yank them along without getting their permission. Can ya do that?

"Let's get started. You can just let Miu and Felicity know what happened and where I'm going. They'll figure it out just fine. They'll alert the others and Vince."

All the while, Felix kept thinking about absolutely having his way with Faith and Goldie. Endlessly throwing those thoughts into the open space of his mind.

"I… okay. Right, then. I can do that," agreed Runner. "I'll check in with the selected and let the others know. Alright."

Runner shook his head, then made a shooing motion toward Felix.

Then in the next instant, he was in an open field of grass wearing his very own birthday suit.

At least Goldie, Andrea, and Faith were all nearby, wearing their own birthday suits.

Chapter 3 - Unstoppable Object -

Unable to help himself, Felix did get more than an eyeful of the three women. He didn't even hide that he gave them a once-over each before he made sure his eyes were head level.

"Goodness. This is certainly an odd world," murmured Faith, causing Felix to look her way again.

The green-eyed, over-sexually-developed Dryad was watching him with some confusion lingering in her face. Her blond hair was pulled back in a ponytail behind her head and every bit of her was on display.

Normally, her skin had a bit more green tint to it but right now it seemed far more normal in tone. Her slightly pointed ears had also shortened down a considerable amount and appeared quite Human.

None of that was what concerned him though, it was the sudden mischievous smile that blossomed on her pretty face.

A smile he'd come to interpret as her contemplating smashing him with a lot of sexual magic.

When she hit him with it, he felt a deep desire to pin her down in the grass and take everything she always offered him. Except this time, it wasn't as compelling as it normally was.

It didn't have the same bite it used to.

In fact, he was able to ignore it for the most

part.

"The air tastes so similar to the way your own world did. Slightly toxic and not as it should be," remarked Goldie, standing not far from him.

Then she turned to look at him head-on along with directing the front of her body toward him. He'd come to realize previously that Dryads and Dragons would always turn to face him completely whenever he was around, unless they were guarding him and looking for threats.

Golden horns came up from her bright-gold hair. She often wore it in a simple fashion that hung straight down without any braiding, ties, or bands. Her elongated ears stuck out from it as well.

Her full, hourglass figure made every other woman that she appeared around look almost masculine. To say it simply, Goldie reeked of a woman shaped from fantasies and artistry.

Thankfully, she didn't show any of the golden scales that typically came along with her Human guise.

It meant one less thing to worry about.

"Field!" blurted out Andrea, then promptly started running around in the grass. Her tail whipped about as she sprinted one way and then the other.

"Well, thank you for agreeing to come with me," Felix said, glancing up at the blue sky above them and away from the women standing around him. As far as he could tell, everything seemed rather normal so far.

"Of course. I'm delighted to be chosen," Goldie said, laying a hand on her well-endowed chest. "Among all of the Legion of Yosemite, I was handpicked by you. I'll not disappoint you, Felix."

"Exactly," added Faith, coming to stand next to Goldie. "I know we Dryads are new to Legion as a whole, but it was very flattering to know that one of us was requested. That I was requested."

Felix gave them a wide smile and focused all of his thoughts on keeping his eyes at the level of their face. He needed to maintain a certain level of awareness with these two.

Otherwise, they'd drown him in their desires while inflaming his own.

Andrea bounded past Goldie and Faith in that moment to jump up at Felix. He had only a single second to put his right foot back and brace himself before she slammed into him.

Her legs wrapped around his waist and her arms went over his shoulders.

Her bright mismatched eyes were wide and staring at him from inches away. He noticed that in her ear was a bronze earring.

"Third?" he asked with some confusion. He certainly hadn't expected Andrea Prime, Second, or Third to come with him. He'd honestly been betting on just a handful of regular Others.

"Nn!" declared Andrea, her ankles locked into place at the small of his back. "We decided you needed our best efforts that we could provide.

"I brought with me Third Adriana and Third

Myriad. Though we can't separate right now. We're still… adapting… to the changes. I know I can separate; I can feel it.

"I just know that I shouldn't yet. Not for a little while at least. It wouldn't be good, I think."

Smiling, Andrea then kissed him quite roughly, only to pull away.

"That's okay. It's nice to have all the Third's in one spot. It's like we used to be now. Somewhat interesting as well though, since all our personalities were so much more well-defined," continued Andrea who seemed completely uncaring about how she was hanging on him. "I'm kinda surprised though. I thought you'd bring Miu along after I heard it all."

"Oh… I did bring Miu along actually," argued Felix as he began pushing Andrea off himself. She didn't fight him and let him pry her off. "See, Miu is exactly who she always was. Always will be.

"I know her. Know her as well as I know all of you. She's going to decide that she needs to be with me. Then she's going to go after Runner. Go after him and become the biggest annoyance he's ever known.

"Every single time she figures out what bothers him, she's going to amplify that. Her powers make that easy for her. Up until the point where he literally will be better off just sending her here, rather than dealing with her.

"Especially since I didn't say goodbye to her. I left it hanging as a question. She'll get paranoid and think everything he says is wrong or twisted over."

"Ah, yeah. I could see that," Faith admitted with a deep chuckle. She moved to the side, popping one hip out and bracing her hand on the other hip. It was an eye-catching pose.

Goldie and Faith often acted in a similar way to how Lily used to. Doing a multitude of things simply to catch his attention and then leveraging it.

"Can you blame us? It always worked for her. It'll work for us," questioned Goldie, reminding him in that moment that she could actually get into his head.

There was a moment of panic in him as he realized Goldie would be able to delve to the absolute limit through his mind and thoughts.

Legion rings don't exist here.

I can't seem to lock her out as her owner, either.

Damn.

"For what it's worth, I'd be happy to fall into such a rut as what you were thinking about previously," purred the golden Dragon. "Though I promise I won't let that happen. We're here for bigger things.

"Here to get back what we lost. I'll be your Lily, Felicity, and Kit, all in one to the best of my ability.

"And to answer your unspoken question… Runner came to us immediately after you vanished. It was only a second or so after. Then he took us off individually. I was the last to be spoken to and by that point Miu was extremely agitated."

"Ah... I see. Then I imagine she'll be here soon enough," Felix mused aloud, lifting his head and peering up into the sky. "He did say it'd cost him too much, but not that he couldn't do it.

"Well, let's see what we have to work with. Then we can plan accordingly while we wait for Miu."

Felix called up his power. He wanted to see the points available to him as he'd grown accustomed to seeing it.

First names, points, bonuses. Just like always.

A blue screen appeared in the thin air in front of him. It was similar to his normal screen, though it also appeared different.

Even the font is a little different.

	Generated	**Remaining**
Andrea	500	500
Faith	200	200
Felix	1,000	1,000
Goldie	1,900	1,900
+Loyalty Bonus	300	300
+Marital Bonus	300	300
=Daily Total	**4,200**	**4,200**
Banked Total	—	**0**

"Huh. Marital bonus," muttered Felix, reading over the screen that floated in the air before him. "And why am I worth so much? In fact, why am I even listed? That's kind of surprising. I see what he meant about it being more like a bank account, though."

"Oh! How much am I worth? Tell meeeeeee," demanded Andrea, bouncing in place directly in front of him. It was terribly distracting and Felix had to force himself to ignore her.

"You're worth five hundred, Andie. Though I think that's you and your Others, really. Perhaps a hundred points per person," Goldie filled in for Felix. "As an example, Faith is worth two hundred. I'm worth nineteen hundred. Though surprisingly, Felix is worth a thousand for himself. Which is very different."

"What? Only five hundred? I'm worth more than that," grumped Andrea, folding her arms across her bare chest.

"Andie, I'm not even worth that much," lamented Faith. "I suppose I'll have to… earn… my keep in different ways."

He felt the cudgel of sexual magic lash out at him from Faith once again.

"Stop hitting him with that 'come hither' magic, Faith. He's right, we need to focus. Go over to that tree line and see if the trees can tell us anything of use," admonished Goldie with a warm, kind voice. She'd even reached over and laid a hand on Faith's back as she spoke. The Dryad gave her a smile and then started off at a light jog toward the indicated trees.

"Andie, start stalking the surrounding area. We have no idea where we are or what's around us.

See if you can't spot anything that might help us in the immediate vicinity but don't get spotted. Remember, this is almost a Human-only world. You and I don't fit in here," warned Goldie, making a gentle shooing motion with her hands at the Beastkin.

"Hai! I'll do that, Goldie!" stated Andrea with an odd military-like salute toward Goldie. Then she took off in a flash, running for the distant horizon.

Smirking, Felix was rather grateful for Goldie being here.

He still regretted not having Felicity, Kit, or Lily with him, but Goldie was clearly working to make that regret non-existent.

"Thank you," murmured Felix as he closed his point screen.

"Of course, Nest-mate. I'll be your everything and do anything," emphasized Goldie with a purr. Then she shook her head a bit and grinned. "I'm going to enjoy this, I think. My poor Dragon had swooned for you so long ago and just wanted to nest. It'll be quite lovely to start an organization with you here."

Nodding his head, Felix couldn't disagree. He was really looking forward to starting over again.

Looking at Goldie, he called up her stat screen. He wanted to see all the ins and outs of her.

Name: Goldie Campbell	**Race**: Progenitor Dragon-Extinct in the Wild

Alias: The Golden One	**Power:** None
Physical Status: Healthy, Ready to Nest	**Mental Status:** Thrilled, Excited, Ready to Nest
Positive Statuses: Ready to Nest	**Negative Statuses**: Ready to Nest

Might:	87	Add +1? (870)
Finesse:	55	Add +1? (550)
Endurance:	94	Add +1? (940)
Competency:	71	Add +1? (710)
Intellect:	43	Add +1? (430)
Perception:	69(Nice)	Add +1? (690) +1 Awareness Type
Luck:	14	Add +1? (140)

I… what?

Awareness type?

Goldie Campbell?

I didn't marry her though. So… what?

Also, why is she listed as a Progenitor Dragon? Have… I ever looked at her stats before? They're also somewhat different than the expectation.

And is fourteen luck low, or average?

I need a baseline; this was almost pointless.

"What's a Progenitor Dragon, The Golden One?" asked Felix as he turned his head to look at Faith's retreating backside.

He pulled up her stat screen as well.

Name: Faith Campbell	**Race**: Nature Sprit (Dryad)-

	Critically Endangered
Alias: None	**Power:** None
Physical Status: Healthy, Fertile	**Mental Status:** Content, gratified
Positive Statuses: None	**Negative Statuses**: None

Might:	23	Add +1? (230)
Finesse:	37	Add +1? (370)
Endurance:	89	Add +1? (890) +1 Stamina Type
Competency:	31	Add +1? (310)
Intellect:	78	Add +1? (780)
Perception:	29	Add +1? (290) +1 Awareness Type
Luck:	17	Add +1? (170)

Okay, right.

I'm married to all three, I bet.

And there's also a Stamina type in addition to the Awareness type.

This must be what Runner was talking about.

Additionally, based on Faith compared to Goldie, it seems like a Human baseline might be somewhere in the ten to thirty range?

Though I didn't expect Faith to have a higher intellect score than Goldie. Maybe that's the competency aspect. One can apply what they have better?

Things to learn.

"Oh. That. I'm just really old, Nest-mate.

Don't you worry about it. I spent most of my early life sleeping and letting the world go by," Goldie said in an offhand way. As if it didn't matter at all that she literally had "progenitor" in her race name. "Not being a normal Dragon, I had no interest in most things and it was easier to doze."

Felix didn't quite believe that and gave her a pointed glance. Then he looked off to where Andrea had vanished.

He couldn't see her.

I'll have to check her screen later.

"Yes, yes. I hear you," assured Goldie. "It really is nothing. I'm just a bit different than a normal Dragon. That's all. I really did just sleep it all away and—"

There was a boom of thunder above Felix, followed by what felt like an insane roller-coaster ride of extreme nausea and vertigo.

As sudden as it began, it ended. With only the appearance of Miu heralding that anything had happened at all.

Standing several feet away, she looked incredibly angry. Angry, cross, and absolutely at her wits' end.

She was athletically built and fit right in the expected body type for her Asian heritage. Her pale skin, dark eyes, and short black hair were all part of that expectation as well.

Where she might have been only cute or pretty several months ago, she'd taken an order he'd given to take care of herself, to an extreme. Miu was an incredibly beautiful woman now who radiated that beauty out around her.

"You left me," came a hissing voice from between Miu's clenched teeth.

Ah… shit.

I guess I didn't think of the fact she'd be angry at me.

Even sounds like when she became a zombie.

"No, he didn't," Goldie countered before anything further could be said. With a shake of her head, she looked at the other woman with a smile. "He actually said he expected you to be here soon. He knew that you'd bother, pester, and annoy Runner until he brought you here.

"It was the very reason he didn't pick you. He knew he could rely on you showing up all on your own. It let him get the best deal he could manage by relying on you."

Felix nodded while holding Miu's gaze. That was exactly what he'd been thinking, in fact.

Goldie had plucked it all out of him like using a net to catch fish in a barrel.

The anger and hurt look on Miu's face fell away in an instant. Her eyes began to twitch and her body started to shudder. Her fingers began to curl reflexively and pull at her own upper arms. Then she started to breathe harder.

"F… Felix, please… look away," she asked instead, all sign of her being upset with him fleeing. All that was left was the mentally broken, shattered Miu he'd known all along.

"Of course, I won't," Felix stated flatly. "I needed my Miu. My Miu came to me just like I knew she would. She did exactly what I expected and needed. I'm going to look at my Miu. She's not Legion's Miu, she's my Miu.

"Aren't you? Aren't you my Miu? My beautiful Miu?"

He knew he needed to push on her just a bit. This would set the tone for her for the rest of their trip here.

If she was his, not Legion's, then he could control her powers to fit his needs. Her being his, after all.

"In fact, your name isn't Miu Mikki anymore," continued Felix, slowly walking toward the diminutive, psychopathic woman. "By coming here, you changed your name. I can see it in your stat screen. Can you guess what your name is? I bet you know. In fact, I bet Runner told you. Seems like it was part of the condition for me to get points from you."

Miu wasn't able to look away from him. Instead, she continued to tremble like a leaf in a windstorm.

"Can you tell me your name, my Miu?" asked Felix in a soft whisper, reaching up to cup her cheek with his right hand. "Because if you have a different name, wouldn't that mean the time for control is over?"

That did it.

There was a sharp twitch from Miu, who then

went completely still. She stared at him now as if someone had just opened a door in front of her.

"I'm Miu Campbell. I… I know my name. He told me I'd have to be your wife to be here," whimpered Miu in a tiny voice, her breath coming out in ragged gasps and sharp exhales. "He also… also told… told me—"

Miu blinked, dove forward, and bit down on Felix's shoulder. Her teeth sank in deep and her arms wrapped around his middle, clutching him with her entire being.

Holding her in return, Felix laid his arms over her shoulders and began to rock her back and forth. The whole time she was gnawing at him.

Which was quite painful, if he had to be honest with himself.

"The Overgod told her to tell you, that while that was a nasty little trick you pulled on him, he'll get you back later. Also that Miu is worth eight hundred points," Goldie offered, filling in what Miu couldn't finish. "From what I can see from Miu's mind, she… really… really made an annoyance out of herself to him.

"Apparently, she even started a religion dedicated to Runner, the fallen god of dirty toilets. There were a number of priests who were already starting to gain faith powers in that belief. That was the point when Runner gave in. It's been about a month by the way. A month in the other world since we've been here. Time is flowing very… strangely."

Unable to help it, Felix snorted at that and just held onto Miu. It sounded rather amusing to him.

Runner was fooling around with time and that wasn't very surprising to Felix at all.

"Feeeeeelix!" called Andrea in the distance.

Turning partly, he looked toward where the call had come from.

Andrea was heading his way at a dead sprint. In her arms was a massive bundle of clothing in a variety of colors.

"Did he tell you all that you'd be my wives, my Golden One?" Felix asked quietly, laying his cheek against Miu's temple.

"I… yes. He did. It was part of the agreement. All your wives. You'll receive points from us unless we divorce you officially by the laws of this land. And just Goldie is fine. Or… or your Goldie. That'd be perfect," Goldie requested, her tone becoming almost pleading at the end.

"My Goldie. Thank you," muttered Felix as he called up Andrea's stat screen. He ignored the fact that it looked like Goldie's eyes were actually glowing.

Name: Andrea Campbell		**Race**: Beastkin(Wolf)-Extinct in the Wild
Alias: Myriad, Adriana, Andie, Ria, Ana		**Power:** Multiple Selves / Partitioned Mind
Physical Status: Healthy.		**Mental Status:** Excited, In Love
Positive Statuses: In Love		**Negative Statuses**: In Love
Might:	17	Add +1? (170)

Finesse:	21	Add +1? (210)
Endurance:	29	Add +1? (290) +1 Stamina Type
Competency:	13	Add +1? (130)
Intellect:	12	Add +1? (120)
Perception:	58	Add +1? (580)
Luck:	97	Add +1? (970)

Stamina type… huh. But only on anything that ends in nine.

Damn. Her luck is incredibly high in this world. I can't even remember what it was previously, but it wasn't that high.

Clearly some stats have shifted around since coming here.

Also, somewhat curious about the fact that being in love hits both the negative and positive sides.

Same thing for the ready to nest status.

By the way, my Goldie, how long have you been holding the reins on that need to nest? I couldn't even tell from the outside.

"You're lucky I haven't tied you to a bed in the vault and taken what I crave from you after ripping out my birth control with my claws," Goldie chirped brightly with a great deal of warmth in her voice.

"He ties me to the bed sometimes," whispered Miu after releasing her bite and rubbing her cheek against his shoulder. "I like it. I give him all the control and let him do whatever he wants."

Andrea came to a stop next to them, her tail swishing back and forth behind her wildly. In her mouth looked to be a pair of women's underwear. She was also smiling from ear to ear.

"I found clothes!" she said in a partially muffled voice. Then spat out the bright yellow panties into the pile in her arms. "Well, stole clothes. Found them, then stole them. They had them on a washing line behind their house.

"I also found a road. There was a sign not too far off. We're about three miles away from a place called Brandonville.

"That and there's apparently a correctional facility on the way. We could probably get some equipment from their armory. It's been a while since I broke into a prison."

Looking thoughtful Andrea than shook her head.

"Never mind, that's wrong. Hehe. I never broke into a prison," she corrected with a wide smile that showed off all of her teeth. "I only ever broke out of them! You'd think they'd have learned after the third time. A super villain is never bound by prisons if they try hard enough."

Ah… yeah. I didn't take a moral compass with me.

I took an ex-super villain, a Dragon, and a Nymph.

Sorry, Kit… morality only plays into effect if it doesn't impede me.

"No. No prison. We're heading to that city. Town. Whatever. We need supplies," Felix stated firmly. "We're going to go into town on Goldie's back, find some businesses that are chains owned by larger companies, and take what we need. All under the cover of night.

"That's the second order of business though. For right now… let's sort through the clothes you've brought and see what we can do. Later on… we'll give something back to whoever we stole these from. It's one thing to rob a company, it's another to rob a person."

Chapter 4 - In the Dumps -

"A lot of churches, not much else," Andrea said loudly over the rustle of the wind. Goldie was very slowly circling over the small location they'd found by following the road.

"Yeah," Felix said under his breath with a shake of his head. What they were looking at really seemed like it was rural.

Very rural.

While he wasn't against such a location at his starting point, it was also something that might prove to be rather difficult. If there wasn't money in the area, there'd be even less for him to take from others.

With his power limited to possession, that meant ownership of material or land. Since people weren't part of that equation anymore, it meant he had to really change things up.

Miu was wrapped around him from behind, Andrea sitting directly in front of him, and Faith in front of her. They were all clinging to Goldie's back by their bare hands and thighs.

She had to go quite slowly so they didn't get thrown.

"That one," Faith said and pointed an arm toward a building off to one side. It looked much larger than any of the other buildings nearby and had signage.

It had the look of a chain or a store that was part of a larger operation.

"That'll work. We need camping gear anyway, since we have no money. Let alone identification," grumbled Felix. "Goldie, get us down there on the roof. We'll break through and take what we need."

"Okay. Please hang on. I'm doing my best," called Goldie as she started to bring them in slowly toward the building.

"You're doing great, Goldie, just keep doing it!" responded Felix with as strong a hand pat on her spine as he could manage. Hitting a Dragon's scales really wouldn't do very much but he had to at least try.

In no time at all, Goldie had brought them down right on top of the building. Before her claws even made contact with the roof, she'd already started changing into her Human version.

Everyone hopped off before that happened.

Everyone except Andie, who clung onto Goldie like a backpack.

"You… are amazing," Andrea said in a tone that was more like a statement. "Truly… amazing to see. And beautiful. Beautiful and amazing. You make my heart beat a little faster. Not as much as darling, but a little faster than normal."

Andrea finished by kissing the Dragon's cheek, though she didn't get down yet.

"Thanks, Andie. I'm flattered. But I'm not interested in women at the moment. Just… just my Nest-mate," replied the Dragon, patting the Beastkin's knee. Then she turned and looked at

Felix, tilting her head to the side while her hands pressed to the bottoms of Andrea's thighs to hold her up. "Now what?"

Andrea was peering at Felix over Goldie's shoulder, while Faith and Miu were both looking to him for direction.

The clothes Andrea had stolen hadn't been enough for everyone because their shapes were all quite different.

A simple shirt and pants for Felix were a bit loose, but workable.

There was also a dress, a pair of pants, and two blouses that'd fit Goldie or Faith.

Faith was wearing what she could, and the rest of items were wrapped up with the other clothes and she was carrying them.

If Goldie wore anything right now, she'd just shred it during the shape change.

There was also a shirt that'd fit Miu, but nothing for her bottoms other than the bright yellow panties.

Andrea was wearing one of the blouses but almost looked like a kid wearing their parent's shirt. There was far too much room in the shoulders and chest.

She was also lacking in the bottoms department as the only other option were the pants Felix was wearing. Those weren't very tail friendly, either.

"We break in, obviously," deadpanned Felix with a shrug of his shoulders. Then he turned and looked to Miu, then back to Andrea. "Would my dear Miu and lovely Andrea please take care of that without setting off an alarm?

"Then if you don't mind, rob the place for us? Faith, Goldie, and I aren't really cut out for this."

"Nn! Happy to help if you promise me I can sleep in your tent tonight," demanded Andrea as she got down from Goldie's back. There was an odd look on her face as she did so, and she gave Goldie a lingering look. Then she gave her head a small shake and looked back to Felix. Except it almost felt like he was looking at Adriana or Myriad, rather than Andrea. "I can do it. Sure. We just need to break through the ceiling, rather than the door or anything like that. There's never anything that can set off an alarm in the ceiling itself."

"I did say one of your Others could sleep with me a long time ago," Felix confirmed with a small smile.

At this point, it'd be harder to sleep without Andrea next to him, than with him.

"That'd work," murmured Miu who came over to stand in the center of the roof. She got down on one knee and then slammed her hand straight down into the ceiling.

Her fist went right through it. Then she moved her arm around and pulled her hand back.

There was a creaking and snapping noise as she quite literally tore a chunk of the ceiling free.

"Good idea, Miu," complimented Goldie,

and then she got down on one knee near Miu and did the exact same thing that Miu had done.

Though she used both hands and tore up a large section of the ceiling.

Shit. How… strong is she? Almost as strong as Goldie?

Felix called up Miu's stat screen.

Name: Miu Campbell		**Race**: Human
Alias: Felix's Miu		**Power:** Multiplicative Base
Physical Status: Healthy		**Mental Status:** Insane, In love
Positive Statuses: In love		**Negative Statuses**: Over 400 items. Click to expand.
Might:	64	Add +1? (640)
Finesse:	71	Add +1? (710)
Endurance:	58	Add +1? (580)
Competency:	33	Add +1? (330)
Intellect:	29	Add +1? (290) +Focus Type
Perception:	61	Add +1? (610)
Luck:	07	Add +1? (80)

Another Focus Type requirement. Yet… I have no idea what that is.

I'll need to look into that as soon as I can. Seems to be a limiting factor to anything moving past a nine. It has to be exactly what Runner warned me about.

"Don't break any glass or anything that might

make a shattering noise," warned Felix. "A lot of security devices in our old world had audio sensors that were tuned to glass breaking."

Goldie made a happy affirmative noise as she wrestled another section of ceiling. There was now a very reasonably-sized hole that led into the building.

"Okay, it's up to you, Miu, Andrea. Do what you need to do. Just make sure you get some rope and something you can attach it to," ordered Felix. "You'll need a way back up and that means Goldie hauling you up here.

"While you're doing that… Faith and I are going to take a look-see around the area since we're dressed for it. Any concerns?"

Miu had already dropped down into the open hole and vanished the moment he stopped speaking.

"Nn! On it, dear, darling, love. We'll be back in a jiff!" Andrea said. At some point, she'd moved over to the hole. Giving him a smart salute, she simply fell backward and exited his view.

"I… shall remain and wait for them," lamented Goldie with clear disappointment. "Though in the future, when we can hide these and I have some clothes… I really would like to go out with you on a romantic walk.

"It isn't fair that Faith and Miu will get all your attention since Andrea and I won't be able to go into public."

"I-alright. I'll make sure to be fair," promised

Felix.

"Thank you, that's all I ask. Now… shoo. Maybe see if there's anywhere else we want to rob. Just go wait over there and I'll come pick you up when it's time," suggested Goldie while indicating a rather dense thicket of trees to one side.

Felix could see that there were other buildings on the other side of it. For two people to hide in there in the dark, it'd be a perfect place to wait.

Nodding his head, Felix and Faith wandered over to the side of the building. Below them was the backlot of the building they'd broken into.

All that was there was some dumpsters, trash, a bunch of cigarette butts, and a back door that was probably the loading bay. There was no way up, or down.

"My turn," Faith said and stepped right up next to Felix. She wrapped her arms around his hips, then moved to the side of the building. Standing on the edge, she gave him a grin.

Then lifted him up into a princess carry.

Somewhat mortified, yet thankful, that neither Andrea nor Miu could see it, he just held onto Faith. More so when she suddenly stepped off the edge and they plummeted to the ground thirty feet below.

When they hit the ground, he felt Faith bend down then simply stand up. As if she hadn't just dropped from a distance that could easily kill someone.

"There we are," whispered Faith against his ear, her arms cradling him. It was at that moment that he realized he'd stuffed his face in her neck during the fall. "I don't mind carrying you, by the way.

"I'm not as strong as Miu or Goldie, but… I can certainly hold you without an issue."

Felix knew firsthand that Faith was actually quite strong.

"I'm good. Thank you, Faith," said Felix and leaned back into her arms and away from her neck. "I… err… lovely view, and all. Quite comfortable. But I do need to walk."

Faith was gazing at him and even before she did it, he knew the sex magic was coming. A second later and it washed over him, leaving him with a strong desire to get touchy-feely with her.

Another thing he'd learned about Faith was that a lot of time her magic did what it wanted without her acting on it.

"Sorry, that one wasn't on purpose," she said quickly, putting him down on his feet. Unfortunately, there'd been no shoes or socks in the laundry Andrea had stolen.

"I know. It's fine," Felix said soothingly, then patted Faith on the shoulder. "Just you being yourself. I get it."

Looking up from where she'd put him down, he realized they were in a darkened area. There wasn't any light that reached them here.

Distantly, across the street and a building

down, Felix saw another person.

The only person, in fact.

The streets were empty and no one was about.

He had the feeling that most of these places had closed up at about seven or eight pm. The area being almost completely deserted by ten, let alone the time now.

He wasn't sure what a clock would tell him, but he'd bet on it being close to midnight.

Felix focused hard on the person, a bare shadow with a Human-like outline at this distance, and tried to see what their stats would be if he owned them.

Name: Paul Mallon	**Race**: Human
Alias: None	**Power:** None
Physical Status: Inebriated	**Mental Status:** Inebriated
Positive Statuses: Inebriated	**Negative Statuses**: Inebriated

Might:	06	Add +1? (60)
Finesse:	08	Add +1? (80)
Endurance:	09	Add +1? (90) +1 Stamina Type
Competency:	13	Add +1? (130)
Intellect:	18	Add +1? (180)
Perception:	14	Add +1? (140)
Luck:	16	Add +1? (160)

Ah, I see. In other words… ten might be the average. That means that… my people are all incredibly exceptional.

Good to have the baseline settled then.

There was a clatter to the side that got his attention.

A rat scurried out from under the dumpster and slunk off into the dark, moving alongside the wall.

A bottle slowly rolled away from the trash having been knocked free by whatever the rodent had done.

Staring at it as it rolled toward him, Felix had an idea start to form in his head. One that entirely depended on a single simple law.

"Faith, what do you know about public domain and trash?" asked Felix and then he bent down to pick up the glass bottle. Rotating it over in his hand, he saw a notation on the back. One he recognized admittedly.

Recyclable.

Smirking to himself, Felix then tried something.

He wanted to make the bottle vanish into nothing and give him the points that it would be worth. For it to be stocked away in his point bank.

It was there one moment, then ceased to exist.

Raising his eyebrows, he called up his point totals.

	Generated	Remaining
Andrea	500	500
Faith	200	200
Felix	1,000	1,000
Goldie	1,900	1,900
Miu	800	800
+Loyalty Bonus	400	400
+Marital Bonus	400	400
=Daily Total	**5,200**	**5,200**
Banked Total	—	**3**

"Uh, what?" Faith asked.

Felix remembered belatedly that Faith was indeed a Dryad. A Nymph.

A sex monster from a medieval, apocalyptic world.

Her view on the world was quite different than his own. What she knew of public domain and trash law was likely limited.

"Anything that goes into the trash is considered abandoned property," observed Felix as he walked over to the dumpsters. "That means anything in these is fair game for me to take, utilize or... destroy into points.

"Come on, my pretty Dryad, come help me with our first harvest."

Grinning like a mad man, Felix stepped up to the dumpster as a man might if he discovered buried treasure.

* * *

***

"I… you… smell," Andrea grumbled, looking at Felix. Her nose was wrinkled and she was looking at him in a most displeased way.

"I do. I'm also much richer in points. For the price of smelling a bit south, I gained two hundred points to spend.

"And before you ask how, trash is public domain. I cleared the dumpsters of everything behind the building."

Felix gestured backward with a thumb toward the building.

Goldie clapped her hands together excitedly at the news, while Miu gave him a small smile and a nod of her head.

"Regardless of anything else, I can at least start scrounging up points like this. While it's dirty, and not exactly… ideal, it's workable," Felix emphasized. "It's points that I can turn into other materials that we can then sell. Possibly just for the gold-melt value or to a pawnshop if I'm just modifying a ring or something.

"It's a starting point. One that most people would fight us to have."

Andrea looked excited now. Her brows were down and she was nodding her head emphatically.

Behind her, her tail rose and partly quivered. A clear sign of her excitement.

"Yes! That's brilliant. Good job, love," Andrea said, though in a tone that sounded a lot like Myriad's. "That's adaptive thinking that we're going to need. This is why I put my faith in you, Felix."

Andrea smiled at him and then gave his cheek a very gentle pat, but did nothing further. She let her hand drop down back to her side.

"I... yeah. So, how'd you all do?" Felix asked, looking at Miu, Andrea, and Goldie.

The last was currently in her Dragon form and trundling their way. There were a very large number of packs, ropes, and things tied all around her body.

It gave Felix the impression of a strange fantasy novel. Where Dragons and other beings might be used to transport goods and people rather than what they were.

Monstrous killing machines.

"Very well," Miu said and then gave him a trembling smile. One that slowly became a wide grin. "I made sure to find good sleeping bags for us.

"Unfortunately, we only found one large tent. All the others were... damaged... somehow. It's a shame."

Miu's eyes skittered away from him and ended up focusing on a point to the left of his boot. Though her smile continued to quiver on her face.

Yeah... you did that on purpose.

But that's alright. That's actually fully within my expectations.

"That's fine. Somewhat of a shame though," mused Felix in an almost offhand way. "There won't be any chance for privacy. But that's okay. We'll make it work."

Miu, Goldie, Faith, and Andrea all looked pole-axed at that. Apparently, they'd considered all being in the same tent, but not the fact that their activities would also have limited them by all being in the same tent.

"I-that is-there might be one in there that isn't torn up," stammered Miu, turning to look back the way she came.

"No… no… there isn't," Andrea groaned with a shake of her head.

"Anyway. Let's get going. We'll see if we can't spot another city from the air and head that way," said Felix with a gesture to Goldie. Grinning to himself, he was enjoying the moment. He was actually starting to get a handle on all these semi-cracked people around him. To the point that he felt somewhat teasing. Something he'd thought of doing, but had never actually done to the Dragon. "My dear Goldie, tell me where I should ride you. Do I grab your horns and hold on tight?"

Goldie's golden eyes swung his way and locked onto him. She stared at him from a few feet away. Her pupils slowly dilated the longer she stared at him.

Until the color fell away entirely and it was as if they were black cauldrons filled with ink.

"Yes. You will do that," Goldie said in a growl while staring at him.

I… right.

Forgot that lesson.

Don't... don't tease the crazy person.

Miu, Faith, and Andrea were all talking about finding more tents and how to go about it. That or working out some type of sleep rotation, Felix wasn't quite sure.

Don't tease the crazy people.

Plural.

Stepping forward, he laid a hand on Goldie's scaled brow and then moved to mount up on her. They needed to get going.

There were only so many hours in the evening and they needed to get a move on.

In short order, everyone got up onto Goldie.

She spent nearly the entire time staring at Felix with a sidelong look. One of her bottomless eyes always focused on him where he sat on her back.

"Goldie, this is on you. You've got the best eyes," murmured Felix while feeling rather awkward. He really didn't know what to do at this point.

Goldie had been staring at him for the better part of three or four minutes.

A lot like a predator would.

"Yes. I'll handle that," she replied, watching him for several seconds more. Only then did she finally look ahead and start into the sky.

The beats of her wings took them rapidly upward.

Thankfully, the motion only pushed them all

down more firmly onto her body, rather than backward. Once she got going forward, she'd have to fly at a much more sedate pace.

"It was better in her mouth," grumbled Faith. "You should ask her to use her mouth."

That was the absolute last thing Felix would be asking Goldie right now. He'd already rang a bell with his horn comment. He didn't need to do more.

They gained altitude and began to slowly move forward.

Distantly, he could hear something thrumming behind them.

A rapid, repeating, deep thudding that came through the darkness.

"That's a damn attack helicopter!" yelled Andrea. "We need to get the fuck out of the sky and now!"

Goldie didn't wait for further instructions. It was obvious she remembered what a helicopter was.

In fact, Felix felt like she'd already started to move as soon as they heard it. As if she remembered the sound quite clearly on her own.

Tucking in her wings partly, she began to bring them down in a controlled dive. She was pitched at a very strange angle and was leading with her clawed feet.

Thankfully, what she was doing had Felix plastered to her spine and unable to move. She wasn't going to accidentally fling him free.

Then they slammed into a small wooded field several miles outside the small city they'd just robbed. Before she'd even fully come to a complete landing, Goldie pushed herself into the trees.

Stuffing the bulk of her body into the leaves and branches, it was almost like a small animal might step into a bush when hiding from an airborne predator.

Her head was low to the ground and she was peering at the sky above her.

Okay, she seriously has some trauma.

I didn't even think about it.

Maybe she tried to grab a helicopter or flew into one directly?

The rotors on that would be pretty strong if it hit her, right?

Twenty seconds later and a v-pattern of helicopters with their lights off blew past overhead. They were in a great hurry and didn't seem to be slowing down for anything.

"Were they here for us?" Miu asked, watching the helicopters as they moved into the distance. It was a straight line with Goldie's own path. "It seems unlikely."

"I don't know… it's something we can't really discredit either. Helicopters take time to get moving and they don't just… put to flight immediately. At least in our old world, that held true.

"However, it's not worth us tempting fate. At least not for tonight," announced Felix. "We'll just… camp for the night and talk tactics. Lots to discuss.

"Faith, have a chat with the trees. I know the last bunch didn't have much to say of use, but here we're just trying to find out if people come out this way."

There was a lot to do still.

Chapter 5 - First Step -

Staring up into the interior of the tent, Felix couldn't settle his thoughts.

This was about the time Felicity, Lily, or Kit would run him down and force him to unburden his mind. Make him pull out everything that was bothering him and force him to inspect it from a different angle.

Except he'd foolishly lost two of those people, and didn't choose to bring the third. While he'd certainly picked the right people to be able to start a strong foundation, a firm base to build off of, he hadn't picked people to help manage himself.

He was going to have to rely on himself to ask others for help. To seek out assistance and have those around him help him because he asked for help.

There would be no one to swoop in on a white horse to rescue him from his own thoughts.

Andrea squirmed around and thrust her hips forward. Which ended up grinding her pelvic area against the top of his head. Once she was closer to him, she went still once again.

For some reason, she'd decided to sleep above him and was practically wrapped around his head. Miu was on his right arm, and Goldie had her back to him and her rear end against his hip.

Felix was actually thankful for the pile of bodies, however. The night had been incredibly colder than he'd expected. When he was moving about and being active, it hadn't been as noticeable.

As soon as he'd laid down, however, he'd felt all of it.

Everyone had fallen asleep, only for Felix to wake up a few hours later with thoughts circling endlessly.

"Miu, I need to use the bathroom. Roll over, go back to sleep. I'll give you a kiss when I come back if you're asleep," commanded Felix in a quiet voice.

With a grunt, Miu nuzzled him for a moment, then rolled over onto her side, releasing his arm at the same time.

He knew from previous experience that Goldie and Andrea could and would sleep through nearly anything. From pushing them off him, to ripping the covers back from their clutches, they'd just sleep on.

Miu was a different story.

She woke if he so much as twitched, then went right back to bed after she confirmed he was fine. It was all part and parcel of her fractured mind.

So long as he commanded her, took control for her, then she'd function better. She'd be able to let herself not fall into the insanity that always gnawed at her heels.

Like commanding her to sleep.

Sitting up, Felix pulled off the unzipped and spread-out sleeping bag. They'd been using it as a comforter instead so Miu and Goldie could get under as well.

Reaching down toward his groin, Felix gingerly picked up Goldie's hand and moved it away from where it rested. Laying it down gently on top of her own hip.

"So possessive, my Goldie," Felix muttered under his breath with a grin.

"Course. Protect my hoard," murmured Goldie in a sleep-addled voice.

Raising his eyebrows at her sleep-talk, and because she'd actually understood him, he got up and exited the tent. They'd left it open in case Faith needed to rejoin them.

She had taken the watch for the night as she could doze in and out while conversing with the trees. No one would be able to sneak up on them without her knowing it before even Goldie or Andrea.

Stepping into the boots they'd stolen for him; Felix grabbed the laces and gave them a tug. He didn't actually want to tie them.

Standing upright, he stretched out his back and then stared up at the sky above.

It was an unfamiliar sky filled with stars that he'd never seen the light of.

"How did it go… like walking into a room and recognizing everyone's face, but realizing that there was no one there that you knew," he muttered to the heavens. "That's what it is. It's all so familiar, yet completely foreign. All of it."

Letting his gaze fall back to earth, he turned his head slowly, trying to figure out which way

Faith had gone. If he was going to get through this world and in one piece, he needed to rely on others.

That meant asking others for help.

Faith had just barely gotten used to his own world when it'd been hit by the religious apocalypse. She and Goldie were likely the two most qualified to help him work through his feelings.

As his gaze rolled across and through the trees where they'd camped, he spotted her. Or more accurately, she made herself visible to him.

Her arms had come up in a wide waving motion as his eyes swept over her.

Folding his arms across his body as the cold began to bite into him, he began moving toward her. Thankfully, she wasn't far off.

"Hey," Felix said, coming to a stop next to Faith. She was sitting down against a tree with her back leaning up against it.

"Grove-husband," replied Faith with a wide smile for him. Her eyes were moving over his body and face in a slow inspection.

The push of her sexual magic once more pelted him. It was almost becoming a constant thing, though he really did feel like he was getting used to it.

"That's a new one," said Felix as he rubbed his hands up and down his arms. Then he got down on the ground and pushed up against Faith. "Stealing your warmth. Frigging cold out."

"Yes. We're heading into fall here,"

murmured Faith and then she wrapped an arm around Felix's shoulders. Her body heat felt amazing.

A second later and heat began to flood into him.

"The magic of nature is very weak here. Very weak. I have a little, but faith in nature is-very… it's almost dead. I do have a little available to me though, so I can at least warm you up some. I think it's partly because I worship a different world's version of nature.

"And yes, Grove-husband. A prestigious title. Vince is also a Grove-husband.

"I was entrusted with turning you into our Grove-husband. Betty is building a Dryad grove for you to bond with on our return. While Evan is quite suitable to many of our needs, he… can't handle that many of us. We deliberately keep a number of maidens out of his grove," explained Faith. "Nor can we plant a tree in him, unlike you. We could easily turn you into our grove itself. So if we can turn you into a grove, and create a new one around you, that would be ideal. Only Dryads who haven't lain with any other man, of course. We have to protect our future, you know.

"I think you'll enjoy being a grove once you accept it. Especially now that you can get points for yourself, which means you can also modify yourself. I imagine being our Grove-husband will give you a great many points.

"As well as some regenerative powers on top of all that. In fact, you might even be able to use a type of our Dryad magic directly in the future as our Grove-husband."

Felix had been stunned to silence.

Sitting there in Faith's warm embrace, he was staring at her bare feet. Her boots were off to the side and sitting next to her.

Modify… myself?

I didn't even try.

What the hell is wrong with me?

It should have been the first thing to try!

Immediately, he tried to call up his own screen. His own status panel.

Name: Felix Campbell	**Race**: Demi-God (Shared Portfolio)
Alias: Felix (Over 50 items. Click to expand.)	**Power:** Modification (Limited)
Physical Status: Healthy, Tired.	**Mental Status:** Excited, Lonely, Concerned
Positive Statuses: Warmth of Arousal (spell)	**Negative Statuses**: None

Might:	11	Add +1? (1100)
Finesse:	13	Add +1? (1300)
Endurance:	10	Add +1? (1000)
Competency:	97	Add +1? (9700)
Intellect:	74	Add +1? (7400)
Perception:	16	Add +1? (1600)
Luck:	08	Add +1? (800)

"You're smarter than I am," remarked Felix as he read through his own status window. He also noted that to increase his own stats was an order of magnitude higher.

But that makes sense. For each one I increase of myself, I probably increase the points I get later. If it wasn't, it'd be horribly unbalanced.

That and I'm a demi-god.

Just... like Vince.

"Of course I am," murmured Faith with a chuckle. Then she leaned over and kissed him briefly and gave him a tender nuzzle. "You're less intelligent than Lily, Kit, and Felicity as well.

"But none of us have your ability, or your way of coming up with solutions so quickly. Effective solutions. Not to mention your political savvy."

Nodding his head, Felix agreed with her words.

"Tell me more about being a Grove-husband, and how I could be your tree," demanded Felix, turning his head to pin Faith with his gaze.

He wanted more points and would get them.

Because more points meant he could do even more.

And that meant he could get Kit and Lily back even faster.

"Never mind, don't tell me, just do it," commanded Felix.

He didn't have time to waste.

Tomorrow they'd be in the small town they'd

flown over. Watching the citizens and trying to figure out how different this world was.

If he was lucky, he could get this Grove business squared away and earn extra points today.

***

Scratching at his chest, Felix was wondering if maybe he'd been hasty. That in forcing Faith to make him her grove, he'd set himself up for longer-term problems.

It wasn't every day that a beautiful Dryad cut open your chest and pushed a tree-seed into it. Only to then close it up as if it had never happened.

This could really be a terrible–

Then his mind smashed that thought like a sledgehammer coming down on an ice cube.

It obliterated it.

No. I'll get Kit and Lily back.

I'll get them back and pull Legion up to where it should be. Where it would've been if it wasn't for me.

If it wasn't for me pumping the brakes on the wrong thing and gunning it at the worst time. It was all on me.

Especially in trying to take on religion. That was one of the worst mistakes I made.

Extra power and points though through becoming a grove?

I'll take it all. Take what it gives me and be thankful.

The simple fact that he'd gained five

hundred points to his own value by becoming Faith's grove had already made it incredibly worthwhile.

He was steadily creeping up on Goldie's own point value.

"It'll feel normal after the sun sets. That's when all plants begin readying for the next cycle, after all," Faith said, catching Felix's hand in her own and then slipping her fingers through it. "And… thank you for making time for me. It was… I can't even begin to describe the experience. To physically have sex with your own tree. At night, on the grass, in a forest. Absolutely wonderful. A real… real toe-curling experience.

"I'll never forget it. I can see what the Dryads in Vince's grove were talking about now. There's no comparison to anything else on the planet."

In retrospect, he hadn't made a conscious decision to bed Faith then and there. There'd been a strange tangle of emotions as her magic flared to life, only for something in him to respond in kind.

His only real worry was that maybe by becoming her grove, he'd made himself a bit more susceptible to her magic.

Miu sniffed loudly and then snatched up Felix's other hand. Grasping it with both of her own, she held onto it tightly.

She hadn't been pleased when he came back to bed smelling like sex. Sex with Faith, no less.

"Miu, it'll look weird," warned Felix as they walked down the street. There weren't too many businesses or shops on "Main Street" but there were more than enough to disguise them.

Travelers from out-of-state paused to stretch their legs and look around.

A man with both hands held by beautiful women was going to stand out, however. There was no way of hiding that.

"Ah, my bad. As I promised, Miu. He's all yours," said Faith, quickly letting go of his hand.

"T... thank you. I'm Felix's Miu," mumbled Miu. Holding his hand as she was currently doing was clearly affecting her. Her fingers were loose in his own as if she didn't trust her strength at the moment.

"Yes, you are. You're doing fantastic, too, Miu," Felix assured her. Then he nodded his head toward a bench in front of them. It was sat squarely in front of two small diners and one looked like a fast-food chain.

It's so very rural.

Though, if I'm being truthful, this is a good place to start. Starting here with nothing means we can actually blend in.

Faith and Miu took a seat on the bench with him. The latter of the two was still holding his hand with both of hers.

"I'm... I'm s-sorry. I'm trying really hard to be in control while being y-your Miu, Felix," whispered the dark-eyed woman next to him. "I'm getting better. Aren't I? P-please don't fix me.

"This is who I am. I've always been this way.

I'm-I'm happy that you accept me for who I am and don't want you to change me."

"I won't. And you're doing great, Miu. My Miu," Felix promised her. He'd long known that part of his appeal to her was that he accepted her exactly as she was.

Other people had told him to fix her. Suggested he do it without ever telling her, in fact.

He'd known that was as wrong as he'd been to put a barren modifier on Andrea, which he later corrected.

"You really are, Miu," Faith declared encouragingly, leaning across Felix to more clearly see Miu. She even managed to catch the other woman's eyes. "I'm actually envious and jealous of you as a woman at the same time. You make me wish sometimes I could take your place. As his Miu."

Whatever positive effect his words had had on Miu were nothing in comparison to what Faith had just said. Miu's shoulders straightened and her body completely squared up. Her head lifted and her eyes flashed as she held Faith with them.

"I mean it," Faith said with a small nod of her head.

Felix was now steadfastly ignoring the two women. They were here for a purpose, not to flirt.

No wrist communicators.

No holographic displays on their phones.

Everything is very physical. Digital, but very physical.

I haven't seen anything that uses energy or energy cells either. They all seem to be battery based or rechargeable batteries.

Looking to the side, Felix saw a group of young people hanging out the back of a truck in a parking lot. They were all gathered around, talking, and drinking what looked to be beer.

Empty cans were tossed into the truck bed. Which sounded like it already had a number of them inside, considering the rattle was audible even from this distance.

Also in the truck bed was a rusted-out barbecue. The top had a hole right through the front of it. There were even char marks running up the front of the cover as if the owner had continued to use it long after it'd developed the problem.

Huh… in such a rural place like this… I can't imagine trash pickup is the same.

If this was an urban jungle, you'd probably just call the trash company and ask for a large item pickup. Is it different here?

I bet it is.

Bunch of young men like that wouldn't answer me if I asked them any questions. However, they'd probably respond to Faith or Miu.

Except… Miu might hurt them for saying something stupid. Faith would just brush it off and it wouldn't phase her at all.

"—rather frustrating," growled Faith in a low tone. "Then I'm just expected to make it happen out of nowhere. If she had that much faith to begin with, she would have granted me my request at the outset."

"That's... that's a g-good point," stammered Miu. Her fingers were flexing in Felix's, holding onto him as if he were a delicate piece of porcelain. "I don't think I'd h-have handled it better. I'd pr-probably have killed her.

"My control is better in some ways lately, w-worse in others. I miss... well, yes. It's harder."

She was going to say she misses Lily. Lily always helped steer her to the right destination. She respected her.

Now... for Faith. She mentioned jealousy and envy.

That means it holds a place in her head as well.

I bet we can use it.

"Faith, I need a favor," Felix said, looking at Faith with a small smile. "I'm sorry to do it too. It actually makes me a little jealous even thinking about asking."

"You're my Grove-husband. There's nothing for you to ever be jealous about. I'm all yours. Only yours. I can have no other," soothed Faith, reaching out to lightly touch his cheek with her fingertips. It was a brief touch that lasted only a second before she let her hand drop.

She was blushing, smiling, and watching him closely now.

Definitely the right approach.

"I need you to go ask those young fools over there where they're going to dump that barbecue. See if you can't find out if there's some type of local drop-off point for large items," asked Felix. He pointed at the young men in question without making it obvious. "We're going to go into the store off to the left of that and ask some questions. Look at prices and see what things cost here.

"Meet us in there when you find out what they're doing with it. Maybe there's some local cast-off spot they know of. I know the… unscrupulous types… just dump wherever they think they can get away with it."

"I can do that. I'll… I'll do it in a way that hopefully doesn't make you jealous, Grove-husband. I would never want you to feel that way," promised Faith. She looked absolutely serious.

"Great. Meet us over there. It's just called The Local. You go first, we'll move second," requested Felix, still smiling at the Dryad. Then he decided to use a trump card he wanted to save for later. He'd noticed she'd had a change in title this morning when he looked at her character sheet. "Move along, my Grove-mistress."

Faith exhaled suddenly and wheezed. Her eyes dropped to the ground and she rocketed up out of the seat. Taking a tottering step forward, she started to move away from them.

It took her another two steps before she'd steadied herself.

A third before he heard her take in a breath of air.

All around her were random pulses and flashes of Dryad magic. It was so strong that Felix could feel it.

That or his newfound status with her seed inside him gave him insight into her magic.

The energy pulses were striking out randomly at anything and anyone near her as she moved away.

A great many of them hit Miu, who made no outward change at all and merely watched Faith as she left. Then she looked back at Felix.

"Off we go, my Miu," he said and stood up. He squeezed her hand and began leading her toward the location they wanted to check out.

It'd give him an idea of what prices were like for goods and services.

Crossing the street at a crosswalk, he happened to notice a gas station as well.

He didn't recognize the symbol next to the price but it seemed fairly straight forward. A gallon of gas ran at a starting point of three and thirty of whatever the currency was.

Somewhat... similar. A little higher than I remember it, but not too far off.

Must be another... what did he call it... point of congruency?

Keeping his thoughts firmly in place, Felix kept them moving.

Amongst all the other information he wanted to find here at the store was also who was the local leader.

Governor, mayor, minister, or otherwise.

If he could find them, maybe he could get some type of drop-off point set up where people could hand off unwanted garbage.

Trash that they couldn't figure out what to do with.

Then I'll just collect and convert it all.

All I need is a public space for them to drop it.

In the meantime, I can go through everyone's trash tonight. Hit up the businesses since their dumpsters are always out.

Then we just have to figure out what day is trash day for these neighborhoods.

Smiling to himself, Felix hung onto Miu's hand and walked into the store.

It was time to get some hard data.

Chapter 6 - Opportunities -

Having gone through the store somewhat quickly, Felix had done what he'd meant to do. He had a fair idea on pricing of goods and objects for this world.

That and a better understanding of what this place was.

It was a commission store for local goods. From produce to socks, and all the way out to infused sesame seed oil, surprisingly enough.

Everything was slightly more expensive than his own world, but nothing he couldn't simply attribute to inflation. They weren't soaring, sky-high numbers that'd push on the population, as far as he could tell.

Well, that assumes salaries are keeping pace.

Given my own history, that's rather unlikely. At least if this world really is much more like my own, that is.

"Gro— Felix," Faith murmured, coming right up next to him. He hadn't even noticed her approach. She seemed excited and was giving him a wide grin. "You were right. There's a dump spot where people throw things out. An old poultry farm. No one likes the owner, so they don't care.

"But there's also a local dump point that's set up at irregular intervals. A company is paid to come and pick it all up. They're due to come, but no one's heard anything about it yet."

Ah.

Well, that works, I suppose.

Then… we'll use one, leverage the other on a sweetheart deal, and look like the local helper. So long as we don't ask to be paid for the city drop-off point, it'll be fine.

They'd want information I don't have; I imagine.

I mean… they likely have something a lot like a National Social Number, just not named the same thing. It'll tie into taxes and provide everyone a digital identity.

"You have a plan," stated Faith, her smile growing larger if that were possible. "I can see it all over your face. You get this… it's a certain look. It's always there.

"Especially if it's a plan you like. It looks like you really like this plan, too."

"He loves this plan," countered Miu, watching him as well. Then her hand twitched and her fingers curled into his, holding his hand tightly as if he might pull away now. "He's even s-smiling a little."

"I… yes. I do. Now… one last bit of information before we go," admitted Felix and then moved over to the shop counter.

A woman with brown hair and dark-blue eyes looked up from her work. She had been doing what looked like inventory to Felix.

"Hi, I'm sorry to bother you, but we're really new to the area. We stopped by here on our way home and… well, it's looking a lot better. A while back, we came through and it looked a lot worse for wear," lied Felix, smiling at the woman. He did his best to lean on what charm and grace he had. He imagined that whoever would run a place called The Local would be all for the area. They'd likely hire people who felt the same way. "I was wondering who's in charge of the change. Or maybe someone not being in charge anymore as sometimes is the case."

The woman smiled brightly and nodded, then laughed as Felix finished talking. She gave a small shake of her head and gestured toward the window behind her.

"You know, you're not the first person to say that!" exclaimed the woman. "As to why, it's our new mayor. His name is Jordan Johnson. He's really helped turn it around for us."

"Well, that's gotta be worth a congratulations then. Any chance you have a way I can let him know the changes were noticed? Card? Phone number? Council number?" asked Felix as he leaned up against the counter. He was doing his best to keep it all simple and aboveboard. He didn't need the woman remembering much more than someone complimented the town.

"You know I do, actually. I'm on the town council!" gushed the woman. She reached down below the counter and pulled out a purse. She rifled through it for several seconds and then held out a card to him. "There ya go. I usually throw a couple in just in case. I mean, you never know, right?"

Felix took the card, nodded his head, and grinned at the woman. He pointed the card at the woman while still nodding.

"You're absolutely right. Thanks for this.

Have a nice day, alright?" Felix offered as a goodbye. Turning, he went to exit the store With Faith and Miu in tow.

Next stop.

Grouchy farmer.

***

The walk to the farm had taken longer than Felix had anticipated. Several hours longer, in face.

The problem had become that walking the road would have made them visible. A spectacle to anyone driving past who might offer a helping hand.

Once again, Felix really wanted to leave as little of an impression behind as possible. The days of taking headlines, being the "business in charge," and generally making Legion well known, were over.

This is going to suck.

These boots aren't broken in and I'm not used to walking through fields and forests. I don't even want to know what my feet look like.

Smirking to himself, Felix looked to the door of the farm ahead of himself. It'd be worth it if they could just get permission to clear the fields.

On the way past the dump spot, Felix had noted there were a lot of things present. A number of appliances that were made out of metal and materials that were still valuable.

Regardless of them working or not, they

could still generate a number of points for him. On top of all that, he'd noticed an abandoned truck amongst the trash.

If they could get that back to the field where they were staying, they could work on restoring it. It'd be a way for them to move about the city with relative ease.

Not to mention, it could be used to cart away trash and other objects they found to convert into points.

Well, so long as we get the appropriate paperwork and whatever else is needed. Still a lot to learn. Almost too much.

Lily handled getting all of this taken care of for our off-world recruits. Yet here I am, an off-world recruit.

Faith was currently waiting in the field where everything had been dumped. Based on what they'd learned about the farmer, Felix was betting that being direct was best. Direct, without guile, and leaving it open to the man.

Faith would be too pretty and cause issues.

Miu was retrieving Goldie and Andrea so they could all meet here. He'd need their help to get everything sorted out and then dismantled. They wouldn't be able to work during the day on this, but would have to work in the dark.

Otherwise, people might see what was going on.

Which meant even if he got permission, it would still take some time for everyone to get here.

Knocking on the door twice with a firm hand,

Felix took a step back and put his hands behind himself. Looking around, he noticed that there was a camera facing the front of the home.

The last thing he wanted to do was show up on a camera feed, but this wasn't something he could dodge. Getting permission to turn all that junk to points was paramount.

"What?" came a loud voice from what sounded like the camera.

Taking another step back, Felix looked up at the camera where he was fairly positive the voice had come from. It apparently served as an intercom as well.

"I'd like to clean up all the trash in your field," offered Felix without any preamble.

"All that trash? Why?" demanded the male voice.

"Because it's a terrible mess and I can recycle some of it for coin," answered Felix. It was an honest reason and also an optimistic one.

People were always more than willing to accept an answer that was self-motivated and optimistic. It was almost always easier than the opposite, or too good to be true.

Optimism is fatal.

"Can't pay you," once more came the angry voice.

"Pay what you can when I'm done. If it's nothing, it's nothing," Felix argued with a shake of his head. "I think you'll find it worth some money though. Or maybe something else in trade.

"But I won't ask for anything up front. That just wouldn't be right. I'll be by tomorrow morning so you can see the work I did.

"That is, if I have permission to clear the trash? All the junk and debris that doesn't belong?"

There was no immediate response from the camera. Which left Felix standing there, staring into the lens and feeling rather uncomfortable.

If this all failed, he'd just leave and never show up in front of this man again. If it became a real issue, they'd just pack up and go to another city.

Felix wanted to at least stay in this area for a little while and clean out all the trash. There was no sense rushing around if they didn't have to.

"Fine," said the voice and offered nothing more.

Perfect. That's all I need.

Turning, Felix left quickly. He just needed to wait for nightfall and the others to arrive, then it'd be time to get to work.

Looking towards the horizon, he realized he had only an hour or two to kill before sunset. Chances were that the others wouldn't get there until just after that given the distance.

Then a sudden thought made him wince.

Shit.

I'm going to be alone with Faith for a few hours.

Let's hope that fear of being susceptible to her as a grove was false.

As if thinking about her caused the tree

growing inside him to take notice, he could feel it shifting around in him. Glancing to his wrist, where it felt like it was creeping into, he was mildly surprised.

His veins looked almost brown in color.

***

Goldie, Miu, and Andrea weren't far away now. Faith had told him so.

The trees had spread the word of their coming long before they arrived. Apparently, the forest was quite happy to have a Dryad with a grove in the area.

Felix was quite happy for the timing because he'd been wrong.

Terribly wrong.

He wasn't just susceptible to Faith's magic; he was at its mercy.

Except so was Faith.

Her eyes had dilated wide and started glowing the moment he got close to her.

After that, it'd become a blur as Faith started a never-ending challenge to see how many times they could couple before the others arrived. Felix had only barely recovered from that a few minutes ago.

"Andrea's going to smell it and tell Miu," worried Felix.

"That's fine. I'll just offer you in exchange to both of them tonight. I'll act as the power source,"

Faith dismissed with a flick of a pretty wrist. "And if they're mad... fine. It was worth it. So worth it.

"I've never really Greened-out like that before. It was amazing. Even better than our first time as Grove and Dryad."

"Uh-huh," grumbled Felix.

It wasn't that he hadn't enjoyed himself.

The problem was he was trying to balance a bunch of crazy people on what felt like the edge of a knife. Any small mistake could result in him with a tent full of problems.

"Oh, well, Andie is almost—"

Andrea appeared through the trees in a whirlwind of speed. She was head down and sprinting right at him.

"Oh, that figures," muttered Felix before Andrea took him clean off his feet and sent him skidding across the grass.

"Dear! I'm so glad to see you! I missed you!" squealed Andrea as she began rubbing her face all over him. Her entire body wriggled around atop him. "Mm, you smell good, Darling. Like sex and earth. I like it."

With a grunt, Felix just put his arms around Andrea and held her. This was the expected reaction if he hadn't seen her in a while. She tended to get pent-up like a shook up can of soda.

"Hi, Andie. Ana. Ria. Others. How are you? I'm glad to see all of you," Felix murmured and just held onto the Beastkin. He'd long ago discovered greeting her as multiple people always helped to get the edge off her. He imagined it tended to make all of them go wild inside her head at the same time.

"Love, we're all fine. Thank you for asking," said Andrea in a throaty voice that sounded more like Myriad. "I… we just missed you. Everything is fine. I promise."

"Thank you, Ria," Felix said, guessing about who was speaking. He felt like it was fairly easy to spot who it was normally but they felt blurred right now to him. "Make sure you take care of your sisters in there. They need you to steady them. You're the Prime of Primes once upon a time. Be that for them."

"I… yes. I will, Love. I promise," Andrea said, then pressed her face into his neck. "I want to tear your clothes off, Darling. I need to scent you."

"Later, Ana. Work to do for now," promised Felix, noticing the speaker had changed once again. He just kept rubbing her back as he held her.

Above him, Miu and Goldie appeared.

"Ladies, we've got permission. Let's get to it, shall we? I want to go take a look at that truck first while you all start sorting everything else. Heavy things for deconstruction, fragile appliances and items to see if we want them, and trash for trash. Is that alright?" asked Felix. "If not, we can rearrange it to something else."

"I'll handle the large items," stated Goldie with a grin that showed off her perfect teeth. Her golden eyes swung toward Faith. "You can assist me, little miss Nymph and in between, start carrying the trash."

"I promise to help his stamina later for you all," Faith said defensively and held up her hands in front of herself.

Goldie didn't respond to that but turned to look to Miu.

Faith got the hint and started moving off toward the field. Apparently, Goldie was trying to play goalkeeper for him at the moment.

"Please handle the delicate stuff? You have the steadiest hands and I know Felix would personally appreciate you doing that. Wouldn't you, Felix?" asked Goldie.

He didn't miss the prompt from the Dragon.

"Of course. I would appreciate my Miu doing that. She's been such a good listener lately. It's really impressive," confessed Felix. He was trying to do it in a way that didn't sound patronizing, but with Miu, that kind of tone worked.

"Yes, I'll do it," responded Miu, who then turned and rushed off toward the dumping field.

"Andie, you need to go watch and make sure no one else is nearby. Do you think you can split yet?" asked Goldie.

"I... I don't... yes. I can split. I can have two Others go out. No more than that," whispered Andrea, nuzzling her face all over Felix's neck.

"Please tell the Others thank you, and I'd really like to express my thanks in person," asked Felix. "So no combining until I get to hug them and kiss them. They came on a dangerous mission just for me. I want to reward them."

"I— that is— err… well, Ria and Ana can come out, too," added Andrea in an almost uneasy tone. It sounded like she didn't really want to split.

"Andie, Ana, Ria, if you don't want to split, don't. Stay joined. If you have two Others who are willing, that's all we need," suggested Felix. "One Other for the farmhouse, one Other for the road, and one with us. That'd be fine."

"Nn. We'll do that, dear. Thank you for understanding, Love," grumbled Andrea without pulling away from him. "It's a very good suggestion, Darling."

Before he could really think about any of that, two Others jumped out of Andrea and went off at a dead sprint. They didn't linger or stick around, but were off in a flash. Running in different directions.

Hm.

Something odd there.

She'll hide it until it's too much. I'll just have to corner her tomorrow at some point. Or maybe tonight.

We need to make sure she knows it's coming.

"Andie, Ana, Ria. We'll talk about it later," Felix said in as soft a voice as he could. His eyes were on Goldie. He knew he didn't have to tell her to say nothing.

She'd see it in his thoughts and tell him what was going on later.

"I-okay. Yes. You… was it obvious?" asked

Andrea, sounding spent. Exhausted but comfortable.

"Only to me. I know my Elex women, after all. Now, get off me. We need to get to work," requested Felix with a playful swat to Andrea's rear end. "Scoot the booty."

Andrea sniffled, nodded, and then got off him. Moving off to the field, he imagined. He didn't get to look at her face, but he imagined it was extremely tearstained.

Something was wrong, he just didn't know what yet.

He had a suspicion though.

"They're merging, aren't they?" Felix asked, getting to his feet, but only after Andrea was far enough away to not hear him.

"Yes. That's what it seems like," answered the Dragon. She was watching him. "Her thoughts were more highly defined when we first got here. As more time goes on, the thoughts are merging and becoming… singular.

"She doesn't want to separate because she's already aware of what's happening. The Third of every Elex in the old world is… becoming a new Elex."

Nodding his head, that was more like what Felix suspected was happening. It was as Runner had warned him. He didn't bring the other Elex girls for that reason.

The fact that she brought Others from the other Elex sisters had made him a little uneasy.

He'd wondered if there would be an issue with it.

Apparently, there was.

Sounds like maybe I'll need to spend my first batch of points on making sure she's unique. Just like I did for Adriana and Myriad.

"Probably. Along with giving her the ability to hide her tail and ears at will. She's far more sensitive to not being with you, Nest-mate," Goldie said in a soft rumble. She'd snuck up next to him and had ducked her head low. One of her horns rubbed against the side of his head as she began to hold onto him as Andrea had. "I can wait to hide my horns and ears longer than she can, but I do need some care."

Checking a sigh and blanking his thoughts—other than to think of how nice it was to hold such a beautiful Dragon in his arms—Felix held onto her. Standing there, he held, and was held.

It took three or four minutes for Goldie to release him so they could get to work. He didn't begrudge her the time.

Everyone was here for him to support his goals. It cost him nothing to help fulfill whatever goals and needs they had.

Moving right to the abandoned truck, Felix attempted to call up the owner's window for it. He wanted to see if he could deconstruct it to absolutely nothing and what points he would get for it.

Not to actually do it, but just to see what he would get for it.

He imagined it this way, just as he had done for so many other things with his power. Shaping it with his need.

Additionally, he truly believed this truck was fair game, and that his power would most certainly work on it.

Because it was abandoned property on a piece of land whose owner had given him permission to remove it. There was no technical owner, other than the old farmer who didn't want it.

A window popped up in front of him.

Type: BB150-1978	**Condition**: Nonworking
Owner: None (Abandoned)	**Action >> Deconstruction**: Yield 1,431 points

"Perfect," Felix said to no one and then slapped the roof of the truck. "I'm going to be able to fit so much trash into this bad boy.

"Though… first we need to see how much it'll cost to fix it. So… I claim this vehicle as mine. And…"

Felix's voice trailed off as he called up the window to repair the vehicle into working, street-legal order.

It didn't have to be perfect, just enough that it'd work without immediately dying or falling apart.

Nothing happened.

Ah, I didn't specify a time.

Enough points so that it'd run for at least two

years without issues. That includes any and all fluids it would require to start up, as well as a key for the ignition.

And to be clear, this is also built into that two-year date.

Oh, and it'd be street legal. As well as changing the colors. Orange and white is very not this century. Nor is it subtle.

A matte black or flat black would be preferable.

A window appeared immediately.

Type: BB150-1978	**Condition**: Nonworking
Owner: Felix Campbell	**Action >> Rebuild**: Cost 7,487 points

"There it is," Felix gleefully chortled and began rubbing his hands together. Only to pat the top of the truck several times. This was the actual starting point. "Let's… accept. Then we can start loading the truck with all the treasures we want to keep. Scrap the rest.

"And we'll name you. Because BB150 is certainly not what I'm calling you. You- you're F-Two. Felix two. The ugly little bastard that we're going to rebuild from. Just as ugly and nasty as your owner, aren't ya?"

Chapter 7 - Change and Changes -

Closing the door to the truck, Felix felt somewhat odd behind the wheel. It'd been a while since he'd driven anything. Andrea had taken over those duties with her chauffeur Other.

Right now, the poor Wolf girl wasn't capable of much more other than existing.

Glancing over to said passenger, he found she was staring at her boots. Her hands rested in her lap and she looked rather lost in her own thoughts.

The two Others who'd helped watch everything were in the truck bed. They'd decided to remain separate for the moment. More than likely, it was to give Andrea space in her head to discuss the situation with him.

Miu, Goldie, and Faith were all going to go back separately by way of Dragon. They were also going to see if they could find a larger city in the nearby vicinity.

Felix would need to know where that was rather soon in order to advance to the next stage of his plan. For now, it was mostly just clearing trash in this small nowhere-town and laying down foundation work.

"Do you want me to start the car and we can drive and talk, or did you want to sit here for a bit first?" asked Felix. He wasn't actually sure which way she'd want to take this.

If she was feeling talkative, this wouldn't be half as difficult as he feared it would be. The opposite held true, as well, because should Andrea not want to discuss anything, she'd just shut down outright.

"Start-uh, start the car, Love. Darling," Andrea said, her voice morphing oddly as she gave him both titles. Then the Beastkin twitched, tilting her headfirst one way, then the other, only to finally look over at him.

Tears were rolling down her face and her eyes wide, as her gaze met his.

In that moment, Felix changed his thought process on how to handle this. It wasn't a matter of being talkative or not, it was going to be figuring out what she actually wanted.

In those eyes, he could see she was incredibly torn.

"Want me to guess first or do you want to open the conversation yourself?" offered Felix with a sad smile for her.

Her brows came down over her mismatched eyes and she gave him a glower that was mostly a pout. Her lower lip even stuck out partly.

"Guess, then. If you're wrong, I'll be mad at you," she grumbled with a firm nod of her head.

"You're becoming a new Elex woman. A woman made of all the Thirds. One third Andrea, one third Adriana, one third Myriad," Felix stated, leaving her without any wriggle room. "Either it's going too well and you're all being submerged, or it's going really bad and you're all fighting.

"Yes," Andrea confirmed, her eyes widening

again as she gazed at him. "It's going too well. We're... we're all being... blended. I'm finding it harder and harder to distinguish ourselves from one another. It's like... it's like when an Other gets really close to being a copy of another one. They end up becoming the same Other and one just vanishes into the other. Then a new Other appears to take its place."

"Okay... so... if you all become one, won't you just end up splitting out again afterward?" asked Felix.

"Maybe? We don't know. We're scared. We might just become Myriad with an Andrea for our world outlook. Where Adriana becomes our libido. Or it could be entirely reversed into something else. I don't know. We... we don't know. What if it's wrong?" asked Andrea more to herself than Felix, he imagined. "We've never had something like this happen. It's always been much easier to split ourselves apart, than it was to bring ourselves back down."

Felix couldn't help but think maybe this was a good lesson to learn, but he didn't want to actually say that aloud.

"Do you want it to happen?" he asked instead. "I mean... Andrea is Myriad, Myriad is Adriana, Adriana is Andrea. As much as I tell you that you're all different, you're also all the same.

"I mean, you heard what our benefactor told you about this world. That while I see you as unique people, the world doesn't. You're all one person. One soul."

Andrea was shaking her head, then started to nod it instead. Her gaze had drifted down to his chest only to flutter back up to his face.

"You… won't be upset if we become someone else?" whispered Andrea in a tentative voice.

"No. You'll still be an Elex woman. I can't seem to get enough of those. If I'm being honest, I was rather disappointed that you didn't have any Others that I could go steal.

"Even if they'd been dead for a while. Take a bone or the like, regrow the Other, then add them to my Elex collection."

Andrea started laughing at that. A low soft noise that was more akin to a chuckle in fact. A sound he'd often heard from Myriad.

"Your Elex collection," she said, her eyebrows raising upward.

"Yeah. My Elex collection. So… if you become a fourth Elex… that means my collection grows," Felix said in a false conspiratorial tone. He was also pitching his voice in such a way to make sure the Others in the back heard it. "I get a new Elex prime, a new Second, and a new Third. Then there's two lovely Others, already."

Felix pointed at the two Others in the back, who were clearly paying attention to him now.

"You'd have to pick a new name. New hair color probably. Platinum blond, maybe? Allison Elex is kinda fun to say as far as names go," he suggested. "Wanna be Allison Prime? Get you a nice gold earring?"

The chuckle had slowly shifted toward an actual laugh that he knew. It was Andrea's laugh. One he knew through and through.

She turned her head and looked at one of the Others behind her.

Something passed between them before the one on the left of the back of the truck reached around to the passenger side window.

There was a fluttering flash as the Other was absorbed and then released again. Almost as if there'd been some type of passing of information.

"I think… yes, I will. I'll do exactly what you've said, Dear," said Andrea with a grin. Then she gave herself a small shake and her entire posture changed. "There. Allison exists. I'm now Andrea, and she's Allison. Allie, for short. She's made up of Andrea Third, Adriana Third, and Myriad Third. A… a new Elex for your collection.

"But she can't come out. She can't come out until we're done. Because I'm still Andrea until that moment. The moment she comes out, I'll be absorbed and you'll no longer have any Andrea's.

"And Felix should always have an Andrea. Always. Though, before you ask, don't change me. Not yet. I don't need to be able to hide the ears or the tail yet. We'll need the points for other things, I think.

"Oh, oh, and… err… uhm, any Other I make from here on out will be Allie. Is… that okay, Dear?"

"Of course it's okay. It's all rather fantastic and I look forward to seeing you, Allie and truly meeting you," answered Felix. He'd always talked to them as if they were all present at the same time. "Be sure to make this Andrea your Second. She's very worthy of that title for sacrificing so much of herself."

Smiling brilliantly at that, Andrea looked unexpectedly excited. To the point that she was practically vibrating in her seat.

"Yes. Yes! When… when I rejoin, I'll be the Second. For now though, I'm just Andrea. Nn!" said the Beastkin with a sharp and pointed nod of her head. "And what I need right now is one thing. I'll need your help to get some, too."

"Pancake mix for pancakes," Felix answered confidently. He knew for a fact that they'd stolen the proper equipment to cook pancakes just for Andrea. Mix was going to be the next thing needed. "We'll go turn all the cans and bottles over to the recycling center and get some mix for you."

"Great! Great. But… ah… yes, I do want pancakes now that you mention it. I'm going to make so many pancakes," murmured Andrea, slowly leaning toward him. "But I want something else right now… and Allie is demanding that I make sure you know that this is our first time so be gentle. It'll be awkward in here but at least it's a bench seat. We'll make it work."

Ah.

Adriana or Myriad is the libido. If it was Andrea, she would've stopped at pancakes.

Such an interesting woman.
I love Elex women.

***

"—and thirty-six cents," said the cashier, placing a large silver coin, a small silver coin, and a small copper coin down on the counter.

Felix took up the handful of blue-colored paper bills and the coins and nodded his head. Walking back to the truck, he was rather happy about the situation.

They'd apparently made one hundred and fifteen dollars and thirty-six cents.

Felix couldn't imagine it would always be that easy to make money.

Especially considering there really was a great heap of things in the farmer's field to take care of. This was a perfect starting point though.

Moving to the truck, he simply held their haul out to Miu. As soon as she took it, he went over to the driver's side door.

"And why am I being given our money?" asked Miu, rapidly reorganizing the bills and coins in her hand.

"Because I trust you with it. Andrea would do something silly. Faith wouldn't completely understand how to use it. And Goldie... well... it isn't gold, so it might not be that big of a deal to her," explained Felix as he got in and buckled his seat belt. "Better you hold it."

"Ah, yes, that makes sense," Miu replied with a small nod of her head. Then she put the money into a pocket and turned to face him directly. "Thank you. I'll be careful to make sure it's used appropriately. What… what do we do next?"

Felix had been eyeing the recycling plant after he finished talking. He watched as a garbage truck filled to the brim with products was brought around the back.

"Not sure. But I think I might want to try and get a hold on this place," he murmured, leaning forward in his seat to watch the truck for a few seconds longer. "If there's no oversight of either incoming, or outgoing, we could get into that spot. Take it all for ourselves.

"Just convert it all to points. Let it build up and constantly rise higher, until using them will be as simple as breathing."

"Still haven't figured out the extra items though, have we?"

Glancing at Miu as she asked her question, he realized he'd forgotten about that. It was a worry he didn't want to gnaw at.

"No… no idea yet. I suppose we'll encounter it when we do. That's fine. We'll get there," muttered Felix as he turned the key in the ignition.

Then he stopped.

Wait, I haven't tried to modify powers yet. Or anything like that, actually.

Can I even do that?

This place is supposed to not have any superpowers yet.

Does that mean I wouldn't be able to modify someone with a power?

Looking at Miu, he stopped and considered that.

Then he put his mind to wanting to give Miu a new superpower. To let her blend in with the shadows at will. To slip away into nearly nothing and be invisible.

Just as she had been back in their original world.

No window surfaced or appeared.

Shit. It refused me outright, didn't it? I can't give out superpowers at all.

That'd make sense given what was explained, but it's still a bit unexpected.

Then Miu was in front of him, kissing him. Her hands were on the sides of his face, holding him as her kisses went from lightweight to her tongue searching the inside of his mouth in under a second.

Letting it linger for a second or two, Felix gently pushed her away while making sure he smiled. Miu was always going to be Miu and he'd been staring at her.

"I-I d-did good, right? That was why you were looking at me so intently?" asked Miu a bit breathlessly.

"Yes, you did well. Thank you, Miu," he murmured. He needed to make sure to keep her stimulated, rewarded, and on good behavior.

If he didn't, there was a strong possibility of her killing or hurting someone.

He'd taken a risk in leaving the door open for Miu to join him here. He could have just as easily told her to not come after him and she would have listened.

"Now, we need to go find a phone and call up our dear mayor and make him an offer. That means a phone booth or someone letting us borrow theirs.

"Pretty sure phone booths don't exist anymore though. Those weren't even in our old world anymore and I haven't seen one here."

"If I get a phone for us, will you take control for me? Tonight?" asked Miu. "I know I don't need it anymore, but I still… I still really enjoy it."

Ah… that'll work.

"Yeah. Get me a phone I can use, but you can't hurt them to get it. Or break anything. Once I'm done with it, you'll have to give it back, too," said Felix, putting the truck into gear.

"Okay, one second then," Miu replied and then opened the truck door.

Felix watched her, putting the truck back into park.

Miu rushed off toward a man who was working what looked like a massive compactor. He had one hand on the controls and the other on his hip.

Waving a hand at the man with a wide, warm

smile as she got close, Miu didn't look anything like the woman he knew.

She looked a lot more like a coed who'd just come off a college campus. She even went so far as to drop her shoulders forward, stick her hands behind her rear end and look upwards at the man from below her hair.

"What an actor," Felix drawled with a grin. "I guess she has to blend in with normal people enough to know how to pull it off."

In seconds, the man was grinning at Miu and handing over a cell phone to her.

Waving her hand at the man, Miu made a small motion off to one side and then wandered back to the truck. She made sure to look back twice at the man as she went, both times with a smile on her face.

"Damn. I'd probably be played by that, too," muttered Felix.

Reaching the car, Miu bent over at the waist, pointing her rear end at the man. The look on her face showed that she was clearly pleased with herself.

Holding the phone out to Felix, she chewed at her lower lip.

"I'm really looking forward to giving you control," she said in a quivering voice. "Very much worth making a hick think I find him interesting."

Felix took the phone from her with a small shake of his head. He often tended to forget just how damaged Miu was because of her love for him.

Not for the first time, he wished she'd let him fix her. However, it wasn't something he'd ever ask her about again. He accepted her for who she was, which included the broken parts.

Dialing in the number for the mayor, Felix pressed the phone to his ear. It hadn't been too hard to figure out how to dial. In fact, it seemed far simpler than utilizing his old wrist communicator.

The line began to ring in his ear almost immediately.

Holding the phone, Felix couldn't figure out if it was him that smelled like trash or the phone.

"Hello, Mayor Jordan speaking," said a bright and cheery voice.

"Good morning, Mayor. My name is Felix and I was wondering if you had a moment to listen to a free service I'd like to provide the township of Brandonville," said Felix in his best schmoozer, middle-management voice.

"Ah… well—"

"I assure you; it really is free. There is no dollar amount tied to it whatsoever," promised Felix after hearing the hesitation.

"Sure. I can hear you out," said the mayor with a soft sigh in his voice.

"I'd like to offer this quarter's large item trash pickup for free," Felix stated in what could only be described as a straight thrust of words. "The only thing I need is your permission, providing a sign or two to that effect, and a location where I can do it.

"Anything brought to that location, anything at all, will be gone by the morning after.

"I'd be more than willing to take anything anyone brought over for an entire week. That way the residents wouldn't have to rush to get it done in a few days.

"I know people were complaining about that last time around. At least this time they won't be able to… ah… whine over that."

Finishing his offer with a laugh, Felix rolled his eyes.

He had no idea if people had actually complained about it, nor could he imagine the mayor would even know that either. It seemed like something people with nothing else to do would complain about.

Which happened often and was quite believable.

"Ah… th—yes! That'd be wonderful. I was just talking to our previous contractor the other day and... yes. Yes, please," the mayor said in a very excited voice. "In fact, can you start it tomorrow? There's a lot of leftover flyers from last year that I can use again. We'll just handwrite at the bottom that I'll last for seven days."

Perfect.

Grinning, Felix leaned his head back and couldn't help himself when he let out a laugh.

"That'd be perfectly doable, Mayor. I'll have a couple of my people there to take everything away each evening. You don't need to worry about anything at all. I won't have anyone on hand to unload, but all the residents have to do is get it off their vehicle. That's it," explained Felix. Then he cleared his throat as an extra thought popped in. "I'm also able to take any vehicles, farm equipment, or just cast-off materials they don't want."

"Really? You can take all of that? Is it going to the dump?" asked the mayor.

"Private landfill I work with. It's out of state," lied Felix. "And yes, I can take all of that. In fact, I can take anything. Anything anyone doesn't want. Just have them all bring it down to wherever you want this to happen. Won't be an issue."

"Perfect then... one second—"

There was a rustling sound in the background followed by what sounded like the mayor asking someone a question. Finally, Felix heard a thump of what sounded like a box hitting the ground.

"Actually, can you start today? I know it's short notice, but I can... ah... you'd probably get five hundred from a donation if you could get it going today," said the mayor in a cautious voice. "It'd be at Leake Park. It's not too far off from Main Street."

"Err, give me a moment to check something," replied Felix, then he just sat there, staring at the windshield. His free hand was over the receiver just to give the illusion of trying to keep a conversation quiet. He was more than happy to agree with the mayor's request, but it wouldn't do to accept immediately.

Or to accept without sounding like it was at least a small inconvenience. After only a handful of seconds, he dropped his hand and cleared his throat.

"Yeah, I can get someone over there in an hour," confirmed Felix.

"Perfect! You came at just the right time," said the mayor with a relieved exhalation. "Thanks, Felix."

"Oh, it's my pleasure. I look forward to giving back to the community. I might not be around during the drop off but my people will most certainly be there though," lied Felix, still smiling all the while.

Chapter 8 - Only a Ghost -

Felix watched from across the street. He was working through a newspaper as if he had nothing at all to do. Just a man with some time to kill.

A man who just happened to be watching two very attractive women waiting in a park for people to drop things off.

Amusingly, there were other men actually doing exactly that. Watching Faith and Miu stand around and accept things from people. Moving them around on the tarp that'd been provided to them by the mayor, or just waiting around.

I should have modified Andrea.

I need someone with me.

Or... well... I wonder if she didn't want to be modified because she's getting used to being Allison. Didn't want to throw other changes into the mix just after she accepted what she's becoming?

That'd make more sense.

Then... Goldie?

Doesn't seem like Miu or Faith need me here. I should get going to the next part.

Time's wasting and I don't really have that luxury. Everything is timed right now.

We've got our foot in the door for our goodie-two-shoes side. Now... we need to start the process for the darker side.

Because how can I control a world if I'm not on both ends of the spectrum?

Folding the newspaper in half, he stood up.

Moving away from the table, Felix wished the paper away into points. He converted it into nothing as if it was an illusion.

He was enjoying the fact that he could stockpile points now and not have to worry about converting them one way, or the other.

He pulled up his points table to see how much he'd earned so far after everything he'd gained and what he'd spent.

	Generated	**Remaining**
Andrea	550	550
Faith	225	225
Felix	1,500	1,500
Goldie	1,900	1,900
Miu	800	800
+Loyalty Bonus	400	400
+Marital Bonus	400	400
=Daily Total	**5,775**	**5,775**
Banked Total	—	**25,139**

I bet that's enough to give a Dragon the ability to hide their horns, eyes, and ears. They already have a shape-shifting ability, after all.

I can't imagine it'd be too far off to add to that.

In fact, it might be really cheap.

Let's go run down our dear Goldie and see if she's willing to go on a trip with me in the truck. This'll be a perfect opportunity to explore a bit, too.

Though… still need to be careful.

No driver's license and no idea on all the rules of the road here. I'll have to keep assuming they're all mostly the same and mimic others.

Pulling the key from his pocket, Felix headed off for the truck. Thankfully, filling the gas tank was as easy as topping it off with points.

This world certainly had its disadvantages to him, but he was fully enjoying using his points however he wanted.

Without suppression, wasting any, or feeling like he had to hurry up and convert things before midnight.

A few hours later, after handling Faith and Goldie's amorous advances, Felix had managed to talk the Dragon into the truck with him.

That'd been more difficult than getting her to agree to be able to hide her non-Human features for some reason.

"Makes no sense," complained Felix as he spotted a sign stating that they were one mile out from the city of Hardysburg.

"I… just don't like being in vehicles," muttered Goldie, her arms folded across her chest. She was wearing clothes that fit her incredibly well and she looked out of place in such a rundown interior.

She must have gotten hold of a sewing kit. Pretty sure that's something that didn't fit her at first.

"Yeah, heard that part. I just don't get why. It makes no sense. You're a Dragon. I ride you like a horse. Doesn't that make you a vehicle?"

"You ride me like a Dragon and a woman. I am most definitely not a vehicle," growled the Dragon. She turned her head toward him and her currently brown eyes began to glow a golden color. "And if you make a joke about my horns being handlebars, then I'll really give you something you need to hold onto."

"No, no joke. Those aren't handlebars. It's where I hold onto my beautiful Dragon because she's too much for me," Felix stammered out quickly. "My Goldie, my Dragon, is far too much for such a man as I. I have to hold onto her horns because of that."

Goldie's eyes slowly faded back down to the false brown they were disguised as.

"You're lying. You were thinking of them as handlebars. You even had that thought when we made love earlier after you were done with Faith," said Goldie in an offended tone. She turned to look forward again and lifted her chin up.

Sighing, Felix nodded his head. He was very much regretting the fact that he couldn't seem to lock Goldie out of his thoughts.

"I'll not be angry at you for your thoughts. Even I had strange thoughts," Goldie said, almost as if she were extending an olive branch. "Besides, you often fantasize about holding onto my horns, even if you think of them as handlebars. I can be generous."

Then thank you, my Goldie, for being generous.

Felix deliberately threw up a number of mental images of her being generous with him only an hour or so previous. From his point of view, at least.

He was aware she wasn't a typical Dragon. How he treated her, how he dealt with situations and was tender to those he cared for, had won her over a long time ago.

For her, it was becoming self-fulfilling.

The more intimate he was with her, the more she fell deeper into that hole, and the more intimate they were with each other.

In a way, she was similar to Miu.

"I… yes. You're… welcome. Now, I can see your plans to a degree, but I'm not as strong as Kit was. Can you elaborate for me?" questioned Goldie. Her chin had come down a bit and her face took on a reddened color. Her shoulders had also lowered and she had partly turned toward him.

A far more inviting and "willing to talk" body posture than she'd had previously.

"Simple. Find a criminal element, exploit it, and turn it to work for us. Except we don't want to be at the head of it. We don't want anything to do with running it.

"We want someone else to run it for us as a puppet. We never want to be seen as anything special," answered Felix. "Just as one amongst many and nothing of any interest. Not a target."

"In other words… we want to do to others what Shirley did to us," deadpanned Goldie, turning to face him now. She'd even lifted one leg and put it on the bench to put more of herself facing him. "You respect what she did. Envy her, in a way."

"I do. I hate her, I admit that, but in the same breath I admire her," confessed Felix as they drove into the city. Then he laughed, feeling a great deal of pain leaving with it. "Hell, she was beautiful. Beautiful, smart, cunning, and dangerous as hell. I wish I could have met her under different circumstances.

"I bet she's an amazing woman, even if I hate her for what she did. That's okay, though. I learned from it. From her. Now I'm going to take what I did previously, expand on it, and build it better."

"Yes, you're going to drop your favorite quote aren't you?" Goldie asked with a chuckle. "I can even hear it in your mind. 'The sum of what we are, our experience, is what we draw upon to make choices. It's what we use to defend ourselves from doubt. We compare them to things we've done previously and judge it based on what the outcome had been then.' Right?"

Felix nodded and pulled the truck into a parking space. They were in a very old, rundown, dirty-looking part of the city.

Except it didn't really feel like a city to Felix.

It felt like a really large town more than anything. The scope of what he was used to and what he was experiencing were extremely different.

"Is this where we'll find our criminal element?" asked Goldie.

"Where you'll find it, yeah," redirected Felix

with a snort. "We're going to go for a walk and you're going to pick out thoughts. We're looking for a drug dealer, preferably. Even a low level one would work.

"Get their home address then go visit them tonight. With Miu and you. You drop us nearby, Miu gets us inside. Have a chat with them, then you get us out of there. It'll get everything we need going."

"Ah. Yes, I can see how that'd work. Alright," Goldie said with a growing smile. "We're most certainly holding hands while we walk, by the way. Because you're right. As I fall deeper into you, my Dragon demands ever more, only to fall deeper. I hope you're prepared."

"You can't be any worse than Miu," Felix argued with a shrug of his shoulders. "She takes bites out of me, remember?

"You just purr, get kind of cuddly, a little kissy, and turn into a giant kitten. It's incredibly adorable."

Goldie went quiet and became the same color as ketchup.

***

Miu grasped the handle in her gloved hand.

Then jerked her hand down.

There was a sharp ping and something inside the flimsy lock gave away.

Pulling back on the handle, the whole thing

came away from the door. Looking into the mechanism, Miu found something and then twisted it to one side.

The door then swung open, letting them into the mobile home. It'd been relatively quiet, so Felix wasn't too concerned about the dealer waking up.

A large number of people in the trailer park had clearly still been awake, despite the dealer they were after actually being asleep. Goldie had mentioned that he preferred dealing during the day, rather than at night.

Apparently, the man felt like he was far more likely to be killed at night by a buyer.

Moving quickly, the three of them entered and Goldie closed the door behind her as best as she could and remained there. Miu kept going deeper, silent as deep space.

Before Felix had even taken a few steps inside, he could hear Miu talking in a harsh whisper.

"Be absolutely silent. Don't do anything stupid. I already took your gun, so don't bother," demanded Miu. "Nod if you understand."

There was a long pause.

"Good," finished Miu, and then went silent.

Ah, that's my cue then. Goldie please free to step in and add anything if it helps.

Felix was quite happy to have someone with him that could read minds. It would make dealing with the criminal underworld a lot easier for him.

There'd be no fear of him working with

someone who planned to betray him, informants, or undercover police. He could theoretically become a godfather and not have anything stand in his way.

Making sure the mask Goldie had made for him to cover his face was in place, Felix came over to stand above the dealer.

"Good evening, Mr. Wiles," murmured Felix in a soft tone. He needed to come in with a much more velvet-like approach after Miu had done her thing. "Congratulations. You're going to be my henchman. You should feel thankful."

Miu turned on a light with a flick of a switch. Lightbulbs came to life in several points around the room. Her own mask was worn just as snuggly over her face as his own.

The man in the bed was nothing like what Felix had expected. Almost not on any level, in fact.

He was heavily muscled and quite fit looking. He had sandy-blond hair that was somewhat bewildering to Felix's eye.

It seemed equal parts deliberate and accidental, giving it a look that would've belonged to a Viking culture from Felix's world's history.

Blinking several times, the man held a hand up to shield his blue eyes from the glare of the light-bulbs.

"Super thankful. Always wanted to be a statistic. Maybe a snuff film, if you've got a phone out," rumbled the man. "Robbing me, murdering me, or both? Pretty sure I didn't do any dealin' on any owned turf."

"No, we're not part of them," Goldie answered from behind Felix. She'd joined him, but remained out of sight. Her figure and body shape would be almost as identifiable as her face.

"Now," Felix chimed in to steer the conversation back to where he wished. "You're going to give me all your drugs. Then I'm going to make them the highest quality possible. You're going to sell your much higher quality drugs at an increased cost.

"You'll put some money aside for me as my cut. You can decide the percentage based on whatever rate you're selling your drugs at, but I do expect you to be fair.

"Does this all make sense so far? Are you following?"

"Yeah... but... no. How are you going to make it better? It's pretty shit. I don't use, but from what I can tell from my users, it's trash," said Jay, getting up into a seated position on his bed.

"Oh, just a little magic. No need to ask any further about it because that's the only answer I'll give you. If you don't believe me, you'll discover it tomorrow.

"Though as I've stated, the quality will go up. Which means the risks go up of overdosing or causing more harmful issues. I expect you to do everything you can to limit fatalities.

"Dead customers aren't customers. I'd recommend doing what you need to, to make it go further. Higher quality attractions more attention, of course."

Felix wasn't really sure what drug the man dealt in. Goldie had said it was cocaine, but Felix had no experience with it.

Nor had he heard of the word from his previous world.

He was more or less operating in the dark here.

He didn't really like getting into bed with an illegal market like this, but he could at least do what he could to limit the damage he was causing. This was something he had to do to have his needs met.

As soon as he could, he'd be exiting the drug dealer market and moving hopefully to something a bit more organized as far as criminal enterprises went. Maybe corporate crime or some type of banking fraud.

Would love to defraud companies of their excess. Especially company owners. I bet I could get a great deal of money from them.

"I… yeah. I'll cut it down and make it last. No point in selling higher quality stuff to them," Jay agreed, looking from Felix to Miu, then back. "If you're really going to make it high quality, I can easily make that go like… three or four times further."

"Splendid. All that remains then is our drugs. Where are they?" asked Felix, gesturing around the room. In that moment, he noticed there were a very large number of books on programing, coding, and general computer science.

There were also a great number of beginner books that looked like they'd once been used extensively, but not much any longer. Covered in dust and other things.

What did look recent were a handful of advanced books. As if Jay had been involved in a full programming career prior to his drug dealing.

Hm. Maybe I can use him further than just dealing.

Jay had gotten up from his bed and moved to one side of the trailer. Getting down to his knees, he started working at one of the floorboards.

Or at least, Felix had thought it was floorboards.

Watching what was happening, he realized it was more like a laminate that'd been stuck down to the floor. At some point, Jay had worked on it, it seemed.

"Programming?" Felix asked in the silence that filled the room.

"Yeah, before all this shit happened. Company shut down about a year ago," Jay said with a shake of his head. The section of the floor he'd been fiddling with came out with a soft clatter. "Couldn't get a job anywhere else. Everyone was hired up and hunkering down to see if it'd all blow over.

"Tried fast-food work but... that just didn't work. Everyone there didn't want to be there and I was overqualified."

"Ah, yeah. Pinch-hitters," cursed Felix.

"You'll end up working a dreary job you hate for not very long before you give up, stop working, or go elsewhere. So a lot of stores just don't bother hiring over-qualified applicants. I get it. It sucks for everyone."

"Yeah. Yeah, that's… that's exactly what one guy said," grumbled Jay, looking at Felix over his shoulder. Then he went back to his work. "Anyway, yeah. Once upon a time, I was a programmer."

"How interesting. Any good? Can you break into a company? Bank?" inquired Felix, genuinely interested now.

"Err, good enough to be a problem. Not great enough to bring down a company, if that's what you're asking," Jay said and pulled out an ice chest from below.

Setting it down next to himself, he opened it.

Or at least tried to.

Miu was on him in a flash with a drawn gun. The tip was pressed to Jay's forehead.

"I've got it," she said in a flat tone. "You go sit down."

"Right, yeah, right. I'll do that," agreed Jay, his hands lifted up at his sides. He went and sat back down on his bed and went still. Not moving quickly or doing anything sudden. "Sorry, forgot. There's a gun in there, too."

Miu then flipped open the lid with one hand.

Inside was another gun, several magazines, and a great quantity of drugs. Or so Felix assumed.

They were all packaged in baggies and were

arranged semi-orderly. There was significantly more than Felix suspected there would be as well.

Miu quickly picked up the weapon, partially pulled back the slide, and then let it go.

"Chambered, no safety. Same as the gun under your pillow," remarked Miu, looking at Jay.

"Dangerous neighborhood. Also why I don't deal out of it," explained Jay with a shrug of his shoulders.

"I'll be sure to leave the guns behind," Miu promised, and put the weapon back into the cooler though she did hold onto the other one. "No sense in depriving you of your security."

"T-thanks," mumbled Jay, clearly unsure of how to take all of this.

Kneeling down over all the drugs, Felix looked through them and then glanced to Jay.

"Is this all mine then?" he asked the dealer.

"Uh… yeah. All yours, boss. Do your thing," offered Jay with a wave of his hands.

Felix nodded his head and then focused on what was in front of him.

He wanted to convert everything in the bags to a pure form of whatever the drug it was. That anything it had been mixed with, would simply become more of the drug.

To remove all the impurities and make it as perfect a drug as it could be. As well as knowing what the value before the action would be, and then after the action.

A window appeared in front of him.

Type: Cocaine / 4 substances Click to expand	**Condition**: Poor Quality
Owner: Felix Campbell	**Action >> Purify**: Cost 1,108 points
Pre-Action Value: $4,349	**Post-Action Value:** $22,913

Ah, that's not so bad to purify it. It must not be too different substance-wise from what it was mixed with.

This is easily going to be expanded three to four times, he said. That doesn't really account for such a massive post-action value, though.

Something else going on here but… whatever. That really isn't my concern I suppose.

Well.

This is all just great. If this is convertible to cash without being able to trace back to me, than it's well worth the cost. I'll need cash like this that leaves no backward identification for me.

"You might want to make some more mixtures of this as you had it previously. Then just put it to the side so I can purify it again later. Whatever condition this was in, was quite easy to work with," advised Felix. "I'll be back in a week to collect my first dividend."

Closing the cooler, Felix made a head nod at Miu toward the door.

"Sorry about the door handle," apologized Felix as they exited the trailer. "You can deduct the cost from what you owe me."

Exiting, Miu set the gun down on the counter and then closed the door behind herself.

Moving quickly, the trio made it to a tree line at a sprint.

They had other dealers to run down. Goldie had found a few that they could work with.

Or at least, probably.

Then... it's cruising the back-alleys for trash.

I can't wait to see what's behind that big box store. Sam's Mart, was it? I bet they have good trash.

Still need to leave an hour or two to clear what was dropped off at the park, though.

Busy, busy night.

"Don't forget you owe me. You promised me," growled Miu from the darkness.

Oh, and that. Yes.

Her control.

Good thing it isn't even midnight yet.

Chapter 9 - Under the Radar -

Yawning, Felix gave himself a small shake. Even though he'd woke up ten minutes ago, he still felt like he was asleep.

"You only got two hours of sleep. It's no surprise," murmured Goldie from his side. She was learning how to clean and dress an animal from Faith.

She'd brought in a rather large deer for everyone. Apparently, she wasn't quite pleased with them eating only the preserved food they'd taken from the camping store.

She believed that they needed "fresh, red meat" to truly operate at full efficiency.

Felix couldn't argue the logic considering that Humans had evolved from omnivores. They had the teeth required to take care of whatever they found.

Eat anything and everything.

"Feels like I only got maybe... ten minutes," Felix grumbled, peering at the distant horizon. The sun hadn't risen yet, but it was starting to push out rays of light ahead of itself.

Miu and Andrea were currently working on breakfast. The former cooking some of the deer that Faith had expertly hacked off.

The latter was, of course, doing what she would always do if given the chance when it came to meals.

"Mmmm! Pancakes!" declared Andrea,

chewing energetically on a pancake even as she made more. As always, it was a wonder to watch her work.

The two Other Andreas with her were on watch right now, moving through the woods surrounding their camp.

"Pan-Cakes. Pan-Cakes. Pan-Cakes," emphasized Andrea, bouncing her hips from side to side with each broken word. Then she suddenly looked up and smiled at him.

She lifted the hand that held her spatula and gave him a little wave with it.

"I love you, Dearlove!" stated Andrea around a mouthful of pancake. Only to immediately go back to chanting what might as well have been her theme song while watching her cooking.

Dearlove? That's a new one.

Must be an Allison thing.

Still haven't seen her or an Other of her yet. She must still be consolidating inside of Andrea for now. That'd make sense.

"Love you too, Andrea, Allison," mumbled Felix, followed by another yawn. "Ergh. Alright... shall we start this? We need to talk about where we are, where we're going, then get moving to tasks."

"Nn! So exciting!" replied Andrea, flipping over the pancake she'd been working on and setting down her spatula. It looked like she was about to judge it finished. "You know, I never thought I'd say it, but I missed being in these meetings. I feel like pulling back from you as far as I did was the wrong thing to do.

"I just let Felicity in by doing that and didn't see you as much. I was so terrified of losing what I had, that I practically gave it all way."

Well. That... that's far more insightful from her than I expected.

Maybe it really is Allison and –

"Pancake!" screeched Andrea happily and then flicked the skillet up with her right hand. With her left hand, she snatched the breakfast food out of the air with a plate, then held it over to Miu.

Who promptly took it and dumped a portion of the sizzling deer meat onto it, then brought it over to Felix with a plastic knife and fork.

Before Miu had even made it to him, Andrea had already started on another pancake.

No. No.

That's... that's Andrea.

"Glad to hear it. Thank you, Miu," responded Felix, making sure to make firm and steady eye contact with Miu. He'd rewarded her by taking control the night before, just as he promised, despite the fact that she technically didn't need it now. It seemed she enjoyed it as its own thing now.

A shivering smile blossomed on Miu's face as she held his gaze for several seconds. Her eyes skittered away from him only to shoot back and remain.

Giving her a smile, he slowly pulled his eyes off Miu, giving her a chance to retreat from the attention.

"Ready," Goldie said, coming over to stand beside him. "Thank you, Faith. That was very informative. I usually just ate everything raw. Human, deer, cow, it didn't matter. Bones digested just as easily as meat."

"Of course, not a problem. And I'm ready as well," murmured Faith as she leaned down over Felix's shoulder and kissed his cheek, before taking a seat in the grass.

Felix tore the pancake in half and then took a bite out of it. He wasn't going to waste time and try to talk between bites. These were all women who'd been through hell and back in their own way.

He didn't need to stand on etiquette with them, thankfully.

"We're moving ahead with the dealers. We have four that will work with us. The fifth decided he'd rather go it alone," started Felix as he chewed. "We won't worry about him and he doesn't concern us.

"The others will be fine for our starting point. We'll use them to get our funding and points for other things. When we can break away, we will.

"I'd much rather get into money laundering, corporate criminal enterprises, and honestly, theft. Those are all much less destructive. We're doing what we can to limit the damage with our dealers as well."

"Nn! Yes!" Andrea piped in, still cooking away next to Miu. "That's good. I... that... I grew up in an area like… kinda… err… I grew up poor. Very poor.

"I saw what drugs did to people. It's one thing to sell it responsibly, but it'd be almost too much to do it without regard for those who are addicted. They can't control it after they reach a certain point.

"They get to it and there's just… it's all whoosh, with a loud bang and splat without any ability to go 'wait, stop'. You know?"

Felix didn't know.

What he did know was that he loved Andrea.

"I don't, but I know that I'll do what I can to make sure you're happy. I'll do all I can to keep the drug side of things clean, safe, and fair," promised Felix.

"That's more than enough, nn. Thank you, Dearlove. Thank you. Oh, and if possible I'd really rather not move into a mobile home later. If possible. Been there, done that, got the trauma. I'd rather stay here in the field," said Andrea with a pent-up breath. She didn't look up from her pancake-making, but he imagined she looked irritated.

"It's likely we'll all stay here in the field for a time yet, Andie. So that's not really a concern. I'd rather trust Faith and the trees than neighbors who happen to be human.

"As to the rest, we'll start getting funding from the dealers relatively soon. Probably a week or so. We can slowly start pushing further with them for a while as well. Take over more dealers and start generating more money," Felix expanded on the previous points. "I get the impression that there are other dealers in the area. Is that accurate, Goldie?"

"It is. I got a couple thoughts from Jay especially. They're apparently rather violent and haven't been very careful with their mixes. They've left a few bodies behind," affirmed Goldie.

"We'll have our dealers eliminate or take them over outright. Have them all become our dealers and keep expanding. Clear the market, bring a stable product, make it work.

"We can bring it together into a cohesive thing," planned Felix after a second to think. "We'll just keep moving the whole thing until we can hand it off to someone and move further away from the front. We can become the 'big supplier' so to speak. At least as long as we have a base of people to work with.

"Maybe use Jay for that. His were the least expensive to modify. We could always find out who his dealer is and go to them, too. They might be more than willing to get us in on whatever they're making to expand their own profits."

"They all had a different supplier," Goldie put in before he could continue. "We'll have to check in with them and see if they share a source. If they do, then it's the dealers who made the bad mixes and Jay is better at it. If they don't, then it's the supplier. We'd go for Jay's. Right?"

"Exactly," agreed Felix. Then he made a hand motion of rolling his hand forward. "That's enough of that, though. We'll need to wait a bit before we can move further. Start with the dealers, see how we do. Supplier will notice they're not buying as much and get curious.

"This and that will line up if we just… hold still for a time. Maybe a month or so. In the meantime that we wait for that, we'll keep pushing with Brandonville and Hardysburg."

Felix had finished the pancake by now and had eyed the slab of deer meat. That would be a lot harder to get into while talking.

"Faith, Miu, how'd the drop point go yesterday? Anything of interest?" he asked and then started cutting into the meat.

He'd noticed there were a number of small electronics, power tools, and odd items he couldn't quite identify sitting in the field behind them. Somehow, at some point, they'd brought everything to the field where they were camping and put them out onto one of the stolen tarps.

Miu had stopped in her work and looked at Faith, then gave the other woman a small nod of her head. Then she went back to work, cooking more of the deer.

"It went really well," started Faith somewhat nervously. Felix couldn't remember her ever being in a meeting like this before. Or at least, not one where she had to talk about how things went. "We had a lot of people come by with just trash. A lot of trash. It was rather impressive how much people had.

"I got the impression they just let it pile up

then bring it over for this pickup. The normal weekly trash wasn't enough."

Felix nodded his head. From the sheer amount of trash that he'd made into points, it felt like there was far more being generated than expected. It also likely provided him with an avenue of approach for another time.

"Other than that, a lot of people just came to… uhm… see us, I guess," Faith theorized with a small shake of her head. "I've never been stared at so much. Not even back home in Yosemite, or in your world. There were people literally just sitting and watching me.

"I don't mind the attention, of course, but it was distracting and rather annoying. I was doing my best to get work done for Legion."

"You did fine. I scared off the ones who lingered," Miu added without stopping what she was doing. She'd just handed a plate of food off to Goldie and was returning to her station.

"I… yes, thank you, Miu. But it went well otherwise. I put all the small electronics and tool things that we could repair and sell in a pawn shop off to the side. Or at least, all the ones that looked like you could probably fix them without too much of an issue," elaborated Faith. She was actually starting to sound somewhat confident the longer she spoke. "As well as anything that uhm… how to say it… ah… it escapes me but anything old that people like to keep."

"Collectibles and antiques!" cheered Andrea while handing another pancake to Miu.

"Yes! Those. I kept anything like that as well. You said you wished to avoid selling gold or silver," Faith said with a grin, her eyes darting to Andrea and then back to Felix. "These are all things that aren't gold and silver and could sell in a pawnshop. I talked to Andrea and Miu about it to make sure I was thinking correctly. I'm still getting used to all these modern things.

"I mean, not that long ago, I hadn't even seen a working lightbulb. It's a lot for me to work through. I'm not Felicity. She's far more intelligent than I am."

"You're doing amazing, Faith. I had to remind myself the other day of that very fact and how well you're doing," Felix said after a hard swallow. He gave her a wide smile and a nod of his head. "In fact, I'd say you're doing incredibly well. As to your idea, I think I'll do just that. I'll go see what's fixable, what isn't, then drive it out to Hardysburg and sell it there. I wouldn't want a resident to see their own stuff in a local pawn shop. That'd be awkward.

"Is there anything else you need to add or say for your side of it? Sounds like it really went extremely well."

"I think I'd like to get a library card or to go to a used bookstore. Someone made a passing comment about how I looked like a felony," Faith said with an odd look on her face. Felix would certainly agree that Faith inspired terrible thoughts. "I took it as a cat-call, but wanted to make sure. I might as well start looking into the legal system here as… well… as we have no one to provide us with counsel. At least so far. Or maybe I'm just being silly."

Lily, if only you were here. I bet you'd already have us a house through some backward magical legal loophole.

"Ah! There was one more thing. The mayor came by," Faith blurted out, clearly trying to push his mind off Lily. "He wants to meet you. I told him it was certainly possible, but that I couldn't speak for your calendar.

"He said he'd want to meet with you sometime after it was all over and to schedule something with him. Though he did mention that he'd have to be out of town for a month or two right after that. He has to go to the capital and work out something with the state government."

"Apparently, Alassippi isn't doing so well with the budget they've been allocated. He mentioned they were deeply overspent. That would likely mean they need more aid from the government if I had to guess," Miu clarified even as she brought yet another steak and pancake set over. This one went to Faith with a smile for the Dryad before she went back to likely finish and get her own breakfast together.

She's eating steak and pancakes. How curious.

I always thought they just did nuts, berries, and the like.

Maybe Betty's group is the odd ones out?

As to meeting the mayor… maybe I can use that to my advantage.

We just need to get all of our identification paperwork together before my meeting with the mayor. I'll need all the certifications people take for granted when they were born in a country.

Hm.

I'll have to think on that. I'm not sure how to approach it just yet but… I'm sure I can solve it.

"He's contemplating that he needs to get our paperwork together. Proof that we exist and are part of the country," stated Goldie while gnawing at the meat she held in her bare hand. "That we can use the mayor, and the budget meeting, to our advantage if we can move fast enough."

One could forget she was a Dragon most of the time.

"Sorry, I don't mean to get caught up in my head all the time," apologized Felix with a small shake of his head.

"It's fine. Goldie helps us keep pace with you," Andrea said and then slammed her rear end down on the grass next to him. She had a plate filled with pancakes and nothing else. "She does Kit's old job and helps us understand where you are. If anything I like the way Goldie does it. She just tells us whatever you're thinking and doesn't try to couch it in nicey-nice words."

Ah. That makes sense.

I suppose with me being shut into myself so often that practically becomes a need.

"By the way," whispered Andrea in her not-so-secret way. "I had no idea you wanted to grab my ears and rough 'em up a bit. Goldie said you do the same with her horns.

"If you'd told Ana, she would have let you, you know. Ria, too, maybe. Not me or any of my Others though. We like it soft.

"But… but if you're especially nice with Allie the first time she comes out, she'll say yes. But you have to pretend like I didn't tell you that, or that she got way more of Ana in that department than we expected. She's bashful, but very curious."

The silence afterward was heavy and had no viable way out for Felix.

Except he didn't care.

Life with the Elex women was an adventure in every possible way. All you could do was just go along with it.

"Okay," Felix said instead with a grin. "I'll do that. Make sure you don't tell Allie about it either. Thanks, Andie. Love you."

"Nn!" grunted the Beastkin around a massive mouthful of pancake. Looking a lot like a cartoon chipmunk, she smiled at him.

***

Felix pulled up to the pawnshop and wasn't really sure how to go about this. He had a bunch of junk in the bed of the truck and he had no idea how to make this happen.

Turning, he looked at his passenger.

Goldie was quickly becoming his go-to

adviser and strategist. The fact that she could read minds in a world that thought such a thing was make-believe gave him incredible leverage.

Miu, Andrea, and Faith would all play their part he imagined, but right now he needed Goldie. Needed her intelligence, ability, and compassion toward him.

He needed his Golden One with him.

"Oh… well, that's rather flattering," Goldie said huskily and leaned toward him. "I do like the possessive edge to it, too. And yes, they're all aware that they can't help as much as they want right now, but know that'll come later.

"Don't fret over them. I'm keeping them suitably involved. As to what to do in there… well, that's more up to you. I'm not sure which way to go with this.

"I can read minds, but I'm not you, nor am I Felicity. I'll support you, but you're the lead. I'm just a Dragon who wants to be a house-wife."

Grinning, Felix realized that was exactly what he needed to hear.

He was the reason Legion rose and fell. He'd be the reason it rose again.

"Thanks," he murmured, then leaned over and kissed Goldie while reaching up to pat her cheek with his left hand. Holding that kiss for a handful of seconds, he eventually moved away from her. "My Golden One, I really appreciate that you were willing to come with me."

"Of course," she replied in a warm whisper.

"Just remember that when I want a vault of gold to nest in and that you no longer get a say in the matter."

Laughing, Felix nodded his head, opened the door, and got out. He'd long since come to the realization that he couldn't get rid of Goldie. Even if he wanted to.

Faith was the same way now.

He just had to play goalie against everyone else. There was no more room in his heart.

Closing the door to F-Two, he went into the pawn shop and had a good look around. It was more or less exactly what he expected.

From what was on sale, to people trying to sell their own stuff.

Felix was suddenly lost in memories of starting out in a store just like this one. Where he, Kit, Ioana, Lily, Miu, Felicia, and Andrea had bled, sweat, and nearly died.

It'd been fun. Hadn't it?

This'll be just as fun. Just as interesting, if not more so.

I just need to make sure Legion doesn't become a target. Soon I can start hiring. Start expanding. Making things happen.

Goldie is my Kit. My Felicity.

Miu is, of course, Miu, but also my Ioana.

Faith is aiming to be my Lily in more ways than just keeping me mentally in check.

Andrea is… Andrea and so much more now.

I can do this. I can make this work.

I have the people to start, now I just need some tools. Starting with money. Because money makes the world go round and –

Felix's thoughts came to a sudden halt.

Off to one side of the pawnshop was a display. It was deeper in the store and had a camera over it and display cases around it.

Laid out along the hooks were what appeared to be prepaid gift cards.

Walking over to them, Felix found that they were exactly what he'd suspected. Gift cards with prepaid amounts and backed by a credit card company.

Next to them, was something even more exciting.

Cards that stated they were prepaid minutes for a cellular service.

One that didn't require contracts, but only to purchase the phone.

Perfect.

Felix grinned and then moved over to the counter where someone was standing. They had been watching Felix with a storefront smile.

"Good morning, sir. How can I help you?" asked the salesman.

"Oh. Well first, I'd like to sell you some items I need to get rid of. I won an auction for a storage shed in the area and it had a bunch of things in it that don't do me any good. I have a few more to get to later this week as well," lied Felix with a warm, convincing smile. "Have it all in my truck bed. Can I get you to take a look?

"Also, I think I'd like to get store credit instead of cash, so maybe you can cut me a better deal than normal? I would love to start a decent working relationship with you and this store."

"Yeah! Let's see what we can do," agreed the man.

Hook… line… and sinker.

Chapter 10 - Rentals and Risks -

Getting into F-Two, Felix let out a slow breath. Turning, he looked over at Goldie.

She was dozing in the passenger seat and slumped low. Her head rested on the glass and her hands were in her lap.

He'd ended up working the clerk over pretty bad on prices, credit, and what he could get from him. It'd taken the better part of two hours to get it all done.

In the end, though, it'd been worth it.

Through all the back and forth, Felix had managed to get two cheap phones, several prepaid minute cards, prepaid gift cards that could be used as credit cards, and two thousand dollars in straight cash.

Faith had done a perfect job deciding what to hold onto and what to trash. Everything that she'd kept had been solid ticket items to sell to the pawnshop.

Unable to help himself, Felix let his gaze roll over the beautiful, sexy Dragon. There was no denying that he was quite attracted to her.

Almost regretfully, he withdrew his gaze and put the truck into reverse. He had things he needed to get done.

The first order of business now that he had a few tools was to get his foundation stabilized. He needed paperwork and identification.

All of that started with having a residence. A

place that you could call home.

At least to a government official.

In his old world, it all began with a home address. If you didn't have one, everything was impossible or, at least, nearly so. This one couldn't be much different than that, he imagined.

He probably couldn't even get a library card without an address.

And if I don't miss my guess, that means I'm going to have to hit up a place like where Jay lived. A mobile home park.

Because if I was looking for somewhere that wouldn't ask too many questions if I paid enough money, that'd be it. I bet the manager of the park might be willing to just… overlook it entirely with enough money.

That's where we'll start first.

I'll just have to wake my poor sleeping beauty when we get there.

"I'm awake, but I'm enjoying listening to all that praise you're throwing at me," murmured the Dragon from where she lay. Her eyes were opened as slits and she was watching him. He could clearly see a golden glow in them. Then she smiled at him. "Can't blame a Dragon for pretending to sleep to hear a little more, can you?"

Looking at her for a few more seconds Felix then grinned at her.

"Nope," he admitted and turned his gaze ahead. Putting the truck into gear, he started them off.

He needed to invest in her just as he had

Andrea, Lily, and Kit. Invest in those who invested in him.

Especially given how heavily she'd bet on him and what he could accomplish.

"When we get a chance, I want to put some very permanent rings through your horns, Goldie. Do I need to buy a drill to do that or do you think you can manage it with those pretty claws of yours?" Felix asked in a curious voice. "Then I think I want to put a number of gold chains through those rings so they spread from horn to horn.

"A very big, very obvious, very expensive display on those horns of yours. Do you think that'd be a problem? Somewhat like Taylor, but less clothes and more horns. Maybe I can upgrade them so they expand and contract with your shape-shifting. That way you never take them off."

He'd almost said "that great rack of yours" but he wasn't sure if her horns were considered a rack or some other distinction.

Felix didn't miss the low rumbling noise that filled the truck interior. A noise that was somewhere between an animal growl and rocks being ground together.

Every time he made Goldie feel especially happy, or excited, he'd heard it. To him, it felt like the Dragon equivalent to purring.

"That's right, purr for me, my Golden One. Purr for me while you contemplate how we can decorate your horns with my gold," said Felix taking a turn through an intersection. "Wearing my gold like the proud Dragon you are."

"Stop before I force you to stop the truck," Goldie said in a low guttural growl that he'd never actually heard before.

It made his skin break out in goose bumps and his spine straightened up.

"Pretty sure there's a grassy lot with trees about a mile before we reach where we're going," offered Felix as he pulled them onto the main highway out of the city, heading toward Hardysburg. Then he firmed up his resolve and his voice. He needed to make sure he took care of Goldie's needs. She claimed she wasn't like other Dragons, and he believed her. But he was willing to bet she also had an itch that'd never been scratched, too. "You're welcome to argue your point there. Though the only real thing to debate is whether we drill holes through your horns to put the rings through, or you wear them like rings on your horns."

Goldie continued to purr, her eyes glowing golden, the entire drive. All the while, Felix force-fed her thoughts of decorating her horns with his gold.

Forcing her to wear it in a way everyone could see it.

***

Pulling up to the front of the community, Felix saw exactly what he was looking for. A simple building that looked more permanent than most of the mobile homes they'd passed by.

There was a sign on the top of the building that read two words.

"Park Manager."

In the window was a small sign that had a phone number and "available for rent" below it. Felix wasn't sure if there was anyone inside, but it wouldn't hurt to go knock on the door.

Worst case, he could dial the number listed in the window. He now had the tools to act almost like a normal person.

Opening the door, Felix got out of the vehicle. Moving towards the small building, he turned around and waited for Goldie. She was going to be acting the part of his wife in this.

He watched her as she stared into the mirror that came down from above and worked at her hair. Trying to adjust it or do something with it.

He wasn't quite sure what she was about, but he saw no reason to not just wait for her.

When she finally did get out of the truck, she didn't look happy either.

"You… you tangled my hair to the point that I need to brush out several knots," she hissed under her breath, coming over to stand with him in front of the door. She looked frustrated, but under all that, he could tell she was pleased.

Very pleased.

She'd had to forcefully cut off her purring rumble several times as they drove to the community. It'd started back up without her even

knowing.

Apparently, the rough handling he'd given her in the truck was indeed what her Dragon had wanted. Perhaps even more so than he'd realized.

Seconds before his brain fired off a retort that would have been along the lines of "now tell me thank you for doing it" he brought his thoughts to a screeching halt.

Smiling instead, he gave her a raised eyebrow.

"I'm not complaining," huffed Goldie with a shake of her head. Apparently, she'd caught where his thoughts were going. "Not really, at least. Just… more horn next time, less hair. My hair can get tangled somewhat easily."

"That's fair, I'll keep that in mind for next time, my Golden One," said Felix and then captured her right hand with his left and gave it a squeeze.

Then he turned and knocked on the door several times.

Unable to help himself, his mind thought about holding onto her horns more. Then it went straight to getting jewelry that would act as a guide on where to put his hands.

"You're… are you actually—"

Goldie's voice cut off as the door opened. A man who looked to be in his thirties was standing there. He appeared incredibly tired and worn down.

He looked like someone who spent more

time than they really should up at night. That or he'd been worked to the point of nearly dropping dead.

He was tall, with dirty-blond hair and eyes that were almost metallic looking. Given his frame, and slim physique, it reminded Felix of the walking dead.

"Hey," said the man, blinking owlishly.

"Are you alright?" Felix asked in an almost reflexive way. The man looked like hell.

"Uh… oh, yeah. I'm alright, just… really tired," muttered the man, finally making full eye contact with Felix and then Goldie. "Hi, yeah, how can I help you?"

"Looking to rent. Willing to pay cash up front," Felix said without beating around the bush at all. "Month to month and hopefully little oversight."

"Yeah, whatever," said the man with a shake of his head. "Come in then. We'll do the simple forms and go from there. You stickin' around for more than a month?"

"Possibly, not sure yet," Felix answered honestly. Pointing at Goldie, he followed up with an outright lie. "We're a bit on the run from her brother. He'd never look here so… good place to be."

Sniffing once, the man looked from Goldie to Felix, then shrugged.

"Fine. You stay longer than a month and I'll need more than just the up-front money. I'm just a manger for the place, I don't own it," explained the man. "Deposit is five forty. Rent is five hundred. Need the rent and deposit up front.

"Don't care otherwise about anything you have to say. Unless it's that you're staying for two months and that's when the IDs need to come out."

"Right," Felix said with a frown, then he shook his head. This was likely exactly what one would expect for the area. It's just how it was. "Let's get that data you need filled in and we'll go from there."

"Yea, course, whatever," grumbled the man. With a sigh, he went back into the small building without saying a word.

Entering behind him, Felix and Goldie stepped inside.

It was a small office with a desk and five chairs. Four were for guests and the desk looked like it was being used more as a place of study. It was almost completely covered in what looked to be medical textbooks and assignment work.

There was a small placard atop the desk with likely the man's name on it.

Treston Cuzzort. Well, you're bedside manner is terrible.

I bet you're a know-it-all, too.

"Names?" droned Treston, staring at a paper in front of himself, pen in hand.

But at least… this is going to go exactly the way I want it. After we're done here, it's a visit to the local library.

They used to have open computers for anyone with a library card. I bet I could weasel a little time out of the librarian.

A simple sob story and there we go.

"—die Campbell," answered Goldie with a small nod of her head. Then she turned and looked at Felix. There was most certainly a faint glow in her eyes.

Apparently, he wasn't off the hook yet for thinking about buying her hand holds to wear on her horns.

***

"Thanks again," Felix whispered quietly as the librarian unlocked the computer. She was an older woman with gray hair and soft eyes. He'd given her exactly what he'd planned.

A simple sob story that he'd been kicked out, rented a mobile home for himself, and was trying to start over. He needed to get some duplicates of his records.

That was all it took for the aging woman to guide him right over to a computer, so he could get started.

"Of course, and good luck," replied the librarian with a small hand wave. "Just lock it when you're done. It'll need a password to get back in."

Felix nodded his head minutely and then watched the librarian leave.

As soon as she was out of sight, he turned to

the computer and sat there for a moment. He was hopeful that the computer system would at least be similar enough to what he was used to that he could make it work.

Grabbing the mouse, he gave it a small flick and found it to be responsive. Looking at the keyboard, he was momentarily concerned about the fact that it was physical.

He hadn't used anything with a physical layout in a long while. His light terminal had never really needed one and they'd fallen out of use since they tended to break.

Putting his wrists to the pad, he laid his fingers on the keys. It felt very strange to have actual physical resistance rather than feedback.

Whatever.

He moved the mouse to one of the icons and then just double-clicked it. He had no idea what the web browser would be named so he'd have to guess a bit.

Almost instantly, an application opened.

It looked to be some type of database for newspapers.

Closing it, he opened another program through double-clicking its icon.

This one opened, flashed a box, and then closed.

So… not that one.

With a sigh, Felix tried the third.

Then the fourth, fifth, and sixth.

It wasn't until he got to the seventh that the

screen flashed to something he did recognize. It looked a lot like the Internet, or so his memory told him. It reminded him of what it'd looked like ten years ago from his own world.

Moving the mouse to the top of the bar, he clicked into it then typed "search engine".

Results were populated immediately.

Picking the top one, Felix felt like he was at least making progress.

I wonder how my Golden One is doing.

Typing out a simple search for "duplicate birth identification", Felix got back a suggested alternative.

A search for birth certificates.

It opened another page and displayed a small box in the middle of the screen. Felix noted that it was asking his location so he simply hit the accept button.

The screen flickered twice more as it did something in the background, then brought up a new page.

Greene County clerk's office. Well, I suppose that answers that. That wasn't too terrible at all, in fact.

There was a note below the location that said that due to the current situation, it was linked to the Vital Records office and could provide all services from its location.

On a hunch, Felix typed in a search for vital records and a birth certificate, which kicked him out to a much more in-depth page and search.

Hm. Seems like I'll need to go there in person and

see what I can figure out. I'm sure there's some type of workaround to get this going.

The question is, would I find it in a random web search, or directed telepathy at the clerk's office with Goldie.

It didn't take him long to realize the answer was simple. Going with Goldie to the clerk's office along with some money for a bribe if he needed it would be his best option.

That was going to be how this one worked out, he imagined.

If it didn't, he'd have to see about getting one illegally through the underworld, rather than getting a legitimate, though still illegal, birth certificate made for him.

Guess that's all I can do about it for now.

Though… out of curiosity… let's try something else first. No sense in leaving immediately for that address.

Felix opened up the search window again and typed in a search on how to get a driver's license. Maneuvering through the websites, he found his answer relatively quickly.

Two forms of residency, social security card, birth certificate.

Okay… residency isn't too hard. Just get something sent to the trailer with a bill. Birth certificate, working on that.

A social security card though… hm. How do I get that one?

Once more, he backed into the search engine and put in another query.

This one turned up an entire listing for the Social Security Administration.

So... birth certificate and driver's license, school record, or medical record.

Alright. Can get the first one, but the license requires the card. So... something else.

Felix scrolled down to the next page to see more examples.

He snorted at the fact he could use a church membership as a form of valid ID to get a social security card. Moving through the list, he found that the most likely answer was going to be a medical record.

He'd just need to find a doc who he could blackmail or bribe. That wouldn't be very hard at all. They were just everyday normal people with normal people problems.

Just get them to bill me for some type of procedure, have them list out my birthdate which will match my birth certificate, get it all registered to the trailer, there we go. That'd be enough according to this.

Then leverage this to get the social security card, and that to get the driver's license. I can get most of this squared away relatively quickly, but... not quickly enough.

I'll have to go slow with the mayor. That or take a different route.

What... does it take to start a business?

Several quick searches later and he managed to get an answer. He just had to get a registered agent to handle it for him. That meant a lawyer who would act as his touch point.

That'd solve most of the paperwork I need, I suppose. Just hit the lawyer with the same shotgun double blast as the doc. Bribery or blackmail, whichever works better.

Leaning back in the chair, Felix was rather glad he'd taken the time to come here. He hadn't been completely sure of how to go about his plan, or how to make it reasonably work given their lack of documentation.

Once I get mine all squared away, we can start working on everyone else. We should be relatively clothed in identity within… a month?

That feels about right.

Smirking to himself, Felix only had one search left to do. Finding a lawyer who could represent them for the LLC.

Except rather than typing in the right search, he put in a broad search for Lillian Lux, attorney at law, criminal justice.

With a single click of the enter key, Felix felt the ground fall out from under him.

On the first result, at the top of the page, was Lily.

Unable to stop himself, Felix clicked that and more information came up.

Lillian Lux and associates. She… exists in this world.

Feeling his mouth start to turn to a frown and his breathing become irregular, he forced himself to look away from the screen. He couldn't look at her smiling face on the page for a single second longer.

It wasn't his Lily, but this world's Lily.

She was a stranger to him, but it still hurt.

Incredibly so.

Glancing back at the page, Felix backed it up so it came off that search. Then he did the most damning thing he could probably do to himself.

He searched for Kit Carrington.

Her name was fairly uncommon but it wasn't unique. The likelihood of finding her was rather small.

Felix clicked on the images selector since he had no idea what kind of job she'd even be in. In fact, he was rather certain this was a waste of time.

Except he found her.

Clicking on the picture of Kit with long hair, smiling, and looking incredibly happy, he was redirected to a new page. One that was about Kit.

Kit Carrington, charity organizer, psychologist Ph.D. Because, of course, she would.

Of course… she would.

Shaking his head, Felix did the only reasonable thing he could. He locked the computer, got up, and walked away.

Goldie was napping in the truck and right now he needed someone to talk him out of his mental funk. She was likely the only one who'd really understand him at the moment.

Fucking stupid, Felix.

Chapter 11 - Surviving First Contact -

It'd been almost a week since Felix had dug up the information he needed and rented the trailer. The time had slipped by since then, one day after another, pushing the deadline Runner had given them ever closer.

Except there really hadn't been much that Felix could do.

He hadn't been able to simply show up at the clerk's office and see someone. He'd tried, in fact. Felix would have to make an appointment.

Any meeting with the clerk had to be scheduled in advance.

That had pushed back a great deal of what he wanted to do. Everything else was mostly dependent on getting a birth certificate.

Stepping out of the doctor's office, Felix sniffed and looked around at the parking lot. Then he looked toward the horizon.

At least that's done.

One medical record with birthdate, medical history, and records of immunization.

Dandy.

Doctor was rather cheap, too. Didn't even have to bribe her.

Just pay out-of-pocket for services that I technically didn't need.

Smirking to himself, Felix started walking back to F-Two. He'd come here by himself as everyone else was busy.

Andrea was watching the campsite while Goldie, Miu, and Faith were working the drop point for the last day.

The latter three had doctor's appointments in the coming days with the same doctor to start up their own medical records. They'd need to get their own paper trail moving as well.

Andrea was still dragging her feet about accepting a modification so that she could hide her tail and ears. Felix wasn't really sure about it, but he still suspected that her hesitation had to do with Allison.

Opening the truck door, Felix got in and contemplated what to do next.

They were due to drop in on Jay tonight to get their first payout, as well as to change the quality of his supply.

Which meant Felix had a few hours to himself and nothing to rush off and do.

It was an odd and rare occurrence for him.

Well… let's check our points. See how we're doing.

Plan for tonight with Jay, and get ready. We're finally past a lot of the setup steps and can start moving things.

Somewhat… disappointing that I couldn't get everything together in time to push something with the mayor. I'll just have to work that relationship when he gets back.

Felix shook his head and called up his personal character sheet.

Name: Felix Campbell	**Race**: Demi-God (Shared Portfolio)
Alias: Felix (Over 50 items. Click to expand.)	**Power:** Modification (Limited)
Physical Status: Healthy.	**Mental Status:** Relaxed.
Positive Statuses: Comfortable with Yourself	**Negative Statuses**: None

Might:	11	Add +1? (1100)
Finesse:	13	Add +1? (1300)
Endurance:	10	Add +1? (1000)
Competency:	97	Add +1? (9700)
Intellect:	74	Add +1? (7400)
Perception:	16	Add +1? (1600)
Luck:	08	Add +1? (800)

Let's… change that luck value. Let's push it up.

If I brought it real high, I could probably make more things happen. More things go my way.

Time to check the points.

	Generated	**Remaining**
Andrea	560	560
Faith	250	250
Felix	1,510	1,510
Goldie	1,905	1,905
Miu	900	900
+Loyalty Bonus	400	400

+Marital Bonus	400	400
=Daily Total	**5,000**	**5,925**
Banked Total	—	**87,619**

That's curious. There's been some increases there. But... why?

Are people naturally growing incrementally without me doing anything? I suppose that'd make sense. It's not like people are locked into something, they could increase it on their own.

I could go hit the gym and try to increase my stats. Couldn't I?

I mean realistically I could... I could... go to the gym... then... take back a hundred points? Huh.

Something to consider, I suppose. Sounds like too much effort.

Let's do my luck for now.

Felix tapped into his character sheet again and then increased his luck. Spending the eight-hundred points to get it to nine, then did so again to get it to ten.

Except a blue-box popped up in front of him.

Target: Felix Campbell	**Action >> Lvl. Increase**: +Luck Type + 900 pts.

"Ah, the dreaded level nine. Time to see how to do this. Can I click or tap or—"

Felix had been poking, flicking, and thinking on the "+ Luck Type" part of the message.

Suddenly it expanded into another box.

"Item considered lucky," Felix read aloud from the small prompt. "So... I need an item that's considered lucky, plus the points, to increase it to level ten.

"I wonder if it's so generic because it's a low level? Feels somewhat easy. Whatever... what's lucky. I mean, is it what I consider lucky, or what this world considers lucky?"

Looking down and out the window Felix stared at the parking lot he was in. Then his eyes slowly moved to the curb and where it met a storm drain.

"Maybe a penny?" he asked no one.

Opening the door to his truck Felix started to walk down along the curb. Looking down at it as he went, wondering if he'd actually be lucky enough to find a penny.

Given his luck stat was technically one point below what he assumed was the average, that seemed unlikely.

Grinning to himself given the situation, he didn't even notice it when he nearly ran someone over. He was so head-down intent on the curb that he'd lost his awareness of what was around him.

"Hey, you okay?" asked a husky voice that snapped right through Felix's thoughts.

Looking up he found a rather attractive dark skinned woman in front of him. She had a curious smile on her face and raised eyebrows.

Unable to help himself, he grinned and

shrugged his shoulders. There was something that always tickled at the base of his skull with a voice like that.

"Ah, I was just looking for a lucky penny," explained Felix.

"What if my name was Penny? Would you try to pick me up? Give you good luck for the day?" asked the woman brazenly.

Blinking twice, Felix had no idea how to respond to that.

Laughing, the woman looked like she found the situation hilarious. Then she reached into her purse, rifled around in it for a few seconds, before dropping a penny on the ground and walked away.

She didn't say another word, though she did linger in his thoughts.

Reaching down, Felix picked up the lucky penny.

Then he made the conversion of said lucky penny and points, to bring his luck up. A box immediately flew up onto his screen.

Message: Congratulations! You've successfully brought your luck up to the second grouping!

"Neat," murmured Felix with a smile. He was rather enjoying the way his power worked now. It felt a lot more natural to use.

Let's head over to the trailer park. Can go see my… home… even if I'm not living in it.

Whatever, getting what I need out of it. An

address.

***

Being at the back of the community was an interesting experience, Felix found.

First and foremost was the fact the he assumed he was the most likely to be targeted by an outsider. Someone looking to make a quick escape. Since the trailer was on the perimeter, literally at the exit, then it was likely he'd be the easiest to hit.

Second, he got to see any and every car come through that was trying to avoid the front entrance. Which was rather interesting all on it's own.

He'd spotted three cars on their way past a few hours ago that were very much out of place driving in. Newer cars without flaking paint, dents, or visible signs of self-repair.

The question Felix had was were they there for him, or something else entirely. He'd told Jay to expect him in about a week, and that would put him at today, or tomorrow.

Kit had often accused him of being paranoid so it was entirely plausible that this was one of those situations once again. Except he didn't believe that.

Right now he was fairly certain that those cars were here for Jay, and by that logic, here for Felix. It meant he'd have to be extra careful on his visit tonight.

A sudden and firm knock on the door

brought him out of his thoughts.

Walking over to it he simply opened it. There was no reason for him to be cautious.

He could feel Faith beyond the door. In fact, he could practically feel her at all times now. As if the seed she'd put into his chest was a constant homing beacon to and from Faith.

Miu, Goldie, and Faith all came into the trailer. They were all dressed in normal street clothes, but dark in color. Goldie also had a small plastic bag with her that likely had all the masks she'd made.

"Saw three cars that didn't belong," Felix started, jumping straight to the part of the conversation that would be relevant. "Looked expensive and new without even getting into the lack of problems on them. Drove through the back and kept going."

"Three?" asked Miu, stopping in her tracks and turning to look at him.

"Mmhmm. Three. Miu Campbell, would you please go look into it for your husband? He's concerned that they're planning something nasty at Jay's place," asked Felix in a warm and friendly voice.

Miu jerked at the sudden use of her name, then began to shiver as he laid out his self-described title on her. Her eyes fell down to stare at his boots even as her body practically vibrated.

"Miu my love, my eyes are up here," murmured Felix with a smile. He needed to get her on the right mental track, but also set hard on a hair-trigger tonight.

His instincts were telling him that this was going to go wrong at some level. He was without his armor, without weapons, and only had those around him to take action with.

In a flash, Miu's eyes jumped up to his own, then widened. Her pupils were completely dilated at the moment. As if she were going to have an eye examination.

"There's my Miu. Such lovely eyes," said Felix, stepping up to her. He reached out and took her hands in his own. Holding on to them he gave them a squeeze. "Miu, go check it out for me? Don't do anything we can't undo. Yet.

"We need to see what they want first. Okay? For me?"

Panting and breathing hard, Miu was gazing at him in a way he knew. This was usually when she got bitey, started licking his blood off where-ever it landed, or just became a gibbering mess.

Brokenly, she began to nod her head up and down.

"Good. Then put the control in place for a short time. When it's all done, we'll figure out how to get you a reward. Alright?" Felix inquired, holding her eyes with his own.

The shivering and panting slowly bled away from Miu. Almost like a bucket with a hole in it. Till the only thing that remained was the iron-clad will of Miu and eyes that burned from the inside-out.

Watching him with a form of dedication that would likely scare off anyone else.

"Yes. I'll do that. Thank you," Miu said without explanation. She gave his hands a squeeze, then exited the trailer. Vanishing into the darkness outside.

"That was very well done, Nest-mate," remarked Goldie, giving him a blazing smile. "You're really pulling out that charm of yours lately. You've got all four of us neatly tied up and begging for more. Even me, despite the fact that I can read your mind.

"That devious mind of yours is always so twisty. It's fun to try to keep up with it."

"Just giving everyone what they want and need, while getting what I want and need," countered Felix. Then he looked to Faith. "You got any healing magic at all? Runner told me it would be pretty weak if it was there at all."

With a grimace, Faith shook her head.

"I have a little. Not much. The only magic I can reasonably count on is sex magic and that's not exactly helpful," answered Faith. Then she let out a soft huff as Felix opened his mouth to get an actual answer. "Before you just ask again, I can probably speed up recovery to half of what it would normally take. That's about it, Grove-husband."

With a nod of his head, Felix turned to look at Goldie. He was going to need her to be a Dragon tonight. It was the best course of action that'd give them the best protection.

"Oh?" asked Goldie, apparently plucking the thought from his mind before he could finish it. She set the bag of masks down right there. "I can do that. It would be a good time for you to look at the piercings I made in my horns. They're already closing so I'll have to keep an eye on them and widen them until we get your gold in. Then we can let it seal up around them."

"Piercings?" Faith asked curiously.

"Piercings for him to weave bridal gold into them. He's going to decorate my horns and I'm rather excited about it. Now, excuse me," apologized Goldie who went to the back of the trailer where the bedroom was. She was already working at stripping her clothes of as she went.

The door shut behind her leaving Felix with Faith.

"Huh. Never seen her so happy. It's radiating out of her," said Faith, looking to him.

"You got your tree, she gets her horn-gold, Miu got my affection, Andrea already had what she wanted," Felix put forward succinctly.

"What about you, though?" Faith asked after a pause.

"I got all of you," he replied with a smirk. "Now, come on Faith. You're my bodyguard, aren't you?"

"I... yes, Grove-husband. I am," she said and then pulled a pistol out of her hoodie pocket. She flicked the safety down, pulled the chamber back partially, then let it move back into place. Sticking her hands, and her pistol, back into the pockets of her hoodie she shrugged her shoulders. "I'm ready."

Huh. Didn't expect that but it makes sense.

Wonder where she got that.

Whatever, good that she has it.

"I'm ready," called Goldie a second before she opened the door. She exited the bedroom nude, her horns visible, and came straight toward him. "See? This is where your bridal gold will go."

She was pointing to several holes that ran up and down both horns. They were perfectly symmetrical, placed dead center, and looked very clean.

"Good. I like the placement. Great job, Goldie," Felix said and meant it. He reached into the bag and took out three masks. He handed one to Faith and stuffed one into his pocket. The third he held onto. "Now, let's get to moving. Time to go get our money. Miu will probably have already infiltrated what's going on. She'll catch up to us by the time we hit the halfway point I bet."

"Think so?" asked Faith, opening the door to the outside and exiting.

"Know so. I know so," Felix asserted. "She's my pet monster. I know her better than anyone else. Even better than I know Lily or Kit or myself."

Exiting with Faith, Felix began walking behind her. Then he reached out and put a hand on her back and grabbed hold. Then he looked backward.

"Keep going," he said when it felt like Faith would stop.

He wanted to watch Goldie transform but not stop either.

Stepping out of the trailer Goldie pulled the door shut. She caught her eyes on him, gave him a wide smile, then walked away from the door. She got ten feet beyond it before she jumped into the air.

Surprisingly fast as ever she became a giant Gold dragon and then launched off into the sky. Her wings flapping down hard and carrying her skyward.

"Wish you'd watch me like that," whispered Faith.

Felix only chuckled and looked ahead, taking a moment to pat Faith on the hip. He knew for a fact she wanted him to touch her.

"I do watch you. Just not when you're aware of it. Alright, let's be ready. This is going to probably get crazy," Felix warned.

"Yeah. That's fine. I'm not your every-day normal Dryad, you remember," Faith murmured. Her head slowly turned as she scanned the area.

True. She's been in some ugly situations. Ioana, Andrea, Miu, and Victoria all said Faith was solid in combat.

It wouldn't take long for them to get close to Jay's trailer.

When they reached the half-way point Felix pulled down the Mask over his head. Faith did the same and then a second after that Miu appeared.

"They're there," she said, coming up out of the darkness from the side. She'd been crouched low, practically invisible, and blended into the shadows. "Jay's there and so is a bunch of others. They don't look very friendly. Lot of guns.

"I took several guards out that were spread throughout the area. Took their stuff. Hid it all near Jay's trailer so we can take it with us. They didn't know anything other than they were coming here to help their boss deal with Jay."

Huh. In other words, Jay isn't the issue.

But perhaps the person supplying Jay with the drugs is? Maybe he tried to lower his purchase rate and they didn't like that much.

Probably escalated from there.

That or it's another dealer who wants Jay's supplier.

Felix held the mask out for Miu and smiled at her.

"Good work, Miu. Amazing, even. I didn't expect you to take care of the guards, too. Impressive," Felix said, holding out a mask to her. "Now we just figure out what the hell is going on."

Miu grinned, took the mask, then moved over to stand next to Faith. Pulling it down over her head she said something to the other woman.

She responded by suddenly veering left and moving off into the dark, leaving Felix with Miu.

Then they were there, standing in front of the trailer. Felix looked skyward and was fairly confident Goldie was up there somewhere.

"Give the door a knock and let'em know we're here, Miu. Be wary," cautioned Felix.

Not hesitating the dark-eyed psychopath who loved him marched up, slammed her fist to the door, and stood there.

"We're here for what we're owed. You can finish your meeting later," called Miu through the door.

Stepping away from it, she marched back to Felix and then stood in front of him. Waiting with him there.

There was no response from inside. Apparently that'd been more than enough to spook both Jay and whoever was with him.

This is… stupid.

Going in there is a death trap.

So… let's not do that.

"Miu, where'd Faith go?" asked Felix.

"Get an SMG. She's on the other side now," she answered.

Felix then made a choice. One that would properly demonstrate how silly this situation was.

Goldie. Pick up this damn mobile-home, me, faith, and Miu, and take us somewhere else. Let's have a chat with these people elsewhere.

We'll make too big a scene here.

There was a strange and sudden stillness to the world.

Then Goldie came down, grabbed him up with a claw and then popped him into her mouth. A second after that Miu and Faith were deposited next to him.

It went exactly as he'd expected. There'd be no way for her to hold onto them while carrying the mobile home.

Then the world went dark even as people began screaming.

There was a sudden wrenching noise followed by the feeling of going up into the sky. All while Felix was pushed up Goldie's teeth by her tongue.

This time he was thankfully facing away from Faith and Miu. Last time he'd been kissed to death by the Dryad.

Felix just sat there and waited with a smile.

This was a far better plan.

Chapter 12 - Parks and Rekt -

"Did you tell her to eat us!?" yelled Miu while inside Goldie's mouth.

"No, I just told her to pick us up. She's done this before. It isn't an issue. We've done this exact thing already," explained Felix.

"I liked last time better," complained Faith. "Goldie, we need to talk about how to make this work out better."

"Mmmhmmm," rumbled Goldie, making every part of Felix vibrate. "'Ai ohn ie eh."

"You don't like it?" asked Felix. He was pretty sure that was what she said. "What, carrying us in your mouth? Goldie, I love being in your mouth."

"Stop flirting with the Dragon," hissed Miu. She sounded like she wasn't enjoying any of this in any way.

Felix only grinned and fell silent.

There was no need to antagonize Miu if she was feeling insecure at the moment.

It only took a few minutes before there was a loud thump. It then felt like Goldie landed on the ground.

Which was proven to be true when she bent her head down and spat the three of them out. Followed by her moving her jaw around.

"Ugh, I hate doing that but... it could be worse, I suppose," growled the Dragon, turning to look at the mobile home. "It certainly worked as we needed it to."

Standing up, Felix brushed himself off a bit but found he was generally better off than he expected. He wasn't as saliva-covered as he'd been previously.

"Okay," Felix said looking at the trailer. "Hello, the interior. Jay and guest. Since you didn't respond, we've changed the location. You'll have to pardon me for insisting.

"I just don't take it very well when people wait for me with weaponry. I'm sure you understand."

Once again, there was no response from the interior.

"Goldie, pop that sucker open like it's a damn cereal box and there's a prize at the bottom," grumbled Felix.

A massive golden claw came out and pulled back the roof of the mobile home. It cracked and creaked as wood shattered. She got a look inside and then let the roof drop back into place.

"They're there and are armed. They aimed at me," complained Goldie, looking at Felix.

Ah, good point. No telling what bullets will do to her in this world.

Even in the previous one, she took damage and she was likely stronger there, than here.

"Shall we talk now, since I've proven I can get to you regardless? Or would you rather I have the interior burned out and I have to go find another dealer?" asked Felix. "Because I can just as easily leave a bunch of burnt corpses in the woods as not. Makes no never mind to me."

"We'll talk!" called a voice Felix didn't recognize. "Can we come out?"

"Yep, come on out then. We'll have a chat about what's going on and what we're doing about it," agreed Felix.

He needed the money and if this was how it had to be, then so be it. He certainly didn't want to become the kingpin of crime which meant he had to keep them alive, or start over.

Being a Godfather of crime didn't bother him so long as he wasn't the one everyone believed to be in charge. He wouldn't repeat the mistakes of the past.

There was no way he'd be a target for anyone if he could prevent it.

Unfortunately, for a situation like this, he didn't have the luxury of choice.

The door to the home opened and nearly closed on itself.

The whole thing was slanted to one side and incredibly lopsided. It was as if the center of the mobile home was cracked in half.

"I might have lost my grip on it and uh... dropped it... at the last second," mumbled Goldie.

Once again, the door opened, only this time held open with a visible hand. Two men came out with their hands raised up in front of themselves.

Felix didn't recognize either one.

A third man exited the trailer and practically

fell out, missing the first step.

When he gained his balance, his hands came up with a very large looking pistol. He lined it up on Felix and pulled the trigger.

Before he could react to the situation, Goldie was there. Her large body practically appeared in front of him.

A number of shots were fired from more than one weapon before there was a brief scream followed by a crunch. Someone else began to scream instead.

Felix was pressed up against Goldie's back leg now. Trying to keep himself out of view. Looking up towards her head, he found she was leaning back in an odd way.

Then he noticed there was a leg sticking out of her mouth, as well as the upper half of another man who was screaming. He was grasping the bottom of Goldie's jaw.

With a shake of her head, Goldie somehow dislodged the screaming man from his hold and enveloped them both completely in her mouth. Then she began chewing, turning her head to look at the trailer once again.

I-yeah. Forgot you're a Dragon who eats people.

No idea at all how you can find a snack like me interesting.

Goldie's head tilted to one side and she paused in her chewing. One bright golden eye was looking at him now.

It doesn't bother me.

You're still my Golden One. My personal glorious Dragon.

I just... forgot what went with being a Dragon.

Still amazing, still lovely, still love you.

Goldie's large reptilian snout wrinkled and she looked away from him. She chewed several more times, than spat the entire mess out to one side.

What remained of the men was a rather hideous mess of crushed flesh, severed limbs, and blood. They were quite dead and had been pulverized by her teeth.

"Ugh. You know, I didn't even think about it when I started to chew," remarked Goldie in an odd way. "It was almost reflexive. Except they didn't taste good. At all.

"I think it was Taylor who mentioned something about it but I discounted it. Now I understand. Having a Human Nest-mate changes things. He really did taste like mud and dirt."

Goldie moved away from him and then stepped to one side. She didn't seem to have anything else to say or do.

As she moved to the side, he could see why.

Miu and Faith had the remaining two people at gunpoint and they were on their knees. Most of them looked terrified and disbelieving.

Apparently, it was one thing to have a Dragon rip the roof off your house, yet an altogether different experience to watch it more or less eat people.

"We'll make this simple," Felix said, coming over to the men. He recognized Jay immediately and made a small wave at the man with his hand. "What the hell are you doing here, and why are you getting into my business? Jay and I were just selling drugs and not bothering anyone."

"I… I'm his supplier," said the man directly next to Jay. "I wanted your contact. You've got some crazy connections. Shit's pure."

"I'm aware," murmured Felix in a bored tone. Then he sighed and wondered how to do this. This was becoming troublesome.

The best and easiest answer was to kill them and leave their corpses here. There'd be no way for anyone to figure out what'd happened.

"Don't, please," pleaded Jay. "Don't kill us. He just didn't get it. We all just want to make money. Right?"

Jay had turned to look at his supplier kneeling next to him while he was speaking.

Walking forward, Felix got close enough to finally see the face of the man.

The man looked to be just an inch or two shy of six-foot if Felix had to guess. His hair was more of a reddish brown. Neither his hair nor his goatee really held much of anything for Felix to gauge something on.

His eyes were a different matter, however.

He was staring at Felix directly and didn't seem to be as completely cowed as the others. His hazel eyes were glaring up at Felix, in fact. As if he were angry about the situation.

"Well, Mr. Supplier," started Felix.

"David Hoerner. Or if you're going to be formal about it, Mr. Hoerner," answered the man.

"Oh? Interesting. Well. What exactly did you want? I'm busy. I was here to collect money, not bury bodies in the woods," elaborated Felix. "Unless you have money for me… well… my night is squandered and I won't be happy about that."

Faith took that moment to bring the barrel of her SMG right up to the temple of the man. She forced him to actually move his head to one side.

"Do anything other than talk and I pull the trigger," promised Faith.

David did nothing as requested and just knelt there.

"No. No money on me. But… I can get you that. I just wanted your contact," answered David. "Yeah, I was gonna take it by force if I had to, too. It is what it is."

"Well, you're in luck then. Because I very much want money. In fact, it's all I want. I don't want anything to do with your business, other than to get money from you," revealed Felix. "I want to make your drugs a better quality, you pay me for the service, and then that's it. Then I want to do it again later, for more money. And then again. And again.

"In fact, maybe this'll work out. Maybe you're exactly what I needed. How about you start bringing me your drugs, make me the owner of them by the way—that's an important and must happen step—then I fix them up to a better quality. You pay me for it up front, at half the cost that you would have saved, then leave. That's the extent of the involvement I want. There's nothing else I can tell you, because that's it.

"The reason? There is no contact. It's just me and what I can do. Me, my bodyguards, and my big, scary-ass, fucking Dragon.

"That's the deal you're getting. You can bring the drugs to a location I'll designate later for you. Leave them there along with the money. I'll have the drugs delivered back to a place you want. Take it or don't."

David seemed to be thinking that one through, his eyes finally moving down from Felix to consider the grass in front of him. Then he nodded his head minutely.

"Alright, I'll take it," he said. "I'll even pay you a one-off fee for this misunderstanding."

"Is he lying? Do I just have a bullet put into his head?" Felix asked, not looking at Goldie.

"I think he's trustworthy," answered Goldie. She was off to the side and partly laying on her stomach now. "He'll hold the bargain."

In other words, he's not planning on doing anything. I just need to make sure I keep Goldie with me in the future. My private, personal, magical eight ball.

"Wonderful. Then… let's get this on the road. I suddenly feel like we're all done here and don't need to worry about this anymore," Felix stated, and then gestured at the trailer. "Jay, do you own… this?"

"Err, yeah, bought it," Jay replied, slowly letting his hands fall down to his sides.

"Alright. Well, it's obviously ruined," Felix said with a frown. Then he blew out a breath. There was no way to really make this work out very well.

"I'll have him put in a new one," offered David. "I own the community. I'll just give him a new one. I'll get the papers on this one and make it so it was mine a week ago. Then I'll write it off as insurance."

"Great, there we go," Felix said, pointing at David. "Thanks for handling that. Appreciate it. Hopefully, this is the last time we meet like this and we can just make money.

"Because that's all I'm after. Money. I don't care about territory, turf, or anything else. Just money. That's all I want. Is that clear enough?

"I just want money. Money is all that matters to me."

"Got it. Money is your thing," said David as Faith slowly pulled the gun back from his head.

Slowly, Faith, Miu, and Felix fell back to Goldie's position. The Dragon was watching everything quietly. Her glowing eyes moved back and forth.

He imagined that most people would look at her and think she was just ready to pounce.

However, Felix felt like there was something considerably wrong here. Wrong and he didn't know how or why.

"Please escort our guests out," Felix said, turning to face Miu directly. He needed her to handle this situation because he really was getting a strong feeling of unease from Goldie.

Miu had never actually lowered her weapon. It'd been trained on the two men the entire time. Now she was rushing toward them, radiating hostility and death.

"Up! Now! I'll shoot you both for no reason other than I don't care. Then I'll let him do what he wants to me to pay off your deaths," hissed Miu.

There was a real promise in her voice that made it sound like they were only minutes away from losing their lives.

Jay and David both scrambled to their feet and started moving at a very brisk walk. Felix wasn't even sure if they were walking in the right direction, but he didn't care.

He trusted his personal psycho completely. She'd take care of them and handle it while he looked after Goldie.

"Goldie, what's wrong?" hissed Felix, coming right up to her head.

Which was now laying on the ground. She was breathing shallow and fast; her eyes looked a bit glazed.

"I don't know. They shot me. A lot. Hurts. Didn't think it was... anything at first. I've been shot a lot before," replied the Dragon. Her eyes were focused on him and seemed wider than normal. "I think-I think... I'm dying."

Faith was there next to him. Her hands rested on Goldie's shoulders and neck. It was obvious she was using what little magic she had to find out what was wrong.

Felix realized belatedly he could do the same.

I want to fix whatever's wrong with Goldie.

Name: Goldie Campbell	**Condition**: Fatally Wounded
If No Action Taken: Death	**Action >> Revitalize**: Cost 67,301 points

"One of the rounds skimmed her heart. Must've been a real big round," exclaimed Faith in a low voice. "It's beating, but there's something wrong with it. I don't… I don't know what though.

"She's a Dragon, so she's tougher than most things out there, but she's also just flesh and blood. I feel like maybe she's weaker here than she would be back home."

Far less magical, much more mundane.

She's more of a beast than a fantastic creature.

"I can heal her," Felix answered the unspoken question. "It says she's fatally wounded. I have no idea if I can bring people back from the dead, either. If she dies, there might not be a coming back."

"What? You didn't ask Runner about that?" squawked Faith.

"I didn't even consider it, to be honest. It's not like you asked him either, so don't give me that," Felix spat back.

"How many... points?" breathed Goldie in a rasp.

"Something like sixty-eight thousand. Near to that," answered Felix, moving over to Faith.

He wanted to see how much it would cost to give her enough power to heal Goldie.

Name: Faith Campbell	**Condition**: Panicked
If No Action Taken: Nothing	**Action >> Empower**: Cost 871,887 points

"Fuck, it's damn near a million points to get you the power you need to heal her," cursed Felix, looking back to Goldie.

"It's okay. Just bring me... back after I... die," Goldie panted with a warm smile. "It'll be... okay."

Shaking his head, Felix refused that answer.

He'd lost enough already; he wasn't going to take another loss here and now.

Okay. Okay.

Ah… okay. How many points would it take to improve Goldie's regenerative powers enough to not die and recover? Just exactly that much regenerative powers.

Name: Goldie Campbell	**Condition**: Fatally

	Wounded
If No Action Taken: Death	**Action >> Alter Race Power**: Cost 31,192 points

Half? Okay. Done. Fuck you and this.

Half it is!

Felix stabbed at the button and then plastered himself to Goldie's head. Holding on to her with his arms outstretched.

"Okay, you big lug," said Felix, his faced pressed against her jaw. "You're going to regenerate now. It was cheaper than fixing it, so I'm guessing you already had something trying to fix it in the background.

"We just need to get you home and let you rest. You'll be fine, Goldie," promised Felix. "My Golden One."

Goldie was breathing hard, but didn't respond. He did feel her tip her head slightly, as if to nuzzle him.

Then she shrunk down to her Human form.

The beautiful and very naked woman lay on the ground with a great deal of blood splashed down her front and midsection.

Reaching down, Felix picked her up and held onto her. He knew he wouldn't be able to carry her all the way back, but he could at least start on it.

"Go get the truck, Faith. We're taking Goldie home," Felix commanded and began trekking in what he believed was the direction of the trailer park.

He had a fairly good idea based on the current position of the moon and where it had been, though he wasn't sure.

"This the right direction?" he asked the Dryad even as he began walking.

"Yes, keep going that way. Keep the moon on your left. I'll-I'll get the truck," Faith said and then set off at a dead sprint.

"You'll be fine, Goldie. Just fine," Felix said, his arms holding her close.

She just rubbed her cheek against his shoulder and said nothing.

Faith came back almost immediately, her SMG still held in her hands. She shook her head as she drifted closer to him.

"I'm not leaving you. Even if you order me away, Grove-husband. You shouldn't be alone. Especially not with Goldie out of action," Faith said with absolute determination. "I'd rather die. So that's just how it is. We'll go back together and I'll make sure you get there safely. After that, you can do what you need to do. The truck wouldn't be able to get out this way anyway.

"Too many trees, ruts, and stumps in the way. It'd just get hung up or ruined. Maybe both."

Felix didn't argue further and just kept going. He wasn't going to lose his Dragon.

Chapter 13 - Flaming Hoops -

Faith pushed open the door to the trailer and Felix entered right behind her. Pivoting, he went straight to the back room that was the bedroom.

Behind him, Faith exited the trailer and closed the door behind herself.

Getting Goldie's clothes and waiting here while Faith got the truck would be ideal. The Dryad would need to get everything that Miu had stashed away and bring the vehicle right into the yard of the trailer.

Going into the bedroom, Felix found an actual bed and dresser there. There were also curtains over the windows, the carpet had clearly been cleaned, and the bathroom it connected with appeared to be in equally good condition.

What?

"I thought maybe I'd get a chance to have you here. Just you and I. By ourselves," Goldie said quietly. She hadn't spoken much while he'd carried her, but he could tell she was already doing better. She was just very weak, still.

Whatever had happened to her had dropped her right at death's door.

If not perhaps in the entryway, in fact.

"Andrea helped me get all this done. We did it without using Legion funds, just what we could manage in-between other things. I swear I didn't spend much and it wouldn't have—"

Felix cut her off by laying her in the middle

of the bed. Then he pulled the covers back and started tucking her into the bed.

"I don't care, nor do I mind," he replied in a gruff voice. "We should probably try to get everyone their own money so they can spend what they want on things.

"It's an oversight on my part that I hadn't even considered it. One that I'll rectify."

On his march back to the trailer park, he'd had a lot of time to himself to think. Time to think about what this little trip was costing him and what he could lose.

His time with Eva had already been severely curtailed with her pushing her studies. As well as learning all there was about Legion and Yosemite.

Then he'd come here and left her behind without even a goodbye. No farewell or anything. He'd more or less cut and run away from everyone for fear of Runner figuring out his plan with Miu.

Sighing, he looked at the Dragon and patted her shoulder, then sat down on the edge of the bed. The last thing he needed to do right now was pity himself.

Goldie had thrown herself in front of danger for him.

Dragons were strong, but they were still flesh and blood. Even in the old world, she'd been grievously wounded by modern weapons.

"They'll all forgive you," promised Goldie, one of her hands coming out to rest atop his. It felt cold and rather clammy against his. "Just as Miu did. You were trying to g-get the best deal you could. So you could get Lily and Kit back.

"No one will blame you for doing what you had to. Besides, we all know Felicity will manage it just fine for you. I'm sure she already had contingency plans in place f-for such an occurrence."

Felix didn't doubt that at all.

His faith in Felicity knew no limits. She was the one person in his life who lived more for his goals than even he did. Because he would neglect himself, but she never would.

"Yes, she's a very good woman for you. Even Lily and Kit got out of her way," agreed Goldie, a weak smile the only sign of warmth in her pale face. "They didn't like it at all, but they did it. If only because you needed someone who would take a firm hold on you and not let go. Regardless of you biting at them or trying to shake them off."

"Ah," grunted Felix with a nod of his head. He wasn't feeling incredibly talkative right now about Lily or Kit. While he wasn't repeating the same mistakes he'd done the last time around, it felt to him like he was making all new ones.

"You're not," argued Goldie, her nose wrinkling. "You're handling us four much better than you did previously. In fact, it's almost eerie how well you're doing.

"You're just second guessing yourself which is normal. It's alright. You're doing well."

Taking in a slow breath, Felix then let it out.

She was right of course.

The Golden One had masterfully speared him and he was only struggling against time. He wouldn't win against someone who could pull out his thoughts as easily as a child with an open cookie jar.

Then he grinned at the golden-eyed Dragon. She'd forgotten to change her appearance.

Looking up at her horns, he reached up and ran a finger along one to where she'd drilled a hole through it. Then he ran his fingertip down along to the base.

"Thanks, Goldie. I really appreciate you. Let's talk more about you, less about me for the moment. I'm wondering if maybe it might not be a bad idea to keep you here," murmured Felix. "Clean bed, no forest bugs, no concerns about temperature. If anything, this might be the best spot for you."

"Oh… yes, that's not a bad idea, I suppose," agreed Goldie, her eyes fixed on his face. "It'd be hard for me to escape if someone came across our campsite. As much as I want to claim I'm fine, I feel sick. Sick, tired, and very weak. It's not as hard to breathe as it was, but it's not easy, either."

Felix was nodding his head at this point. Everything she said made perfect sense to him. It matched up with his own thoughts.

"We'll just… move from the camp to here. We'll just have to be really careful coming and going so that Jay and David don't notice us. Shouldn't be too hard," planned Felix aloud.

"Probably time to bring it indoors anyway. It's getting colder by the day, I swear."

"It is," Faith said from behind him. He'd felt it when she'd entered the bedroom and merely stood behind him. The feeling he'd gotten from the seed growing inside him was that Faith didn't want to interrupt his talk with Goldie. "And yes, she'd do better here. She's a Dragon, she can survive almost anywhere.

"If she were healthy and hadn't just had a near death experience, that is. Right now, her being in a warm, safe, and controlled environment is better for her. Andie won't argue if that's our reasoning."

Faith entered the bedroom fully and came over to stand on the other side of the bed. The Dryad reached down and laid a hand on Goldie's head.

The Dragon's smile had slowly been dwindling as she listened to Faith. Her eyes starting to dip closed even as she tried to follow Faith as she walked in front of her.

By the time the Dryad's fingers made contact with her head, Goldie looked like she was sleeping. The rise and fall of her chest was the only sign of her being alive.

"She's exhausted," reported Faith, letting her hand fall back to her side. She gave her head a shake and then sighed. "She'll be fine, but it'll take time. Her body is fixing itself. More or less what you said.

"It's just doing it in a way that'll put a

burden on her and will keep her weak until it's done. Even then it might be a bit of time after it's over before she's back to normal.

"But... in the fullness of time, she'll be fine. Of that I'm confident. As if nothing had happened at all and she hadn't almost died."

"That's exactly what I wanted," confirmed Felix. Turning his hand over, he contemplated Goldie's hand in his own.

Then he let go of it and started to get undressed. Stopping when he was down to his undershirt and boxers, he then clambered into the bed.

Her skin felt very cold to him but that wouldn't last. Pulling the blankets around himself, he snuggled up to Goldie's side.

He'd act the part of a heater at least for tonight.

There wasn't anything he could do about anything until the morning came anyway.

"Oh, good idea. Slumber party," Faith said and immediately started stripping as well. Except she didn't stop until she was absolutely naked. "When Miu gets back, we'll just invite her in, too. We'll all keep you company."

Felix didn't argue. He just wanted to keep his poor Dragon warm.

***

"I'll be fine," promised Goldie with a grin.

She was looking quite comfortable in the bed now. She'd slept until just after nine o'clock.

That was entirely because Andrea had taken over the kitchen and was in the process of cooking pancakes. Though she was also apparently planning on giving Goldie a number of deer steaks.

Lightly seared, almost raw, deer steaks.

"You need to get going. Lots of things to do and you can't sit around here moping over me," advised the Dragon with a grin. "As much as I do enjoy the attention, I'm also not going anywhere. You can come back to me as much as you like.

"I'll be perfectly fine here. Andie already brought me a bunch of books. That'll keep me occupied, if not busy."

Goldie made a little hand wave toward the corner where a bin of books had been set down. He had no idea where she'd gotten them, but he would bet on her having stolen them.

"Nn, Doctor Andrea is here for duty!" said an Andrea in the corner with a sharp salute. Another Andrea in the opposite corner saluted as well.

"Nurse Andrea is here to support!" said the second one. "We'll make sure our amazing and beautiful Dragon recovers completely!"

The Andrea in the kitchen—who Felix could just see the back of—froze in place. Then she stepped into view, with both hands held in fists in front of her.

"Nn! We'll make sure our amazing and beautiful Dragon is perfect!" called that Andrea before she went back to cooking.

"I think you left an impression on them," Felix remarked dryly, turning to look back at Goldie.

"Oh, it's nothing. It's just an infatuation she has with me. She'll be over it soon," dismissed Goldie with a deep chuckle. Then she turned and gestured at Miu, who was sitting at the edge of the bed. She'd only had a chance to linger in the last ten minutes. Before that, she'd been going back and forth repeatedly. Transferring all their gear from the campsite to here. "Now, Miu. You clearly have something you want to tell us and you've been patiently waiting for the right time. Thank you, by the way."

Miu had taken Goldie's wounding very seriously. If Felix didn't miss his guess, it was because she'd willingly stepped into the line of fire to protect him.

He knew that Miu tended to look with favor on those who were dedicated to him. Especially those who just accepted her as she was.

Being a mind reader, and never having pushed at Miu at all, probably rounded out her willingness to be friendly to the Dragon.

Smiling at Goldie, Miu nodded her head once then turned to look at Felix.

"David gave Jay two bags of cocaine. As well as two bags of money. It happened just after I dropped them back off here at the park. They asked for me to remain for a time just so that they could start the deal. David put Jay in a new trailer. It's…

on the other side of the park near the wall. It's very remote in the layout," explained Miu with a growl edging her words. "If I'd known about Goldie I wouldn't have stayed. I would've—"

Goldie made a small motion with her hand and tilted her head to one side minutely. Something unspoken clearly passed between Goldie and Miu and it brought the latter up short.

"Anyway," continued Miu after taking a short breath. "Anyway. Jay has our money and the drugs. He's offered to be the middle point for both us and David. His pay for doing so is that he's going to get his supply from David for free."

Huh.

That works out, I suppose. It's a middleman who was forced by both sides to do their bidding. He'll be happy with his cut because it means everything he sells it pure profit.

Not to mention he becomes a much bigger, and safer, player to both sides.

Seems like David thought this one out on his way back.

"Fine. We'll go take care of that and then move on to the next piece. Today is my appointment with the clerk for my birth certificate," said Felix. "The money was the important piece of what we were aiming for last night. If we're going to bribe the clerk, we'll need it.

"Though I do wish you could be there for it, Goldie. I can't let you, though. I won't lie and say I don't feel more confident with my mind reader around."

"I know. Thank you for relying on me. I wish I could go as well," argued Goldie while holding up a hand in a stop motion. "But you already declined that. You want me here resting. To be honest, I want to lay here and rest, too. I feel so incredibly weak. And cold. I feel really cold."

"Time to eat!" Andrea said, handing a plate off to the Other who had called herself the nurse.

That Other bounced right up onto the bed without even a bit of hesitation.

She scooted forward until she was straddling Goldie's lap and then sat down on it. On the plate she held was a large, steaming portion of what could only be deer steak.

"Dragon Nurse Andrea will now feed you!" proclaimed Andrea.

"Goldie, it's now time to eat. Then you will drink a lot of water. Then it's nap time, followed by another steak. This is your prescription," declared the Other who had said she was Doctor Andrea. "You'll be our beautiful and amazing Dragon who's healthy real soon!"

"Yay!" cheered all three Andrea's at that.

Shifting around in the Dragon's lap, Andrea got comfortable and then set the plate down between them. She began to diligently cut the meat apart with a knife and a fork.

Looking amused and frustrated at the same time, Goldie just shook her head and then smiled. Then she opened her mouth and gave Felix a "long suffering" look.

"Your teeth are pretty," Nurse Andrea declared as she worked at cutting up the steak.

"Yeah. I've been through this," Felix said, remembering being force fed by Andrea. He could only give her the advice he could have wished for. "Just… get it done quickly. She'll ease up after a day or so, once it's obvious you're not fighting her."

Andrea promptly stuck a piece of steak into Goldie's mouth and then lifted up a napkin to daintily dab at the Dragon's mouth.

Goldie just began to chew while nodding her head.

"Felix, can we talk for a minute?" asked Doctor Andrea. She'd come over to grab his forearm while Nurse Andrea had been cutting.

"Of course," Felix said and then turned, leading the Other out of the bedroom. Faith and Miu came along as well, the last closing the door behind herself.

Leaving the Dragon alone with her nurse to handle her needs.

Except Andrea pulled Felix toward the front door and stopped him there.

"Uhm, Faith? Miu? Can I talk to him alone? Please?" Andrea asked, looking between the two other women. "It'll only take a few minutes. I promise."

"Okay," Faith said then opened the door and exited the trailer.

Miu hesitated, looking between Andrea and

Felix.

"Miu, please? Just a few minutes," Andrea asked again.

Grimacing, Miu shook her head then went to the door.

"Thanks, Miu," Andrea said as the other woman exited.

"I… sure. We're in this together, Andie," said Miu, pausing just in the entryway. "I love Felix. But I can't… behave as I did previously. I have to be better. We're all depending on each other. We're alone in this world. Just the five of us."

Stepping out, Miu closed the door behind herself.

"Nn, she's really growing," Andrea said, looking to Felix with a wide grin. Her eyes moved back and forth across his face as she stared at him. "You've really turned her into a person again. She's crazier than she's ever been before, but also the most Human she's been.

"In a very long time. I have no idea how you've managed it. But it's amazing, Felix. Amazing."

Grabbing him by the front of his clothes, she leaned up and kissed him. Then kissed him again and wrapped her arms around him after.

Laying her head on his shoulder, she rubbed her face against him.

"I'm ready for you to modify me. Just… err… don't tell me what it says about me. I don't think I want to know right now. I'm not ready for it whatever it says," stated Andrea.

"Is it going to say something it shouldn't?" Felix asked, curious now.

"I don't know if it'll say Allison or Andrea. I'm not really… sure, anymore. The strange part is I feel more like Andrea right now than I ever have in my life before. More like… I guess… more like when I was whole.

"When I had all my others, before Myriad died, before we-we were… we were used as a kid and had to split the Adriana's off into Others. Before all of that. I feel like me and I don't… know… what it'll say when you look."

Hm.

Identity crisis.

It was always rather obvious Andrea had gone through a lot. Far more than anyone would have expected.

It makes sense that she already had all those personalities in her before they became actual people. Protecting the core of herself as she went through life.

"What do you want it to say?" Felix asked while calling up her screen.

"Just that I-err, I want it to say Andrea. Not Allison. Or Adriana. Or Myriad. If it says Andrea, then I'm still just… Andrea. Just… Andrea who's more reliable. I don't have to rely on my sisters so much."

A box appeared in front of Felix.

Then flickered and vanished before he could really read it. Except it came back a second after that.

Name: Andrea Campbell		**Race**: Beastkin(Wolf)-Extinct in the Wild
Alias: None		**Power:** Duplicates / Partitioned Mind
Physical Status: Healthy.		**Mental Status:** In Love, Terrified
Positive Statuses: In Love, Self Awareness		**Negative Statuses**: In Love, Terrified
Might:	18	Add +1? (170)
Finesse:	21	Add +1? (210)
Endurance:	29	Add +1? (290) +1 Stamina Type
Competency:	16	Add +1? (130)
Intellect:	14	Add +1? (140)
Perception:	59	Add +1? (580)
Luck:	97	Add +1? (970)

Felix noted that there were some obvious changes to Andrea. Ones that he couldn't hold back from her.

He had no doubt in his mind that the fact that her aliases were gone, as well as that her power now said "Duplicates" rather than "multiple selves", had significant meaning.

"You've uh… changed," started Felix. "We'll start with the obvious one. Your name is listed as Andrea Campbell. You have no alias anymore. They're all gone."

Andrea began to vibrate in place against him.

Shifting her weight back and forth from one foot to the other as her tail swung wildly back and forth behind her.

"Your stats have increased in several areas as well. You have a positive status at the moment of Self Awareness, but you're also Terrified," Felix summarized quickly. "Lastly, your power... changed. It used to read as 'multiple selves' but now only says 'Duplicates'. I'd say... whatever happened, whatever you did, definitely strengthened yourself."

Sucking in a quick breath, Andrea began to scream with her mouth closed. Her eyes were pressed tightly closed and she was swinging her whole body back and forth. Stamping her feet against the ground.

Then she went still and quiet. Leaning against him and breathing through her nose.

Soft laughter escaped her and then she sighed.

"Allison gave her life to me. She was so very much like the ideal me that it hurt me. She existed for a time, then merged it all back into me. She was much smarter than I was," babbled Andrea. "Knew what we needed to do and how to do it. Then she just whooshed into me and brrrred us until it was all... normal. Until I was Andrea and Allison was... gone. Adriana and Myriad are gone too.

"I'm just... just me. I'm Andrea. All the Thirds gave themselves to me and became... me. I'm Andrea. As I probably... should have been.

"Oh god, what'll happen to the Andrea's who

were left behind? Adriana and Myriad?"

"Eh, they'll probably want to share an Other with you to figure out what happened, then just be happy for you," prophesied Felix. "They're your sisters. They're very different from you now, but they're still you.

"You'll just be a much more stable version of you now. I think it's exciting. You grew as a person. You're Andrea Elex and you can stand proudly next to Adriana and Myriad. The current Prime Andrea will probably want you personally, then incorporate you outright and become you."

"Yeah! I'm Andrea E... Andrea Campbell. I'm Andrea Campbell and I can stand with my sisters proudly. And you're right. Andrea Prime will definitely take me back and might incorporate me directly! I'd become Prime with her! Nn!" declared Andrea, gazing up at him. Then she gave him a wicked smile that looked a lot like something that would have been on Adriana's face. "Now, kiss me, make me wish we had more time and privacy or that Goldie was willing to share her bed with us.

"Then... then modify me so I can hide the best parts of me from the world. You and I are going to go see that clerk as soon as we're ready for it!"

Chapter 14 - Exchanges -

Felix really wasn't sure how to feel about the fact that he had Miu go collect the drugs and the money in broad daylight.

He believed in her ability to do it without being seen, but there was no way to really know she'd managed it. There was no magical indicator to tell her if she'd been spotted.

Admittedly, she'd only had to hop over the community wall, go into the trailer, and come right back out, but it still felt like an incredible distance.

Sitting there in the bushes, wearing a mask, Felix felt really awkward. Unsure of the orders he'd given her.

Then Miu oozed out of a bush right next to him. Her masked face didn't hide the fact that her eyes were practically staring a hole through his head.

His fears about her being spotted were completely obliterated.

As was his heartrate.

It was beating hard and fast in his chest now. She'd gone full horror movie on him in that moment.

"I think I've gotten better at this, even without the abilities," she murmured. She began pulling bags through the undergrowth and setting them down in front of him.

"Yeah, you definitely are," agreed Felix. "Damn, Miu. We should hire you out as an assassin or a thief."

"I'm whatever you want me to be. I'm yours, Felix," whispered Miu, her voice pitching a bit oddly. Then she grunted and dropped the last duffel bag in front of him.

Leaning over, Felix lifted the bottom part of Miu's mask. He gave her a brief kiss and patted her cheek. It was a simple enough action, but it would go a long way to making Miu feel appreciated.

Twitching as he pulled away, Miu just crouched there, her eyes now fastened to the grass and dirt beneath them.

Pulling the mask back down over her mouth, Felix laid a hand on her knee and then looked at the bag in front of him. He had no idea what was lying in wait for him, but he imagined David was probably going all in on this.

The duffel bag looked to be stuffed to the point that the zipper was straining to keep itself shut. In fact, when he looked at it, it almost looked like the teeth might be slipping.

Using one hand, Felix tugged at the zipper and found it to be stuck.

Before he could take the hand off Miu's knee, she'd unzipped the bag. As if doing so would keep his hand right where it was.

Laying inside the bag were a number of hard, plastic-sealed, white bricks. There were a large number of them in the bag. Felix didn't really want to bother counting them.

"The... that... ah... two other bags are filled

with drugs, too. I was wrong. Only one is filled with money," corrected Miu quietly. With her right hand, she indicated a bag that certainly looked different than the other two.

Her left hand however had landed atop his own. It felt like she wanted to cage his hand right there.

To be fair, I haven't been intimate with her since we got back here.

Admittedly, that was her choice and feeling shy around the others but… she probably needs the physical connection.

Pulling his hand away from her knee, Felix set it down instead in the middle of her lower back. He began to lightly stroke her as he moved forward to the bag she'd indicated had held the money.

When it popped open, Felix found hand-packed money. It was all in one's, fives, tens, and twenties. There was no note or indication of how much it was.

Some of it looked like it'd been pulled from other last-minute sources, and several bundles looked like they'd been pulled open and had some bills removed.

He did it in a hurry based on what I told him. He didn't want to wait for the next step in the deal. This was all done based on what he could do in a hurry.

He probably had a lot more drugs as well, but not enough money to cover it all. I should probably expect this to be much bigger next time.

Felix concentrated on the money. He wanted

to know how much was there and who owned it. Additionally, he wanted to know how much it'd cost to purify the drugs.

Two windows popped up for him.

Type: Fiat Money	**Condition**: Unmarked
Owner: Felix Campbell	**Value:** $197,880.50

Type: Cocaine / 2 substances Click to expand	**Condition**: Medium Quality
Owner: Felix Campbell	**Action >> Purify**: Cost 17,983 points
Pre-Action Value: $201,349	**Post-Action Value:** $541,010

Holy shit.

Well… that'll… certainly help. Money talks, bullshit walks.

Need a lot of money to get the plans in order as well.

That won't even cover the cost of a new garbage truck, but… might be able to get one used. Then I can move forward with my plans.

After we spent thirty thousand to modify Andrea, though, this'll bring our points down to about five thousand. Not a lot left.

Whatever, money first. Points will flow in as we go.

Earn points, spend points, make money, get even more points.

That's our loop.

Continuing to stroke Miu's back intimately, Felix converted the drugs. The money would be useful immediately.

He'd probably have to bribe the clerk and there was no telling how much that'd take.

Except regardless of the price tag, so long as it was in a hard currency, he'd pay it. He needed a birth certificate.

***

Andrea quietly opened the door to the clerk's office and stepped inside. She was taking her role of bodyguard seriously at the moment.

Given what'd happened to Goldie and her choice to change, she'd gone all the way back to how they'd first been. She was his bodyguard and personal secretary.

She looked over her shoulder and gave him a wide smile, holding the door open for him. He was still getting used to seeing her with Human ears, rather than her triangular Beastkin ones.

She was dressed in one of the hoodies that Faith preferred. More than likely, she had a pistol in the pocket as well as several magazines in another.

Surprisingly, she even had a purse.

In all the time he'd known Andrea, he couldn't actually remember her carrying a purse.

Though if he had to bet, she probably had an SMG in it, knowing her.

Their haul of weapons from David's goons had been useful to say the least for the gun-users in their group. Felix had accepted a small pistol that only had a single magazine to go with it.

It wasn't something the others would rely on, but it was something he could use if he had to.

Beyond that, he knew he could rely on what'd been drilled into him by Miu, Ioana, Victoria, and Andrea in hand-to-hand fighting. He wasn't at the level they were, but he could hold his own against an unpowered or Special Forces.

Oh.

Actually.

Doesn't that mean more or less almost everyone on the planet? How interesting. I never considered that.

Entering the lobby, Felix went right up to the desk and smiled for the young woman behind the counter. Andrea came right up beside him and took his hand in hers.

She was an older woman with a dark bronze skin tone. Her dark hair was pulled behind her head in a short ponytail. Her warm brown eyes had been measuring him since he walked into the office.

"Hello, ma'am. Good morning, that is. I… uhm… we have an appointment. About my birth certificate. Or, ah, that I don't have one," said Felix, trying to work an uncertain and unsure angle. He knew that more often than not the secretary or receptionist could end up having pull all on her own.

If they decided you needed to be run around in circles, they'd make it happen. If they wanted you to be helped, they could open doors you never knew were closed.

The receptionist blinked, then smiled back at him.

"Name, sweetie?" she asked.

"Felix, ma'am. Felix Campbell," he replied with just a hint more spine in his words.

"Right. You just go take a seat. I already have all your information from the form you filled out on the portal. I'll let him know you're here," she said and then spun in her seat. She pulled out a folder from a filing tray and then got up.

Andrea grabbed him by the arm and dragged him over to sit down in one of the seats. She plopped down right next to him and scooped up his hand in hers, though after glancing down at her own rear end.

"It's so weird with it not being there," she said with a frown on her face. "I normally have to be kinda careful with chairs so I don't sit on it or crush it against the wall."

"You'll get used to it, I imagine. Though... do you hear any different? Is it better? Worse?" Felix asked with genuine curiosity.

"You know, I hear about the same, if I'm being honest, but it feels weird. It's not the right place at all but it sounds the same," she said, reaching up to touch her very human ear that didn't exist this morning. Normally, she just had hair there where a normal ear would be.

Sticking a finger into her ear, she then pulled at her earlobe.

"I don't like that I can't tune into something. They don't move. I have to turn my whole head," Andrea complained, turning to look at him.

"You're still just as cute as ever, Andie. Whatever ears you have doesn't matter," he assured her.

"Oh? Well. Maybe I should—"

The door next to them opened and the older woman gave them a smile.

"He'll see you now. He's ready. Just be direct with him. He's pretty helpful so long as you're direct," warned the woman.

Felix and Andrea got up and followed her as she led them down a short hall to another door. She knocked twice, opened it, and stepped aside.

Sitting behind a very cluttered and well-worked desk was a man in his late thirties. With dark-brown hair, and eyes that were a blend between blue and green, he looking exactly like a clerk.

Thin, intelligent, and awkward.

Smiling, Felix walked in as the man stood up.

"Ah, hello, Mr. Roberts," Felix said. He'd already confirmed the name on the door matched the one he'd found online, Dylan Roberts.

Reaching the desk as the man stood up, Felix

held out his hand to him.

"Mr. Campbell, it's good that you put in your request when you did. With everything normalizing to a degree a lot of the temporary measures were starting to run out," said the clerk, shaking Felix's hand, though with some hesitation. "In a few months, it'll be just as hard as it used to be. We had a lot of mad shuffling going on as people popped out of the woodwork all over the place."

Felix had no idea what the man was talking about, but he only smiled and nodded his head. It was starting to sound like he'd just missed a massive event in this world.

Not for the first time, he felt like he wanted to sit down and question someone. To find out what'd happened. Though whatever it was, it didn't particularly seem to be holding him back.

For now, it was more of a minor footnote that something earth-changing had occurred, but that wasn't going to impede Legion's rebirth.

"Yes, yes, I imagine. Uhm… I just… hopefully I'm not part of the mad shuffle for you," Felix said, then turned to indicate Andrea. "This is my soon-to-be-wife, Andie. Err, Andrea, that is.

"Problem is, we can't get married 'cause I don't have a birth certificate. When I asked my ma about it, she said I never had one. Not at all. None of my brothers or sisters had one, except Dolly but that was because it happened when she was shopping."

Andrea had reached across the desk and

shook Dylan's hand after being introduced.

"Point of truth, she doesn't have one either. We just... it never really came up. Ya know?" asked Felix in an odd tone.

"I do know, actually," Mr. Roberts agreed and then indicated the seats. "We call them delayed birth certificates. We just need some paperwork from a few places and we can actually get moving on that.

"I'm pretty sure Theresa sent you a document request? Did you happen to get that?"

"I... don't... err..." Felix faltered, realizing that he'd given an email address in the form but hadn't actually checked it.

"We don't own a computer," Andrea said, stepping into the silent gulf that was growing. "Had to use the library one to get stuff done. We're renting a trailer now though, so we can probably get a library card.

"We do have some medical records though. Medical records, statements from our parents, and a couple other things that might help. Not sure."

Andrea had pulled the purse she'd been carrying around in front of herself. She opened it, rifled through it for a second, and then came up with a large pack of papers.

Dylan took the papers and laid them out on his desk. Slowly, he began to work through them. He was even nodding his head as they went.

Glancing to Andrea, he saw her look back at him.

She gave him a wink, a smile, and stuck her tongue out at him for a moment.

Still Andrea, but... also not. How interesting.

"You know, we might actually be able to put in for a delayed birth certificate with all this. Well, not really, actually," confessed Dylan with a chuckle. "But there's enough here that I can get it to happen. Won't take much more than a little wiggle on my part and having Theresa grease a wheel or two. She's got more connections than anyone would suspect."

"There'll be some fees, of course, and—"

Felix took out the envelope he'd prepared and set it down in front of Dylan as the man changed the subject. He knew exactly how much the fees were for this kind of thing.

It would total out to be around two hundred dollars, give or take the cost of postage.

The envelope however had five hundred in it. On the outside of it was written "500" as well. It wouldn't be needed, really, but it would give Mr. Roberts a chance to simply accept it without counting it.

"This is what my da gave me to pay for it," said Felix as he set it down in front of Mr. Roberts. "For both of us, that is. We really appreciate your help, sir."

Dylan looked at the envelope for several seconds, then opened it. He thumbed through the money inside, pulled out what looked to be about two hundred dollars, then gave the envelope back.

"That'll be enough," said Mr. Roberts, giving Felix and Andrea a wide smile. "It'll take about four to six weeks, but it'll happen. I'm pretty sure you included your address in your file, so we'll send the documents there.

"I'll need to hang onto all this for a time. To fill in some things here and there, that is."

Dylan had gestured at the paperwork on his desk while speaking.

"Of course, we expected that. It's perfectly fine. We'll be workin' anyway," Andrea said and stood up, pulling Felix up with her. "Well, tryin' to work. Still lookin'. Any suggestions?"

Blinking, Mr. Roberts looked thoughtful, then gave her a sad smile.

"Lot of entry-level openings right now. Whatever you get into though you'll probably be overworked and underpaid. Lot of people quit recently. Across the board.

"I'd say check with the rec-plant. With everything that happened, they're struggling."

"Thanks!" Andrea said and then gave the man an energetic wave goodbye. Felix was pulled physically from the office.

They were outside faster than he realized with Andrea pushing him into the passenger seat. She skipped her way around the front of F-Two and got into the driver's seat.

"Oh! That went so good!" she said with a rapid clap of her hands together. "The timing stinks on how long it'll take, but that was rather easy!

"He was a bit too trusting, but I can't fault him for that. It's just how the world is with those who are kind."

Felix nodded his head.

He was still thinking about what the clerk had said though. That the rec-plant, or recycling center that was, was having some issues.

I wonder if I could swoop in and take the contract. What if I could become a government service on one side, all lower end things that just help, without taking control?

That'd balance the underworld side of things quite well.

It'd fit in with my plan to buy a garbage truck. Steal people's trash for myself and convert it all to points.

Speaking of the meeting with the mayor is later today.

What do I do until then?

A thought bubbled up from the back of his mind. Faith could bring in small game and things, but there was no way she'd be able to grab an entire deer like Goldie could.

That meant they were going to run out of fresh red meat, which was very likely what Goldie would need to recover.

"Need to grab a quick suit from that local thrift store. I'm sure they have one that I can modify to fit me and clean up a bit. Then visit a butcher as well. We need to get some red meat," Felix said, turning to look at Andrea who had been happily humming to herself and doing a little dance in her seat. He pulled the truck key out of his pocket and held it out to her.

"A butcher? Wh— ah! Goldie! Nn! We have to care for our lovely and amazing Dragon!" shouted Andrea, who took the key from Felix's hand and stuffed it into the ignition. "Meat, meat, meat for our Dragon!"

Turning the key over, Andrea brought the engine to life and got them moving. She did it while obeying the rules of the road as far as he could tell, but she did it with a great deal of speed and her driving style belonged in a high-speed chase.

Felix wasn't going to complain, though. Andrea was as she was and would never really be anything different.

No matter which Elex it was, no matter what her first name it might be, she was always the same woman to him. He could always tell them apart, but to him, they were all one and the same.

In time, he imagined they might even recombine into a whole person again.

A whole, healthy, singular individual, instead of one fragmented out into three different people.

All of which he suspected were built from a traumatic and violent childhood.

Then Andrea ran over a stop sign as she blew through a dirt road intersection.

"Oopsie!" she squealed excitedly while turning the steering wheel end over end to correct for the drifting turn they were now in.

Felix hung on tightly to the 'oh shit!' bar

while bracing his feet on the floorboard. Though he did smile the whole time and couldn't help it.

Andrea was Andrea.

Chapter 15 - First Volley -

Feeling much better about the situation, Felix was quite happy to sit there in front of the small, locally-owned coffee shop.

A truck bed containing an ice chest filled with fresh meat was on the way back to the trailer with Andrea behind the wheel.

They'd also stopped off to get a used suit for Felix, a map of Hardysburg, and while they were there they found some used appliances as well. To be specific, a freezer and fridge that Felix bought and was having delivered to the trailer today.

Reaching up, he ran a finger along his jaw and watched a group of teens move past him. One and all, they appeared to be males around fifteen years old.

They looked fairly normal for the area. They wore jeans and t-shirts, somewhat worn, but not overly so. Although Felix noted that they were on the lookout for something and their heads swiveled around visibly.

Felix didn't have to think very hard about what they could be watching for. The simple fact that their eyes kept drifting over to where Miu, Faith, and Goldie had been collecting items at the drop-off point gave it away.

Not that he could really blame them, if he was being honest. The simple reality was that they were incredibly attractive women. The type that wouldn't normally stop in a small place like

Brandonville.

Even in a place like Hardysburg, they'd stick out terribly.

When he thought about it, even if they went to LeFleur city, there'd be few who could compare to them. The simple reality was that none of them belonged to this world.

Faith and Goldie came from a world where sex and violence were king, and Miu was a superhero.

"I'm probably the closest thing to what belongs here," mused Felix to himself and then picked up his cup of coffee and took a sip.

By the time he put it back down, he'd spotted what he suspected was the reason for Felix being here.

Heading his way was a man who stood out as nearly as much as Miu did.

Dressed in an expensive suit that Felix would have picked out from corporate boardrooms was a man in his middle years. He was also taller than average and looked to be at least six-foot-four from Felix's best guess.

He was rather pale as well, with blue eyes and brown hair. He really didn't fit in with the local populace for more than just that though.

His shoes were brand new, his hair styled, and his wrist had a watch that looked pricey. Everything about this man screamed that he was originally far removed from this place and was here not completely by his own volition.

Must be the mayor.

Few other people would dress like me in Brandonville as a general rule. Nor would they show up to this part of town as such even if they did dress so.

Standing up, Felix reflexively worked the top button on his coat and then took two steps from the table. Holding out his hand to the man, Felix put on his best middle-manager smile.

"You must be Mayor Jordan," assumed Felix as soon as the man was within a casual speaking distance.

"Ah, yes. Indeed, I am. That makes you Mr. Campbell," said the mayor, and then made a small hand-waving gesture, ignoring Felix's hand. "Forgive me, I'm still wary of shaking hands."

Felix felt his brows draw together for a split second and then let his hand fell. Once more, he felt like he was missing something, but didn't want to push.

"Of course, not a problem. I didn't order you a drink because I had no idea if you'd actually want anything," Felix apologized and gestured at the other seat at the two-person table.

Felix unbuttoned his coat without realizing he'd done it and hitched up his pants from the knees.

Taking his own seat, Felix immediately took another sip from his coffee. It was a good opportunity to force a response from the mayor.

To put it simply, many people would jump to fill a silence all on their own. Adding to that a situation where one couldn't talk and others would take it on themselves to fill the void quickly.

"Ah, yes," the mayor said, nearly repeating his earlier words verbatim. Then he took the seat that'd been offered and made a small hand wave at the table between them. "I… no, I don't need anything from here."

Hm.

I wonder if he feels like maybe this place is beneath him. He certain dresses like it is. Does it match the mentality?

I wonder if I could use him as a pawn. Further my goals without putting myself in any deeper.

Something to certainly consider.

"I'm glad you were willing to meet with me. I wasn't sure given how… aloof… you'd been about this so far," tested the mayor, leaning back in his chair.

"Oh, well, I figured it'd be a good time to let myself be in public," Felix said as if he were allowing something to happen that was a bother. "It wouldn't have been very polite to offer such a service, then decline to meet you. That's no way to make a lasting relationship."

"No, it most certainly would not," agreed the mayor with a chuckle. Then he folded his hands in his lap and crossed one leg over the other. He looked far more at ease all of a sudden. "And may I ask where you got that suit? It's rather impressive. It looks like it was hand-tailored?"

"Why thank you. A one-off, I'm afraid. My

seamstress is a real… Dragon… with her work and secrets. I had to spend some points to get this made on short notice," murmured Felix with a grin. Mixing lies and truths was always his favorite weapon. The lies were easier to obfuscate later if it was all tied into truth.

The mayor smiled.

Felix smiled.

Both men eyed each other, letting the silence build between them.

How curious. Maybe he isn't so dissimilar from myself.

Felix picked up his coffee and once more took a sip from it, setting it back down and then looking at the surroundings.

He could let the silence build for a few seconds further, but then he'd need to move the whole thing along. He wasn't looking to put this man over a barrel or get anything from him.

At least, not yet.

"Well, I must—"

"If you don't mind—"

Felix paused mid-sentence when he realized the mayor had started talking as well. Apparently, the man really was quite similar to himself.

Smiling, the mayor gestured to Felix to indicate he should continue.

"The little drop-off event went rather well," continued Felix. "As far as I can tell, there was a solid need for it this time around. Brandonville had trash to get rid of across its population.

"We even had someone bring in a small tractor. I believe he called it a Bobcat, though I'm unsure, to be honest. That was a bit of a surprise, but we got rid of it all within the limit of the event."

Felix had indeed been surprised with that one.

He'd almost considered trying to fix it and sell it elsewhere but realized the points would be more useful. It'd been scrapped with all the rest.

"Yes, it certainly did go well," murmured the mayor with a small nod of his head.

"Is there an issue with a local business? It seemed like something that could have been done easily by someone else," asked Felix. He wanted to pry into this as he felt like it could be an angle he could use. Then he reached into his jacket and pulled out the envelope he'd prepared for this meeting.

The mayor had already made mention of giving him a gratuity for taking on the job. Which meant he wasn't against the idea of handing over money.

That most certainly hinted at the idea that he took money, too.

"Oh, I meant to give you this previously. My apologies. It's the green contract we spoke of in regards to the event. I'm sorry that it slipped my mind until just now," Felix said setting the envelope down in front of the mayor. "All two thousand words for such a simple contract. It's a wonder how lawyers can muck everything up, isn't it? Shouldn't involve them for anything."

The mayor looked confused for only a fraction of a second before his face smoothed out. Then he smiled and picked up the envelope and tucked it straight into his own jacket. Likely in a similar pocket to the one Felix himself had.

"You're so very right, Mr. Campbell," agreed the Mayor once again. "You know, I think I can guarantee we'll have a useful relationship with your sentiments on that alone.

"As to what happened, more or less what you already intimated. A local business that normally took care of it wanted significantly more for the contract. To the point that we just couldn't afford it. Unfortunately, they were the only ones we could go to. You bailed us out at just the right moment."

"Glad to be the white knight. Though, I hear that there's similar issues cropping up with the recycling plant," Felix offered and then tilted his head to one side. "Would they happen to be the same company, the same problem?"

"Different company, same problem. The city owns the plant, thankfully, and it's operated by employees of the city. Except that most of them are all asking for more money.

"I'm fairly certain that the company that handled collections for the recycling plant, which is indeed the same company as the problematic one, is behind the issues. They've offered to purchase the plant from the city and are offering up a number of solutions that seem impossible to deliver on."

I see.

That sounds somewhat like a hostile takeover of sorts. I wonder if that's their intention. Squeeze the city out of a few jobs and services and then push the price up.

Somewhat similar to what we did, but more aggressive.

This might be an easier push than I thought.

"I'd love to make a bid on that recycling plant. As well as the trash collection contract," Felix stated, getting straight to the heart of the matter. He'd been fairly direct with the mayor so far and he felt like this was a perfect place and time to continue that. "Though I wouldn't want to own the plant. No, that wouldn't be acceptable at all. I'd prefer it to remain part of the city, just handled by my own company. Almost like—"

Felix froze mid-sentence. He had no idea if post offices operated the same here as they did in his own world.

"Well, do you know how the postal service leases a building from private individuals, then pays them for it? Covers almost the entirety of it including damage to everything?" asked Felix, then frowned deliberately. Trying to hedge his words. "Well, at least, I think that's how they do it."

"No, no, you're right. That's exactly how they do it. I had to negotiate a contract with someone for the damn roof practically caving in," complained Jordan. "Wanted the city to pay for it."

Grinning, Felix gestured at the mayor. An open-handed gesture as if he were giving something.

"Just so. I want to give you that sort of contract. I'll lease the building from you and all the equipment. You'd be responsible for upkeep of a certain amount of equipment per quarter, whether repair, purchase of new, or otherwise.

"You would, in turn, contract me to handle the running and maintenance of the location and all the services that would be required for it," explained Felix. "You get oversight of the facility as you'd own it. I'd be responsible for the services and making sure everything is running the right way.

"If we parted ways in the future, you'd cancel the contract, I cancel the lease, we both can go on without the other being too far out. No lingering problems for either.

"As for the details, just write down whatever the current contract is with the company and the promises made. I can fulfill anything they have written in as it stands today with no change. Though each year after that would need a contract arbitration to make sure we meet whatever rising needs may be.

"As an example, you might need more large-item pick-ups in the future. Or add more neighborhoods. Perhaps even more trips between other plants and locations.

"Or costs for wages and the like might go higher as an average across the state. We wouldn't want to be behind what other companies can offer. There's never really a labor shortage, just a shortage of correctly paid labor."

The mayor digested all of that with what

looked a lot like forced deliberation. As if he had wanted to answer instantly, but had fought it down.

There might be something or someone else that was a problem here.

"Though, I'd want the collection and transportation contract at the same time," added Felix. "So we'd have to wait for that contract to come up for negotiation. Off the top of your head, would you happen to know the timing on that contract?"

"I… I think it's about four months, to be honest," the mayor said after another short period of thinking. "I'm sure I could get the other parts of what you wanted ready for that. Are you sure you can actually meet what you've said though?"

"Easily. Without even seeing what they've promised. So long as you put the same exact contract down in front of me that you have with them, I can meet it to the letter," Felix confirmed. He had no doubt he could make it work regardless of whatever it might be.

"Well. I… that's a lot for me to consider. A lot. I think it'll be easy for me to meet your request positively, but I can't promise it. I do have to do what's best to remain the mayor, after all," Jordan confessed with a tired-looking smile.

"Why aim so low?" asked Felix, jumping to the next part of the conversation he wanted to touch on. There's always the possibility of becoming the governor or perhaps a senator of Alassippi.

"I can imagine that someone such as yourself wouldn't set themselves such a low bar as the mayor of Brandonville. It can't be your endgame, can it?"

Jordan was staring at him in a blank, completely shut down, unsure how to respond, kind of way. Whatever his plans actually were, Felix had struck at a point he hadn't considered, or very much wanted to do.

"Just food for thought," Felix said and tapped the table between them. "Now… if you excuse me, mayor, I do need to move on to my next meeting. It's been a real pleasure talking with you. I'd love to have another sit-down with you.

"I heard you might be heading out of town for a little bit though. Problems with the state as a whole is the scuttlebutt."

"Err, I… yes. I'll be out of town for a while. I can get everything else worked up in the meanwhile. Is there a way to stay in direct contact with you as I start going through this? I'm sure you'll want to see the contract long before we get to the signing," asked the mayor.

"Just so. Here's a number I can be reached at. As for the contract no, I don't need to see it until I sign it," Felix declined while standing up. He once again buttoned the top coat button and then pulled a small card from a pocket.

It only had a phone number on it with no other information.

Not his name or anything else.

He set it down in front of the mayor and tapped it once. Then he gave the man a smile, stuck his hands in his pockets, and began walking off.

He didn't need to speak with the man anymore and he'd gotten across the points he wanted to make. Everything else would need to wait for the man to come back into town.

Well.

The question becomes, who's in charge of the company that handles the recycling plant, trash pickup, and transportation? Why're they pushing for more?

Is it greed? Need?

Power?

Something to work on while I wait.

For now though, I need to focus on what I can.

Points, cash, and paperwork.

I need to get it all squared away in time for this deal with the mayor.

I'm on the clock in more than one way.

Shaking his head, Felix kept walking. His eyes slowly picked over the scenes around him.

Then he saw what looked like a bookstore. One that had probably been in the same location for a long while, in fact.

Opening the door, Felix stepped in and was immediately reminded of his childhood. Coming into a store just like this with his aunt.

He'd go pick out a few used books while she always went straight to the romance section.

Full of scantily clad men and most of a torso on the cover. Sometimes with a certain long-haired blond man on the cover.

"Hi! Welcome in," said a young woman

behind the counter.

Felix met her eye and gave her a smile and a nod. He moved to an aisle and then looked at the listing taped up there.

Fantasy, to the right.

Well. What else would you buy a bed-ridden Dragon, but fantasy novels? I'm sure she'll appreciate the irony.

Smirking, Felix grabbed one of the handbaskets, then turned and walked down toward the indicated aisle.

Squat down in the middle of it was a young man. His clothes looked like they were on the more worn than average side, his pale-green eyes moved across the page of the book he held in his lap. His dark-blond hair was cut short and springing up in every direction on his head.

He looked quite "down on his luck" Felix would say, though there was clear intelligence in the eyes.

Additionally, Felix noted that the young man seemed to be rather underfed for a teenager. He'd judge him to be about seventeen given the way his face looked, but far too skinny for him to be absolutely certain.

Out of habit more than anything, he tried to call up a window for the kid to see what his stats were and what his power was.

These were the types of people he'd hunted down to join Legion in the past. Those he could pick up and dust off, then hand a purpose.

Name: Edmund Wilhelm	**Race**: Human
Alias: None	**Power:** Latent
Physical Status: Ailing	**Mental Status:** Nervous
Positive Statuses: None	**Negative Statuses**: Wounded, malnutrition

Might:	07	Add +1? (70)
Finesse:	05	Add +1? (50)
Endurance:	06	Add +1? (60)
Competency:	81	Add +1? (810)
Intellect:	43	Add +1? (430)
Perception:	19	Add +1? (190)
Luck:	03	Add +1? (30)

Standing there, staring at the young man, Felix had no idea what to do. While he'd done it accidentally, he now was presented with new information.

The fact that his power was "latent" meant this young man would indeed become a Powered on the day of Awakening.

On top of that, his competency and intellect were significantly higher than most everyone else Felix had come across. In fact, the young man's stats were very similar to Felix's own.

Looking up at Felix, the young-man stared at him for several seconds.

"I'm… not hurting anyone," he said reflexively. Defensively, in fact. As if he'd had people push him around wherever he went.

"I know you're not. Was just curious about the book. Sorry," Felix lied, motioning at the book in his hands. "Though... you seem familiar. But you're not from around here, are you?"

"No," admitted the young man with a head shake. It looked like he couldn't decide if he wanted to shrink into himself, or run away. "I... doubt you've ever seen me before. I'm not from here. Like you said."

"Mm. Which community?" asked Felix. He was very interested in Edmund, but had to take this slow and careful. Otherwise, he'd come off as a creepy bastard.

"Community?"

"Trailer park community," elaborated Felix.

The young man flinched at that, then let his eyes drop to the ground.

"Forest Ridge... I swear I'm just here to read."

"I don't doubt it. Forest Ridge," repeated Felix. He had no doubt the boy had actually told him the truth. "Buy a few books on me. Feel free to come back in a week from today and maybe I'll buy you a few more. I remember doing the same thing you're doing.

"Never really made the owner happy with me, but he didn't throw me out either."

Felix reached into his back pocket, pulled out his wallet and quickly thumbed out two twenties. Dropping them down next to the man, Felix then went to what he was actually here for.

He looked over the shelves of books and started going through them. He'd have to make sure he got a few decent ones for Goldie.

"I can… recommend a few," offered Edmund, having already picked up the money, put it away, and stood up.

"Oh? Fantastic. Please do," Felix requested. He'd half expected the man to scamper off. "Romance would be preferable. She has a maiden's heart."

Chapter 16 - Going Shopping -

Felix looked at the map in his hands and carefully drew a black sharpie through the alleyway they'd just gone through. It was no longer viable and given the trash pickup schedule, which they were one day ahead of, they wouldn't have to come back for a week.

"Okay. Next is... across this intersection, then into the parking lot. We'll be checking the back of those," mapped out Felix, sliding a finger across the paper to what he'd just described.

"Alright," Miu said and then pulled F-Two out of the parking lot they were in. She made a left across the street and pulled up to the intersection.

Sitting there, Felix looked at the light, the cars going back and forth, and then at Miu. She seemed quite pleased at the moment, though she was clearly watching their surroundings.

"You good, Miu? You look good. Look happy. Healthy. Less... well, crazy," asked Felix, his eyes moving along her profile.

Surprisingly, Miu laughed at that, a wide smile spreading over her face. She looked at him and wrinkled her nose, then she looked back at the road ahead.

"Yes. I'm very happy. Very healthy. Not... less crazy, though," she murmured. Her fingers drummed from left pinky all the way across to the one on her right hand and went still. "I still want to kill Andrea. Kill Faith. Goldie.

"Drink their blood and eat their wombs. Devour anything of them that might have been part of you. Take you for myself.

"I wish you'd just… leave bites all over my neck and shoulders and claim me in a way that everyone can see. Then I want you to ravage me atop the corpses of all the other women. Push my face down amongst their bodies.

"But I know I can't do any of that. We need them more than my desire to take all of you for myself.

"I guess… in the end… I'm just happy, I suppose. That's all. I'm happy. Happy with my coworkers, my love, and what I'm doing."

Please… don't. No.

You can't treat me touching something as seasoning.

"Really," Felix stated in a flat tone. "Happy with your coworkers that you want to kill and have me sex you up on. That seems rather counter to happy, doesn't it?"

"Not at all," Miu said with a flick of a hand. The light hadn't yet changed. "I am Miu Campbell. I'm your Miu, specifically. I want all of you to me. I would go to great lengths to make that happen.

"I won't actually do anything, mind you. I would never do anything that would harm you. Nothing that would ever make you unhappy. That's my limitation, really.

"So while I want to kill every woman who looks at you, I can't. The world is fortunate that you're a kind and caring man. Otherwise, it'd be half a population as I'd cut the eyes out of every woman's head who looked at you."

"And the happy with coworkers part?" prompted Felix, turning his head and looking toward someone standing at the crosswalk.

He noticed that the timer was counting down for how long someone could cross to the other side. He imagined when it got to zero, the lights would change.

"I'm very happy with who I'm working with. They're so very much like me that I'm not alone. I'm not… not dealing with Kit and Lily giving me weird looks.

"Where I have to constantly walk a line between what I can do versus what they don't want me to do," growled Miu with a shake of her head. The light changed and she eased them forward into the intersection. "They were against me watching you with anyone else. Against me collecting your… your wastes. They wouldn't let me collect your… genetic material from them.

"It was all no's and don't do that. A never-ending line of them. Thankfully, that all ended with them vanishing.

"You took away the control and told me to be me. So I am. I'm me and I get everything I want."

"My waste and genetic material?"

"Yes. Don't worry, I now understand why I wasn't allowed to take the first. It isn't sanitary, despite me wanting it. It wouldn't have been healthy for me either. I have to take care of myself, so that's off-limits," Miu said matter-of-factly while driving them into the next parking lot. "My coworkers now all understand me though. Understand my needs and concerns.

"They literally have similar mental conditioning to my own in most cases. You apparently feel that Goldie is a self-replicating loop of care for you. Much more similar to myself than she would like.

"Faith has gone full Dryad with a grove in you and thinks the world is blessed where you walk. I have no doubt she'd do much the same I would for your attention."

Felix noticed she didn't mention Andrea in any of that.

"Andrea's not as crazy as we are, but as devoted," Miu clarified as she started pulling the truck around the back of buildings. As if needing a moment to think on the Beastkin. "I mean, she splits herself into new people, constantly trying to figure out how to be the perfect Andrea for you. It isn't like she did this before you."

Huh. That's... a valid point. She might actually be seeking a version of herself that I am particularly happy with.

That'd make sense.

"Okay, first one," Miu said with a small nod of her head toward a dumpster on their right.

Felix nodded and then leaned out his open window just a bit and focused on the dumpster.

He could just barely see the interior as they drove past it.

Focusing on it, he tried to activate his power set to clear everything out of the dumpster. Leaving nothing behind at all.

It was all junk that belonged to no one and had no owner.

Much as it'd happened every time he used his ability this morning, there was an odd popping noise. It was followed by the trash simply vanishing.

The interior of the dumpster also became quite clean.

Even the stains on the interior could be considered trash, which meant it was cleaned off, too. Nothing was left behind.

"You know, this is a lot easier than trying to own people," mumbled Felix as Miu started them forward again.

There were some things next to the dumpster that he couldn't clear, unfortunately. Unless it was in the dumpster, it could still technically be claimed as property.

Even if he put it in the trash himself, it wasn't considered abandoned property.

"I imagine it is. Not to mention, it's a lot less overhead for you. You were managing a massive empire in the end, but we saw less and less of you," complained Miu. "Even if we expand our operations now, so long as we do what you've been doing, we'll be fine."

Felix could only nod his head as they passed another dumpster. He once again emptied it entirely.

Unfortunately, those were the only two he could see in the alley.

"Alright. That finishes this alley," he reported almost to himself and picked up the map again. Taking the sharpie, he crossed out the alley they were in. "Next is—"

***

Felix hadn't forgotten about Edmund.

In fact, he'd been diligently counting down the days.

Collecting points by destroying trash, spending time with his group, and generally relaxing had been his day-by-day plan.

Right now, he was feeling the most relaxed that he had in a long time, in truth.

Even without all the niceties and luxuries he'd had previously, or the sheer amount of manpower he could throw at any problem back on Legion Prime.

None of that compared to how he felt right now, working to build everything up. Maybe it was the "starting something new" aspect that truly appealed to him.

Which is why he really was looking forward to talking to Edmund today. The young man was a resource he couldn't let go of easily.

Felix really didn't want to have to run him down, but if he had to, he would. That's how vital the young man felt to the Legion cause right now.

There was no way he would let someone so talented escape. Especially with the fact that he would have a superpower later.

Walking into the bookstore, Felix looked straight at the woman behind the counter. She was the same one he'd seen previously. Her name tag said Cindy.

He couldn't imagine she didn't know Edmund, or at least, knew of him. The way he was sitting in the back wasn't something that would go overlooked or unnoticed.

Given his response, it was likely others had complained about him in the past.

"Hi, did Edmund come in today?" Felix asked, meeting the girl's eyes squarely with a smile. "He and I had gone over some books recommendations last time and I wanted to pick his brain a bit more. My wife loved his choices. Absolutely loved them."

The woman gave him a cautious smile, then slowly shook her head.

"He hasn't been here in a few days. Which is really weird. One of the books he ordered came in," said Cindy.

"Ah, that's fine. I'll pay for it and take it over to him. He's still out at Forest Ridge right? Number o— uh, actually. Now that I think about it, I can't remember the exact address."

Felix was thankfully dressed in much more casual wear today. He blended in perfectly with the general public and wouldn't be out of place at a trailer park.

Pulling out his wallet, he set down two twenties on the counter.

"Could you give me his address? I'll go drop it off for him. Oh, and while I'm here, do you have any type of a discount card, repeat customer card, or anything like that? I imagine I'll be coming back repeatedly," Felix asked with a warm and wide smile.

The store clerk couldn't quite keep up with Felix, but instead nodded her head.

He'd hit her with something she didn't want to answer, then with something she did. His hope had been that she'd be more willing to do the first as she'd agreed to do the second.

A few seconds later she pulled out a book and a clipboard while taking the money off the counter. Lifting her eyes back up to him, she gave him a smile.

"We have a book club," Cindy started. "I'd love to get you down for a year's membership. I get a commission for everyone I get."

Ah, clever girl.

I like her. I'll have to keep tabs on her, too.

Grinning, Felix gave her his information.

***

* * *

Looking from the address to the mobile home, Felix realized he'd under-estimated how bad off Edmund was.

While many such places had bad reputations, they didn't always live up to them. Felix had already found that his own community where he was living went against his preconceived notions.

His direct neighbors were actually quite kind and had even come over with homemade chicken wings as well as a large case of beer. They were an older couple who just didn't have enough money to keep up with their previous lifestyle and had changed their lives to fit their ability.

Goldie had made fast friends with them since she was home all the time. She'd even been quick to share some of the stockpiled meat with them.

On the other side of them was a younger family whose children had developed a strange game of hide-and-seek with Andrea. Where she'd stalk them around the yards and then catch them.

Miu had inadvertently been dragged into it when one of the children had managed to find her. Now the two of them had started up a massive game of "hunt and stalk" as they called it.

Creeping around the community, while all looking for one another.

What Felix had in front of him was the opposite of that.

It was every bad flavor, stereotype, and rotten possibility one could conjure up with a mobile home.

"Shit," Felix said under his breath, the bag in his hand mostly forgotten. He hadn't expected it to be this bad.

Faith shook her head and looked to Felix. "This makes our own home feel almost like too much," she muttered. "I know we've done what we could without buying the trailer to fix it up. Spent some money on some decorations but… this is… it makes me almost feel ashamed."

Nodding his head, Felix tried to ignore the rusted-out exterior, the holes he could see through into the interior that was clearly missing insulation.

He did his best to not focus on the fact that it was dangerously sagging to one side as if the running gear was bad. Not to mention, a number of the skirt panels were just missing outright.

What mattered to him was finding Edmund.

A resource who was quite literally rotting away in a place like this.

He'd have to get in touch with Treston and rent a trailer out for Edmund. This was simply too much of a problem for Felix to leave alone.

"Hey there, pretty," called a voice from the side. "Watcha doin'? How about you come talk to me?"

Faith turned her head and looked at the speaker.

Apparently, she wasn't really in the mood to deal with something like this as she turned around and opened the door to the truck. Reaching under the seat, she pulled out a short bat that one could only call a billy club.

Standing up, she gave it a waggle with her left hand while looking at the man who'd cat-called her.

"Come on over to talk to me instead," she replied, her right hand in the pocket of her hoodie. Chances were she was more than willing to draw her pistol and shoot these people if she deemed them to be an issue.

The baton was just a polite warning given what he knew she was capable of.

Apparently the threat of the bat wasn't enough to deter them and was more like toilet paper you'd find at an entry level bathroom at a corporate HQ.

Flimsy and without any material to it.

In fact, six or seven men started moving over toward them.

"I'm sorry, Felix," apologized Faith with a heavy sigh. "I thought that'd steer them clear. Anything you want me to do?"

"No guns, please. If we have to dump bodies in a swamp later, it'd be better if they just vanished.

"Kind of annoyed that we're bringing problems to Edmund's house, but it's not like we didn't try to stop this," Felix warned her.

"Can't promise that, but I'll try. Starting to feel a lot like home here. My old home that is. This was rather normal. A regular Tuesday, you could say," muttered Faith, then went silent. It felt like she was a spring that was winding up.

As soon as the goons got close enough, Faith brought the club around in a wicked swing. She wasn't here to play around or listen to them trash talk.

The club slammed into the original speaker's temple and sent him crashing to the ground. Laying there unmoving, the man was face down on one of his friend's shoes.

"I'm not playing, and I'm really over this," Faith said a second before she pulled out her pistol. She leveled it at those who were standing around. "You've got five seconds to pick up your friend, or I turn all your bodies into gator grub. I know a perfect swamp to dump you all into."

Following Faith's action, Felix put his hand around the pistol in his pocket. Holding onto it, he finger-checked the safety and then flicked it to the off position.

The rather disreputable gang of lowlifes looked like they were considering rushing Faith. Which meant he no longer had a choice.

He dropped the bag with the book in it and then pulled the pistol from his pocket. Taking a second to rack the slide, he then pointed it at the closest individual to him.

"Gator grub it is," Felix muttered and started to squeeze the trigger.

Before he'd really made the choice to shoot, everyone began running away as fast as they could. They didn't even bother to pick up their friend.

Faith sniffed loudly and then stuck her gun back into her pocket. Walking over to the downed individual, she rifled through his pockets.

She came up with a wallet, a cell phone, and a set of car keys. The phone and keys both got dumped out on the man while she flipped through the wallet quickly.

Pulling out a gift card and what looked to be several ten-dollar bills, she then tossed that on top of the man as well. Pocketing her gains, she looked back at Felix.

"At least we didn't have to waste ammo. Hard to get without paperwork trails," she said, then bent down and slammed her billy club into the man's right forearm. There was a sickening crunch as the bone broke under the blow. "There, that'll be a good reminder for him. He can give himself a stranger with his left hand."

Felix snorted at that and looked back to the mobile home. There'd been no noise or response from anyone inside.

If there was anyone inside.

Momentarily, he had a thought that maybe Edmund had lied to him after all. Maybe that he'd managed to sidestep Felix in the end.

Walking up to the door of the mobile home, Felix contemplated what to do. It looked to be bigger than the one where he was staying, which meant that there was certainly room for more people.

He just couldn't shake the feeling that this

wasn't the right time or place. That this was already the wrong action to take, given what'd happened.

Except Felix just couldn't shake the feeling that he needed to try and reach out to Edmund. The sun had just set a short while ago which meant this was technically still a decent time to call on someone.

We'll just play it off as a delivery.

That'll work.

A free promotion for no reason.

Felix lifted his hand and knocked on the mobile home door. Then he took a step down from the stairs and stood at the bottom.

Seconds ticked by and Felix could hear someone shuffling around inside. Though they didn't come to the door.

Nor did it seem like they were in any hurry either. Eventually, whoever was inside settled back down and moved no more.

After an entire minute passed, Felix realized they weren't going to answer the door. If Edmund was here, which realistically didn't seem likely anymore, then he wasn't answering the door.

The fact that Edmund hadn't been spotted at the bookstore had been odd to Cindy. On top of that, there were some goons outside waiting nearby.

Were they here looking for Edmund or was it just coincidental?

Now the address where he supposedly lived at felt wrong. Which meant he'd had to have lied to Cindy as well.

Maybe it was a lie so well practiced that I took it as truth.

But why would he have to lie so often that it felt like he was giving an answer that was honest? Something to consider.

Nothing I can do for now. I'll just have to try this one again later.

Or from a different angle.

Sniffing, Felix walked back toward where Faith stood near the truck. He did pause for a moment to bend down and pick up the thug's wallet. Flicking through it, quickly he pulled out the man's driver's license then tossed the rest back down.

Slipping it into his pocket in case he needed to know more about the man later, Felix got into F-Two.

"Hey, I want to do some testing with this regeneration power you said I'd have as your grove," he said, looking at Faith as she got into the truck. "I need to test a few things without you hitting me with the magical whammy."

"Oh? Wonderful. I'd be happy for you to experiment on me," Faith said with some excitement as she turned the key in the truck's ignition. "After that, we can do some minor testing on cuts and things to see how you heal up."

"I didn't mean..."

Felix let the words die unspoken.

He saw no reason not to test if he could recover in that way quickly, either.

It'd be good data.

Chapter 17 - Shadow War -

Groaning, Felix rolled over onto his side.

Or at least he tried to.

All he really managed to do was end up putting his face in Goldie's throat. To which the gold Dragon responded by putting an arm around him and then laid still.

No sooner than she went unmoving, Faith pushed up against Felix's back to close the distance.

She squirmed around against him until her lap was pressed up to his rear end and he was being spooned. Then she put an arm around Felix and Goldie both, nuzzled the back of his head, and went back to sleep.

You know... considering the heater isn't working, I'm kinda glad for the body heat but this is a bit much. There's no reason that –

Andrea thrust her hips against Faith's head, which only forced the Dryad's head down against Felix, then ran her hands up and down Goldie's back, causing the Dragon to also push closer to Felix, then the Beastkin stopped moving as well.

Felix could feel her torso against the top of his head and her breathing in and out.

Once again, she was sleeping as if she were the top of a capital letter T in their pile of bodies. Somehow not bothering anyone while doing it.

You know... it's not as bad if Miu is here.

When she's not, it just becomes a pile of sweaty arms and legs.

Unable to help it, Felix felt his lips turn up into a smile. These were people he trusted absolutely. Their wants and needs were minimal compared to what they offered him.

"Alright, my loves," Felix murmured quietly. "I'm going to get up. I'll come back with coffee around nine if you're all still asleep."

Goldie said nothing but continued to softly snore.

Andrea made a grunt and then stuck a hand down to pat Felix's face. She then ran her fingers through his hair and got comfortable again.

"Lots of creamer, please," Faith asked from behind him, then kissed the back of his neck several times.

Regretfully, Felix pulled himself out of the very warm and comfortable bed and wriggled his way down off the foot of it.

By the time he'd gotten to his feet, Andrea had taken his place and was face planted in Goldie's chest with Faith snuggled up behind the Beastkin.

Watching for several seconds, Felix gave his head a shake and left the bedroom. He closed the door behind himself and passed through the small kitchen to the living room.

Miu was sitting on a couch they'd scrounged up and was reading a newspaper. Next to her looked like some sort of radio component that'd been in a car.

Honestly, to him it looked like it'd been torn

free from its placement outright. As if she'd just ripped it clean out of a dashboard.

Several wires were spread out around it and one went up to the wall where what looked a lot like an antenna had been taped.

In the corner, behind all the mess, was a car battery which everything had been hooked up to. Which meant his earlier thought was right.

He could faintly hear what sounded like radio chatter from a police drama coming from it. Someone was trying to report something that'd happened, with some sort of numerical code attached to it.

Looking up from the newspaper, she stared at him in the way only Miu could. A way that felt like she equally wanted to lick every inch of his skin while also draining him of blood so she could bathe in it later.

Only to drink the bloody bathwater, then sleep inside his corpse.

Flipping the newspaper over, she folded it and set it down next to herself, putting the entirety of her attention on him.

"Did you break into a police car?" Felix asked, coming over to sit down next to Miu. He reached out and took her left hand in his right and leaned into the corner of the couch.

He found holding hands to be quite comfortable for him as of late. Regardless of it being Andrea, Goldie, Faith, or Miu, he quite liked holding hands all of a sudden.

Miu's hand squeezed his right up to the point of causing him pain, then relaxed slightly. Holding her hand was always a lesson in how vast her grip strength was.

"Yes, I did. I wanted a police scanner and some equipment. Took the ballistic vest he had in the trunk. Shotgun, and all the shells for it as well.

"The app I was using to listen in found the frequency for the county easily enough, but it was encrypted. I couldn't hear anything," she explained, her pupils widening as she stared at him. Her hand started to tremble in his but it didn't get out of control. "I needed a radio that was set to that encryption so… I took one. I made sure there isn't any way that they can track it back to me.

"I ripped all of that out and took only the components I needed. It was part of my physical training when I joined the Guild a long time ago. These are much less sophisticated than what I'm used to, but it wasn't too hard.

"I… I didn't do wrong, did I? I didn't injure the officer. I just waited for him to park, broke into the vehicle, and took what I needed. I made sure to not leave anything behind. I wore a mask and gloves."

Felix wanted to scold her for her actions, because they might bring undue attention to them, but he couldn't really blame her either. What she was doing was exactly what she needed to.

She was keeping an eye on the situation around them to stay aware of events. Because they were dealing with a criminal element, they would need to be ready and aware of a response to said element.

"No, I can't blame you. I'm just surprised and nervous, that's all. You know how I am," Felix said soothingly. He didn't want to push her off balance at the moment.

Miu had been performing incredibly well lately.

"Anything interesting?" he asked, before leaning in to kiss her briefly. Almost akin to a greeting, he enjoyed a quick kiss on seeing anyone after a break.

"I-that-err… no," Miu stated with a slow breath. It was obvious she hadn't wanted it to stop. "There's just a lot of bodies turning up, it seems like. Gang violence.

"Lot of it. Seems like we're in a location with a high murder rate on top of everything else. People like to point at big cities for murders but where we came from, it was the south with high murder rates.

"Double in some locations. I'm wondering if this is maybe an offshoot universe to our own that took a slightly different path. There are so many things that I know from the old world that's true. So many things that feel similar."

Felix hadn't actually told anyone but Goldie that he'd found Kit and Lily, or at least their duplicates, on this world. There was the distinct possibility of their being another Miu here as well.

Andrea was rather unlikely since her species died out previously.

"It's a similar universe," agreed Felix and then sighed, giving Miu's hand a squeeze. "I found this universe's Lily and Kit. They're quite well. A lawyer and a psychologist. Distinctly possible there's a Miu Miki in this universe as well."

Miu stopped moving, her eyes locked to his. She didn't breathe or move.

I didn't think the possibility of meeting an alternate version of herself would make her shut down. That's rather strange.

She mentioned before that her childhood was off. Filled with training and danger, but never really opened up about it.

I wonder –

Shouting from outside broke through Felix's thoughts. People shouting in a way you could never mistake as anything other than hyper-aggression.

This wasn't your everyday disagreement type of shouting.

Felix felt like it was a "crazy person getting a gun to kill a neighbor" kind of shouting. Except that it didn't stay shouting for long.

It now sounded a lot like screams, grunts, and howls.

Jumping off the couch, Felix walked by the coat rack near the front door and pulled his pistol free from the hoodie there. He didn't need to pull the slide to know he'd chambered a round in it previously.

Pushing the safety down, he opened the door

and went outside.

Or tried to.

Before he'd even gotten a step towards it, Miu had simply flown out of the doorway. She breezed past him and out into the early morning day.

"No gun," she said, even as she vanished from view.

Pushing the safety back on, Felix stuck it in the hoodie then rushed outside behind her. He emerged right into a mad brawl that was occurring practically on his doorstep.

He could see that it was a number of kids from the community engaged in a straight-out melee with people who were unfamiliar to him.

Miu had walked right up to someone who had a knife that was going for a teen. She snatched it out of the man's hand, reversed it, and slammed it home into the man's knee. It slipped in easily and went right up to the hilt.

Felix moved forward toward three men who'd circled around a young woman. They hadn't done much other than try to pin her up against Felix's trailer.

Not bothering in the least to figure out what was going on, Felix did as Miu had. He simply attacked the first person he came to.

They'd looked his way when he came out, then turned toward him. In their hand was a short length of metallic pipe.

The man made a swing at Felix as soon as he

got within range.

But it was clumsy.

Slow.

It took so terribly long to reach him that Felix misjudged the timing. He was used to people who were incredibly proficient in combat.

Not this.

Rather than block the attack, Felix ended up striking the man's forearm. It sent the attack backward and knocked the man off balance. His feet stuttered beneath him to get his bearings.

Stepping in, Felix threw out a left jab and caught the man in the chin. Dropping his shoulder, he then struck a hook in deep against the man's floating rib. Right where his liver should be.

Tucking in tight, Felix then threw a left uppercut, aiming for the man's chin again as his head shot forward from the body blow.

Felix's fist landed perfectly and there was a pop as the man's head snapped upward. Then he went down in a heap with what looked a lot like a broken jaw.

Stepping past the man, Felix threw out a kick while rotating his hips and putting maximum force into the strike. Aiming it at the side of another man's thigh, right above the knee, Felix blasted his foot into it.

The man's leg went to the side due to the force and he started to fall backward. Felix stepped in closer and brought the blade of his right elbow in with a short strike to the man's face.

There was a crunching noise followed by the man being thrown backwards and to the ground. Blood was gushing down from his flattened nose and split lip.

Turning, Felix looked to the last of the three men he'd engaged. He looked like he had a bit of proficiency as he held his hands up in front of himself.

Looks like a striker? Maybe?

Play into it and go!

Felix held up his hands in a similar way and then moved forward. He kept his eyes on the man's torso, right below his arms and beyond his fists.

A sudden, swift jab came out and Felix simply bobbed to one side, letting it pass him by. Then he stepped in and brought his foot down right on the top of the man's knee.

He'd locked it into place when he'd thrown the punch and it wasn't going anywhere. Felix stepped into that kick with the full weight of his body and all the force he could muster.

The man's kneecap folded in on itself and bent backward in the wrong direction. Trying to step backward, the man practically collapsed even as he began to scream.

Felix shot out with his left hand and grabbed the man behind his head. Then he shot out a knee-strike with his right leg.

It slammed into the man's shrieking face, right where his cheek was. There was an ugly thump and the man was sent to the ground just like his two friends.

One of the three was rolling around on the ground, screaming into his hands.

Stepping toward him, Felix put a kick into his gut that folded them up around his leg and knocked the wind out of them completely.

Looking up, Felix found Miu had downed six attackers in the time it took him to work through three. Glancing over his shoulder, he saw the young woman who'd been surrounded not far off.

She was watching Felix with wide eyes, her hands held up in front of herself.

"Go home, say nothing. You saw nothing," Felix stated, then nodded his head to the side. "Get moving before more show up or the cops do. You don't want to be here."

Nodding her head, she was off in a flash, sprinting between two mobile homes. All the other teens had also scattered and fled in every direction as Miu and Felix had waded in.

Coming over to him, Miu had a wide smile on her face. She looked quite happy despite the fact that blood was liberally splattered across her face.

"You did good! Very good," enthused Miu. "I was so happy to see it. You used your training well."

Her smile was ear to ear as she stood there. As if there weren't a number of people laid out around them in various states of injury.

Her head snapped to one side and she looked toward the center of the community. As if she could see or hear something that way.

"Go inside. Someone's coming," commanded Miu. "I'm going to watch. See who's looking around."

Felix did just that, going straight into the trailer without another word. He didn't want to be standing around amongst this mess.

Especially if it was cops or something else entirely.

Though he did feel rather stupid.

He'd just been thinking of the fact that Miu could have done something to bring attention to them. Only for him to rush out to play hero and do just that.

"That was a great fight!" Andrea said when he entered the trailer and then she bounced up to him. She wrapped her arms around his neck, pulled her feet off the ground, and hung onto him. "Nnn! So good, so good! I loved it."

He had about a second to stiffen his back and plant his feet lest he be pulled right to the ground. Both his hands went under Andrea's rear end to hold her upright.

"I'm not that fond of hand-to-hand fighting, but that was well done," agreed Goldie from the couch.

Says the woman who could punch a brick-wall flat.

Goldie still looked pale and was rather weak, but she was also clearly recovering. At this point, she was more or less able to care for herself, which was why the Others who'd been watching over her were now more on scouting and guard duty.

"We'll need to get the Second and Third in to see if they saw anything," said Felix, concentrating on Andrea. "Are Four and Five ready for a job?"

"Yes! We're here and ready," Andrea said with a dip of her head a second before she flung her thighs around his hips. She settled in against him and tilted her head to one side, watching him. "Is it time for a four-way? It's been a while."

"Sure, just not right now. Any chance you two could go see if there's anything else going on in the community? These jokers don't look like they're from around here," asked Felix.

A second later and two more Andreas appeared, stepping out of the one clinging to him.

Both looked at him and then gave him a crisp salute, though the one on the left had her tongue sticking out to one side.

"Nn!" they said in unison. "Scout, reconnoiter, assess, report, four-way!"

Both Andreas then exited the trailer. Though they did so by going to the bedroom and pulling up the trapdoor they'd cut into the flooring. Slipping down into the hole, they vanished under the mobile home.

He was fairly certain there was a section of skirting they'd undone that was now just leaning against the home.

"Nothing on the radio," Faith said from where she sat on the couch. Exactly where Miu had been. "No one's called anything to the police. This is good news, right?"

"Cops don't care. They just want to fill out a report. Then they get curious about everything else that they shouldn't," grumbled Andrea, still hanging onto Felix. "Parks aren't dens of crime. It's not where all the bad people go.

"It's just where bad things can happen a bit easier. Cops can make things worse. My dad always said you 'settle them cases yourself' and don't bother with the law. Bringing in the law just brings them into your home."

Hm. I like that.

Sounds like a solid motto to give to my Legionnaires once we start moving.

Though… seems like my original plan is shifting.

I'm going to have to really think about how to make this work.

I need to rebuild Legion, but only of those I trust. Also how to build it up as an organization that isn't technically in charge. One that doesn't call the shots.

But a group that people go to, to ask for permission to make a risky shot. I don't want them to look to me to tell them what to do, but they should ask for us to say it's fine.

That'll mean –

Felix's thoughts were dashed completely when Andrea started kissing him. Her tail started to swish back and forth behind her lightly as well, which meant his ability to ask her to do things was going to run out soon.

Breaking the kiss, Felix rested his cheek to

her temple.

"Ah, okay. I need to—"

Miu opened the door at that moment and stepped inside. She looked from Andrea to Felix, and then closed the door gently.

Marching over to the Beastkin, she simply stared at her from a foot away. Not doing anything else.

"Uhm… want a turn, Miu?" Andrea asked, reaching up to lightly toy with a lock of hair.

Several seconds passed before Miu nodded her head.

"Okie. I get him back afterward for a four-way though. You can watch if you want. I'll even let you clean him up after," Andrea offered.

"Yes. Yes, please, Andie. Thank you, Andie," whispered Miu with a tiny smile.

Andrea hopped down out of Felix's arms, then grabbed Miu by the rear end and tossed her up at Felix.

She simply clung to him in the exact same way Andrea had.

"Those were thugs from a rival drug… supplier… dealer… group… I have no idea what to call them," complained Miu and then promptly laid her head down on Felix's shoulder. "They were rivals to David. Remember that body count I was talking about?

"I believe he's the reason. I think he's attacking another group and taking things from them. We're probably the cause. Or something along those lines."

Ah… I see.

Time for a meeting.

Miu was slowly inching forward and clearly getting ready to bite him.

He intercepted her with a kiss instead.

Chapter 18 - Neutrality -

Felix had been sitting with Faith for a little while now. They were simply watching from the top of Jay's mobile home to see the comings and goings of everyone.

Miu had gone earlier in the morning to tell Jay to set up a meeting with David. There'd clearly been some changes in the local scene and Felix wanted to know what was going on.

He'd also been clear with Miu that she needed to convey to Jay that this wasn't a demand. This wasn't a command.

This was a request from an involved party and nothing more.

The last thing he needed was David thinking that Felix was actually a problem or a solution. His entire goal was built up around the idea of simply not being a target for anything.

"He'll come," Faith whispered. Most of the lights in the community were out by now. People had gone to bed a while ago and turned in.

Morning alarm clocks waited for no one after all. Regardless of who you were.

"He's just making sure this isn't an ambush or that you're working with whoever he's fighting against," continued Faith, her head rotating from one side to the other. Her eyes picking across all that was laid out before them. "In fact… I'm pretty sure that's their cars in the distance. Before you ask, yes, I really can see that far.

"The… my… you're my tree, Felix. It is literally growing within you. You are growing in power, as it grows in power, which in turn gives me more power.

"I'm already twice as strong in magic as I was when we first arrived here. While that isn't saying I'm back to my original power, it's saying a great deal.

"I've also noticed my skin has gotten softer, my nails are much harder to break, and my hair has a lot better bounce to it. I'm really loving how tight the skin on my face feels. Betty never mentioned any of this, but… I think their grove is weaker than… er… than my grove.

"That's not to say they're unhappy with Evan, just that he isn't the same sort of power you are. Ugh, I'm making a mess of all this."

Grinning to himself, Felix couldn't deny he'd expected her to make mention of other things, like having more strength, being faster, or having greater stamina.

There were times that he forgot Faith was probably the most feminine of those who were with him. Second to that would be Goldie but she often felt more like a house-wife.

Andrea didn't typically care about most of what a modern-day woman would. Or at least she didn't seem to.

Miu's routine was steeped in everything that involved self-beauty, self-care, and upkeep of oneself, but nothing at all for anything in regards to anything feminine in nature.

Faith was his girly girl.

"I get it. Though you never answered me when we first… err… made me a grove. Is it just you and me?" Felix asked, staring out to where Faith had indicated. He was pretty sure he could see movement but no headlights.

"Uhm, depends on how many Dryads Betty has set aside for you by the time we return," answered Faith. She lifted her hand and pointed at the spot where Felix was looking. "Their headlights are off. They're coming."

"And how many do you think Betty will set aside?" Felix asked. He'd known getting a power increase from Faith could run a risk like this and he'd deemed it acceptable.

"Probably ten or twenty to start. She won't think you can take on as many as Vince can. At least… not at first. You're more mental, he's physical," Faith answered with some reluctance. "You might be able to get it to stop at that so long as you convince all the Dryads in your grove that'd be best.

"Though, now after having experienced it myself. I think you could easily handle as many as Vince does. It isn't your… err… way of fighting that dictates that. Just your innate power. You're both very similar from what I can tell."

"You're the Grove-mistress, consider that your first order of business. I don't want others. I've got too many as it is," Felix said and then stood up. He adjusted the mask that he had already been wearing and made sure it was resting suitably over his face.

Faith stood up a second after that and then the three Andreas on nearby roofs all looked at them. They were there to make sure no one did anything stupid.

Goldie had wanted to come, but she was still clearly on the mend.

"Let Shadow know we're going," muttered Felix and then moved to the edge of the mobile home's roof. He jumped off and landed lightly. Moving forward several steps, he parked his feet on a spot that'd make Miu happy.

Close enough that David would see him, far enough from them that Miu could act if she needed. On top of that, he was wearing the ballistic vest she'd stolen from the squad car.

Anything less than a headshot that hit him in the brain and he could get away from it. The regeneration testing he'd done previously had revealed that he was a lot more like Goldie now given his status as Faith's tree.

Her grove, as she called it.

He'd even gone so far as to cut a small chunk out of his forearm.

The injury had filled in and healed completely over without even a scar left behind.

Right now, he was feeling far more potent and able than he had in his previous life. Being able to modify himself had opened almost too many doors for him.

Stepping out in front of him, Miu eased

herself up to stand just before him. In her hands was an SMG. The arsenal they were picking up was increasing and he wasn't quite sure from where.

"Robbing people?" Felix asked under his breath.

"No. Illegally purchased. No paperwork, costs a bit more, better than not having it though," she answered. "I've got written records for all our expenses and where it goes if you—"

"Nope," Felix said, resting his hand on Miu's waist. "You're our money person. I trust you. You know what my goals are and I'm sure you've budgeted it all out appropriately."

"I-yes. Thank you for trusting your M… your… your me. Thank you for trusting your me. Your me loves you and can't wait to—"

Miu's rambling, chaotic words stopped dead. The cars Faith had pointed out were pulling up now.

Two Andreas and Faith all came out of the darkness around the other side of Jay's home. They were all holding SMGs, but they all had them against their chests. None of them were pointed, nor were they held in an aggressive way.

Felix wanted David to know that he had more than just a "pet Dragon" so to speak. That he had normal weaponry and people as well.

There was a soft rumble in the distance that caused Felix to look up.

A light sprinkle of rain began to fall, washing down and over everything. Standing there, Felix wasn't very happy about that, but scurrying inside wouldn't do him any good at this moment. It'd just make him look weak.

The trio of vehicles came to a stop and everyone got out.

Surprisingly, David was one of the first to pop out. He waved a hand at Felix as he did so.

"Ah, good to see you. I'm actually glad you called this meeting. I hope you don't mind, but I brought a bunch of product for you to do your thing with," David said with more than a little excitement. He pulled up the collar of his coat and then motioned toward the door to the trailer. "Let's go in, it's just going to really start pouring here in a bit."

Felix nodded his head and followed David into the trailer. Faith, Miu, and the Andrea all came with.

Reminder to self, make sure to brush out Three, Four, and Five's tails. They're going to get soaked in this. That'd be a nice reward for them.

They'd love that.

Jay was seated in the corner of his own living room. He looked rather nervous as he leaned forward with his hands pressed together. His eyes were also on the floor.

It was obvious he was trying to "not be there" despite reality not permitting that. Jay was the focal point for the meeting as he was their in-between.

"Something wrong?" Felix asked, looking to

Jay. He was already rather positive that those he'd put down had all been here for Jay.

His current posture made it easy to question him directly.

"I know there was an incident in this community earlier. I heard about it from someone I pay to watch over the area," Felix offered as a lead-in to the conversation. Walking over to one of the couches, he sat down in it and then crossed one leg over the other. "I take it you were the target, Jay? I've also heard a lot of corpses are turning up lately."

"Uh, yeah. About that," David said and then grunted as he sat down on the love seat across from Felix. "Yeah, I'm at war with a contact I had in a cartel. One of his dealers, too. They really don't like the fact that I don't need to go to them anymore.

"They've lost the power they had over me. They can't control my expansion anymore. Can't hold me back. They're trying, obviously. Not doing so well.

"Already killed at least forty or fifty people. Most of them were from my original contact, Stephen, who got me my stuff. He brought up a lot of thugs from the south.

"They didn't really fit in well with the population though. They stuck out so bad we just started shooting them on sight. Soon as they met up with their local contact."

David laughed and shrugged his shoulders, holding his hands up.

"You'd think Stephen would have figured it out. It was obvious who they worked for. Executed them the day they arrived, most of the time. I'd been planning something like this forever. Just never had the opportunity," explained the man.

Ten duffel bags had been brought in and dumped to one side of Jay's home. Another several were brought in and put on the other side.

"You mentioned the quality didn't matter much, so I spread it around a lot. Then re-bagged it and brought it over," continued David with a chuckle. "You know, your rates are so reasonable that I raised them myself. I don't want you thinking I'm taking advantage of you. You're a lot cheaper than Stephen and a hell of a lot nicer to deal with.

"All you want is money. Money? I've got money. Lots of it. Happy to give it to you. Best deal I've made in years."

Felix glanced at Andrea who was standing near the bags that were probably filled with cocaine. She immediately realized what he wanted and she began dragging them over to him.

He was fairly certain he had the points to spare to convert it all. Not to mention he wanted the money.

Cash was exactly what he needed right now.

It left no trace of how he got it or where it was going.

Perfect for all the things he needed to do and to keep himself off the radar.

"Of course, I didn't involve you or mention

you as you said you wished no part of any of this," David promised and then sighed. "They did come for Jay though, thinking that he somehow had something to do with this."

"We can't use him then," Felix stated firmly and then opened up the bag. It was exactly what he expected. Letting his eyes move to the other bags, he figured it was all the same.

He wanted to change all the bags to a pure quality at the same time. Using whatever they were blended with as points to help fuel it.

Type: Cocaine / 14 substances Click to expand	**Condition**: Very Low Quality
Owner: Felix Campbell	**Action >> Purify**: Cost 41,017 points
Pre-Action Value: $141,874	**Post-Action Value:** $979,987

"You said you were paying me more?" Felix asked, contemplating the window.

He'd been slowly building his points back up by patrolling the city and emptying dumpsters.

Pushing at his power, he pulled up his point balance.

	Generated	**Remaining**
Andrea	670	670
Faith	400	400

Felix	1,605	1,605
Goldie	2,473	2,473
Miu	1,025	1,025
+Loyalty Bonus	800	800
+Marital Bonus	400	400
=Daily Total	**7,373**	**7,373**
Banked Total	—	**81,771**

Everyone's scores went up again.

They're all functioning at full power, yet I'm getting all the points for them. I wonder if that'll change after the day of Awakening.

Probably.

"—increased it significantly. You've got about four hundred thousand dollars in those bags there. Well more than half of what I would've saved and I still make a lot of money," David confessed. "That and I stole a lot of that from Stephen. I'm sure he's raging right now."

Felix spent the points and gladly so.

That much money was what he needed. He could easily start pushing things.

"Done," Felix remarked in a dry tone and then zipped the bag back up and pushed it to one side. "Now, as to Jay. We can't use him. We need a new neutral ground.

"Got any properties in Hardysburg that we could utilize? Preferably someplace where we can kill intruders at if they decide to try and crash the party."

David clapped his hands together and then rubbed them against one another. He looked incredibly pleased.

"I have no idea what kind of voodoo that you do, but I don't give a damn," David chortled. "You know, I won't lie, if I hadn't seen a Dragon turn some of my people into chewing gum, I'd say this is all crazy.

"But… whatever. I'll take it. Never look a gift… Dragon… in the mouth. As to Hardysburg… no. Nothing. I've got a warehouse up there, but you wouldn't want to go there. Damn FBI is watching it like hawks. Anyone I send there is just so that they can get tagged."

"I see. Well. I'll see about acquiring a location up there," Felix said in an offhand way. "In the meantime… we'll use an out of the way place. There's a swamp… where was it?"

Felix turned to look to Faith. He knew she'd been talking to the trees and they'd been relaying locations to her that would work out for them.

One particular question had been a good place to dispose of a body.

"Between Hardysburg and New Augusta. It's off the road, but you can drive right up to a farm that backs up to the land."

"I know the place," David put in quickly before Faith could continue. "I can meet you there easy. I haven't put any bodies into that swamp, but it's definitely out of the way and not somewhere people go."

"It'd also let us know if someone is coming for us. There's hardly any way to get to that farm without taking the only road to it," Felix added and then gestured at the money.

Andrea moved to the door and opened it. She stood there for several seconds, saying and doing nothing.

Then she shut it and came back over.

Before he could ask her what was going on, two more Andrea's entered. They were masked of course and wearing SMGs.

They looked to their Prime, received an unspoken command, then picked up the three duffel bags between them. Then they were gone without a word.

"Your people are… very good," remarked David. His eyes had followed the Others as they worked, only to move back to Felix. "It's a wonder you aren't… interested in other things."

"They're my Legionnaires. I run an organization called Legion. We don't get involved in the day-to-day stuff. We just want money," Felix confirmed again. "We support no one but ourselves and don't want to get crosswise with the government either."

"Legion First," stated Miu, Andrea, and Faith in unison.

He'd forgotten that the typical response to any mention of Legion almost always brought out the motto.

Both Jay and David were looking at the

masked women. After a handful of seconds passed, they ended up looking back at Felix.

"What does that make you?" Jay asked, looking up from the corner and peering at Felix curiously.

"A Legionnaire, of course," Felix replied with a grin that they wouldn't see. "Now... is there anything else I need to know? Is this contact of yours going to be a problem for me?

"It seems like he came to Jay to try and find out how you were getting your product. I imagine that means getting to me."

"I'd say yeah," agreed David. "Chances are, you're right. He was looking for a way to get to you and Jay was a means to an end. Probably just put two and two together after talking to some folks.

"He might try to continue to make trouble for you. Sorry about that. I'm working on it. Stephen is a tricky little shit at the best of times. When he decides he wants to make an ass of himself, it just gets a bit much."

"Fine. You might want to send him a professional courtesy note. He shouldn't look into what you're doing too deeply," warned Felix and then stood up. "Because I'd be a problem for anyone who wanted to come looking.

"And for problems, well, I don't have much control once I get to solving one. I can't stop until I'm satisfied the problem won't ever be coming back.

"Because I really don't like problems. People

shouldn't come to me with problems. They should come with answers.

"Because unfortunately, I solve problems in a way that doesn't leave room for them to become a problem again. I will go to extremes to make sure the problem doesn't come back. Often that includes anyone who was part of the problem from top to bottom simply… going away."

David and Jay were now watching Felix like a person would eye a wolf that was inching closer to them.

"It's a lot like a cavity. You get rid of it and then eliminate the material around it. Make sure only the good bits remain. Anything even possibly softened by that cavity gets drilled out," Felix said and then looked at his people. Then back to David. "Also, would you be willing to sell me gear? Equipment? I imagine you probably can get me a better price. My people go through it rather fast.

"They're not very… gentle… when it comes to things. They can be a bit klutzy and break things."

"Like a Dragon dropping a mobile home," Faith pointed out helpfully.

"Just so," agreed Felix and then turned and made for the door. "See you in a week, David. Just send any messages by way of Jay until we get the farm setup."

Exiting after Andrea pulled the door open and went out first, Felix kept right in line behind her. His eyes were on her shoulders as she led them out into the rain.

She made a small hand gesture with her left hand and then turned right, pulling them along the side of the home.

Another turn and they were going out the back of it.

Walking straight out into the pouring rain, into the dark itself, Felix did so with a smile. He knew that other than himself, his people would see in the dark well enough.

I should upgrade myself with that, shouldn't I?

Night vision.

Humans don't normally get an easy free pass like Miu. She just focuses on what she wants and how she views it and it's multiplied.

Even small things can become massive for her.

Well… farm next. Lay a trap. Have Miu and an Andrea get ready to welcome guests there. Because I'm willing to bet David has a spy.

An insider who's passing on information.

He's underestimating how much his opponent knows of his organization.

With any luck… we'll find out who this Stephen is since he's decided to become a problem.

Take prisoners, bring them to Goldie, and let her ransack their minds.

Lemon Peesy, Easy Squeezey.

Smirking to himself at the murdered colloquialism Felix was feeling quite happy about everything. Only Stephen was the issue at the moment.

Oh! I need to brush some tails.

Where's my poor waterlogged Elex ladies?

Turning his shoulder, he found Miu on his left, Faith on his right, and behind them were four Andrea's.

They were all in their true forms, tails, ears, and all.

Looking ahead, he found the Prime's tail looked quite soaked as well.

Well. That's what he meant when he was talking about them. They clearly weren't Human. Oh well.

That'll throw him off the trail of finding us.

Tail brushings for all.

Chapter 19 - Knife Fight -

Felix sat down on the couch and did his best to stifle a yawn. They'd all woken up with the sunrise. There was a lot of work to be done today.

"Coffeeeeeee," said an Other while holding out a cup to Felix.

"Thank you, Three," he replied, giving the Andrea a wide smile.

The Andrea blinked, smiled, and tilted her head to the side. She watched him for several seconds.

"How'd you know?" she asked finally, bouncing in place a little.

"As I told you when you came back with Myriad. You were formerly Myriad Three. Before that a Death Other. We met for the first time when you were working contracts of captured Heroes.

"I know my Elex Women. You can't hide from me," Felix said and took a sip of the coffee.

"I... you knew I... really?" asked the Other, now looking shocked.

"Yes? I know all of you," agreed Felix. He'd gotten much better at knowing which one was which as time went on. After their home world fell, he knew them all at a glance. Even if he'd only met them once before.

"Okay, what... nn..." the Andrea took a shuffling step to the side and another Andrea popped out of her. Pointing at the Other, she looked very serious. "Who's she?"

"Five, now," Felix said after looking at the Other. "She was Adriana's Third. Before that she was Andrea sixty-four. She died in the back of the car saving me. It was really hard to watch you die, Five."

"I… yes! Yes, I am!" squealed the new Other. She began to dance in place and then jumped into Felix's lap, nearly spilling the coffee he'd just been given. "You really do know us! You were sad watching me die? But we come back!"

"I mean… yeah, I was sad. Coming back or not you were still dying, Five. And yeah, I really can tell you apart. I believe I've said that repeatedly," agreed Felix.

Faith, Miu, and Goldie had all joined him and were taking seats throughout the living room.

Miu had sat down right next to him and was now glaring a hole through the Other's head.

"We just… didn't realize you really meant it," called Andrea from the kitchen. She took a step away and met his eyes. A grin had spread across her face that looked ecstatic. "It's amazing. Do… do you know who was with you last night?"

"Your Second, of course. Who's currently with you, right now. I don't know where Four is," Felix said then looked to the Others. He had a fair sense she wasn't with any of them. "No, she's not here. Where'd she go?"

"She-she's on watch," all three Andrea's said in unison.

Then the Others all went and combined with

Andrea, who was watching Felix in a very curious way. Leaning back into the kitchen, she set to her task of making pancakes for everyone other than Goldie.

The Dragon was still on a red-meat diet.

"Is it time for a bored board meeting?" asked Faith who sounded rather excited.

"Board… board… meeting?" Felix responded, not quite sure what she meant by that.

"As in, you're bored, so you want a board meeting," elaborated Goldie.

The Dragon sighed, then went over to the couch. She made a small hand gesture at Felix to move down.

Miu shifted down and started pulling at Felix's arm.

No sooner than there was enough room, then Goldie sat down. She leaned in close to him and then rested her head on the couch and his shoulder.

"I guess it's that," muttered Felix, taking another sip of coffee. "I just wanted to talk about our plans. We have a lot going on."

"Mmhmm," Faith said, watching him with a wide smile. "You don't have to justify it. I like being here for these things. I'm not just… a… uhm… what'd you call it, Goldie?"

"A side character," answered the Dragon. Her eyes were closed and her left hand was now hanging onto Felix's left sleeve.

"Yes! I don't feel like a side character in my own story anymore. Being here and being part of this means I'm finally the heroine of my own story!" Faith gushed, sounding a lot like a kid being told they were getting ice cream.

"Right," mumbled Felix. He cleared his throat and then nodded his head, as if restarting his mental process. "We're moving on the 'evil' side of the plan first. We can't really push ahead with the 'good' side until we get those documents.

"That means cash, prepaid cards, prepaid minutes, and everything that doesn't leave a trace. Good thing we got paid by David."

"Yes, it was a lot of money. We're now able to make a lot of things happen with cash alone," Miu agreed from his right. "I'm starting to put some aside for the trash truck you wanted."

"Trash truck. Remind me what we're doing with that again?" asked Goldie with a yawn.

That's... why are you asking that, Goldie? You can see the answer in my mind as clear as day.

Goldie responded to his thoughts by rubbing her cheek against his shoulder. Whatever her plan was, it was for someone else's benefit in the room.

"It's part of the 'good side'," Faith answered before anyone could speak up. "Help out the cities and towns with low-cost solutions that also benefit us. We don't step up to the same level of visibility of Legion, but ingratiate ourselves into the system. Then we just keep spreading out. Undercutting others and utilizing our abilities."

"Exactly that," Felix said, pointing at Faith with a smile. "That's right. But as I said, that's for later. We need a lot more documentation for those things to work out for us.

"Right now, we can only really work on the underworld side of our plan. It's all Legion to anyone inside, but two organizations from anyone outside."

"Okay. So… what are we doing about that?" asked Andrea as she trooped in with three plates of pancakes. She handed them off to Miu, Faith, and Felix. "Just a few minutes more, Goldie."

Andrea took a moment to pat Goldie on the head and then went back to the kitchen.

"What we've already been doing, really. Forcing a change in the drug scene while expanding in the background," explained Felix. "I don't want to be working with drugs, but we don't have a choice. Criminal enterprises seem to be focused around theft or drugs. The last thing I want to do is rob any of these people.

"They already have very little. That'd just be adding misery to their lives. No sense in being cruel."

"Nn! Good! Yes!" called Andrea. "Drugs are okay because the people doing them would do them anyway. If you can make it less lethal and regulate it a bit, that'd be good. Kinda like how Skipper did it with all vices and made them industries.

"Though it's kinda funny how you don't even try to keep them guessing with how you change the drugs. Pretty sure they think you're a wizard or something."

Felix couldn't deny he'd seen how that'd worked out with Skipper at the helm. Things had been regulated, commercialized, and held to a higher standard. Skipper's government had a vise-grip on everything and had forced all to bend.

Or break.

"Well, we'll keep moving in the drug world. Since I only need a little bit of whatever they're dealing in to purify the rest, it makes it easy. I don't even have to import anything or run the risk of dealing with borders," continued Felix. "Past that, we'll just keep moving out. Expand into other things.

"Gambling, black-market goods, anything that we can do without hurting people."

"What about prostitution?" asked Faith.

"Problem with that one is that it's harder to force our view on it. We'd have to step into a spotlight to make that one happen. Either in the underworld or going through the political route," argued Felix. "Everything else is just letting people do their own thing.

"If we get the opportunity though, it's definitely worth getting into that business. Just not something we can move to at this time."

Andrea came in and then gently touched Goldie's face. In her other hand was a large steak that looked just barely seared. It was a very large chunk of meat that took up the whole plate.

"Just like you like it," Andrea said in a warm tone.

Goldie groaned softly, then sat upright. Taking the plate from her, she picked up the steak with one hand, held the plate in the other, and began eating. Tearing a mouthful off with her teeth.

Felix noted there was no cutlery there anyway.

Interesting.

You're cute when you're feral, my Golden One. Should I put a collar on you with a pure gold tag on it?

"Yes," Goldie said around a mouthful, chewing determinedly while staring at him now. Then she swallowed hard and cleared her throat. "Yes, you should. A necklace though, not a collar. Pure gold, of course.

"Now, move to the next part of the plan. Dealing with this… Stephen… fellow."

"Yes, Stephen. Stephen Chernishoff. Local big contact for all things cocaine in the area. He doesn't do anything else, so he's obviously heavily invested in what we're trying to take from him," Felix elaborated. "More or less sounds like he's the cartel guy for a large part of Alassippi.

"It's one of the reasons I wanted to have that farm as our meeting point with David. There's only one road in, it's backed up to a swamp, and there's no way to really get to it otherwise.

"I mean, I think there's a really large open field you can go across to get there. But at that point, you might as well drive. Or at least, that's what you heard, right Faith?"

"Yes, that's what all the trees told me.

They're rather eager to talk to me here. Eager and very chatty," confirmed Faith with a small nod of her head. "No one's been to that farm in a very long time. Whoever owns it has forgotten they do.

"Or died and it's just... lost. That happened back in my old world, but that was more because death was always close."

"There we go. We'll set up a nice trap for them there. We just have to decide who to send so they can welcome Stephen's people when they arrive. I really have no doubt that there's someone in David's organization who's feeding Stephen information.

"They'll show up looking for a knife fight and I'll have mined the arena. Simple as that."

"I should have been there," growled Goldie as she continued to chew and eat.

"And you will be. Even you yourself said that you think you'll be back to normal in a few days more. You're not draining your own stamina anymore to regenerate," countered Felix quickly.

"Yes. I... yes. I'll be ready very soon. Doesn't matter if I'm ready or not though, I'm going to that damn farm," the Dragon stated firmly. Apparently, there was no room for argument from her. "Also, I have a request. I want you to alter what you did to me as well as the regeneration power."

"Oh?" Felix inquired; his curiosity piqued. "Please, tell me what you're thinking."

Because I love your mind, my Golden One.

One half lovely and warm woman who wants to be

cared for and to care for another. One half brutal and truly awe-inspiring Dragon.

Goldie was staring at him now, her golden eyes glowing as she held his gaze.

He just smiled at her in return. He really was rather fond of his Dragon.

"I… yes," continued the Dragon. Her eyes were not moving from his own. "I want you to make it so I can change my scales' hardness when I wish. You've given me a regenerative power as well as the ability to modify my shape-changing as I wish. My horns that is and the like.

"I imagine to alter it to do a third thing based on those two wouldn't cost you very much. As, of course, hardening scales would be a form of shape-changing, and letting it stop when I wish would be regenerative. At least, to me."

"Nn, I like that. Oh, oh, oh, I also want you to change me and we need to do a test!" Andrea blurted out. She'd sat down next to Faith but leapt out of her seat. Moving over to the door, she opened it.

Leaving it ajar, she walked to where the living room, kitchen, and entrance joined together. She put her hands on her hips.

"I've been practicing!" she stated. "First, I want to show you how good I've gotten."

"Good you've gotten?" parroted Felix. He had no idea what she was talking about.

"Yes! I figured the better I could control my Others and I, the easier it'd be to expand us. I know that I have at least three Others in me that would love to exist. But I can't!" Andrea stated with a stamp of her foot.

Then Four came in from outside and went straight into Andrea, vanishing into her.

Putting her hands on her hips Andrea stood there looking almost confused.

"Oh, this'll... be harder... without music. Whatever," she said and then shook her head.

Stamping her right foot out, she threw her hands out to each side. Thrusting her hip forward and toward Felix she gave him a solid profile view.

Her tail stuck up from behind her and curled around her middle as well.

She leaned her shoulders back, pushed her chest out, and angled her rear end out. Giving her entire body almost a snake like writhing movement. Putting her hands out in front of her, an Other appeared. Then one more in front of that one.

All three Andreas began to move in sync. They crossed their arms in front of themselves and pressed their arms together to push their chests up and forward.

Then Felix couldn't quite follow the action very well as Andrea continued to dance, appearing Others and drawing them back in as she went.

Creating an almost optical illusion as she practically flung herself back and forth in the highly suggestive motions. Others popped into existence with a flourish, only to draw another one to themselves, or to vanish again.

Then she suddenly came to a stop and all the Other's came back into her.

"See? See? I'm really, really good at controlling my Others now!" she said and started hopping in place. "You should give me the ability to have five more. I bet it's cheap. If I had ten, I'd be so much stronger."

Andrea held her arms up and flexed.

She actually did have a good amount of muscle on her. He could easily forget how much of a terror she was in combat when she was acting cute like this.

"I... sure," Felix remarked. He really had no idea what was going through Andrea's head at the moment.

Wanting to escape the situation, Felix focused on upgrading Goldie's power first. To give her shape-shifting the ability to harden her scales as much, or as little, as she wanted.

Right up to the point that she could probably stop any ballistic weapon cold. Making her more on par with what she'd been in the old world.

Name: Goldie Campbell	**Condition**: Pleased. Heat will occur.
If No Action Taken: None	**Action >> Alter Race Power**: Cost 4,821 points

H... heat will occur? Goldie?

Heat like as in "in heat"?

Do I need to know something?

"Oh, that's nothing to fret over," Goldie said with a laugh, disregarding his thoughts outright. "Wonderful! Now, how much does Andie's cost? Having five more of her would be rather helpful.

"And by the way, Andie, that was a nice dance. I liked it. Was that what we watched on the television the other day? Thank you for bringing that again, by the way. It was a nice change of pace."

"Nn! Nn! Yes. I made the Others practice and then bring it back to me and we just kept doing that," chattered Andrea excitedly. "It would've been better with Myriad's dark hair."

Felix was feeling a bit nervous about the message in regards to Goldie going into heat. He knew that Dragons weren't Human and they did have animal needs and urges.

Doubly so that he knew she wanted to nest.

If her heat was like Andrea's, than he was in trouble.

She tended to get wound up once every two or three months to the point that she was nearly insatiable.

"Something like that, yes," Goldie murmured and patted Felix on the knee. Clearly following along with his thoughts. "It'll be fine. Now... Andie's power?"

Shit.

Felix focused on pulling up the same window, but for Andrea. He wanted the costs to modify her power and allow her the usage of five more Others.

Name: Andrea Campbell	**Condition**: Excited. Heat will occur.
If No Action Taken: None	**Action >> Alter Power**: Cost 7,194 points

"Perfect! Yours is only seven thousand, Andie. Mine's four thousand. I'll just carry Felix over to a different city tonight and we'll go ransack some dumpsters," Goldie suggested. "That'll replenish our points to a degree. I don't think Stephen's people will make a move tonight. Likely they'll make their first advance in three days, I'd say."

"Agreed," Miu said firmly as Faith nodded her head. She'd been mostly quiet the entire meeting. "That's when I would strike."

"Nn, nn, likewise!" Andrea said, rotating back and forth like a little girl would. She looked incredibly excited. "Did I mention I'm really happy that we're all… combat types?

"I always felt like some of the magic users were a little too nose-in-the-air for me at times. That they looked down at me for using my fists, feet, and guns."

"I'm very happy about it," Faith pitched in. "I like everyone well enough, and I'm quite friendly with them. But it's nice just to be with combat-oriented people. It's very nice."

"Yes, it is. I feel… good… with you all," Miu

added to the conversation.

It was an unexpected confession on her part.

Before anyone could react, Andrea darted across the room and snatched Miu up in a hug. The Asian woman's face was pulled straight into Andie's cleavage.

"Oooh, Miu, I'm so glad you said that," Andrea practically howled. Her arms were wrapped around the back of Miu's head. Her hands rested on her shoulders. She began to rock back and forth, holding her face in her chest. "I've always wanted to get closer to you.

"After you stopped killing us, that is. You were always so mean before that."

Miu had struggled against Andrea for a second, before going limp. Her arms came up and she just hung onto Andrea and let herself be manhandled by the Beastkin.

"Miu, Miu," Andrea said in a loud whisper. Then she bent her head down a bit. "Let's split Felix tonight. Okay? I bet we can really make him squirm between us. Maybe let me hug and cuddle you a bit, too?"

Miu's body flinched, then her head nodded incrementally.

"Awesome. We're gonna have so much fun," whispered Andrea at a speaking level and stood up again. She started rocking Miu back and forth again, her face still buried in her chest.

The psychotic assassin who wanted to eat the wombs of the women in the room just held onto

Andrea. Her arms wrapped around the Beastkin's hips.

"You know. Even though I can read her mind. I still can't tell if it's on purpose, or not," remarked Goldie, chewing methodically at her steak. Then she turned and looked to Felix with a wide smile.

He didn't have to ask her what she was grinning about. It'd been an idle thought that'd crossed through his mind.

That he'd almost rather spend the evening with Goldie than get stuck between Miu and Andrea.

Of course, she'd taken that thought from his mind and would likely offer to keep him out all night with her.

She'd have her own price for him to pay. But he couldn't fault her for that. He'd do the same, of course.

Naturally, a service should always have a price.

"Naturally," Goldie agreed, putting her arm on his shoulder and leaning closer. She kept eating with her other hand.

Chapter 20 - Prepping -

Felix really didn't like the farm where they were setting up the trap.

Calling it such a thing was actually grossly inaccurate.

There were only three standing walls that remained upright. The rest was an actual ruin. There were trees and brushes growing through its broken floors.

Nature was reclaiming it and from what Faith had heard from the trees, it was more than happy to do so. Whoever had worked the farm hadn't left positive memories in the nature they worked in.

"Can we buy the farm?" Faith asked, turning and looking to him.

"What? It's as ramshackle as they get," countered Felix immediately.

"It… most certainly is. It's a little more than a vacant lot with a ruin on it," agreed Faith. "But still… I think this'll be a good thing to have. Or something like it.

"I just think the swamp, approach, and area, is actually quite good. Even its location in relation to the other nearby cities and towns is good. Not to mention, as a Dryad, I can tell you this is a perfect location for one.

"I can start working at clearing some livable spaces in the middle of it as well. A refuge for… well… Dryads."

Felix shook his head. He really didn't want to

waste money on something like this. A farm was definitely not something they needed at any level.

Except he knew he owed it to Faith.

With Miu, it was addressing her as his, taking control from her despite her not needing it anymore, and generally just touching her.

Being with her and showing her honest affection for who she was.

For Goldie, it was a possessive address, promising her gold, discussing how to wear it, and generally being kind and loving toward her.

Treating her as a house-wife with a dangerous side to her and wanting more of it.

Andrea, it was everything he'd already been doing and would continue to do. She needed the least amount of investment.

Faith had always been the question mark in a way.

Sexual, but extremely combat-oriented. Loving, but more than willing to pull someone's guts out to get an answer. Incredibly beautiful, yet knew how to field dress and gut a Human like they were a deer.

He'd gotten a win with her, and for himself really, when he let her put her tree in him. Giving her a simple farm seemed like the next step to investing in her.

That and it never hurt to get a smile out of the lovely woman. Often it was worth doing something if only for that.

"Fine," Felix said with a soft sigh. "I don't get

it. I don't want it. I think it's wasteful, but... okay. Only because you want it, Faith. Because I want you to be happy."

"Really?" asked Faith excitedly. Then she wrapped an arm around his hips and pressed herself to his side. She kissed his cheek and then nuzzled him, her other arm coming around to quite brazenly fondle his crotch. Her eyes were a brightly glowing green right now. So much so that her pupils weren't visible. "Thank you so much, Grove-husband. I love it when you let me get what I want if only to make me happy. That... err... I love you."

Felix stood there for several seconds before he realized he needed to stop Faith or he'd end up "tilling her soil" as she called it.

Given her admission he didn't want to move away, but he had to. If she hit him with the sexual whammy that was her nature, he'd have no power to stop her.

Clearing his throat, he gave her a pat on the lower back, then moved away from her. He couldn't quite bring himself to respond to her statement, but he felt like he might be able to soon.

"It's on you to find the owner, Faith. I have no idea where to even start with that," stated Felix, putting the onus of the job on her. As he stepped away from her, her eyes started to clear up gradually. She'd clearly been affected in a similar way he had. "If I have time, I'll look into it. I promise.

"Just kinda caught up in everything right now. I will do what I can though."

"It's fine. I plan on just taking the land anyway. Nature will help me and gladly," countered Faith with a dismissive wave of her hand. "There's not many Dryads left. Having a grove changes things.

"The very land here will fight for us. They'll have to take market value for the land when they finally do show up, because anything they try otherwise, will get thwarted."

At the end of her little speech, Felix heard the inflexibility of steel in her words. She knew for a fact that nothing could stop her from keeping the farm once he'd said they'd buy it.

Even the glow that'd almost vanished started to come back to her eyes.

"Right. You uh... just... go all nature's wrath and vengeance. I support it entirely. I'm going to check in on the Andreas. All the cameras and electrical setup should be nearly done," Felix said with a thrown thumb back towards a tool shed.

It appeared rickety, barely standing up, as if it would probably fall over if someone slammed into it.

Or at least, it did on the outside.

Andrea had already shored up the interior, rebuilt a frame into it, plumbed it, and got it hooked up to a solar power source and battery.

If he was being honest with himself, he'd vastly underestimated just all that Andrea could do. When he'd asked her to do this, he hadn't expected it to be at this level.

Pulling on the rope that acted as a door handle, Felix peered inside.

It looked like something out of the old Legion buildings with computer workstations for two people, a trapdoor in the back, and very new looking drywall that only needed to be painted

He also suspected they'd put up materials to limit small-arms fire. They probably didn't have enough time to get in protection from larger rounds.

There was an Andrea sitting in the chair and she spun toward him with a smile.

"Hey, Seven," Felix said and nodded his head at the Other. "Where's your Prime? She said she wanted to do a test?"

"I... she's out by the farmhouse," murmured the fresh Other. She looked surprised.

"Great, thanks. Also, hi, Eight. You good?" Felix asked.

There was a strange look on the Other's face before another Other popped out of her. She was staring at Felix with what looked to be shock.

"Nn. I'm fine. Yes," murmured the Other. "How... do you know? How did you know I was with Seven?

"We all know you did it earlier with the first five but... we're new. You've only known us a short time."

"I always know," Felix said with a smirk. He couldn't actually explain it anymore. He really did just know who was who, and if they were inside another Andrea. "Thanks, you two."

Closing the door, Felix went back toward the ruin of the house. With the surveillance in place, all that was left was some traps and creating kill zones.

He found Andrea Prime right where her Other had told him she'd be.

She'd been talking to her Second and Third when he came around the corner. They were rapidly chattering with one another, flicking into one another as they were absorbed and then put back out, while also using hand signals.

"Ah, Prime, Second, Third. Good to see you all," Felix said and came over to them. Their conversation stopped as soon as he spoke. "Seven and Eight said you'd be over this way."

All three Andrea's were watching him.

"You shouldn't know who we are," said Second. "Even... we have problems sometimes knowing who's who."

"We're really happy you can tell us apart, it's just... you shouldn't be able to," added Third.

"Nn, very happy. It's just... I... how?" asked Andrea Prime.

"I just know. I didn't at first, but... after the second year I could kind of guess who it was. Wasn't until we lost our HQ that I knew at just a glance. I know my Elex women.

"Anyway. How's it going? Looks like everything is moving along. Can we call this done?"

Prime, Second, and Third all nodded their heads at the same time.

"I'm going to stay here with Third," said

Second. "Seven, Eight, and Nine, as well. Backup and security watch."

"Prime, Four, Five, and Ten will all remain with you," Third added.

"Mm. Can I swap Ten and Three? No offense to Ten, but… well… I have a great respect for Death Others when it comes to combat," Felix said and pointed at Third, who looked incredibly surprised. "They went through so much and still keep going. I love that mentality."

"I… uhm… Prime?" asked Third, looking to Andrea.

"Nn, sure, no problem," said Andrea with a wide grin. She looked incredibly pleased at the situation. "Did you know that… err… well, I was going to be the next Death Other? Before you changed us, that is."

"That makes too much sense. You weathered a great deal without making it too obvious," Felix said and reached out to gently pat Andrea on the shoulder. Then to gently run his fingers through her hair and gently brush against her triangular ear. She was still all smiles for him right now and her tail started to swing back and forth. "Now, you said you wanted to do a test?"

"Nn!" the three said in unison, their hands balling into fists and pumping them at their sides. "Death test!"

"Death… test," repeated Felix.

"Third is going to kill Second, I'm going to absorb her after you see if you can bring her back to life," Andrea explained happily. "Then we know if you can bring us back from the dead!"

"Ah, that makes sense. Let's not have Three, or Third I suppose, do that though. No reason to give her that memory of killing another Other.

"Besides, I know someone who would actually enjoy killing Second. You could even phrase it as a favor to you, Andrea. Especially after you two bonded the other night."

We'll need to make sure she can still selectively limit her memories and give that back to her soon if she doesn't have it.

I like Death Others, but there's no need to torture them.

All three Andrea's eyes lit up. Each one smacked a closed fist into an open hand with a pop sound.

"Miu," they all whispered.

Then Andrea Prime pulled out one of the phones they'd purchased and tapped in a number quickly. Holding it up to her ear, she waited.

Felix hadn't managed to dodge Miu and Andrea the night before. Goldie had been browbeaten into bringing him back lest she face a united front of Andreas and Miu.

She'd apologized to him, then took him to them.

It'd certainly been a memorable experience, though also very strange. He'd never imagined Miu showing her absolute submissive self in front of Andrea.

Andrea was staring off at the sky while holding the phone to her ear. It looked very strange with how up on her head she held it, but it wasn't as if she had a Human ear.

"Oh! Miu honey, I need a favor. Can you help me, sweetie?" Andrea asked, smiling to herself. "Yes, he's here. Mmhmm. No, it didn't come up. I'll ask him."

Andrea dropped the phone from her ear and Felix could clearly hear Miu shrieking "no!" on the other end of the line.

"Did you like what we did last night? Miu's nervous," Andrea asked, ignoring the endlessly shrieking phone. "I thought it was rather sweet how willing she was to do anything you wanted. Especially when you got aggressive with her."

"Yeah, I did. I enjoyed it. You… should just get back to her," Felix said, pointing at the phone, trying to minimize the damage. Miu was still yelling on the other end. "Might want to move to the 'will you kill me' phase of the conversation."

Felix had no doubt Miu would gladly murder Second and it might just soothe her a bit.

***

In the end, the test had been successful.

Miu had strangled Second, then Third, and also Seven and Eight. After that, she'd apparently been appeased.

Even going so far as to hug Andrea prime

and kissed her cheek. Whatever ill will she might have had was gone.

Felix had been able to bring each of them to life thankfully. The point cost had been minimal as well since she'd only just died.

He hadn't, of course. Andrea had just reabsorbed them.

Exiting the jewelry store, Felix felt better. He'd finally followed through with his promise to Goldie. He had the golden chains and the starting rings to put through her horns ready.

Amusingly, it hadn't even cost that much to get them. He'd used cash to get pure gold rather than use points to convert it after the fact.

He'd already have to modify the gold so it extended and expanded rather than broke when she shifted forms. He couldn't imagine that being expensive, but not cheap either.

"You know… I might not be a mind reader like Goldie, but even I can see what you're doing," commented Faith from beside him. She'd been particularly attentive to him after he promised her the farm and her confession.

"Do tell me, my beautiful Dryad. What am I doing?" asked Felix, looking at her. He could feel something boiling away behind her.

Sex magic, likely. Formed from not being able to corner him for two days.

"Other than you, that is," Felix added before she could respond. "Clearly, I've neglected you for longer than you deserve.

"Would you prefer to go to a field again? Home? Truck? Somewhere else? Could probably rent a room with cash if you wanted a private room."

Faith blinked rapidly, her cheeks taking on a slow blush. Her eyes began to glow from the inside as well. They slowly turned a very bright green color.

To the point that her pupils vanished once again.

He'd heard someone call it "Greening Out" in the Dryad circles. Before them, he'd only ever heard that reference meaning someone who took way too many edibles.

"Yes. All of those places. Truck, the field, then home. In that order," demanded Faith. Then she took in a short breath and held it. "I'm worth it. You know I am."

"Yes, you are," he agreed quickly.

It looked like she was just holding her breath even as her face slowly grew redder now.

At about the twenty second mark, her eyes started to lose the color. Filtering out to their normal state as if it'd only been a trick of the light.

"Not fair, Grove-husband. You did it to me just now," hissed the Dryad and took his arm. She began leading him down the sidewalk back to where they parked. In the end, Brandonville had what he'd been looking for and at a good price. "I… that is… I know what you're doing to us. What you've already done.

"You're giving us no room to even think about doing anything other than what you ask of us. You give us what we want even if we don't ask for it and corner us.

"Goldie, the mind-reading Dragon, is more like a small puppy on a leash trailing along behind you. She can even see what you're doing to her and she can't escape. Doesn't even want to try."

"We're here by ourselves for a long while," Felix said, not answering her in a direct way. "A long while. Years. I'm… going to miss a lot of things back home. Almost too much, really.

"All I can do is invest in those I have with me. The love they're giving me. Take it, give it back to them, and get more back in turn. All while rebuilding Legion. Then we can get Kit and Lily back."

Felix hated thinking about what he was missing out on.

What he'd never get to see and suddenly how deeply it was affecting him.

When Andrea and Adriana had their first litter, he wouldn't be there for it. He'd miss the first four or five years of the children's lives.

It wasn't a loss he'd been prepared for and he'd done his best to block it out of his mind. Lately though, it'd been preying on him in the quiet moments.

Chasing him endlessly.

Added to that, a large number of mewling Elex women who would miss him. Regret that he couldn't be there for the birth of their very expected and excited-for litters.

Shaking his head, Felix cleared his thoughts.

"Well, anyway. That's all I can do," Felix finished. "Move forwards, build Legion, invest in… invest in you all."

"And I'm so happy to be invested in. Do till my soil regularly and invest in me. Lots," Faith demanded, squeezing his arm against her chest.

Her head snapped to one side and she took a step away from him.

Her hand dropped down to the pocket of her hoodie and he heard the click of her pulling the safety. She was staring straight ahead of them to where an alley was.

"Shouldn't have come here at night," complained Faith. "Just asking for trouble. I let your damn smile influence me."

Felix realized now what she was talking about. Coming to a jewelry store just at closing wasn't a great idea. Coming out of there with any sort of package would make you a target.

He could vaguely remember that there was a time when people were targeting big box stores in his home world. They'd watch for people to buy a light-terminal, put it in their car, and then go shopping elsewhere.

All a thief had to do was bash the window glass in and take it.

This felt similar to him.

Or at least, from the outside looking in. He

had no idea what Faith was actually reacting to. For all he knew, it was just a bunch of people who didn't belong.

Unfortunately, their truck was past the alley. When they'd arrived earlier, the parking lot had been fuller than expected.

Now it was empty.

Faith pulled the pistol from her hoodie and moved to Felix's right side putting herself closer to the alley. When they walked in front of it, she'd already brought the weapon up to a forty-five-degree angle. The barrel still pointed at the ground, but it was ready to be brought up quickly.

"Six people circled around two others. One of the two is on the ground and heavily wounded. It's obvious they're contemplating how much further to take it," Faith whispered, letting the gun point directly at the ground. "Not our issue."

Felix frowned as he thought about that. This was actually a perfect opportunity to push forward the other side of his plan.

There would be a dark Legion that rose in the underworld. One that would become a center for non-violent crime.

On the other end, Felix needed to build his own counter. So that he could control the conflict from both sides.

This was beyond just making a Villain and Hero's guild. He needed to even balance the scales in his own organization.

Internally, they'd both be called Legion, of

course and even have cross-over operations. Each side knowing the other existed.

Just never to the outside world.

Heh. We'll just call both Legion outside, too. That'll confuse the population greatly.

As well as those who would want to see one or the other harmed. We'll just make sure it's only confusing from the outside.

Actual Legionnaires would know one another.

This is a perfect time to cause some whispers.

"Faith, put on your mask. Go stop whatever's happening and give anyone who deserves it a broken leg," commanded Felix. Reaching into his back pocket, he pulled out his mask. Moving into the alley before he fitted it to his head, he put the bag of jewelry down behind a trashcan as he went past.

He'd pick it up on the way back out. Right now, he needed both hands.

Faith pulled her own mask on when he did and then moved forward at a light jog. Her pistol was held low in front of her.

"Stop!" called Faith as she got closer. "Everyone disperse! I won't ask again. First and final warning!"

Her tone had the ring and phrasing of Legion security manuals.

Second warnings only mattered if they were Legion.

Everyone else was just meat.

Faith came to a stop and raised her pistol. Up

ahead of her were a group of people who looked like they were considering her words.

"Well, fuck y—"

Faith's pistol shifted a fraction and she pulled the trigger. The boom of her weapon was loud in the alley.

The man who'd spoken squealed and his hand shot up to grab at his upper arm. Apparently, she'd put a round right through his shoulder.

"Anyone else want to get a free pass to being left-handed?" asked Faith. "Leave, now. Legion will be managing the area. You're not welcome in Brandonville."

Well. More aggressive than I originally wanted, but not wrong.

Nor was I really wanting her to announce Legion but… that's fine, too. I suppose. This'll be a good way to start growing both at the same time.

Lots of confusion.

This'll work well.

Rather than arguing with Faith, they scattered, fleeing in every direction. Including the man who'd been shot.

Faith stood there, waiting, watching them all run.

Only after they were physically gone and almost twenty seconds had passed did she finally lower her weapon. She reached down and picked up the spent casing and tucked it into her pocket.

"Are you alright over there?" Felix asked rather calmly as he came to stand beside Faith. "Do you need us to call for medical assistance?"

"I... uhm... no. We're okay," called a female voice. Felix couldn't quite make out who it was he was talking to. The shadows were deep and pooled around them. From what he could see, it was as Faith said. One person was sitting upright, and another was laid out flat on the ground. "Just... just beat up bad. We'll be fine.

"Thanks-thanks for stopping them. It's gotten a lot scarier out here lately."

Mm. I'll send a note over to David through Jay.

Let him know that I heard a report that violence is on the rise and is bringing civilians into play.

See what he says to that.

Anyway.

Felix turned and began walking away. There was nothing more that needed to be done here.

Picking up the bag of gold jewelry on his way out, Felix pulled his mask off and dumped it inside. Faith did the same and guided him to F-Two.

Getting inside, they sat there for several seconds, then Faith let out a long sigh.

"Pretty sure they would have killed the man, raped the woman, then killed her," said Faith, turning to look at him. "I don't think it was our problem, but I'm not against the action we took."

"I liked it," said a muffled voice from behind them.

Peering at them through the rear glass was Edmund. He waved a hand at the two of them and grinned. He was in the truck bed and had apparently seen everything.

"A lot. I also heard what you did back at my… err… at the community. That was kinda funny to learn about," Edmund continued, looking from Faith to Felix. "So… why did you wanna talk to me? And where are we going?"

Huh.

I like him.

Felix grinned, feeling like he'd found someone he could work with.

Chapter 21 - Messy -

Entering the mobile home, Felix found Goldie and a few Andreas in the living room. They were watching the television in the corner.

To the side of it looked like a cheap laptop that was streaming directly to the TV.

Playing on the screen were a bunch of dark-haired women of Asian-descent dancing in a very similar way to how Andrea had been. Their motion included a lot of hip movements and posing.

Felix couldn't deny that it was rather fun to watch.

"Felix! Welcome home!" exclaimed Andrea, bouncing out of the seat next to Goldie and rushing over to him. She wrapped him in a hug and began dragging him over to the couch. "I got the internet set up. We're stealing a signal from the leasing office.

"Goldie was helping me find a new dance to learn and— oh, hello. Who are you?"

"Uhm, I'm Edmund," said the young man who came in after Felix. Faith was behind him and had been holding onto the billy club.

While she was willing to let this continue, she'd been very direct with the young man that she'd kill him faster than Felix could say to stop. To her, nothing was more important than his life.

"Edmund? Oh! You're the one Felix was looking for," Goldie said and then waved a hand at him. She turned to look at Felix with a smile and then froze.

Staring at him as if he'd sprouted a horn between his eyes, Goldie seemed transfixed. It only took him a moment to realize why.

Yes. Your bridal gold and the attachment rings are here. I modified it on the way over. I'll give it to you later.

Privately.

Goldie began to immediately growl loudly. The low rumble filled the small space. The smile on her face was more akin to the opening of a hinge. It seemed like her head might tilt back and fall off just above her nose.

Her eyes had flashed to a brilliant golden color and there was a heavy presence that filled the mobile home.

"Now," she demanded and stood up.

"Edmund, have a seat!" Andrea said brightly. "I'll make pancakes! Pancakes make everything better. Or… actually, would you prefer waffles or french toast?"

"Uhm… I like all those. Whichever is easier?" Edmund tried as an answer. He looked like he wanted to crawl into a corner and hide.

Not that Felix could blame him. Dragons were killing machines to most inhabitants of any world they were on.

Goldie had taken him by the elbow and was guiding him to the bedroom.

"He'll be right back," Andrea said, waving a hand at Edmund. Two Others popped out of her and started going into the kitchen while Andrea remained standing in front of him. "Now, can I get you a drink as well? We have some sodas, water, a couple—"

Andrea's voice was cut off as Goldie shut the bedroom door behind them.

"Decorate me!" Goldie demanded in a voice that sounded far more like the way she sounded in her Dragon form. Her horns had instantly sprouted up. "Put on my bridal gold! I've waited, I've been patient, I'll wait no longer! If I can't nest, I will be at least decorated!"

Felix wanted to be annoyed, but he couldn't.

As a Dragon, Goldie had been more patient than one could have ever expected from her. To the point that any other Dragon would have called her stupid or crazy.

Placing the bag that was in his hands down on the bed, he began to pull everything out. He set the boxes down in a small pile.

Not hesitating, he pulled out the golden chain that'd move through the lower part of the horns after being attached to the golden rings at the base.

When he turned around, he found Goldie inches from him.

Breathing hard, she was practically staring through him. To say her eyes were glowing was an understatement.

They were more like two suns blazing through him.

She was growling so loud that it made his

whole body vibrate.

Felix didn't get the chance to start putting the gold in her horns. Goldie had lost control and instead threw him onto the bed.

***

An hour later, and after a shower, Felix felt like he could brave the world again.

Though he wasn't sure he could live down the embarrassment.

Goldie had been so loud that he was certain their neighbors had heard her commanding dirty talk and high-pitched moans. His only saving grace was they'd all been demands for him to treat her dominantly.

Opening the bedroom door, and leaving behind the sleeping Dragon who now had gold through her horns, Felix rejoined the others. They all looked at him as soon as he exited.

Giving them a smile, he closed the door behind himself and then came over. Edmund was eating what looked to be french toast. Though Felix had distinctly smelt pancakes and waffles as well at some point.

Leaning over the arm of the couch, Andrea put her hand up to her mouth.

Ah… no… please don't, And–

"Felix," whispered Andrea loudly. "It sounded like you really hit the right spot for her. Good job!

"I look forward to our own turn! I'm in heat, too! So is Second, Third, Six, Seven, and Ten. We'll need Faith to help us out!"

Sighing, Felix let his eyes drop to the ground.

He stood there, wondering what to do for a few seconds.

Then he realized the answer was the same as always when it came to Andrea.

Onward.

"Edmund, I'd like to hire you," Felix said, looking at the young man and ignoring Andrea's words. "I think I'm going to need someone to operate as a point of contact for me with important figures here in Alassippi.

"I'm not always available, so I need someone who can stand in. Someone who knows what's going on at a low level but is smart enough to operate in a higher social circle if needed.

"Given that you ran me down the way you did, I'm guessing you're not as… simple… as others might believe you to be."

Swallowing hard, Edmund looked at Felix for a moment before shrugging his shoulders.

"I'm not twenty-one yet, so I can't move out. They could probably call the cops on me," Edmund answered.

"I'm sure that's not an issue. We'll just hire someone to represent you and force the court's hand," Felix said dismissively. "I'll put in an email to someone to see what they think of the situation.

"Any other concerns? Anything else that'd

prevent you from moving forward with Legion?"

"Uhm… so I'd just be… a contact for others? That's it?" Edmund asked.

"More than just that, but that's the obvious and early role. I'm sure more job duties would be added in time. Along with your pay," advised Felix. "And before you ask, we'll start you at fifty thousand a year. No benefits at all, all cash, no taxes.

"We're a bit of an underground organization at the moment, though that'll change with time."

"I… err… yeah, I guess that'd work. I'm just not really—"

A radio crackled to life from where it sat next to the police scanner. It caused Edmund to fall quiet.

"Shadow. Trap sprung. Engaging. Requesting Gold-coin and… more Pancakes," Miu said over the line. She was still very unhappy with Andrea's choice of code name.

"Time to go!" Andrea blurted out and shot to her feet. Several Others jumped out of her and started zipping around the room getting things in order and generally arming themselves.

Four had already pulled open a section of floor that'd been cut into a trapdoor. Then she dove through and vanished.

Third came over and knelt down over the trapdoor while Five pulled things out of the closet that looked a lot like ballistic vests.

"I'll stay with Edmund and Felix," Andrea

said cheerfully. The young man in question looked to be unsurprised by what he was seeing.

Given that Andrea had been operating this whole time with her tail and ears out, maybe he was already past the point of concern.

"I'm going. I need to be there. I need to get some answers out of the survivors. I'll stay out of harm's way and keep back," Felix said and then moved back to the bedroom.

"No!" said all the Andrea's at the same time.

"Yes, not arguing. Faith will come with me and act as my handler," declared Felix and then opened the bedroom door.

The Dragon was still asleep, her bridal gold glittering as it hung between her horns. He hadn't realized it at the time, but he'd probably bought too much.

It looked like a very intricate spider-web of gold.

"Goldie, I need you," commanded Felix in a flat tone. "I need my Golden One."

Goldie's eyes snapped open, her shimmering gaze fixing on him.

"Of course. Anything for you, Nest-mate," mumbled Goldie, sitting up in the bed. She looked rather pleased and had a sleepy smile on her face. "As much of me as you want. Thank you for needing more. On the bed again?"

"Ah, no. They walked into our trap. I need my Dragon. I need her to crush my enemies," clarified Felix.

A blink or two after that and Goldie stood up. Her shoulders were squared and her spine ramrod straight.

She had the look of a very imperious and dangerous woman in that moment.

"I shall do so. A perfect opportunity to display my adorned horns," Goldie declared and then marched out of the bedroom.

Following her, Felix got ready as well.

***

Riding on Goldie was always an adventure.

Tonight was no exception to that.

This time, he was holding onto the golden chains that were strung between her horns more like reins, though. It was a different experience and he felt more secure for it.

Goldie had frozen up as soon as he'd grabbed on, but then relaxed. He got the impression she was quite happy with the situation.

That him hanging onto her bridal gold fit a tiny nook in her head she didn't know existed, until she found it.

Pressed in behind him was Third, who had all the Others. Behind her was Faith. Each woman was clinging to the person in front of them.

"We'll be there momentarily!" called Goldie as she flapped her wings. "I'll drop you all off near the swamp, then engage!"

Felix nodded and looked ahead. He could

see what looked like flashes of light that could only be gunfire.

There was no sound that he could hear, but he wasn't sure if that was due to flying through the air or the distance.

Moving into a dive, Goldie tucked her wings backward and angled them. Felix had no idea how that all worked, but he knew they were rapidly descending now.

When Goldie pulled up in a sudden stop near the swamp, Felix practically threw himself off her back. He took Andrea with him, who ended up pulling Faith with her.

Goldie was clear of passengers before her feet had even touched the ground.

Flapping sharply, she pulled back up into the sky and then went upwards, vanishing in the darkness.

Felix got down on the ground and laid himself out on his stomach.

"Faith, Third, stay with me," Felix stated. "All Others proceed to assist Second and Miu. Wound where you can, so we can question them before they die.

"Otherwise, they're just meat. Legion first."

"Legion First," they all responded, several Others moving off at a run. In their hands were SMGs and they were outfitted for a firefight.

"Felix, why did you want me to stay?" demanded Third. "I… I should go help!"

"Because I need you here with me. You were

a Death Other. Then a Myriad. Now Andrea. Is there anyone as fluent with weapons as you? I know you all share abilities, memories, and thoughts.

"But I've seen some are better than others. Can you claim any are better than you? Truly so?" demanded Felix.

"I… uhm… we're not supposed to talk about that," muttered the Andrea.

"I'm right though. Now… if you're the best who's the most qualified to keep me alive with Faith? You, right?" pushed Felix.

A silence began to grow before Andrea sighed loudly.

"Yes. Prime won't be happy. We're supposed to pretend we're all the same. So you don't take favorites," she mumbled. "Especially now that you can identify us."

"I love you all equally. I just know how to use skills better than you want to admit," Felix replied. Then he leaned over and kissed Andrea's cheek and put an arm around her. "Thanks, Third. I appreciate you."

"Where's my appreciation?" demanded Faith, laid out on the ground next to him.

"You ate it this morning," deadpanned Andrea, still sounding upset.

Felix tried to focus on what was ahead of them. He could hear gunfire now, but it was oddly muffled. The only thing that made sense to him was they were using silencers.

They were still quite loud, but just not as

loud.

"Oh, I suppose I did at that. Hm," Faith replied reflectively.

Rolling his eyes, Felix leaned over and kissed the corner of Faith's mouth just to shut her up. Then he put his attention ahead once again.

"Nn. This is bad. Real bad. It's a lot of people," Andrea said quietly. "Way more than we were expecting. I'm pretty sure most of myselves that were there already are dead.

"Maybe even those that just left. Too many people and we can't split more than we are. We're not used to being outnumbered."

Frowning, Felix pulled his arm off Andrea and then patted her back.

He wanted to keep her here with himself, but he knew that wasn't the right answer in the end. She'd been initially right.

She should have gone with the Others.

"Go. Get the fallen back up. Absorb and redistribute," Felix said. "Keep yourself safe though. If they're all dead and it's just Miu, and you go down, we'll have to wait for Prime to get here."

At that moment, a brilliant golden flame jetted out from the dark sky. It splashed down over a wide swath of the fields. Washing down and over, and then it kept going as Goldie made a long pass.

Numerous flashes of light and gunshots filled the air. Shooting at the Dragon as she cut her breath off and banked hard, then began to gain altitude.

There was a great deal of shouting now as the attackers panicked.

"Faith, go with her. I'll just stay here," commanded Felix. Reaching into the holster on his chest, he pulled out his pistol and made sure it ready.

"Fat chance of that, Grove-husband," demurred Faith. "I'd sooner share you with another grove than leave your side right now."

Andrea was off at a run now, sprinting into the mad gunfight. Her head was down low and she was moving at an oblique angle compared to where the first Andrea's had gone.

"There are other groves?" Felix asked. He was curious about the Dryads of this world. He knew there were some which was rather interesting to him.

"No, not really. No groves. Their trees don't… survive. Not for long. From what I can tell, the Dryads of this world have to pick up and move every decade or so. They stay clear of Humanity for the most part," explained Faith. The sound of gunfire was ongoing. "Every few decades they'll pick a man, breed up, have their daughters, then disconnect.

"Right now, there's an entire generation who haven't been with a man. Their mothers were wiped out when a forestry company bulldozed their grove down. Didn't even mean to do it, they were just clear-cutting.

"All the young ones had enough time to escape and start a new one. They've been trying to figure out what to do for a while now. Then we showed up.

"Trees gossip. Far and wide they're talking about the Dryad who isn't from this world and her grove."

Felix frowned and then looked at Faith.

He suddenly had a really bad feeling. One that he often got when he was dealing with the Dragons and Elves back on Legion. That they were setting him up for some type of plan and he couldn't escape.

Not far off, a loud burst of what sounded like rifle fire went off. It was only twenty or so feet away.

No one in his group used rifles and no one would be coming this way either. They'd avoid this direction so as not to attract attention to him.

That left only enemies.

Without thinking, Felix pulled his pistol up, sighted it on the target, and pulled the trigger. He got off three rounds before the individual dropped.

There were several shouted curses and more people appeared.

Faith had pulled up her SMG by this point. Squeezing off a single burst, she moved it to the left, pulled the trigger, then did it again, and again.

In the time it took for Felix to register the enemies, she'd already dropped four of them. No other enemies appeared.

"There really are a lot of them. Damn," muttered Faith.

Disengaging her magazine, Faith flicked it onto the ground and put in a new one. Once it was settled in place, she hesitantly picked up the old one and gave it a once over. After a pause, she stuck it into a pocket.

Goldie came back again, appearing in the gloom as a glowing beacon of light. Her head came back and then went forward.

Golden flames started to flow over everything once again.

All the light made the gold in her horns glitter and shine quite brightly.

It was an amazing sight to behold.

Flapping her wings twice in rapid succession, Goldie cut off her impression of a waterfall of flames and flew back upwards.

"We'll stay here until we get the all clear," grumbled Faith. "Not moving until then. Way too many enemies."

Felix couldn't argue that point.

The response from Stephen was out of proportion to what Felix had been expecting. Which meant whoever was giving Stephen information had overhyped Felix's capabilities, or Stephen was incredibly high-strung.

In either case, it really was obvious now that there was a mole in David's organization. A mole hunt would have to happen.

Chapter 22 - Chores -

Gunfire continued for another ten minutes or so.

Goldie came by for another fire-sweep before she started circling out further. Moving around as if she were conducting an area search.

Likely preventing anyone from escaping the farm, in fact.

Felix even saw her dive down toward the ground at one point.

He didn't see what she did, but she was airborne roughly twenty seconds after that.

Unfortunately, he mostly just kept his head down.

Everyone here was using guns and the like. Things that would kill him very quickly if he was unlucky.

Despite having confidence in his hand-to-hand, getting lucky enough to survive a firefight wasn't something he wanted to push.

"I think that's it," Faith murmured from beside him. They hadn't heard any gunfire for a while. Nor had they seen Goldie.

Faith did a quick check of her SMG and then resettled it in front of herself. She held it snugly and was clearly ready for someone coming their way.

Either everyone on their side was dead, or the enemy was wiped out. Until they got a signal, they could only assume that their own side was eliminated

"I'm pretty sure we got them all. Just not sure if we'll need to get Miu up again or not," muttered Faith. "She's the most vulnerable in our team. My own regenerative ability has increased significantly since planting my tree here. Even you have some regeneration. She doesn't.

"Even Andrea has her regeneration back since you gave it back to her along with her ability to wipe memories."

Valid point. Maybe I should consider giving her an ability that would help that.

Tie it to her main ability.

The more medicine she takes, the faster she heals. A multiplicative on consumables, so to speak. If I can get it to attach to her main ability, it might not even be that expensive.

In fact, I bet if I make it so that it only works on restorative items then it wouldn't be too bad. Leaving it open to any item would be prohibitive, I bet.

There was a soft hiss that Felix barely heard. It lasted only for a fraction of a second and it was so quiet that he first thought it was imaginary.

Faith leaned to one side and reached down to her side. Unclipping the radio there, she pulled it up to her side and glanced at it.

She thumbed a button for a fraction of a second and let go then did it again.

Looks like this is some type of security protocol. I wonder if they worked it out back before we came here, or if this is new.

"Pancake, clear," came the voice of Andrea

over the radio. It was very quiet. As if the volume was as low as it could go. "Collecting Batter."

Ha. Batter.

She means her Others.

To make more Pancakes.

"Shadow, clear. Injured," Miu replied. "Rally point bravo."

"Gardener, with Throne. Clear. Had contact. Request recon," Faith whispered into her radio.

"Pancake for Gold-coin, going," answered Andrea.

In other words, Goldie was with them and has no radio. Makes sense.

The golden Dragon appeared in the distance. Coming right out of where Felix suspected the ruins of the farmhouse was.

She flew over toward them then began circling around.

Suddenly, she tucked in her wings and came straight down like a meteor. Falling toward the ground at full speed.

Her wings snapped out just as she neared the ground and her landing was little more than a rumbling thud rather than an earth-shattering kaboom.

She hadn't landed too far away from them. Felix felt like it might have even been where they'd dropped the enemies earlier or around that area.

Tilting her head one way, then the other, she looked like she was focusing on something. She reached out with a claw and grabbed at something.

A scream followed as she leaned back and sat on her haunches. Held in her hand was a man. He was either wounded or had been hiding.

"Clear," stated Goldie, her golden eyes turning to look toward Felix. She held up her claw with the struggling man in it. "This one was hiding. I'm sure we can question him, too."

Felix nodded at that and then got up with a sigh.

"Let's… round up all the bodies, check for survivors, get the gear, and start in on questioning. I'm going to go find Miu and see if I can't help her," commanded Felix. He then looked from Goldie to Faith. "Need anything from me?"

"No. The way is clear of people or bodies. You won't have an issue," promised Goldie. She swung her head toward Faith. "Please handle the gear? It's hard for me to pick up. I'll take care of the bodies."

"Sure, no worries," Faith said, having stood up as well.

Deciding this was the time to leave, Felix set off at a jog for where Miu would be. He wanted to try out his idea about using consumable items.

Pulling at his power, he wanted to see what his current point totals were.

	Generated	**Remaining**
Andrea	680	680
Faith	410	410
Felix	1,625	1,625

Goldie	2,502	2,502
Miu	1,025	1,025
+Loyalty Bonus	800	800
+Marital Bonus	400	400
=Daily Total	**7,442**	**7,442**
Banked Total	—	**21,121**

Felix was suddenly not very happy about the number of points he'd spent on Goldie's gold. He didn't have as many as he wanted right now.

If he was going to modify, Miu he'd have to hope it was on the cheaper side.

Thankfully, he wasn't scheduled to do any conversion work for David for at least a few days. He could try to rebuild his points by doing some dumpster diving after this, but it'd probably be close.

I can't let this linger. I have to squash this and then pass it off.

Probably to David.

I can act and fix it the way I want. The way I like, but I can't remain in the lead.

We can't be a target.

Turning a small corner, Felix found Miu.

She was slumped against a wall, an SMG at her side, and the radio in her lap. She'd clearly been shot more than once, but was also alive.

Her pants were quite bloody and he wasn't sure how much of it was hers.

"Hey there," Felix murmured coming over to

her. He got down on one knee next to her and looked at her closely.

"Hi. I killed a lot of them. Tried to wound as many as I could so we could question them," replied Miu, smiling at him. There was blood coating her teeth.

Let's just fix whatever's actually going on with her.

Name: Miu Campbell	**Condition**: Severely Wounded
If No Action Taken: Lasting Organ Damage	**Action >> Revitalize**: Cost 16,907 points

"Well. Can't be too bad. Only seventeen thousand, give or take," Felix joked and reached out to cup her jaw. "Won't even die from this.

"Though I want to modify your power a bit. I want it to change so that the more… mm… restorative… things you take, the faster and more completely you heal.

"So if you had a bad burn, the more burn cream you put on it the faster it'd heal and more completely. Does that make sense?"

Miu only nodded her head, watching him.

"Do you care if I do that? I want to do it in such a way so that you can make a full recovery," Felix asked.

"Go ahead," she answered, still gazing at him.

Felix focused on doing exactly what he'd just

described.

Modifying her original power so that it would also allow her to get multiplicative results from medicine and restorative items.

Where a full recovery was completely possible.

Though, he did make sure that the quantity on this request to change was reasonable. He didn't want her to have to take a million bottles of probiotics to build her resistance.

He honed in on the idea that she could fix everything that was physically wrong with her right now within a month given enough items.

On top of that, he made sure that his request didn't address her mental issues in any way. She'd been quite firm with him about never changing that.

Name: Miu Campbell	**Condition**: Severely Wounded
If No Action Taken: None	**Action >> Alter Power**: Cost 12,642 points

"Well, more expensive than Goldie or Andrea, but well worth it," Felix murmured and then accepted the change. "Because I need my Miu."

Miu's eyes widened as she stared at him.

Almost as if she were staring through him, in fact.

Everyone had always said it felt like he was punching a hole through their thoughts when he made changes to their power.

"Oh, I see," Miu mumbled. Then she reached into the vest she was wearing. She fished out several bottles, vials, and what looked like some type of bandages.

Popping open a bottle by crushing the top of it with one hand, Miu then upended it. Downing its contents in one go. Then she did the same to the next.

Picking up one of the plastic vials, she ripped the top off it rather than getting a syringe for it. She simply pushed it into a spot in her leg that looked particularly bloody.

Once that was empty, she flung it to the side and then started working at dressing the wound with the bandage.

"I… can I help in any way?" Felix asked in an unsure tone.

Miu grunted and shook her head. The bandage she'd placed on her leg, atop her clothes, had sunk into her. Vanishing away completely.

She pulled out another bandage and went through the exact same process again.

"Just need to use everything I have on me. Then scrounge up more," said Miu as another bandaged slowly sunk into her leg. From what he could see, the wound beneath was already significantly smaller in size. "More like a video game character now. I wonder if I sit down and eat a hundred wheels-of-cheese if I'll be fine."

Felix raised his eyebrows and wondered

what she was talking about.

All he really cared about was the fact that it seemed like she'd be fine.

Leaning in, he hugged Miu, holding her. He pressed her face to his neck while his hands pressed on her back.

"Uhm… I… F-Felix… no-not right now. I'm a m-mess and I need to fix m-myself and—" Miu's voice trailed off in a groan. Then she just clung to him, holding him for dear life.

Then she started crying, which made Felix extremely worried. Worried and nervous.

He'd never seen her cry or heard of her crying.

All he could think of was that whatever he did to her power set had changed her more than he intended.

Need to talk to Goldie.

Felix just held her and let her cry.

***

"Prisoners, prisoners, they're always… a dilemma," murmured Goldie as she began to slowly walk across the front of the arrayed prisoners. Her golden eyes swept back and forth across them.

She clearly was peering through their minds as she did so, rifling through their thoughts. Using their directions on herself as a way to focus their minds.

Andrea made a happy little chirp from where she stood off to one side. She had a pistol in her hands and looked like she was here to play guard to Goldie.

That or executioner.

Of everyone who'd come to the farm, there had been eleven people that were coherent and able to be questioned.

There were thirty-some-odd others who were dead or unconscious. None of whom would ever leave alive.

Off to one side, all of the other Andrea's were excitedly stripping everyone of gear and rounding things up. The items were sorted out and put into various piles.

He'd already looked it over and found there were certainly a lot of things they'd needed and were now provided for them. From communications equipment to weaponry, magazines, grenades, and everything in between.

Pulling his eyes off the Others as they worked, Felix looked back to the Dragon.

She'd come to a stop next to Andrea.

Goldie was naked.

Her hands were braced on her hips with her gold shining brightly in her horns. She looked down on their fallen foes laid out in front of them with contempt.

The Dragon looked imperious and statuesque. She gave the impression that these enemies were all beneath her. As if looking at her nakedness would shame the viewer, not her.

With a sigh, Goldie moved over and bent down in front of a prisoner who'd been shot through the arm. They'd been bleeding profusely and looked very pale, though they were conscious.

"It's always a question of how much pain to apply to get a reasonable answer. Too much and they'll give you whatever they think you want. Not enough and they think they can hold out," Goldie continued in a tone that sounded more as if she were talking to herself.

Reaching out, she dragged her thumbnail along the edge of the bullet wound for a moment before jamming it straight in.

Tilting her horned head to one side, she ground her thumb around, twisting her hand one way and then the other as the man writhed around on the ground.

Goldie never actually asked the man a question. Instead, she stared at him with cold eyes the entire time as he screamed unendingly.

When it seemed as if he couldn't yell anymore, when he slumped to the ground and seemed unconscious, Goldie turned and looked to Andrea.

"Do put this one out of their misery," asked the Dragon, and then she stood up and moved away from the fallen man.

"Oh, poo," Andrea whined and shook her head. Looking at Felix, she pouted at him. "You completely forgot to ask him anything. You should try to do better next time."

As she spoke she waved the pistol at the second man in line. He'd actually been uninjured and looked intact.

Flinching back as the barrel was directed his way and then moving in the opposite direction, he was clearly trying to stay away from her.

Then Andrea sighed, walked up to the man Goldie had been torturing, and put a round through his temple. It caused the man's head to bounce once against the ground and then blood began pooling blood around him quickly.

Ah… that's right.

Andrea was technically a villain. As Myriad, she took on any contract she wanted and more or less did as she pleased.

Even blew up a number of buildings killing everyone inside them.

This is all quite normal for her and probably far less than she's done in the past.

Smiling, Felix shrugged his shoulders. Given that his goal was to turn one half of the world against the other while controlling both, he needed exactly these kind of people.

"It's fine. I'm sure she's doing what she feels she has to, to get the right information," he said. This was all for show anyway. Goldie was rifling through their minds even as they spoke. All of this was just to get her to what she felt she needed, he imagined. "We have more than a few left over. It'll be fine.

"Soon as we find out what Stephen knows, the better. We just want the mole in David's organization after all. That's it."

"Okay!" Andrea said happily, then looked toward the prisoners. She watched Goldie as the Dragon began to move up and down their ranks.

Felix noted she was focusing on someone who really didn't look good. They were hunched to one side with an arm on their middle. They had a bandage there and he was holding his hand over it.

Calmly walking over to the man, Goldie stepped up behind him and laid her long fingers to his throat.

"Good evening," she greeted the man. "Do you know who the mole is we're looking for? Can you provide me with more information about Stephen?"

"I… I don't know any of that. Please, I just —"

With a sigh, Goldie flexed her hands. One tore the man's throat out with a casual twist of her wrist. The other had grabbed the back of his neck and flexed wildly.

The sudden snap of his neck was loud as his head suddenly tilted backward.

It was rather grotesque.

"You didn't even let him finish. There wasn't even a chance to ask him anything proper," Andrea chastised Goldie and then skipped off to stand near Felix. "You know, it's been a really, really long time since I did something like this. I used to do it so often that I had Others just dedicated to cleanup duties.

"It's always so incredibly messy. Everything always kinda gets everywhere. Then you find like… a tooth or a chunk of skin a month later that's all shriveled up and kind of ewwww."

Goldie had made her way back to the front, her cold and uncaring gold eyes moving over each and every prisoner.

Andrea bounced over to the Dragon and skipped around her in a circle, gave her a hug, and then veered off back to Felix.

Coming to a stop behind him, she put her chin on his shoulder. Her mouth was right next to his ear.

She'd done it in such a way that her mouth was on the far side of the prisoners. They wouldn't be able to see her face really.

"They were both already dying. They wouldn't have survived the night. They made great examples though," whispered Andrea in a barely audible voice. "You're not… sickened or mad, are you? We know we can't leave them alive and we'll be quick when we can. But we do need information. We can't get it all through just mind reading."

"No. This is more akin to what I'd heard about you when we first met. As for our Golden One… well… it's what she is. That'd be like expecting a predator to not eat meat," Felix answered in a low tone. He'd turned his head to try and disguise his words in case there were any lip readers there. He reached up to lightly scratch at

Andrea's head. "It's a surprise because I'd forgotten about it for the most part, not because you've done anything wrong. I'm sure Goldie is getting lots of good information."

"Nn, nn!" enthused Andrea before giving him a loud kiss on the cheek.

Moving away from him, she went back to the prisoners. They were all staring at her now with wide eyes. Clearly thinking that the only way to get out of this was providing her with information.

"Okay! Round robin time!" she declared and then held the pistol up in front of herself, pointing at the crowd as a whole. "Who wants to tell me what I want to know? They get to live and —"

The weapon discharged as if it were on accident, a round slamming into the ground in the middle of all the prisoners.

Felix didn't believe for a moment that she'd fired that on accident.

"Oopsie doopsie! Anyway. They get to live, and everyone else gets a bullet, then a ride in the swamp out back! It'll be a fun game, right?" demanded Andrea, pointing the weapon at the ceiling.

Felix didn't need to be here for this. Andrea and Goldie had it under control. Him being here was actually a distraction.

"Let me know when we get the information," Felix called and then left, exiting the ruins of the farm.

Faith followed along after him, leaving the

scene behind.

Walking out, he found Miu not far away.

She was going through any and all medical supplies they'd found on their enemies. She was systematically taking everything.

Even a bottle of kid's chewable vitamins.

Looking up as he approached, she gave him a grin. She was in the process of applying an entire box of band-aids to her leg.

The crying had stopped a while back and she seemed fine.

In truth, she appeared extremely happy. In a better mood than she'd been in, in a while.

"This is really nice, Felix," she said with a nod. "Really nice. Thank you. I'm going to have to rob a pharmacy, I think. I bet I can use things to improve myself now.

"Like medicines to push my stamina, or to increase muscle mass, or improve concentration. I bet they'd all work on me. Not very much but… enough that in very large amounts it might be noticeable.

"Though… did… you make it so this would change my mind at all? If I take medicines designed to help… combat… what's wrong with me?"

"No. I didn't. I specifically avoided it. I only wanted you to be physically healthy, Miu," Felix said with a shake of his head. "I didn't ask for any other change whatsoever. Because my Miu is exactly who she is. There's nothing to fix or change."

Grinning ear to ear at him at that, Miu hit him with probably the most beautiful look she'd ever had. It felt like Faith had just struck him with her sexual magic.

"I love you, Felix," whispered the psycho before she went back to tending to her wounds.

"Love you, too," Felix admitted, then started walking again.

He wanted to think by himself for a bit.

They'd get the info.

The mole would be found.

It was just a question of how to deal with it.

Chapter 23 - Unfilial -

"Feeeeeeeelix!" Andrea trumpeted out a second before leaping onto his back. Her legs wrapped around his middle and her arms encircled his shoulders and neck.

Though her wrists ended up right atop his throat.

"Nnnnrrrgh!" he exclaimed and did his best to keep himself from toppling over. He had to lean forward and nearly face-planted into Faith's chest.

The Dryad grabbed him by the shoulders and steadied him.

She did of course take the opportunity to sneak in with a kiss as she did so.

"Felix, Felix, we did it, we're all done," cheered Andrea. Then she tucked her head in and started sniffing at his ear and neck. Her breath came in little, short puffs that made him want to hunch away from it. "You smell really nice right now. Like… sex and Goldie. Or sex with Goldie?

"Whatever, I like it. Like it a lot."

Andrea began to lick at his neck. As if some other thought had blasted through her head.

Grunting, Felix got his feet planted more securely, then reached up and held Andrea's hands down. It kept them from riding up and choking him.

Faith just shook her head with a smile, her hands holding Felix's shoulders for a few more seconds before she let go and stepped away.

"Sorry, Nest-mate," apologized Goldie as she came up from behind them. "She's just excited because we really are done. It got messier than I expected and realistically, no one actually gave us anything useful. At least... not verbally."

Turning in place with a few hobbled steps, Felix found Goldie with his eyes. She came to a stop just a few feet away.

Blood was splattered across her face, as if she'd been around a red spray can that had exploded. There were several trails across her breasts as well.

Over her thigh and down her leg was a bloody handprint that trailed downward. As if someone had been trying to beg her for mercy from below.

"You look like a horror movie villain, my Golden One," remarked Felix without being able to stop himself.

"Yes. I'll need a shower and a good scrub, I'm afraid. I have been sprayed with the blood of the unworthy. I'll have to bleach and clean the shower after I'm done," grumbled Goldie, gesturing at herself then sighing. Next, she pointed to her horns. "I did manage to keep my bridal gold quite clean. As well as my horns.

"I really do like how they jingle and tinkle when I move my head a little bit. I think I might put a few little bells in them so they make more noise."

Goldie tilted her head to one side, then the other. He heard the faint click and slither of the gold moving across itself as she did so.

"Oh, I like that idea," Faith agreed. "I don't have your lovely horns to wear them in, but I bet I could get a black lace choker with a bell or two on it that'd work. Or just braid them into my hair. It's been a while since I did some braid work."

"Would give away your position," countered Miu from where she sat nearby. She was still going through the bandages that they'd recovered from their fallen foes. At this point, she was almost at full health, so to speak.

"Ah… while I can appreciate this conversation and find it mildly interesting, I would very much like to learn who the mole is," Felix redirected.

"David's son did it. Sent Stephen emails," Andrea said simply and then resumed licking all across his neck. She started at the base of it and went all the way up to his hair line.

"Exactly that. We also know where this group was supposed to go after they finished up here. It's a warehouse in a rundown commercial park.

"We can't let this problem linger. I assume that's where we'll be moving next to make sure it's over," elaborated Goldie, turning to look at Felix again. "It was actually somewhat difficult to get everything out of them for some reason. There was some odd… interference. It made it rather frustrating at times, but I think I got most of it.

"And by the way, I'm able to make my skin as hard as I can my scales. I'm now as durable in this form, as I am in my true form. I am now much more formidable and can do more. One of them tried to stab me and it just skittered off."

"Good to know. I'm sure you'll be far more effective," agreed Felix.

"You… you should praise me more, Felix. Nest-mate," whispered the Dragon. "Praise… praise your Golden One who wears your bridal gold, more. Praise her more."

A low rumbling purr started up from the Dragon.

I… oh… they're both in heat.

Both the licky monster on my back, and the one in front who wants praise.

Turning to Faith, he gave her a hopeful smile. With any luck, the nymph might be able to cool their jets.

As soon as his eyes met hers, he realized she'd be no help. Her eyes were glowing green from the inside out without a pupil.

Whatever Goldie and Andrea were feeling had influenced the Dryad.

Damn. I knew better than to put these four together with me, but I prioritized power and points. Now I must shepherd it.

"You did wonderful, my Golden One. You look beautiful wearing your bridal gold, as well. We'll have to get a charm or two to hang from it as well as those bells.

"Now… let's pack it up and get to the next location. The night is young and we have rats to exterminate. Gear up and get ready."

Felix let go of Andrea's hands, reached down behind himself, and then slapped his hands to the Beastkin's rear end.

The loud smack of his palms hitting her rather lacking-in-padding rear end was quite loud. Andrea yelped and hopped down from him, whining loudly.

"Down, Andie. Get the Others moving. Time to go full Myriad. You'll be in charge of this. Miu will assist you," commanded Felix as Andrea continued to whine pitifully. "Faith is my bodyguard and Goldie is our rear guard. And no, I'm not staying behind. I need to be there to identify corpses and we're all staying together. I'll be careful."

The mood had changed drastically in those few seconds. From lust and general good feelings to tension and the anxiety of an impending fight to the death.

"Let's go," he said.

***

Felix felt rather comfortable with the sub-machinegun in his hands.

He'd never been quite comfortable with full machine guns, rifles, or shotguns. In the end he had always felt the best with a pistol, personal defense weapon, or SMG.

This one was actually quite similar to one he'd trained on extensively with Andrea, in fact.

He'd already memorized the name of the company and planned on seeing how they fared on the internet.

Though I wonder what kind of name is Heckler. How does someone get a surname that is more or less a stigma.

"P-Seven, set," came the voice through the headset he was wearing.

The comm gear that the op-forces had had made the Andreas quite happy. They were now able to function almost identically to how they did when they were a supervillain.

Just with a lot fewer Others and adding in a Dragon.

He'd been overruled in one of his placements.

Miu was now the rear-guard as she could take care of anyone who appeared while remaining unseen. Goldie was the spotlight target.

The show-stealer.

Now that she was a Dragon in Human form at a defensive level, it meant she could be far more active in these situations. Andrea was going to use that to her advantage.

"Gold-coin, set," declared Goldie with a great deal of excitement.

She might claim she's unlike other Dragons, and she is, but I'm positive she still enjoys all the things a normal Dragon does.

Just not for the swooning part.

"Yes, that's fair," Goldie said over her

headset.

To no one.

Are… are you reading my mind from that distance? I didn't say that out-loud, Goldie, you beautiful doof.

Do you seriously just tune in to me that often at this point? Am I your favorite radio station?

There was an awkward pause on the frequency they were using as everyone sat there. Clearly trying to figure out what that meant.

"Disregard. Correction, Gold-coin, set," Goldie mumbled a second or two later.

Is this a good time to discuss that I'd like to put some golden wedding rings on your bridal chains? Do you think that'd be interesting to you as a Dragon?

Show bridal gold with Human wedding customs of wedding rings?

Even as he thought it at the Dragon, he realized he was making a massive mistake. He'd forgotten the biggest rule for dealing with people like this.

Don't tease the crazy person.

Easing forward, Felix peeked out at the large warehouse. He was just across the street from it. Once it was clear enough for him to enter, he would do so. This part of Hardysburg was quite silent at the moment.

No sooner than he got eyes on the front of the warehouse, and Goldie, then he realized he really had made a mistake.

A big one.

Goldie was staring right at him. Her upper body twisted around to look his way. The rifle in her hands was held up close to her chest.

Her eyes were like golden spotlights right now, they were glowing so brightly even through the mask she was wearing.

I'll take that as a yes. Now cool those pretty high-beams of yours and get ready!

Goldie blinked rapidly which literally made him feel like he was trying to read Morse code. Then her eyes did indeed lose a great deal of their intensity as she looked back to the door.

"I think I felt her lust from here," muttered Faith from behind him. She laid her left hand on his back and then pushed in close to him. Her thigh was against his rear end and the middle of her against his right side. "Whatever you're doing to her, knock it off. She needs to concentrate."

"Yep, sorry, my bad. Just a little nervous and my thoughts ran away from me," Felix apologized.

"Not me you need to apologize to," she replied, her eyes scanning the warehouse. "Probably about time that—"

"P-Two through P-Ten, twenty second delay to engage. We have ten minutes until it's likely emergency responders will arrive," commanded Andrea. "Gold-coin, dynamic entry."

Goldie stepped up to the sheet metal garage door. As if she were kicking a field goal she brought her booted foot back and then cracked it into the bottom of the door and upward.

With a screech, the door broke, a great deal of the metal tearing away and twisting around. It had also ripped it clear from whatever fasteners had been holding it in place.

Bringing her foot back, she put another kick into the door. This time it made a cacophony of noise. As if she'd cleared an entire shelf of pots and pans.

It also jumped away from her giving her an opportunity to enter.

Lifting her rifle, she did so, stepping into the breach. He saw her point it to one side before it sounded off. The loud bark of it in a quick pulse of rounds being discharged making the previous racket seem quiet.

"Shadow to Throne, shift ahead," requested Miu.

Ahead? Weird.

Something we must've overlooked.

Acknowledge and act.

"Wilco," Felix said and tightened his hold on his SMG. Then he stood up, turned the corner, and sprinted across the street. Faith was on his left and matching him pace for pace.

"Disregard all previous. New directive. Full engage. Repeat, full engage," Andrea ordered through the line. "Throne and Gardener, dynamic entry, clear, hold. P-Two to P-Five, watch crossfire with tactical two entry."

Well, something definitely changed.

We're going to end up bumping into some Andreas

going in this way, but we're just holding the room after entry.

Felix and Faith stacked up on the simple door. Faith was already grasping the door handle. It shifted partly in her hand and seemed like it was unopen.

Giving it a full twist, she looked to him and nodded her head.

Thankfully, he'd trained more than enough for this situation. Andrea had run him through it countless times.

Grasping the grenade-like item off his vest, Felix pulled the pin free, held onto it and looked to Faith.

She opened the door partly and Felix tossed the flash-bang into the room, after which Faith closed the door. There was a muffled question inside followed by an ear-splitting boom.

Faith jerked the door open, then peeked inside and went in.

Felix followed her.

They were in what looked like a front entry office with no ceiling and most of the back wall missing. The smoke was rapidly fading but there were bits of dust and debris raining down from above.

Faith immediately went left with her SMG sweeping the distant back corner and moving to the left corner. She pulled the trigger twice as she did so, knocking someone off their feet with two bursts.

Felix was on her rear, his own SMG flicking

to the back-corner for a split second on the left where she'd started and moved to the right. He scanned it rapidly and his eyes focused on two people.

One man was standing there with his hands on his ears, a gun in hand, and the other was on the ground. His hands were over his eyes and he was rubbing at them. A gun was directly in front of him.

Unthinking, Felix sighted on the center mass of the first man and squeezed his trigger for a brief moment. Shifting to the second person, he did the same.

Both went down to the ground and began writhing around.

The immediate not-really-a-room that he was in was now clear.

Looking at the gaps in the walls, Felix could see two more people with guns firing on what was likely Goldie.

Taking cover behind a desk, Felix braced his SMG, sighted more cleanly through the red-dot sight and exhaled. His finger depressed the trigger for a moment.

Then he re-aligned and fired again.

The second burst did the trick and sent one of the shooters to the ground. By the time he'd gotten the RDS to the second one, they'd suddenly been enveloped by what looked a lot like a flame thrower.

Following it back to its source, Felix could see the ballistic-vest-wearing, rifle-carrying blond

Dragon. Even as she exhaled fire, she knocked the magazine out of her rifle with a fresh one, jammed it home, and pulled the bolt handle, chambering a round.

Drawing it back up to her shoulder, she cut off the fire breath and marched forward again. Lining up on someone or something, she again fired.

"God damn, she's fierce," Felix said with a smirk. Putting his back to a wall, he looked at a doorway that Faith was beside. The door itself was closed and she was aiming towards the gap in the wall next to Felix.

He settled into his current position, and aimed toward the door. They'd cover each other like this.

"Throne to all, tactical two held. Entry disallowed without announce," called Felix through the radio.

"Gardener relays Throne is in intact state," added Faith.

"Shadow en—" Miu's voice cut off and what sounded like a shotgun blast went off in her mic. It was followed by two more and someone screaming. "Shadow engaged. Enemy expected a counterattack and was marginally prepared."

The door next to Faith opened suddenly.

Felix didn't wait and put a burst of fire through the doorway. Followed by another.

He couldn't see what he was shooting at it, or whom, but he was fairly certain he'd just given them too much to think about.

He and Faith couldn't remain where they were now that the enemy knew they were in the room. A flash-bang could just as easily be used against them.

Felix held up his right hand and made a chopping motion to the door, then stood up. Following the right wall, he moved around to the door.

"Gardener and Throne shifting from tactical two. Exiting into attached offices," reported Faith. Felix could only just barely make it out over the ringing and gunfire.

Only the quality of the headphones they were wearing had made it possible so far to hear anything. He felt like his hearing was going to go out from all this.

Pulling out his last flash-bang, he pulled the pin, glanced at Faith, and then tossed it into the hall. Faith had shifted over to the door at this point, though she was still watching the gap.

Before the flash-bang could go off, Faith froze and then fired.

Then the boom went off and Felix realized Faith was covering their exit. He needed to move.

Shifting over, Felix entered the hall.

A group of people were bumping into each other in front of him. Some moved toward him, some moved away. Others were on the ground.

Felix kept moving forward and began cycling targets. Flicking the barrel from torso to torso, after putting in a burst of gunfire into each.

At this distance, hitting center mass wasn't an issue.

He wasn't even truly aiming at this point.

Enemies fell away and collapsed to the floor.

Storming forward, Felix continued to clear the hall. He only paused briefly to orient his SMG on someone on the ground who was moving around.

A brief pull of the trigger ended them and Felix's internal head count told him he was near empty, or empty.

Glancing to the front of his weapon, he saw that the bolt-hold-open feature had engaged and he hadn't even noticed it. The blood exploding out of the other side of the man's head as Felix fired had been a bit too distracting for him, if he was being honest.

Pausing for a moment, he slid his finger forward against the guard and pushed the detent to drop the current magazine. It fell away with a gentle shake of the weapon, even as he pulled a new magazine from his vest.

Snapping it into place, he then slapped the charging handle forward and into position. Grabbing the front of his weapon, Felix began moving forward again. Ahead of him, he saw no one and nothing standing in his way.

"Legion?" challenged a voice up ahead of them.

"Yosemite," answered Felix with the correct

response. Moving ahead toward the voice, he exited the hall into a T-intersection. One led off to where Andrea Four was aiming down. Andrea Three was aiming down where Felix had just come from. Next to them was Andrea two.

"Hey Third, Second, Four, good to see you all," Felix confessed and gladly moved into their ranks, and then partway down the hall they'd come from.

Andrea Five was slumped against a wall, but holding her rifle up in front of herself. She didn't look like she was doing well.

"Gardener, check Five for me," Felix commanded and pointed to the Andrea. Getting down into a kneeling position, Felix lifted his weapon and aimed it down the hall.

"Gold-coin, warehouse clear. Moving to next," growled Goldie, sounding very aggressive and determined at the moment.

"Shadow, counterattack cleared. Moving to intercept Throne and Gardener," Miu reported.

"Continue operation. P-Six through Nine, move to phase three," ordered Andrea. "P-Ten, hump the green-box."

They're going to start trying to flush the rest out. Andrea Ten is going to capture anyone who runs.

These are the people we want information from. The ones who think they're above dying here while the foot soldiers perish.

In other words... proceeding as intended.

Now I just hunker down here for a bit.

Chapter 24 - Origin Story -

"G-G-Gold coin, c-clear," puffed Goldie over the radio several minutes later. She sounded extremely winded. As if she'd been running a marathon and had crossed over the finish line and would now collapse.

"All teams have reported clear, retrieval has already been underway. All objectives met; secondary retrieval will cease. Emergency responders are now en route. Use green-box and follow the first route. End communications," directed Andrea.

Sure took them long enough to get rolling.

Andie had been right though. Really need to make sure she runs these sort of things for us in the future.

Only Andrea Five of the Others had remained with him and Faith. The rest had gone to collect and capture.

Reaching down, Felix stuck an arm under Andrea Five's arms and then stood up.

"Come on, Five. We need to go," he said, grabbing hold of her vest and holding her tightly. She'd managed to survive whatever had happened to her and kept her gear. Faith had stabilized her a little bit and now they could be gone.

"Nnnuuugh," groaned Andrea Five as she began stumbling forward at Felix's insistence. "I can't even tell that you're grabbing my boob. Everything hurts."

"Well, we'll get you out of here and then

have someone absorb you," promised Felix. The other Andreas didn't really have the time or luxury of being able to pull Five in. They'd been busy holding the intersection and then moving on to begin grabbing everything they could.

"Nn. Please, yes," groaned Andrea Five. She turned her head and just pressed it to his shoulder. Faith hesitated for only a second before going around to the other side of Andrea and supporting her.

Much faster now, the trio exited the T-intersection. They headed through several locations that were still burning as well as past chunks of what used to be Humans.

The fighting had gotten visceral at a literal and figurative level.

Exiting out the large and obvious exit at the back—the same one they'd left open as a golden bridge—Felix saw Andreas hurrying around in every direction.

Third spotted him and gave him a grim smile.

"Thanks, Dear," Andrea Third said as she came over. She was moving at a light jog and went right through Five, absorbing her and catching her gear as it fell to the ground.

Moving around Faith with a stutter-step, Andrea pivoted and went back to a bread truck. Everyone was busy loading gear, corpses, or each other, into it.

Goldie popped into view outside of a

second-story window. She looked around, spotted them all, then simply stepped out and fell to the ground.

Landing with a slap of boot heels on concrete, she started walking to them. Her landing had looked strange to him as she hadn't bent her knees very much. However, she looked unharmed.

Other than moving slowly, she seemed fine.

"I'm so tired," she muttered as they all met up at the back of the truck. "Shape changing certain parts of me wears me out so fast. That and breathing fire as a Human. That took a few tries to get right, but… it was worth it.

"Never thought it would have been possible without trying. I know Taylor and I both tried it out back in our old world but… things are different here."

Stepping up to the truck, Goldie pulled the mask off her head, then the magazine from her rifle. Then she cycled the bolt and caught the cartridge that was ejected. Putting it all in the truck, she then started to work on removing her vest.

Suddenly, she burped and a small tongue of flame came up from her mouth. Washing over her own face.

It did absolutely nothing to her.

"Ooh, I'm… excuse me. I'm so sorry. That's just so rude," complained Goldie and waving a hand in front of her mouth. "There's so much of me right now that's part-Dragon and part-Human that I think my body is just confused."

"You look beautiful and amazing to me. So half-Dragon, half-Human, whatever. You're lovely and I wish I had time to kiss you and give you're a horn-rub," answered Felix. He'd seen what Goldie was doing and was going about the same thing. Unloading everything into the truck.

He was sure Andrea had already given instructions, he just hadn't caught them or been told yet.

Goldie began to purr again, a smile playing across her lips as she worked at her vest. Her eyes were glowing again.

"Why thank you, Nest-mate. I do love the attention as of late," demurred the very warm-hearted Dragon. The more attention he paid her, the more he invested in her, the more he got back from her and he was determined to abuse that.

Just as he did with Miu.

"I'm sure it's hard to be put next to the beautiful Dryad beside me as often as you are. It's hard to compare with her," Felix said, pulling his mask off and flipping it on top of where Goldie had put hers down. "You're just as wonderful in ways that even a Dragon would be impressed with."

Goldie's smile grew wider at that, her eyes hovering on him for several seconds and her purring growing louder.

Felix started to work at unbuckling his vest and stole a glance over at Faith.

She was working at her own gear, though her eyes were glowing from the inside out again. His words had clearly hit both and quite well.

"And before you get upset, Miu," Felix muttered, without looking to the top of the truck. He'd known for a while that she was on top of it, watching him. "I'll remind you that I wore you like a damn cape just to have you near me despite being a very… fragrant… corpse.

"All for the sake of making sure you were with me. Even in death. I needed my Miu."

Only when he finished talking and had pulled the vest off, did he look up.

Miu was peering at him from over the edge of the truck. Only her eyes and up were visible. He could see the crinkle at the corners of her eyes though.

She was smiling at him.

"You came for me," she whispered. In a voice that sounded exactly like she did when she'd been dead.

"And always will. For all of you. Because you'd all come for me," answered Felix and then got up into the truck directly. He dropped his vest into a pile of similar gear and looked at an odd wooden crate in the corner.

"Thumbs!" said Andrea Seven, rushing by him to toss six or seven thumbs into the box. "Easier to have you identify thumbs than corpses. We can take 'em with us!"

She gave him a pat on the shoulder, spun around him, kissed his cheek, and bounced out of the truck, literally kicking off the edge of the wall panel and going over Goldie and Faith.

"She's energetic," growled Goldie after getting out of her vest. She started to rub at her chest with both hands. "My boobs hurt so bad. They shot me so many times in the chest. And before you ask, the regeneration is a little slow right now because I'm so spent."

Felix was contemplating offering to help her out with her issue, but wasn't sure how well that'd go over at the moment.

"Shit," Miu said from above. "Police are here. A lot of them. Faster than we expected. We should have had a few more minutes. That's… not normal."

Suddenly all the Andreas came flooding back. They were all pulling masks on as well.

Shit.

Felix bent down and grabbed his own mask then held out Goldie's to her. He met the Dragon's eyes with a smile.

"I'll offer later?" he asked her, knowing she had most certainly been listening to his thoughts.

"You better," she replied with a smile and took the mask. She pulled it down over her face and then her horns appeared. Holes tearing open magically in the mask. The Dragon sighed. "Damn, I can't control it. I'm so darn tired."

Thinking quickly, he realized this was actually something he could solve. This situation was one that he was made for perfectly.

He reached out and laid a hand on Goldie's

face.

His intent was simple. Recharge Goldie with power. He wanted to use himself as a conduit and his power as the system to transfer.

Name: Goldie Campbell	**Condition**: Exhausted
If No Action Taken: Remains Exhausted	**Action >> Recharge**: Cost 4 points

Is it because I'm Faith's Grove? She said it would change me.

Have I become a battery, just like Vince did?

Raising his eyebrows, Felix didn't hesitate.

He activated the power. Letting his hand slip away from Goldie, he put it on Faith's cheek. She hadn't managed to get her mask back on yet as she'd been halfway through getting her vest off.

"Grove-husband? What're—"

Felix unloaded his power into her. Wanting to recharge her just as he had Goldie. The cost was even less, at two points only. She had only been "very tired".

Faith's words died instantly and her eyes flashed bright green.

Looking at the two women who were staring at him, he found their eyes to be glowing as if someone had put LEDs in them. Both of them were bright to the point of looking cartoonish.

"Miu, all Andreas, absorb up and get over here," Felix called. "Our plan is simple. They won't have many cops that can respond to a situation like this. I bet none of them could deal with us as a team.

"Better still, they probably don't have a helicopter, armored vehicle, or anything else, in fact."

Miu dropped down and landed directly in front of him between Goldie and Faith. Felix reached out and put his hands to her cheeks.

As soon as he touched Miu, Andrea showed up with all her Others.

Felix blasted Miu with the same exact request. Hers was a single point, as her stamina hadn't been taxed much at all.

Laying his hands on Andrea's face, he once more did the same.

Name: Andrea Campbell	**Condition**: Critically Exhausted
If No Action Taken: Remains Critically Exhausted	**Action >> Recharge**: Cost 8 points

Hesitating only for a moment, Felix did the same thing to her. He filled her right up to full. Then he pushed on his power, wanting to change it so she could receive excess power.

To become a reservoir of sorts for anything he didn't need. To transfer it to her automatically on command.

Almost as soon as he thought it, he realized it was too broad, but also not defined enough. It needed boundaries or the cost would be too high

He wanted to be able to syphon off his extra power by touching Faith, Goldie, Miu, or Andrea. To put it into them so that they could use it as they saw fit, if they had the room for it.

To that end, he wanted it so that they could store that extra power.

Name: Andrea Campbell	**Condition**: Empowered
If No Action Taken: None	**Action >> Alter Power**: Cost 142,917 points

Damn.

Whatever.

This is fine, this'll be more than enough. I can always charge them up again.

"Take care of the cops. Swiftly. Then we leave," Felix asked of them. "No fatalities. Do it without killing them or maiming them. Andrea, hit us with a plan from that big sexy combat brain of yours."

Andrea was staring at him with extremely wide eyes. As if she were looking into the end of the world.

She suddenly shivered and but her gaze remained fixed on Felix.

"Goldie, march around the corner and go straight for the cops," said the Beastkin, staring at him now with a strange dedication. "Do it with a sexy saunter. Like in those dances we watch. Don't run. Draw their fire to you. Let them shoot at you and soak up their threat. Harden your scales appropriately, so that it just bounces off entirely.

"Miu, rooftops, then down atop them once they're truly distracted. Hands and feet, non-lethal, non-maiming, just as Felix asked.

"Faith will remain with Felix. She's best suited to keeping him healthy.

"I'll go around the far side with my pack and flank once Goldie has them. Third will drive the truck partly into position."

Nine Andrea's all stood together an instant after stepping away from Miu, Goldie, and Faith. One Andrea broke away and got into the truck.

Faith hopped in and then guided Felix to a point where he could sit down.

Felix caught sight of the Andreas forming up into a wedge and setting off at a mad sprint around the far side of the building.

Then the truck engine turned over and they slowly began to nose their way out from behind the building. Andrea Third was moving them in a very non-threatening way, but still getting them ready.

Because of the way she'd done it, they were not in line with Goldie anymore. If she was fired on they'd be out of the line of fire.

Goldie was sauntering toward the police slowly. Her horns glittered and the gold sparkled and shifted with every step she took.

Straight toward five police cars, a swat truck, and a lot of guns that were all pointing at her. They were entirely focused on her.

Watching her, he found the look of her rather awe inspiring. From how she carried herself to her impressive figure, to the absolute lack of concern she held for the police.

"—will shoot!" screamed a policeman at the front. They were all shouting, but Felix managed to hear that one for some reason. "Stop now!"

Goldie didn't stop. She just kept moving right for them.

Felix couldn't see who fired first, but it was instantly joined by everyone else. Every single officer began unloading their weapons at Goldie.

She just kept walking forward, though she did lift her left arm and held it across her chest. Apparently, she didn't want to get shot in the chest anymore.

It gave her a very villainous look as she just kept walking. There wasn't even a hitch in her fluid strut that rolled her hips as she approached them.

Someone suddenly slammed the swat van into gear and aimed it right for her.

Either the horns or her glowing eyes had suddenly given someone a very deep-seated need to kill her quickly. Not that he could blame them.

If he were in their position, it'd likely be the same.

When the van was right on top of her, Goldie lifted her right arm and back-handed it.

The whole vehicle was knocked to one side, one of the wheel broke free, and the front was crushed inward where her hand had touched it. Smoke began spewing up from it, immediately followed by a high-pitch whine and then a muffled boom.

Followed by the vehicle going silent even as more rounds were being poured on Goldie. As if a cylinder had just detonated itself inside the engine and caused it to die.

Miu took that opportunity for what it was and flashed into view on top of a light post. Then she dove off it and vanished into the ranks of policemen.

At the same time, the pack of Andreas—still in their V-shape formation—came around the far side of the building. Somehow they had made it all the way around. They waded into the cops and began throwing kicks and punches.

Goldie kept going, drawing so much fire that almost no one had noticed what was going on in the back.

An officer stumbled out of the van and collapsed to the ground. He was on his hands and knees and started to throw up bright-red blood.

"Damn," muttered Felix. "Faith, any chance you can reach him with some nature healing magic from here?"

Not bothering to hear an answer, Felix reached out and laid his hand on her hip. He began to try force-feeding her a never-ending stream of power. Just wanting to dump power into her.

"I-ungh-errgh-Felix-I—" Faith groaned and

got out between clenched teeth. Putting her right hand on the floor of the truck, everything around them suddenly became a neon-green color.

The same color as her eyes, in fact.

Felix just kept trying to pour more power into her. It only cost him a point or two each time and didn't seem to bother him at all.

Every single time he did so, he watched Faith shiver, her eyes only growing in intensity by the second until it was like looking into the sun. To the point that he gave up watching and closed his eyes it was so bright.

"Enough, Grove-husband! I'm full!" begged Faith.

Stopping, Felix opened his eyes and looked out to the fallen officer.

A tree had sprouted from where he'd thrown up and another was not too far away. He was wrapped in vines and nearly cocooned in them, as if he were in some sort of natural hammock.

From this distance, Felix could clearly see the man's chest rise and fall as he stared up at the sky above them.

Green nature energy pulsed and vibrated, radiating out from that point, wanting to envelope everyone and everything around and smother them in regrowth.

Grass, weeds, plants, and everything that could be considered flora was growing. From long-dead dried-out leaves to dandelions.

Felix couldn't see Goldie, but there were

several cars that'd clearly been knocked out of her way as well as a trail of officers laid out on the ground and across the vehicles.

Andreas were rushing over the downed officers, and robbing them of anything that could be taken quickly. One of the Andreas was driving a squad car with the trunk open. Things were being tossed in quickly as it paced alongside the other Andreas.

"I'm so full," groaned Faith, who then slumped down against the back of the driver's seat. "I need… I need to go grow trees. I have to go empower my farm. So… full.

"Feels great but… too full."

Andrea Third took this as an appropriate time to call an end to it all. She laid on the horn for several seconds, then tapped it once.

All the Andreas broke away from their looting to hit the squad cars and swat van. They continued to strip everything clean as they went.

Miu and Goldie were now visibly moving through the crowd of downed officers. They were carrying several between themselves, in fact.

They dumped them off at the imitation Dryad grove where the van had crashed, before starting to head back to the truck.

Goldie was only wearing tatters of her clothes at this point. Most of the fabric had been shot clean off her.

Miu looked unhurt.

"Back to the farm then," mumbled Felix.

"Then go see David and his son. By the way… did we get any prisoners?"

"Yes, Andrea Prime took them all away after she killed the comms. They're all at the farm. Along with a lot of the loot we grabbed early and what we took from them.

"Uhm… Edmund… was with her as well. I'm sorry. She's going to drop him off at the trailer. We didn't really know what to do with him and you invited him to join and we just—"

"It's fine, Third," stated Felix firmly, interrupting her. "It's fine. He'll be Legion very shortly. We'll need him down the road.

"Others, too. We'll need to start recruiting. Primarily for our underworld side but… need to start recruiting."

Andrea Third honked the horn again for several seconds, then beeped the horn three times.

"Nn, nn, okay. Time to gooooo," she chirped excitedly.

Chapter 25 - Fallout -

"Nope," Felix mumbled and tossed a thumb out the truck door. It sailed for a short distance through the air before landing in the brackish water of the swamp behind the farm.

Picking up another thumb, he checked the name.

It wasn't Stephen.

"Sorry, Bubba," apologized Felix and then flicked the thumb away. Much as he'd done with the last eleven of them.

"Hey, hey, hi. No luck so far?"

Felix looked up from the box of thumbs and found Andrea Prime standing there. The golden earring that designated her as such was very visible, though he knew it was her anyway.

"Not in any way. Though all these names are quite local sounding to me," answered Felix. He had his back resting against the interior of the truck and was seated right at the edge of the rear exit. "How about you? Any of the prisoners Stephen?"

Andrea shook her head with a frown.

"I only got here a minute or two ago, but Goldie already checked them as we loaded them up," explained Andrea. "She was pretty certain even then that we didn't have him. She did a check again just now and no Stephen. We did get his second-in-command, though. As well as a number of key people to him.

"His only resource now is the other supplier

he was leveraging against David. That's it. He's done otherwise. We'll... process the prisoners and go from there."

Felix plucked out a thumb, checked the name, and then tossed it as soon as he saw the wrong name.

"They were ready for us. Or at least, expecting to be attacked. It was fairly obvious, or it seemed so to me," murmured Felix, looking at Andrea for a moment.

"Nn, agreed. Definitely felt like they were expecting problems. Maybe not that we'd attack them the way we did, but that they were prepared," affirmed Andrea. "We took them down no problem, though. You even got into the mix I saw and acted well.

"Even when you cared for me. Or, Five, that is. You were performing better than most people who go into the military. Maybe not as good as special forces or anything, but still very good."

Felix had already seen that Andrea was alone, there were no Others with her. That didn't mean she hadn't already absorbed all Others and redistributed everyone back out.

"Why thank you, I tried. I've been doing all this training with everyone for so long that it almost felt second nature," he replied, picking up another thumb, checking it, then tossing it. "Most certainly paid off. I'm glad for it, though also a little nervous.

"I haven't done much training since we got here. I might be slipping a bit on the physical side."

"No, you're good!" Andrea said shaking her head almost comically. "The tree thing is burning up lots and lots of calories. You're thinner now than you've ever been before. If anything, we should be force-feeding you calories.

"In fact, you look pale and thinner than I remember at the moment. Did that empowering thing drain you?"

Pausing, a thumb held between his fingers, Felix considered her words.

He hadn't really put too much thought into it, but now that she'd directed his attention there, he felt she was right. About all of it, in fact.

He hadn't really felt like he'd gained any weight despite eating a lot more than previously. On top of that, it felt like he was gaining muscle mass yet hadn't worked out or trained at all.

Lastly, he did feel tired. As if he'd just gone for a jog with Andrea, Miu, Victoria, and Ioana. A several mile fun-run meant to increase his endurance; except he hadn't done any of that.

"Huh. I think you're right. Faith?" asked Felix.

He was fairly certain the Dryad was nearby. Probably dozing in the grass and waiting for sunrise. She did better during the day, he'd realized a long time ago.

My little sunflower. Without the sun it's hard for you.

She used up all that power and then fell asleep.

"Sleeping. Not far off. Should... should I

wake her?" Andrea asked, her head tilting to one side.

"No. Leave her be. She's been up for a while and she could use some sleep. We'll need to wait a few hours anyway, because I do have an order I need to give. One for you and one for Miu," said Felix, checking the thumb in his hand and then tossing it. "I need you to get a message to David. We need to meet here at the farm. Let him know that chances are this little… war… is over.

"Because I'm done with it. I don't want any part of it any longer. I'm going to solve it today and that'll be it. The moment I was involved, it was no longer going to continue."

"Nn, nn, got it!" said Andrea with a crisp salute. "Should I go get Miu?"

"She's here," Felix said with a shake of his head. Checking another thumb and disposing of it. "Aren't you, Miu?"

"Yes," came a response from above. As if she were laying down on top of the truck and peering down at him again.

"I… nn… not good… grrr. I need to work on my awareness. I got soft," growled Andrea, peering up at Miu. "Feral friend Red would be laughing at me."

"No, you didn't get soft. Miu is just that incredible. She's even getting better, aren't you Miu?" asked Felix with a grin.

"I'm… I'm just… Miu. Felix's Miu," responded the shadow assassin. "I need to go find the Miu of this world. Can I go get her when we have time? When we're done with everything immediate?"

"Sure," Felix agreed, another thumb tossed. "I'll give you a week to get it done. You can use some funding as well, but try not to spend too much.

"Though, I do have an order for you. Are you ready, Miu?"

"I'm always ready," she growled.

"Go get me the supplier David is fighting against. The one Stephen was using," murmured Felix, his checking of thumbs paused. "Kidnap him and bring him back here for me. I want this done.

"You can take Goldie with you if you need her. Otherwise, I need it done before David gets here tonight."

"I understand. I'll make it happen," she promised.

There was the slight sound of metal crinkling as she likely stood up or got down off the truck. There was nothing further to be heard.

With a sigh, Felix went back to his rather unsightly job. He wasn't having much luck, nor did it seem to be going very well.

It needed to be done though.

"I'm going to go help my Others. They're still sorting through all the gear we recovered. They also robbed the squad cars and swat truck," Andrea muttered. She seemed entirely displeased that Miu had managed to sneak up on her.

"Have fun. Don't get too down on yourself. You all have your points of strength," Felix consoled her.

Plucking a thumb from his box, Felix held it up and asked for the name of the owner.

"Jim-Bob. My apologies for the name as well as the fact that you're no longer in the world," Felix lamented dryly and then discarded it.

***

Felix stood with his hands behind his hips. The sun was rather high in the sky at the moment. It was almost an hour past noon.

David had responded eagerly, stating he'd arrive around one in the afternoon.

Which was why Felix was out here waiting.

Miu and Goldie had returned with the opposing supplier and dealer. The one who Stephen had been leaning on.

A rather unassuming man by the name of Zachary Nahrstadt.

He was currently kneeling in the grass next to Felix, along with all the people they'd captured in the raid on Stephen's base.

Held in Felix's hand was a pistol an Andrea had provided him.

On his right was Goldie.

To his left, Faith.

Both were armed with SMGs and wearing ballistic vests and their masks. Though Goldie had been forced to make a new mask for herself. The previous one had too many bullet holes in it.

Miu was somewhere in the fields and the Andreas were spread out all over. They were working security to make sure no one else tried to join the gathering.

Law enforcement, criminal, or otherwise.

"There he is," Goldie murmured, her head turning slightly, the gold in her horns swaying. "You were right."

Faith had already told them that David was on the way. The trees were always eager to relay any and all information to Faith as quickly as they could.

What'd surprised Felix the most was that apparently even other things were getting in on sending her information. Bushes, shrubs, anything that could live longer than a season, was trying to help her.

From what he knew, that wasn't the norm. That was typically a tree-to-Dryad type of situation.

"Of course," Faith replied simply. "They're more responsive in these lands than they were in my original homeland, or... or before here. It's rather nice.

"Eager to talk to me and tell me anything they can."

In talking about that, Felix had a sudden thought triggered. He'd wanted to ask her about something she'd said and that it felt abnormal to him.

It seemed as if she'd been saying there were Dryads on their way to this farm. That he'd have to deal with more Nymphs.

Except what he wanted to ask wasn't something he could do right now. Not with Zachary right next to him.

It'd have to wait.

"He wants to ask you about that, you know. He suspects it," Goldie murmured, as if she were reading both their minds and finding the same thoughts on both ends. One as a question, and the other as an answer. "Best you come clean about it before they start showing up."

Faith let out a shuddering breath that sounded a lot like a sigh. Followed by a tongue click.

Then she nodded her head, either in response to his unasked question or Goldie's words he didn't know.

"How many?" Felix asked, realizing that it was exactly what he'd been afraid of.

"Two… tomorrow, I think. They were the only ones in this country that I wanted," answered Faith. "Another… three next month. After that, only four more. A lot more wanted to come, but I was being very picky. We won't have that many but more than enough to plant a full and true… colony.

"I spoke with Meliae, Vince's… wife, extensively about what she did to grow it. What precautions she took and what uh… what… traditions they kept."

It sounded like she'd wanted to say "Grove" but couldn't, given that Zachary was present.

"Everyone else will be arranging themselves in a second colony. Not far from here. I promised them that Legion would guarantee their lives," admitted Faith. "In return, they'll provide strength similar to my own. More so once the right day comes."

Ah... yes. That'd work out just fine.

We pay up front now for their power later. We're investing in a future resource.

Good planning there.

"Sounds good. Shame that there aren't any like our golden friend left," Felix mused aloud, his eyes moving to Goldie.

"Well, I could probably find some skeletons if you want," offered Goldie, turning her head to look at him from the sides of her golden eyes. "If you own their bones, then that'd work, would it not?

"Though I have no idea how useful they'd be. They might not be able to cope with this... this."

Another good idea. I like that.

In fact, can't I just go collect corpses and start doing that? Just has to be somewhere that I can claim ownership of it.

"Do that. I'm sure you can dominate them all easily if I bring them back," commanded Felix.

"It'll be done."

Goldie's words ended abruptly as a car swung into view at the end of the road.

Everyone went quiet and remained so. Nothing was said as all eyes were on the car.

Waiting.

"Pancake for all Pancakes, no extras," declared Andrea on the frequency they were still all on. In the end, it was easier for them all to keep the radio on them with the attached earpiece in. They could keep in contact significantly easier.

"Shadow, no extras," Miu responded. "Shifting."

David's car pulled up and stopped not far away.

Felix was surprised to see it was Jay driving and David riding in the rear. There were no others with them and they didn't look armed.

Opening the doors, David and Jay both got out.

They both looked at Zachary, then at Felix.

Hm?

Glancing down at the man, Felix saw there was nothing out of the ordinary there. Blue eyes, brown hair, male.

Everything as it should be.

Looking back at the two men, Felix raised his eyebrows at them.

"You're meeting me during the day and that's... Zachary," David muttered, coming over to stand in front of Felix. There was a nervousness to the man that was obvious to a casual observer.

"Indeed, and those are all employees of Stephen," added Felix, indicating the row of men off to one side, then let his hands fall to his side. He wasn't going to hide the weapon.

Faith took that as her cue to go fetch the second-in-command for Stephen.

"I'm tired of this war. I'm ending it. I want you to both go back to your original territories. I want you two to start working together. I don't care how you do it, but there won't be fighting anymore," stated Felix and then pressed the barrel of his weapon to Zachary's temple. "Zachary. Is your little war with David over?"

"I— yes. Very much. Very over. Not a problem. Work together, go back to how we were to one another, war's done," Zachary agreed quite quickly.

"Splendid," Felix said and pulled the handgun away from Zachary's temple. "Now, David—"

Felix paused to take a breath.

"War's over, got it. Peace and working together. I'm sure Zachary and I can pull together a quick plan to dominate everyone else," interjected David with some excitement. "Not a problem at all."

Nodding his head with a smile, Felix felt relieved.

"Splendid. Splendid indeed. I'm so glad to hear that," he said as Faith pushed down Stephen's second-in-command down to his knees.

Faith then started working at untying Zachary and pulled him to his feet. She pushed him roughly so that he'd stand next to David.

"Now, I'm going to say it in a very simple way," continued Felix, looking to Zachary, David, and Jay. "I'm a businessman. I want business and money. That's all that I want.

"I don't want leadership. I don't want to tell you what to do. I don't want to be involved in stupid things like what just happened.

"I'm not interested in it at all. I have two interests and two interests alone. Money and business."

"Yep, you got it," David said, holding his hands up and waving them a little. "No arguments from me. Happy to just do business."

"Perfect. That's all I needed to hear. I expect you to give Zachary all the requirements I have and teach him what ratio to bring me product in so I can fix it."

David and Zachary looked to one another.

"No overdoses. Nothing killer. Can't be a mad doc about it," David rattled off rapidly. "He wants you to bring him trash coke. Really stomped on shit. Load it up in kilo bricks. He… he makes it into pure stuff. Pay him half of what the difference would be. We both make money. No middleman.

"Recut your stuff and sell by a standard. I'll give you my own ratios and we can sell the same products. Just make sure you keep some in reserve so he can do it again. Repeatedly. I bring him like fifty or sixty now."

Zachary was staring at David as if he were a

mad man.

"Don't… don't question it," offered Jay. "Just do it. It isn't worth it."

Though Jay and David were clearly cowed, Zachary looked like he wasn't completely sold.

"I'll kill you and pull your intestines out and use them as a garland if you finish that thought," growled Goldie, taking a step forward.

David and Jay immediately stepped away from her, though they didn't seem to be the target of her ire.

"Yes, I can read your mind, you stupid bug," Goldie said in a voice that was growing deeper. "If you don't want me to hose you down with fire, you should agree to what's being told to you.

"Serve Legion or serve the worms. Your choice is simple and free of complications. Blessed you are for being such a simple directive."

Smoke was actually wafting up from Goldie's masked face now. Coming up and off her in clouds.

"I'd listen to the Dragon, Zach!" David said in a strained voice.

Jay was nodding his head rapidly.

Zachary began nodding his head rapidly.

"Yes, do exactly that, Zachary. Exactly what you're thinking. Otherwise, maybe my friend and I will go visit your home. Your real home," threatened Goldie. "It's in… Runnelstown? Yes. Runnelstown. A cute little place off Lacey Drive. I see it now. That's a really good-looking dog, too.

Do you think it'd be tasty?

"Or... your wife, maybe? She looks like she's bite-sized."

There was an unmistakable bright, gold glow coming from inside the mask that could only be Goldie's eyes.

Standing there, Goldie stared at Zachary for several seconds as the man just kept nodding his head, only to start shaking it as he realized Goldie's question had changed.

After a long pause, the Dragon finally moved away from him, taking her place next to Felix again.

"So, that's that. I want business. I want money. I want nothing else. I don't want to run your organizations. You don't work for me. I work for you. It's that simple," summarized Felix. "David, your son sent information to Stephen. I have no proof of it, but he's been sending out emails with information.

"It's your organization, so I don't care what you do with that information, or what happens to him, but I felt I should at least warn you since I work for you.

"Now... are there any questions that I can answer for you? Otherwise, I'd like very much for you two to go back to your homes. David can give you a ride, Zachary.

"Jay, stay behind for a moment. I want to make you an offer to become a Legionnaire. It's time for me to increase my numbers and you seem reliable."

"Uhm... I do have a question," Zachary said hesitantly. He looked from Felix to Goldie and back.

"Certainly," allowed Felix, waiting.

"When... when I bring the product, will you be providing us with directions? What we should do next? I think that you as the bo—"

Felix lifted the pistol, pointed it at the man who'd been Stephen's second-in-command, and pulled the trigger.

With a splut, the man's head went to the side and blood began pouring out of the wound. Then he collapsed forward onto the ground, red crimson arcs spraying out of the hole in his head and into the grass.

"I'm sorry, I couldn't hear your question. I was busy taking care of a problem. I take care of problems quickly. I make them go away," Felix flatly stated in the silence after the shot rang out. "It'd be a problem if I was your boss. Or in charge of your organization. That's why I don't own your organization. I'm not your boss. Nor am I someone who will order you around in your business.

"My business is product, moving lots of it, and giving customers a known and stable product. I want to make a lot of money off it.

"Now... what... were you going to ask me again?"

Standing there, Felix wondered if Zachary was about to be shot in the face. The man clearly hadn't understood his point before, there was no telling if the man would finally understand.

"I... no. No problem. My organization, my people, my problems. Sorry," Zachary mumbled in a soft voice.

"Goodie. Thank you, gentleman. Have a nice day," Felix offered.

"Have... have a good day, L-Legate," David said and dipped his head to him. He took the car keys from Jay's very pale hand and hustled off to the driver's side door.

Legate?

Felix had no idea what David meant by calling him that.

He wasn't completely certain, but he was pretty sure that Legate was an old title from the Roman Empire. It literally was the person in charge of a Legion.

Legate... hm. I suppose I do need a name this time, since I'm not Felix.

The Legate.

He who controls the Legion.

"Come along, Jay. Let's talk numbers. I'd like to hire you on as a personal contact for me. Beholden to me and no one else. My first real Legionnaire," explained Felix. He was going to recruit him and pay him to be the underworld version of Edmund.

Speaking of, where'd he end up?

Chapter 26 - Fifteen Minutes -

Walking into the trailer, Felix found Edmund sitting on the couch.

The young man looked rather chipper for someone who had been dragged around with Andrea Prime. Apparently, there'd even been an issue with their own getaway that they'd had to deal with.

A brief chase with the police, in fact.

"Hello, Edmund," Felix said, entering the trailer fully and then walking over to the love seat. Sitting down on it, he let out a long sigh.

He'd been on the move for more than thirty-six hours at this point. Calling him tired was an understatement.

Right now, he just wanted to crawl into a bed and sleep for a while.

"Hi, Felix. Did Jay take the offer?" asked Edmund.

I... what? Hm.

Someone must have told him.

"He did. He'll be the underworld version of you. He's now aware of what we're doing and how we're going about it," answered Felix. "I'm not exactly thrilled with it, since I can't enforce his loyalty in any way but that's how it goes."

Edmund looked rather confused at that, his entire face screwing up in an almost comical way.

"Hahahaha, Edmund! You might as well have a speech bubble with 'huh' above your head.

Like something out of a comic book," remarked Andrea as she skipped into the trailer. She waved at Felix and Edmund both and turned hard, heading into the kitchen.

He could see that she had most of her Others with her save two.

Miu and Goldie came in after that.

"Errr… I see," replied Edmund, who then looked like he was trying to school his face.

I suppose his confusion is normal. Especially for such a mundane world.

I was spoiled by magically-enforced loyalty. It's easy to win people over when they don't have an opportunity to say no.

I'll just have to put on my super-middle-manager hat and really work the people over. Make sure they're happy and cared for.

Not to mention, being very selective with who I hire.

Jay will be fine.

He didn't rat David out when his life was threatened and he didn't run away either. He's pushed on despite losing what sounds like most everything.

Edmund is… I'm sure Edmund will be fine.

"Faith stayed behind at the farm," Goldie proclaimed and then wandered off to the bedroom. "I have to go get her tonight on the way to Hardysburg to dump the truck."

They'd traveled back in two groups. One with the legally obtained truck which consisted of him, Miu, and Andrea, and one group in the truck that wasn't so legal with Goldie and Faith.

He hadn't even noticed that Faith had stayed behind. His mind just wasn't keeping up very well right now.

"She's working on the farm to prepare for the new arrivals," offered Miu.

The dark-eyed psychopath looked at Felix, then quickly away. She then went and sat on the far side of the couch with Edmund.

She's as tired as I am if not more, I bet. She had to go wrangle Zachary away from all his people and do it without too much in the way of commotion.

Probably has almost zero on her ability to keep herself from acting out right now.

Goldie came back into the room with what looked like Felix's clothes, including a number of shirt's he'd picked up as well as a pair of his jeans, and some slacks.

As well as a suit jacket he'd only just picked up from a goodwill store the other day. It'd mostly been in his size and looked new enough that it was hard to pass up.

With how hard they were trying to save money at the moment, he couldn't really justify going and buying high-end clothing. Especially for meetings that might happen, but also might not.

Sitting down next to him, she pulled out a small sewing kit. Examining the sleeve of the jacket, she then turned it inside out. With only a few tugs and a snip from her small, very sharp-looking scissors, she'd already begun pulling the sleeve off entirely.

Humming to herself, she started to sort out the kit in her lap as well as the jacket.

Looking up, she gave them all a somewhat embarrassed smile.

"I'm sorry, I'm afraid my work is never done. Housewife, Dragon, and Legionnaire. I wear many hats, so I'm forced to be economical with my time," said the Dragon, even as she rapidly pulled the sleeve away from the jacket. The gold in her horns tinkling prettily as she worked.

She didn't get it completely off, but up to a point. Looking at it, she seemed to be gauging something visually before she went back to her kit.

"Well… thank you for it, Goldie. You make my life significantly easier," Felix thanked her earnestly. "Just need to find more people to hire and get moving.

"Hopefully, Jay will find us some useful candidates. I'll need you for that meeting most definitely, Goldie."

Goldie only made an affirmative humming noise to that. She was stitching the sleeve back to the jacket now. Her head was bent close to her work.

"I can probably find some trustworthy people. If you trust me, that is," Edmund offered.

"I-yeah, alright. Bring them around sometime. Just give me a little warning so I can plan it," agreed Felix. "Make sure they know it'll likely have some danger involved as you yourself know."

"Yeah, sure. No worries. I know a few people that could probably get into this kind of life," Edmund said. "And thanks for getting me a trailer. It'll be nice to be on my own."

Felix wanted to groan. He'd forgotten about that.

Reaching up, he rubbed at his eyes and ended up partly leaning into Goldie. He wanted to push his hands right through his head until his eyeballs fell out.

Felix needed to go speak with Treston before he did anything else. The problem there was he'd need to ask the man to rent the current trailer they were all in for a longer period of time as well as another one for Edmund.

Treston had said he'd need paperwork at that point and Felix was unfortunately still without that. Likely Edmund was probably without that paperwork as well.

Money talks. Especially to someone who's going to end up paying off medical school.

Right?

Let's go talk to Treston, give him a solid bribe, get Edmund moving, and go from there.

Letting his hands drop, he sighed and nodded his head.

"Yeah. Need to get to that. Not a problem. I need to bribe him into letting me stay here longer without paperwork, anyway," confessed Felix.

He hadn't opened his eyes yet and was just leaning against Goldie, listening to the swish of fabric as she worked on his jacket. It was something he'd heard a number of times when she snuck into his room.

Late at night to work on his clothes so that they'd fit him better.

Without even realizing what was rapidly rushing toward him, Felix succumbed.

He fell asleep.

***

"Felix," came a quiet voice. "We need to head over to the leasing office. They open in about thirty minutes."

With a grunt, Felix shifted around. Then slowly opened his eyes.

He realized he was in bed now. At some point, someone had carried him over and put him in it.

Focusing on the person in front of him, he found it was Faith.

Except she wasn't supposed to be here. Last he remembered, she was at the farm until tonight.

"Faith?" he mumbled, levering himself up to a seated position in the bed.

Looking around, he saw that it looked like there was light outside and no one else was with them in the room. It didn't seem like he'd been asleep that long, but he felt rather well-rested.

"I… wh… how long was I asleep?" he asked, looking at the Dryad fully now. He'd noticed that her clothes had changed. On top of that, she looked as if she had taken a shower.

"Half a day or so. It's... well, you slept the rest of the day, the night, and now it's morning," replied Faith. "Now we need to go give Treston a bribe for the two trailers.

"Goldie filled me in about everything when she picked me up last night. I stayed with you over the evening and night.

"Goldie slept with us in the bed, but left this morning. She's with Miu and the Andreas at the swamp farm right now. Edmund left yesterday.

"Apparently, to go get those people he mentioned to you and the others."

Felix appreciated her giving him so much information and so quickly. He now had a decent idea of what'd happened after he'd fallen asleep.

Looking at the pretty Dryad, he wasn't sure what to say.

"You're looking better," Faith said quietly and then leaned forward. She gently took his face in her hands. Her fingertips were gentle and just a little cold.

They were quite firm as she peered into his face.

Her fingers moved slightly, shifting his head to one side slowly, then back the other way. Looking at him all the while.

"Look up for me?" she asked in a quiet whisper.

Felix did so, looking up toward her hairline.

"Down please," she continued, leaning in a bit closer to him.

Once more he did as she asked and looked down at her hips.

Her palm rested briefly on his cheek and she leaned in close to him. With her thumb, she gently peeled back his lower eyelid. Then she brought her other hand over and rested it against his brow.

Just as carefully, she pulled up at his upper eyelid.

Pulling up just a bit on him, she ran her fingertips along his jaw. Pushing and feeling at the sides before moving up to check behind his ears.

Her fingers trailing along the front of his throat and neck as if she were checking something there.

Pursing her lips, Faith took hold of his jaw again and leaned away from him.

"Say ah, Felix?" she requested, her voice soft and warm. It gave him a rather tingly feeling along his scalp.

Opening his mouth, he looked into her face and promptly did as requested.

"Ah."

Clicking her tongue, Faith peered into his mouth.

Then surprisingly, she leaned in close to him.

She sniffed as he exhaled, doing it twice before she leaned back a few inches. Next, she put a fingertip in his mouth, running it along the inside of his gums and under his tongue. Then she put that same finger into her mouth.

Felix didn't even react to it, he just stared at her with his mouth open.

She tapped his chin with two fingers, causing him to put his teeth back together.

"You need a little more salt. Some sugar, too," she whispered in a way that was almost more to herself than him. Then she blinked and looked rather surprised at herself. "I… huh. I went full Dryad and just treated you like my tree. Sorry, Felix. Grove-husband.

"It was almost an instinctual thing rather than a thought process. It just felt like I needed to check and see how you were doing. Like I used to do with my old tree."

"Oh, well, didn't really bother me. Was actually kinda nice. I do like attention, after all.

"And as far as I can tell, I'm getting a lot of benefits from being your tree," mused Felix with a smirk. "So it doesn't bother me for you to… err… take samples to test, I guess. That's what you did, isn't it?"

"I suppose it is," she admitted with a smile. Staring at him for a few more seconds, she then took his wrist and pressed her fingers to his pulse point. He also felt her push a tendril of what felt like her power into him. The tree that lived inside him responded eagerly. "I'm rather glad I took basic field medicine now in Legion. Rather helpful to combine it with my magic."

A few seconds passed before Faith released

him and stood up.

"Calories, sugar, salt. Nothing terrible and all easy to solve. A few of those 'hydrating' drinks that Andie likes would do it," remarked the Dryad with a grin. "We'll talk to Doctor Andrea later to make sure that's right. Anyway, we should get going."

Felix just nodded.

He'd felt rather calm talking to her. He knew that she would gladly listen to him regardless of what he said.

That maybe she wouldn't judge him.

He could talk to her and share what was on his mind freely. Rather than relying on someone to drudge it up because he was too stupid to rely on others.

"Faith, can I talk to you about... everything?" Felix asked suddenly. "I don't have anyone I can really talk to at the moment because I'm trying to be everything to everyone.

"You're a little different for some reason, though. I don't know how to describe it, or even really the right words for it, but I feel like I can talk to you. Even about the others."

Faith stared at him and blinked several times.

Then she gave him a grin and a waved a hand at him.

"First, thank you. I'm so flattered that you trust in me. Especially with something like that that I know you guard closely. I'm very thankful.

"As to our relationship, of course! I'm your

Dryad. You're my tree. We're bound to one another. As long as you live, I live. My tree lives in you and feeds off the nutrients in your blood. The carbon dioxide you create is simply taken by the tree.

"It's all going to… wait... Felix, have you looked in the mirror lately?" she asked suddenly. "You do realize you're getting younger, right? You don't think Vince always looked young, do you?

"It's regenerative. It's cumulative, too. You're going to live for quite a while. I just need to tie more Dryads to your grove.

"Now come on, we need to get moving. Time's wasting and the day is fleeing from us. As soon as we're done, you and I can have a nice chit-chat about everything you want."

The mirror…? I didn't, no. Not really.

I'll have to check on that.

"Check later. For now, we need to go," she said, as if realizing he wanted to look in the mirror. She pointed at clothes that sat at the foot of the bed. "Dress, I'll get you a cup of coffee and something sugary to eat on the walk. I've already put together a decent bribe for Treston."

Faith ran the backs of her fingernails along his cheek, then gave him a small kiss.

Leaving him there with a tingling that ran along his skin, she exited the bedroom.

Just in telling her he wanted to talk to her, he already felt better. Because he'd be able to unload everything onto her and let her talk him through it.

Getting up, he grabbed the clothes she'd

indicated.

Before he'd done anything at all with them, he heard Faith say something.

"Felix?" she called, a second later. "Better come see this."

With a frown, Felix exited the bedroom.

He could see in the living room the television was on and tuned in to the news. There was a shaky video being played on the screen.

Getting closer, he could see it looked like a building that had seen better days. There was fire licking out of one window and there was a battered garage door at the front of it.

Then it clicked.

Holy shit, that's where we were.

The video eased back and got a bunch of cops arriving. Multiple squad cars all pulled up and disgorged policemen.

Then the swat truck rolled onto the scene.

The video sped up just a bit. As if the news team was moving it along. Felix slowly got closer to the television screen.

"—when things really got strange," proclaimed a reporter. "Almost surreal, in fact. We haven't had confirmation that this isn't photoshopped, but the police agencies involved aren't denying the incident claims, either."

Goldie appeared around the corner and came toward the police.

Her dark black clothes and mask were a glaring contrast to her golden chain adorned horns, and the bright glow of her eyes behind her mask.

Andrea had told her to walk with a strut, and the video certainly caught that. Goldie was moving toward the police with a hip-rolling gait that looked more like it belonged in a music video.

Lifting her arm, she held it across in front of herself and looked absolutely villainous. A malevolent promise of violence heading toward the police and the cell-phone camera.

Everyone opened up on Goldie.

There was no mistaking that rounds were actively hitting her. Most of them simply fell to the ground after the impact, though some struck her horns and bounced off and away.

The swat truck darted forward and went straight for her only to be slapped to one side. Her walk continued in an undisturbed line.

Then the Andreas appeared. Their tails were quite visible as they literally plowed into the back lines of the police. The camera focused in on them as they punched, kicked, and battered their way through the ranks.

There was a brief flash on the screen as Miu dove off a light pole and into the middle of the mad battle that was ongoing.

The video paused and backed up very slowly until it froze on a single frame.

Miu in midfall.

Dressed in the same way Andrea and Goldie were, she looked like some sort of dark assassin. Her gloved hands were held wide as she aimed for the ground.

Then the video resumed and the battle continued.

Goldie had been very careful in the fight. It looked like she mostly just slapped people very gently and moved vehicles out of the way.

Miu was not so kind and looked to be seriously injuring people. Her fists and feet slammed officers about even as they tried to shoot at her.

The Andreas simply worked like a football team. Bowling people over, pummeling them once they were down, and moving on.

Clearly several of them fell—wounded or dead—only to be absorbed and shot right back out.

"Obviously, there's a lot going on here and we'll be breaking it down afterwards with several experts," offered the reporter. "Additionally, we found out that there were a few grievously injured officers we.

"This is only known to us because a second person showed up and took a video from a different angle. We were able to get footage of that as well."

There was a brief flicker of shadows and light as a cell phone was brought upward. The view focused in on the other side of the swat truck.

Two trees were rapidly growing out of the ground and the injured police officer was wrapped in the nature magic. Shortly after that, pairs of Andreas came over, dumping officers into the growing green field and then leaving them there.

The camera person focused in on one particular policeman who had a long gash across his face and a broken nose.

Even as the video continued, the cut began to close itself and the nose reformed. A squashed and broken thing was slowly straightening out to where it should be.

"Clearly, there's something to be said for this and we're going to be covering it all," said the reporter. "Next we—"

There was a slight delay as the video came back to the reporter behind the desk.

"Wait, what?" asked the reporter a second before the feed died.

Hm.

Well.

That's one way to enter the world, I suppose.

Though… it does give me a really good idea. A really good one.

No one can stop us right now. That won't always be the case.

Eventually, others will step up. Others that might be able to give us pause.

That means we should make hay while the sun shines, right? Act now while no one could possibly even prevent us from doing what we wanted.

Smiling to himself, Felix looked back at Faith.

"We're going to start the supervillain group," Felix said suddenly.

Rob anything and everything we want.

So long as we're fairly certain it's insured and those involved won't be harmed by our actions. There's no reason to not make this work for us.

Hell… we could even go for something like… an armory.

Or a mint.

Thinking over the situation, Felix let his mind wander. Circling the subject repeatedly.

If they did rob a bank or a mint, it was very likely they'd have problems getting rid of the cash afterward. He had no doubt that there was some type of system to organize the serial numbers of all the money they had on the property.

If not all, likely some. Certain marked denominations or bundles, more than likely.

Thinking about that, Felix realized he could probably identify anything that was earmarked for surveillance. A simple check to see if he could make it untraceable. There would likely be a cost for something that was marked or recorded, and none for one that wasn't.

Though, we can't really keep operating here in Alassippi as a villain organization. It'd put too much pressure on the locals.

This needs to go somewhere that the weight of such a blow could be shrugged off.

Somewhere like… well… I wonder where this world's gamblers go. That'd be the place to really sink our teeth into.

Goldie could rake it in all on her own for certain games. I could probably sort through any number of 'find the prize' type of scenarios.

Except all that needs paperwork. Paperwork and the ability to identify oneself.

Smiling to himself, Felix shook his head. That meant his original thought was still correct.

Smash and grab. Maybe start with something simple like… an armored car.

Just have Goldie pick it up and carry it off.

Seems like it's time to really create both sides of the coin.

Good and evil.

Snorting to himself, Felix suddenly needed to talk to his Dragon as well as look into the classified ads on the laptop they owned.

That or buy a new one just for himself.

The amount of dance videos Andie has downloaded has really clogged that one up.

"Treston, pawn shop for a laptop, breakfast at that coffee shop with Faith for a chat, put together a planning meeting, push forward," mused Felix aloud.

Chapter 27 - The Hardest Part -

Sitting down at the table, Felix put his coffee down in front of himself as well as the several pastries Faith had made him purchase. They looked like far too much to eat in one go to him, but she assured him he'd be able to eat them all just fine.

Faith sat down a second later, putting down her own coffee as well as a single pastry. She was wearing a sweater with a zipper, or a cardigan as she'd insisted, and most certainly was wearing a shoulder holster under it.

What Felix found amusing about that was that most people would stare at Faith's chest, yet never suspect there was a gun snuggled up close to her in that area.

"You know, it's kind of nice to have you to myself. It doesn't happen as often as I'd like," murmured Faith, unwrapping the plastic knife and fork she'd picked up. "So often one of the others is around. While I don't mind it that much, and I certainly don't care if they're there when we're intimate, it does make it hard to have a good talk with you."

Felix could only grin at that and nod his head.

They were living in a single-wide mobile home with five people. They were almost always on top of one another. There wasn't much room to spread out.

Before that had been a single tent which

ended up with much the same challenge as far as space went. He'd tried to put up boundaries and rules about privacy and intimacy with so many people at hand.

That'd lasted all of two hours.

"I get what you mean. Feels like we're all living in each other's pockets," agreed Felix. He carefully pulled apart the utensils he'd gotten for himself. "It's definitely closer than I've been… with anyone, really.

"Even before this, there was always a layer between me and everyone else. You should know, you were part of that layer for a while there."

"I was, I was. Now there is no layer and it's just us as a whole. Do you regret it? Being so much closer to everyone and everything?" she asked, glancing at him as she leaned forward and took a sip from her cup.

Felix blinked and honestly considered the question.

In that moment, he realized that the question itself was much more than it seemed. Deeper and uglier than the surface of the inquiry.

"I honestly don't know," he muttered with a shake of his head. Picking up his cup, he took a sip to stall for a few seconds. Faith merely smiled at him and began to delicately pick at her pastry. Her eyes moved to anyone who came near them and clearly weighed out if they might be an issue.

Setting his cup back down, Felix realized that his answer wasn't concise. It didn't feel solidified or structured.

More akin to a liquid sloshing around that needed a lot of time to settle.

"I wouldn't worry too much about saying yes or no, Felix. This is more about talking about how you feel," offered Faith. "How you feel can easily change even mid-sentence. Sometimes even as you talk about it.

"I'm not looking for a perfect answer, either. Just how you're feeling. What you think about it in this moment."

Rather than think about what she said, Felix tried to simply do that. He forced his tongue to move and put words to the thoughts he was having.

"I don't know. Some days, I feel like I'm unable to act as I used to. Where I could make a decision, set it down, and move to the next," he began. "Now I have to pick it right back up and almost redo it sometimes because someone needs something from me.

"It could be money, resources, or just my time, but suddenly I can't make a clean choice and be done with it. I have to rebalance it and redo it.

"There's a lot more middle-management type of work going into this and less CEO level things. I'm trying to cope with it and keep moving. Keep on track.

"But I find it getting harder and harder to push forward. I have to spend ever more time thinking and talking than doing."

The words sounded like a bitter child's

complain to his ears. The whining of someone with too much who only wanted more.

"I mean, that's all true," murmured Faith with a slow nod after swallowing what she'd been chewing on. "Everything you said really is happening. It's all correct.

"As an example, I asked for the farm. You had originally planned on it just being a place to dump bodies as a one-off and be done with it. Never worrying about revealing the location to Stephen and considering it just a temporary thing.

"Now, you have to reconsider it. Work out a long-term defense for it, build up a plan to legally acquire it. Then worry about how to get to and from it without creating a security gap that someone could use against us.

"It's exactly what you were talking about and real. A legitimate complaint, Felix."

Felix had taken a rather large bite from one of his breakfast pastries as she spoke. His chewing slowed as he listened to her though.

Especially when she used herself as an example. One that rang very true for what he'd been talking about.

"Previously, you really were at CEO-level decision making. Set and forget," continued Faith with a laugh. "You had everyone around you to squish the details and make it happen.

"Now, we're just a small ma-and-pa business. A start-up with resources coming in, but few tools to really utilize them. That'll get better in time, obviously, but for the moment, it's an undeniable truth.

"Now... what about us as a relationship? Last time, you were fairly circumspect with everyone in the build-up phase. This time you don't really have a choice. We've forced it on you.

"And while you start thinking about that, how are you balancing your right and wrong in your head? Obviously, none of us are Kit or Eva and we don't care about anyone that isn't Legion. So that somewhat falls on you for your own needs."

Unable to help it, Felix felt his entire face turn down in a frown. Thinking hard about what she'd just asked him.

Then he realized he was about to do the same thing as earlier.

Hit the end of his thought process, realize he didn't have a concrete answer, and shrug his shoulders. As she'd already said, that wasn't the point of this.

"I'm enjoying it. I mean, who doesn't like sex? Sex is amazing. Especially with such beautiful, fantastic women," he said, trying to force the thoughts out as they came. "The relationships are... it's... I didn't have them the first time around. As you said.

"It's new for me. I'm trying to give you all attention and provide care for you. It's especially hard to do so for a very aggressive beast who wants to nest and who can read my thoughts."

"For what it's worth, she's very happy. We

talk often," confided Faith. "She tries not to read all your thoughts all the time. Especially when it's casual or non-essential.

"As to her need to nest... the gold helped alleviate some of that. She'll be fine for a while. Get her those gold rings you threw at her mentally and you'll buy yourself a year or three. Gold does wondrous things for Dragons.

"For Miu and Andrea, you're doing equally wonderful. They're better than they've ever been previously. You're doing a great job of building them up in a stable way without breaking them down."

Smirking, Felix nodded his head and swallowed. He'd already polished off an entire pastry just listening to her. Picking up his coffee, he took a drink and set it down.

"Yes, I don't think I have the Machiavellian tendencies needed to psychologically break someone down then rebuild them," admitted Felix. "I also don't exactly have the best name for something like that either. Need a title. A moniker. Like being a count."

"I... yes. A name like Alexander would fit," Faith conceded. "As to me, before you ask, I'm quite happy. I have a couple Dryads coming today who I need to meet up with and get squared away, but that's my only concern.

"I have a tree, a Grove-husband, and I have so many... so, so many babies I can choose from. I've already caught at least thirty or so pregnancies from you. I spend a couple hours here or there just sorting through them all. I never realized how fun it could be just to pick through my children.

"Oh, and speaking of the Dryads, they'll… they'll need to plant their trees in you as well. Immediately. It'll give you an increase in power and regeneration."

He'd wanted to talk to her immediately about this pregnancy thing, but his mind jumped tracks quickly. Having more trees put in him and getting power from it sounded perfectly fine to him.

The regenerative power of Faith's tree alone had been rather new. Adding two more to that would be splendid.

"Now… what else is going on in that head of yours? Talk to me. I'm your Dryad-wife. Your Grove-mistress. I'll be with you until the end, you know. Can't hide from me," purred Faith with a smile for him. She picked up the last of her pastry and popped into her mouth and washed it down with a drink.

He was still mildly surprised that she had a diet that was so much like his own. She seemed very "unDryad" like in that.

"I… that is…" Felix felt his words start to dry up and then forced himself. "I'm really regretting that I won't see my kids with Andie as they grow up. They're pregnant and… I'm not there. I won't see them through so many firsts.

"Eva is going to grow up while I'm gone and by the time we get back… who the hell knows, she might even be married. She might meet someone and then what? What do I do then?"

"You do exactly what you're likely already planning to do. Do your best to make up for lost time, apologize to them sincerely, then… move on," Faith answered simply with a shrug of her shoulders. "Because let's be honest, everyone is well aware of the fact that we need to get Kit and Lily back. It's not even a question.

"The Originator gave you an opportunity to do so. A really good one. One that would let you add to Legion by building a new one. A new cohort.

"We'll literally have three sources to draw from after this. Legion Prime, Yosemite, and this world. That's an amazing pool to draw from. We were handed a perfect chance and you're taking it. They'll be sad, angry even, but likely won't fault you for it. I imagine the happiness of your return will outweigh the anger that you left very quickly."

Nodding his head, Felix knew that her words matched his own thoughts. That'd been his plan exactly as she'd said.

"Oh, and before you really get worried about it, I'm keeping everyone as they are. No pregnancies are allowed to continue. We really don't need babies running around at the moment," Faith told him almost as an afterthought. "That'd just be terrible for us all right now. Aren't you glad you brought me along, now?"

Blinking, Felix only now realized that he'd been relying on them to be taking birth control. Just as they had been in the previous world.

Except none of them would be able to get a prescription yet. They wouldn't be in the systems and would need to be entered. That'd take paperwork that they didn't have.

Ah… yeah.

"Very glad, Faith. Though not because you're a living form of birth control," he said and then reached his hand out across the table to her. She laid her own hand within his and squeezed it. "When the world came to a literal end, you and Goldie were the primary pillars of support for me.

"It was easy to pick you, Goldie, Andrea, and Miu. You're all people who've been through the worst with me."

Faith wrinkled her nose, grinned, and squeezed his hand tightly. Then she patted it, picked up her cup again and leaned back in her seat.

Her eyes shifted to a group of people heading their way. She didn't look away from them until they passed.

Ever my bodyguard… I'm not sure what god I pleased to have you put in my path, Faith, but I'm thankful for it.

"Now, what else is on your mind, my Grove-husband? Anything at all? I'm willing to listen to it, whatever it might be.

"Otherwise, we need to head off to the swamp farm. My new Dryads will be there in an hour or so. They're both coming in from the south. They've had a long walk and they're quite weak from abandoning their trees," Faith stated. "Then we can have them plant their tree in you and go from there. You said you wanted to have a planning meeting and also recruiting."

With a grunt, Felix nodded at that. He'd been wolfishly eating, pushing down two pastries in almost no time flat. Picking up his coffee cup, he drained it of its remains and set it down with a soft clatter.

"I'm ready, yeah. Thank you for talking with me. I don't really have anything else to share," Felix promised with a smile. He felt considerably relieved after talking to her. "Though I'm a little nervous about this planting. I don't have to immediately… err… till their soil, do I?

"I'm kind of full up on relationships at the moment. I'm not looking for more. I'd really like to just… stick with what I've got."

"Ah… you'll have to at least once in the next seven days or so. Then again here and there as time goes on. Not very often. It can probably be stretched out for months at a time without any ill-effects.

"If you didn't want a relationship with them beyond just being their Grove that'd be perfectly fine, too. I know they'd be disappointed, but they'd accept it. I warned them in advance you already had some pretty heavy relationship commitments."

"Great, that'll be… that's great," Felix murmured with relief. He didn't want Kit and Lily to come back to him neck deep in women.

If he could keep it down to those who were with him, they'd probably be accepting of the situation.

"Do I have time to scan a few listings in the classifieds, see if there's any contractors I can hire?" asked Felix indicating the laptop bag at his shoulder. They'd picked it up at the pawn shop after bribing Treston.

Thankfully, the med student had been more than happy to take ten thousand dollars to look the other way for three months.

Faith tilted her head to one side, toward a tree that was rather close to them actually and paused. Her eyes slowly floated up to a space above Felix.

She was clearly communicating with the tree and not really seeing anything.

"Maybe thirty minutes," she said, her eyes snapping back to him. She gave him a wide, almost predatory, smile. "We have to be there when they arrive though. They're very tired, Felix. Very tired.

"They'll feel better the second their seeds are planted in you. Even more so once you… plant your seeds in them. As their Grove-mistress, I'll be sure to fight for their rights with you. Don't hate me down the road for badgering you to give them time.

"You'd probably tell me it's my job as their boss to do so, I imagine. Unless I miss my guess, which I don't think I have."

Unable to help himself, Felix grinned and nodded his head.

She was right.

Not wanting to waste another second, he pulled the bag into his lap. He was going to hunt for a number of positions.

Two web developers for web pages. He needed one for each side of the coin he'd own.

One website for the League of Villains.

A second website for the Guild of Heroes.

With the birth of the Legion super-villain group, there'd be people banging the drums of war. Sounding the trumpets and trying to gather people together to fix a "big problem".

They were right, of course, but Felix needed to be the person to bang that drum. To call everyone in to fight the bad guys.

While also being the very same bad guys.

In addition to the web developers, he'd have to hire a number of people to write articles. Articles in favor and against what'd happened with the police.

Those who would argue that the only ones harmed were criminals, but not anyone who didn't deserved it. That they were clearly vigilantes and working to better the world.

On the other side, he'd have them labeled as villains the likes of which one could only see in comic books. That there would need to be a task force, a group, to combat such terrifying evil.

And if I'm both the good guys, and the bad guys, then I control it all.

All while never putting myself into a leadership position.

Never a role that could be traced back to me. I just need to make sure that I put people in charge that can lead and do what I want.

Without ever telling them what I want.

Smiling to himself, Felix knew that this was the start of it all. It was happening faster than he'd anticipated but he was his own catalyst this time.

There was no reason not to act on this. The timing was almost perfect given the circumstances.

Legion will run along both sides of the fight. Providing for both and guiding them without ever being in charge.

All while slowly turning the whole world to my point of view.

Then… when it's all said and done… I put a puppet on a throne of my choosing. Of my design.

Of my wishes.

With that done, I can dominate and clear the way.

Whatever Runner needs to happen, will happen. Then… then I can go get Kit and Lily.

Chapter 28 - Soiled -

Pulling up to the swamp farm in F-Two, Felix finally looked up from the laptop. He'd spent most of the time traveling here writing up job descriptions of what he needed.

While the classified ads, and searching the internet directly for people, had provided some results, he didn't want to rely on only that. He would also need people who weren't completely self-established or knew how to market themselves.

People who were just trying to get by and would hunt for job advertisements.

Thankfully, it looks like they all take credit cards to pay for the listings. Getting everything running would be nearly impossible without the prepaid cards.

Closing the laptop, he tossed it up onto the dash, opened the door, and got out.

Standing directly in front of him were two women. Their skin had a clear green tone to it though darker in complexion than he expected.

Faith's had disappeared after she'd planted her tree in him, now that he thought about it.

One had hazel-colored eyes that shimmered brown one moment, then red the next. As if they couldn't decide which way to go. Her long, brown hair looked windblown and hung in a single braid behind her back.

The outfit she was wearing looked like everyday clothes he'd seen all over. Though she did fill it out in a way that was very similar to Faith.

There was an undeniable beauty to the woman.

At her side was a woman who looked very similar with an equal amount of undeniable attractiveness, though her eyes were deep, dark brown. Except with the light hitting her as it was, they looked almost dark red instead.

Her hair was a much lighter color, trending toward light brown. Her skin tone was a few shades lighter than her companion as well.

Though her physical features were very similar to the other two Dryads.

Her clothes looked a bit more intact than the other, and also of a slightly higher quality.

They both looked incredibly tired and worn out. Like they were dead on their feet, in fact.

"Ah! We made it right on time. They just got here seconds ago, Felix. Alma, Carlota, I'm so glad you two made it here safely," Faith gushed as she slammed the truck door closed and came around quickly. "Felix, these are your new Dryads, Alma and Carlota. Ladies, this is your Grove."

Faith came to a stop next to Felix and then began pulling his shirt off. She didn't wait for him to even get a word in edgewise.

He remembered in that instant that she'd already told him she'd need to have the two new girls plant their trees in him. That meant cutting open his chest again, he imagined.

Faith, of course, had bright-green, glowing eyes now.

Surprisingly, the other two Dryads had eyes

that glowed red in color. A vibrant and rich red.

All three of the Dryads were staring at the hair-thin scar along his ribs from the incision mark.

Faith lifted a fingernail and drew it along the exact same scar. The same point where she'd put her seed into him.

Watching, Felix was surprised to see his skin part so easily right at that point. He didn't even feel it, in fact.

A single drop of blood leaked down at the corner and then traveled down him for a few inches. It didn't get far and seemed to have already run out of "juice" as it were.

Looking up at the two Dryads, he saw they both had a glowing seed pod in their hands. Ones that looked somewhat dried out and a bit worn.

Not hesitating, and before Felix could actually react, they both pushed their pods into the wound. As the two seeds vanished into his body, he felt rather horrified but also fascinated.

Faith ran her fingers over the incision and the skin knit itself together. It closed together cleanly, without a new scar or any scabbing.

Faith brushed her fingers across the bloody trail and then held it up to her mouth. She licked at it daintily while using her other hand to rub the rest of the blood into his skin.

"Mm, those pastries helped," she said. "Still need more salt. Or something like it. We'll need to get you another one of those gator drinks. That seemed to help quite a bit."

Faith let her hand fall and then pulled Felix's shirt down.

Both she and Felix looked turned to the other two Dryads to find they already looked improved. The dull, listless look in their eyes was gone.

They looked more like sleepers, slowly waking from a heavy dream. Blinking and looking around, as if a bit more aware of what they saw.

Though that lasted only for a few seconds.

Both women's very brightly glowing eyes returned to Felix and stayed there.

"I'm so… so pleased to be here, Grove-husband," said the one on the left.

"To have a Grove, as well as a place of safety," the right murmured.

"Yes, well, welcome to the Legion," Felix said with a tight smile. He wasn't sure who was who.

Rather than worry over it, he called up their character sheets instead. It'd be an easier way to see into them.

He started with the hazel eyed one on the left.

Name: Alma Campbell	**Race**: Nature Sprit (Dryad)-Critically Endangered
Alias: Maiden of the Grove	**Power:** None
Physical Status: Sickly, Infertile(Recovering)	**Mental Status:** Relieved, gratified, satisfied
Positive Statuses: None	**Negative Statuses**: Polluted(Recovering)

Might:	15	Add +1? (150)
Finesse:	19	Add +1? (190) +1 Agility Type
Endurance:	54	Add +1? (540)
Competency:	21	Add +1? (210)
Intellect:	65	Add +1? (650)
Perception:	84	Add +1? (840)
Luck:	26	Add +1? (260)

Much weaker than Faith. Only her perception is better. Definitely useful though. She's far better than a normal Human. Decent Intellect.

We can work at improving her levels accordingly.

That and I'm sure she'll grow naturally with a leader like Faith.

Concerning that she took on my last name. I wonder if that'll change my points. If maybe I'll get more now.

Is it because she's technically married to me since I'm her Grove?

Things to consider.

Turning his eyes to the other, he noted she was actually an inch or two taller than the other one.

Name: Carlota Campbell	**Race**: Nature Sprit (Dryad)- Critically Endangered
Alias: Maiden of the Grove	**Power:** None
Physical Status: Worn-out	**Mental Status:** Relieved, aroused, horny, randy

Positive Statuses: None		Negative Statuses: None
Might:	38	Add +1? (380)
Finesse:	41	Add +1? (410)
Endurance:	91	Add +1? (970)
Competency:	13	Add +1? (130)
Intellect:	15	Add +1? (150)
Perception:	16	Add +1? (160)
Luck:	09	Add +1? (90) +1 Luck Type

Holy fuck, her stats are higher than Faith's on the physical side. How does one even have ninety-one endurance? That's almost as high as Goldie's, isn't it?

Quite a bit less on the mental side.

Seems like she took one of each and is trying to build out something. How curious.

Also… why are there three different ways to say she's excited.

"Alma," Felix said, dipping his head to the left. Then he looked to the right. "Carlota. I'm glad to have you both. Thank you for coming, my Maidens of the Grove. I welcome you formally and am glad to have you here.

"Is there anything you need immediately? Anything that you must have taken care of? Other than… other than tilling your soil.

"That'll have to wait. We have a meeting to attend to that you're welcome to join in on. Though… I wouldn't find it odd if you wanted to lay down in the field and doze in the sun."

Felix lifted a hand and pointed out toward the back of the farm. He'd seen Faith sleeping in one particular area over there repeatedly.

Both Dryads had perked up at the title he called them by. Their eyes slowly grew in intensity as they gazed at him.

Although Carlota did look quite downcast when Felix said he couldn't take care of their physical needs. Alma seemed somewhat disappointed, but also quite eager at the idea of taking a nap.

Both nodded their heads wearily.

Even their hair looked like it weighed far more than they wanted to carry at the moment. They were simply drained.

Hm. I charged up Faith. Why not them?

This'll be a good test.

Reaching out, Felix laid his hands on their shoulders.

Then he tried to force power into them. He wanted them to be full of energy, and not polluted or worn down.

"Felix, I—"

When the message popup came to him, it said he only needed to spend six points. To which he agreed to immediately. That was a minuscule price.

Ignoring Faith, Felix was eager to see what would happen.

There was a thump in his chest, followed by a very warm, tingly feeling that spread throughout him. A heat that made him feel quite nice, if he was being honest.

It felt a lot like the trees were intertwining themselves quickly and forming together. One helping the other two to stabilize and how to fit correctly inside him.

Alma groaned and her hands shot down to her lower stomach. Both of them pushed against her clothes in obvious discomfort. Or more accurately, right above her pubic mound.

Carlota let out a low moan and reached up with both hands to grab Felix's wrist where it rested on her shoulder. Both Dryad's eyes were shining as brightly as Faith's had when he'd restored her.

"There we are," Felix murmured with a smile. "That should have fixed you both right up. And… uh… and… err…"

Felix's voice trailed off as Carlota began to kiss and nuzzle his hand, letting out little soft whimpers all the while.

Alma was on her knees now. Both of her hands pushed up between her legs and groaning in what sounded like pain.

Unsure and thinking maybe he'd done something wrong, Felix looked to Faith.

"They weren't-you just forced their trees to mature in you," she answered the unasked question quietly. "Alma… Alma had some issues in the past. You just kind of... well, did really, forcibly correct it for her. If she was as healthy as Carlota was, she'd be reacting the same way as she is right now.

"I told you they'd need their soil tilled in a week, right? Well, guess what? Your night's going to be busy tonight or tomorrow whether you like it or not, now. Way to go."

Faith slapped him on the ass and then gathered up Alma and Carlota, leading them toward the back of the ruined farmhouse.

Oh.

Huh.

Whatever. It'll be fine. Andrea and Goldie will be leaving tonight. Miu and you will be busy moving resources.

I can handle Carlota and Alma. It shouldn't be—

Two waves of extreme sexual energy pounded through him. They came from Carlota and Alma respectively. Both Dryads were eyeing him hotly with eyes like lasers as Faith escorted them away.

Each was more than powerful enough to get his body to respond without him wanting it to.

Ah… yes.

Hubris, hello, my old friend. How are you?

I'm great, great. Real busy lately. Punishing you constantly. How're you?

Oh, I'm good. Good. Fantastic, even. Just, you know, making more work for myself. Gotta stay busy.

Sure, sure, I getcha. Yep.

Growling at his own stupidity, Felix began following after the Dryads.

When they reached the back, Felix found Andrea, Miu, and Goldie all waiting for him. They were actively gathered around a laptop and watching what looked a lot like the footage of their escapade.

The area had a table, multiple chairs, area heaters, and several coolers positioned around them. He even noted that the camping gear had been unpacked and set up accordingly.

Including the grill-top and Andrea's cooking station.

"Feeeeeeeelix!" shouted Andrea excitedly. He could tell she had all her Others with her as well.

"Hello, Andie dear. Hello Second, Third, Four, Five, Six, Seven, Eight, Nine, and even Ten. How are you all?" he asked, making sure to address the Others as well.

There was a strange moment of panic on Andrea Prime's face and her eyes nearly went in different directions as the smile froze on her face. Then she did a small shake of her head and practically ran over to him.

Leaping at the last second, she slammed into him and wrapped her legs around his middle. She kissed him and locked her arms around his neck.

Walking forward—as he'd expected this reaction—he kissed her back and carried her over to the table.

Breaking the kiss with a gasp, Andrea stared at him from a few inches away.

"You shouldn't call to all of us like that. It's hard for us when we're trying to not crowd everyone," whined Andrea, wriggling around against him.

"It's fine. I'll give you all a hug and a kiss individually after the meeting. All my Elex girls. Okay?" he said, grinning at Andrea. "Each and every one of you. And no cheating this time. I know a few of you lined up twice when you were still part of the other Andrea."

She was the one person he would willingly go out of his way to spoil. Even if it cost him things to do so.

Andrea suddenly had a grin on her face, her tongue sticking out to the side as she looked at him. She looked very guilty.

Mostly because Prime had been one who would do exactly what he'd just accused them of.

Setting her down on the table, Felix put his hands on her shoulders and looked at the others. He smiled at them and dipped his head.

"Good afternoon, my Miu, my Goldie," Felix said possessively. He wanted to hit that note a little hard right now, knowing how well both of them responded to it. "It's a pleasure to see you.

"I'm glad everyone's here because I wanted to tell you what our next objective is. Right now, at this moment in time, we can push forward with one side of our agenda.

"Our League of Villains route can be rapidly sped up. To the point that no one can even deny that there are supervillains out there and that the world needs to prepare. We'll be able to create a fabulous fiction out of all of it and turn the whole thing into a spectacle.

"Something for the general public to latch onto, put their viewpoints onto, their morality, and spin it all into a focal point. One that everyone will be glued to, a part of, and forced to participate in."

Felix had absolute belief in his own plan. Convinced that it would absolutely succeed.

It'd be complicated, difficult, and somewhat awful in more than one way.

But it could and would work.

"Oh, I see. I like it," Goldie said with a growl in her voice. "I like it a lot. I wouldn't mind doing any of that."

Andrea frowned, turned, leaned over and then grabbed Goldie by a horn. She pulled on it a little bit and actually caused the Dragon to bend her head a bit.

"Hey, how about you tell us what he's doing since we can't read his mind," demanded Andrea.

"It's simple," Felix interjected. "You and Goldie are going to be a founding duo for the League of Villains. I want you two to head somewhere that there's a lot of money, and start robbing them of it.

"Preferably a location that has gambling, so you can really get things going. I was thinking that if this place still has armored vehicles making bank drops than it'd be incredibly easy for Goldie.

"They have no idea that someone could just swoop down and pick something like that up and carry it off. If you figured out armored bank courier routes, you could snatch up quite a few of them in a day or two and work your way across the country.

"We'll just pile up all the cash and start laundering it out through cash services and things on the back end. Or through other people. Like David and Zach."

Andrea was watching him now. She looked rather interested in the idea and excited.

"That sounds like fun," muttered Miu. "What… what do Faith and I get to do? You said duo. So I assume she and I would be doing something else."

"The opposite end of the spectrum, of course. Superheroes. You'll need to start curbing negative actions in the public and doing things to bring a positive and glowing light to your deeds.

"I'd suggest taking on things you can easily handle with your abilities Miu, or Faith's magic. I can always supercharge her and send her off.

"Natural disasters, disaster relief and rescue, things like that.

"Eventually, we'll need to have your duo go up against Goldie and Andrea. We'll have it be a draw, but the encounter will need to happen.

"While all this is going on, I'm going to have some out-of-country websites made, as well as some resources put into place. We need to start up the idea of both the Villains' League and Heroes' Guild long before they're needed. That way, we control them.

"Have puff pieces put together, blistering reviews, scathing editorial attacks, all the normal things you'd expect. Just directed at one another while being the puppet master behind both.

"We'll end up tying the government's hands together long before they even know it. When they start to even have a clue, when they just begin to suspect it could be far more than they think, it'll already be too late."

Everyone was looking at him. They didn't seem surprised or worried.

A sudden thought popped into his head.

Looking at Alma and Carlota, he pointed at them.

"Do you both have your identity paperwork? Are you legal citizens here?" he asked, feeling excited.

"I... yes?" answered Alma. She looked like she was feeling better but still wasn't feeling well.

"Uh-huh," Carlota said in a low tone.

Perfect!

I can use them to create shell corporations. I can get this whole thing up and moving quickly. They can just pay cash for everything and anything. A bunch of shell corporations to get things created and progressing.

Cash for everything and keep it rolling.

I'll send Andrea and Goldie to go on a spree. Miu and Faith will go start playing happy helpers when they get a chance.

I'll stay here and work from the laptop through Alma and Carlota.

Yes, this'll work wonderfully.

Just to make sure, though, another question or two.

"Did you both have jobs? Paid taxes? Did all the things a normal citizen would do?" he inquired further.

"I worked in customer service," Carlota said, a slightly concerned look on her pretty face. "I was just a shift-lead though. I did everything as a normal Human would though, yeah."

"Sales," Alma said with a lovely smirk. "Watches. It was always fun to try to upsell men who had too much disposable income. A couple comments, a smile, a little push, and it was done. I'd get a bigger commission.

"But yes. I was living as a Human as well. There was no reason to try to not to. The uh… those who live in the groves don't… do as well, I think."

Hm. How curious.

I wonder if Faith was targeting Dryads who had integrated into society better than others. It wouldn't be surprising, I suppose.

"Can I use you two? I need you," Felix asked, looking at the two Dryads.

"I really wish you would use me," Carlota replied, leaning toward him. She did it in such a way that forced his eyes down to her chest. Her eyes flamed with a bright red glow within a second. "With Alma or just by myself, I don't care. Use me."

"That's not what I meant and you know it," Felix replied quickly with a dismissive wave of his hand. "We're going to go start buying things.

You're going to be doorways.

"First… lawyers. Lots of lawyers. Lawyers make everyone unhappy. Even me. But you can't run an illegal organization without them."

Chapter 29 - Trashy -

Felix let out a soft sigh and shifted around in the truck seat. Right now, Alma and Carlota were attempting to carry out a goal he'd given them.

All he could do was sit here and wait.

Contemplate all the ways he'd failed in the past and how he was working to fix them. Often to the point that he worried he couldn't actually catch up.

"You're getting stuck in your own head, Grove-husband," warned Faith from the passenger seat. "Stop. Talk to me instead. If I'm going to be your worry rock, you should probably hurry up and start... fingering me?"

Letting out a short laugh at that, Felix looked over at Faith now. She was grinning at him with raised eyebrows.

"You use a thumb on a worry rock, but... I appreciate the wordplay," he replied with a smile of his own. Looking back out the front windshield, he wasn't sure how to feel.

Right now, everyone was more or less engaged in work. Going about one task or another to keep things moving in the right direction.

Miu and Andrea Prime were working at sorting through all the money they'd made so far from their dealings with Zach and David. Going through it all, getting a firm count, and getting it ready for him.

He'd need to go through it all and make sure

there wasn't anything marked or tagged for tracking. If it was, he'd need to see if he could spend some points to have it cleared.

If he couldn't, then that money would need to be handed off in exchanges that would deflect interest away from him and Legion. His best idea for that so far was charitable or political donations.

Goldie and the Andrea's were robbing their way across the country. From what he'd heard from them on the disposable phones, Goldie was already twelve or so armored cars deep.

She would swoop in and pick them up, carry them off, then deposit them somewhere for Andrea to handle. The security guards that they captured were all being detained at the moment but would be released in one big group.

Apparently, they were planning on giving up on the strategy in the next day or so and switching to another one. One that apparently included a large number of casinos that had very thick vault doors.

They were a little nervous that the government would start having fighter jets on standby just to intercept Goldie as she flew off with an armored car.

It wasn't as if she was faster than a jet plane, after all. They'd be able to catch up to her fairly quickly.

Instead, they'll just brute force it on the ground.

She's just going to punch her way into a vault, then fly away to an area nearby with Andrea in her mouth.

Dodge any type of aerial response completely.

Ha. If ever there was a time to be a super-villain, it's when there aren't any heroes.

Felix and the Dryads were trying to get rolling now that they had some legal identities to work with. Carlota and Alma were the jumping point for a number of shell corporations being made.

Companies within companies within companies. Many of them anonymous listings with fraudulent people at the top who had no idea what was going on. Their names and information were little more than figments of the imagination.

It wouldn't hold up if someone really started to dig into things, but for now, as a starting point, it'd work. He'd have to go through and redo everything with real names, actual patsies, and dead-ends that went nowhere.

"I'm fine," Felix murmured after a few seconds. He hadn't meant to leave Faith hanging. "Just… worried. Always worried. Terrified. What do I do if this all fails?

"Nervous. The normal existential dread that I'm sure everyone feels. Just not able to shake it, really."

"That's fair. And yes, I imagine most everyone feels it in some way or another. Some of us more acutely than others," Faith agreed. "An example of that is Carlota and Alma. They've been watching their very world die. Their belief in this world's earth spirit is fatally weakened. Crushed down by those in power and forced to bend too far past a point that it could return to."

"Oh," Felix stated in a flat tone. A question he'd wanted to ask had likely just been answered. "That's why their eyes go red, instead of green, isn't it?

"Your belief in nature and the earth spirit isn't as weak as theirs. Your eyes have remained green and you seem far stronger than them. They... err... how do I put it kindly..."

Felix's words trailed off as he considered how to describe what he felt from Alma and Carlota. They were certainly the same thing as Faith, but also felt incredibly different.

"I'm a wolf, whereas they're starved, scrawny, beaten dogs?" Faith supplied. "Scurrying away from someone who even looks at them wrong?"

With a wince, Felix nodded his head. That was a fairly accurate way to phrase it.

"If there had been Dryads in your home world, they would have been the same as these or worse. Unfortunately, it seems that inhabitants of worlds with a higher tech level eventually turn against their own home," speculated Faith. "Or at least, at this stage of technology. But yes, they're very different than I. However, you'll notice they're already looking considerably healthier.

"All it took was planting their seed in you and then you planting your seed in them a few times."

Grimacing, Felix had been doing his best not to think about his evenings as of late. It'd been a very awkward experience with the three Dryads over the last several days.

As if summoned by his thoughts, Alma and Carlota were heading back their way. They looked somewhat satisfied, so he was hopeful they'd been successful.

Getting out of the truck, he stuck his hands in his pockets and hunched forward a bit. The weather was getting colder and colder.

Pretty soon, they'd have to stay in the trailer most of the time or have the swamp farm truly fixed up. They couldn't remain outside in the growing cold.

"All done?" he asked, walking toward the two women.

Much as Faith had already pointed out, both Dryads looked better since he'd met them. The aura around them was much more akin to Faith's.

It was a strong, earthy, natural presence. One with the promise of nature's greatest gift—sex and the birth of the next generation—running throughout it. Life existed in a way that would always require another generation.

While some individuals might not reproduce, a species must to survive. Dryads were part of that reproductive promise, it seemed.

"Done," Alma said and raised the manila envelope she'd been holding close to her side. "Got him to sign everything. The deed is here, too. He's packing up right now and should be gone in five minutes.

"Never expected this to be a poultry farm. It looks really different than the farm on the swamp. Then again I'd never seen one or the other before. I grew up in a city nothing like this."

Carlota nodded her head, as if that was exactly what she'd wanted to say.

"We already own the land, though. He won't be coming back," promised the Ironwood Dryad, picking up where Alma stopped. Much of her strength and durability came from the fact that she was a rather rare type of Dryad. "He said he's getting his dog and moving to Florida."

Carlota shrugged at that and gave Felix a smirk. She seemed far more straightforward and brazen compared to Alma.

"If he wants to head over to god's waiting room, more power to him. He can wait to check out with the rest of the filthy apes."

Alma frowned and then turned a sour look on the other Dryad.

"You practically jumped into a filthy ape's bed," Faith countered with an amused chuckle. "You sounded quite happy about it as well? Begging for more in fact?"

Carlota blanched and looked at Felix. Her eyes slightly widened as she clearly realized that her words did include him.

"I didn't mean it, Grove-husband! I'm… you're so different and—"

"Humanity is filthy," Felix said dismissively and cutting her off. "Anyway. We're good? It's all done? We own it as of this moment?"

"Yes," agreed Alma, offering the paperwork to him. "As you're my Grove-husband, this is also your property. I recognize you as so by the rights inherent to this land, long before a Human government tried to claim sovereignty."

Huh. I wonder if I can use that to my advantage.

In fact, could I technically find out if there were any natives to this land before the current government? Would they be considered the original and valid government?

Or is there a passing of ownership after a certain number of years?

At what point does an upstart government become the ruling government? Can a warlord eventually become recognized as the rightful government?

Ah… so many questions. I'll have to poke at it when I get the chance.

Taking the envelope, Felix glanced at it, then just held it back out to Alma.

"Hang onto it. You and Carlota are going to be the owners for a while until I get my own paperwork," he advised her. "Until then, all of this rolls up to you two. When I finally do get my official identity, I'll remake Legion.

"Now… let's go see if I can't revolutionize the world. Because I bet I can disguise my superpower in a fun way."

Glancing at the land nearby, Felix tried to call

up who owned it. He wanted to modify it by removing some trash off the land, which meant he'd need permission.

Or so he made his intent and desire known to be.

His power responded to intent more than it did his thoughts.

Type: Land (Agriculture Zoned)	**Condition**: Indefinite Fallow
Owner: Alma and Felix Campbell	**Cleaning**: Yield 197 points

"Perfect, we own it," he murmured, looking to Alma. "Alma Campbell, would you grant me majority ownership of our land?"

"I give you everything, Grove-husband," Alma said immediately. There was an intensity in her words that he'd only seen from her in one situation.

When they shared a bed.

"Anything I have is yours," added Carlota, throwing her arms out to her sides. "Even me. I'm all yours."

"Yes, that, too," Alma agreed. "I'm yours."

Felix just shook his head with a grin. He found Dryads to be ride or die partners.

They're really perfect for Legion.

"I accept, of course, and appreciate your words," murmured Felix.

Looking back at the land of the former

poultry farm, he focused on the part of it that was right next to them. He needed to start here. This was the entrance to the property and would remain so.

If his plan worked, this would be where everyone drove past to get inside.

Taking in the entirety of the land, and everything in it, he wanted to modify it. He owned it and all things on it, which meant he could do what he wanted, even if it was technically illegal.

We'll need to push and bribe people to get this listed as a landfill for non-hazardous trash. That we'll take on all concerns for it and whatever fines may arise.

Get it zoned appropriately. All the permits for the buildings put in retroactively. So much to do.

But that's something we can do after the fact. Especially since we won't be asking for anything other than providing a service.

Hell, we may not even have to bribe anyone for this to become a landfill.

Pushing his attention to what he wanted, Felix focused a single thought into an image in his mind. He wanted a small detached building here. One that would hold a single person to be on duty.

It would have a small space to monitor the area, rest in, and store weaponry. A single guard post as it were, for someone to admit guests, check names, and watch the property.

A window popped up in front of him.

Type: Building (Guard Building)	**Condition**: New

Owner: Alma and Felix Campbell	**Construction**: Cost 97,004 points

Perfect. Now… what if I wanted to do the same thing, but utilize the trees in the area. The rock, the dirt, the trash. The home the farmer once lived in and anything in the soil beneath us that could assist.

As well as fabricating tools to make it all happen.

How much would it cost if I simply sped up the work we would do with our own bodies, using the materials on hand.

There was a pause that Felix could practically feel. As if the world was coming to a grinding halt as it considered what he was pushing at his power.

Suddenly, there was a pop and the world jumped back to life.

It felt like when he'd learned how to drive a manual transmission as a teenager. He'd managed to pull the whole thing out of gear while driving on the highway and trying to shift to a higher gear. Only to go with the "grind it until you find it" route and getting it back into gear.

A new window popped up along with a small text box beneath it.

Type: Building (Guard Building)	**Condition**: New (Materials and work provided)
Owner: Alma and Felix Campbell	**Construction**: Cost 2,889 points

Whoa.

Well, that was unexpected. You managed to soft-lock the world. I had to kick the damn thing just to get it to start again.

I know you have a way of breaking shit, but do me a favor and try not to make more work for me.

-Uncle/Architect

P.S. Red-eyed Dryads are really hot. If you can introduce me to an unpartnered one, I'd be very grateful.

Raising his eyebrows, Felix felt concerned at the note from the man known as "Uncle". An incredibly powerful Mage that Felix suspected was much more than he seemed.

"I… could probably do that. No preference as long as red-eyed? Also, how's Al?" Felix asked aloud, wondering if Uncle was around.

A new text box fluttered up from nowhere.

I mean, I just want the introduction… anything past that would revolve around my wives liking them or not. I don't have as much time as I want right now to find one and dig into them so you'd be saving me the time and trouble, really.

Al's fine. Still working on that project of his. I think he's expecting Runner to do something stupid. Stupid, sudden, and early.

Chances are, he'll go forward with his plan in that moment.

I can only begin to imagine how bad it'll all go.

"Ah, yeah, he… err… my benefactor seems to have a patience issue," Felix agreed. "Anyway, I'll see what I can do. Thanks for the assist."

There was no response to that and Felix couldn't help but wonder about how convoluted his life was.

"You… okay?" asked Faith, a foot away. She had a hand up and it was pressed to his brow, as if checking for a fever.

Alma and Carlota were right in front of him, as well. All three Dryads looked concerned.

Er… I guess I was talking to myself in their eyes.

Faith pressed her hands to his face and pulled his jaw open with her thumbs. She leaned in and sniffed his breath.

Alma and Carlota moved in to do the same. The three of them sniffed at his breath as he exhaled.

Knowing what was coming next, Felix just kept his mouth open. Faith let him go and peered into his eyes for a few seconds.

Then she did what he'd been expecting. He even managed to not flinch when Faith stuck a finger in his mouth and then popped it into her own.

Alma immediately did the same, the two

Dryads watching him closely.

Carlotta instead leaned in close and kissed him, pushing her tongue into his mouth for a second, before pulling away from him.

Which was rather nice if he was being honest.

The three Dryads all looked to one another.

"Needs a little organ meat. Like liver. That's all though," Faith murmured to the other two Dryads. "Otherwise, he seems perfectly healthy. Thoughts?"

"B6," Alma corrected with a nod. "He's lacking B6. That's why you think he needs organ meat. Maybe a little B12, as well, but that goes back to liver. So you're absolutely right, but that's the underlying reason.

"And before you ask, I briefly did some work as a nutritionist and personal trainer. Since I never gain weight anyway, it seemed like an amusing job to have.

"Became a problem with how much I was asked out by clientele. Then they'd get angry with me for turning them down."

"Blood," Carlota said simply. "Liver and blood sausage."

"I'm fine. Was just talking my thoughts out loud," promised Felix when it seemed like the Dryads would continue. "Promise. Now… let's continue."

Stepping away from the triad, Felix looked back to the window that was still floating there.

He pushed out a need to see his points as

they stood right now. He'd only had a single day to bank some points since converting a load from David and Zachary.

Nor had there been an opportunity to go trash hunting.

	Generated	**Remaining**
Alma	250	250
Andrea	685	685
Carlota	270	270
Faith	420	420
Felix	1,700	1,700
Goldie	2,605	2,605
Miu	1,050	1,050
+Loyalty Bonus	1,000	1,000
+Marital Bonus	600	600
=Daily Total	**8,330**	**8,330**
Banked Total	—	**11,101**

Hm. Dryads count as wives, so I get points for them.

Interesting. I'm not sure I want to go whole-hog on Dryad wives, but… it's something to consider. I do hope Lily and Kit will forgive me.

I hope.

Felix accepted the cost with a shake of his head. Right now, he was stretched too thin and didn't have the time or luxury of being able to easily replenish his trash points.

There was simply too much going on as there

always had been.

Even something simple like working out was too much for any of them to really contemplate. There was always more to do and never enough time.

There was a sudden rush of noise as several trees nearby vanished. They simply ceased to be.

At the same time, a building came into being before them along the road. Exactly the way Felix had imagined it and wished it to be.

"Perfect," he said as the building now existed. It looked absolutely right. "And that answers my question. I can disguise my power set. I can be the Constructor or something.

"My superpower is to finish buildings in a single… look. Ha. That means I can just buy up a whole bunch of properties and really let loose on them.

"Next though… a landfill. A big open pit with a cliff face people can just throw stuff into. Real deep pit. Deep enough that it'll be hard for people to truly see the bottom.

"Then… start clearing the trash out and harvesting points. A dump for the locals and anyone driving by to use. Next up after this is the recycling plant, that way I can collect everything for that contract.

"After that… garbage collection and transportation. Then just have everything brought here and dumped. This'll be my farm. My point farm."

Felix nodded his head with a grin.

Next, he needed to call the mayor. It was time to push his political agenda and get his pieces moving.

Chapter 30 - Sponsored -

Carlota, Faith, and Alma had spread out through the nearby cities with flyers.

They'd spent a little money to have them done up at an office store that provided print services. They were simple things, inviting anyone and everyone to come dump whatever they didn't need. It wasn't classified formally as a landfill but all non-hazardous materials were welcome.

Felix wasn't charging people; he was inviting them to dump their trash. He wasn't zoning it as a landfill, just stating that he was willing to take whatever they didn't want.

It was a skirting of the law in more ways than one, but it'd work for the time being. At least until they could get the zoning changed, permits done up, and get approval from the local government as well as a few agencies, he imagined.

That was all well and good for later on, but for now, he just wanted trash. All the trash he could get his hands on.

Watching a rather beat-up truck roll toward the edge, Felix quirked his eyebrows. He was watching from a small ranch home he'd put together on the edge of the property.

It had a view of the landfill, but was screened quite heavily by trees. If someone stared long enough, they could probably spot the home.

For Felix though, he could see the drop point quite easily.

When the truck came to a stop, the passenger got out and jumped up into the truck bed. Swinging around slightly, the driver angled the back of the truck closer to the pit and the log dividers to prevent people from going right off the edge.

The tailgate was missing, so all the passenger had to do was shove things out.

Amusingly, the bed was filled with boxes, broken furniture, and even what looked to be an oil barrel. All of it was shoved out into the pit without any thought whatsoever.

Hopping out of the truck bed, the passenger got back into the truck and then the vehicle pulled off. They drove out toward the exit road from the dumping point which would lead them back toward the entrance, and then the exit side of the entry booth.

Felix happily flicked out two fingers in the direction of the pit. As if he were moving a drink to the side he then moved them to his left.

At the same time, he wanted to turn everything in that pit into points. Regardless of what it was.

He wasn't interested in anything they could dumpster dive and use, but only the points. Money likely wouldn't be an issue relatively soon, but points would always be a needed resource.

Then he opened up his point window. He was curious how much he'd gotten from this load.

	Generated	**Remaining**

Alma	260	260
Andrea	685	685
Carlota	280	280
Faith	435	435
Felix	1,705	1,705
Goldie	2,605	2,605
Miu	1,055	1,055
+Loyalty Bonus	1,000	1,000
+Marital Bonus	600	600
=Daily Total	**8,365**	**8,365**
Banked Total	—	**34,097**

Huh. Definitely getting points from the trash so far this morning.

This plan is working perfectly.

Though… Alma, Carlota, and Faith all went up in points in a noticeable way.

I can understand Goldie and Miu going up, they're out there actually doing things. The Dryads didn't do anything yesterday at all. They were with me all day and night.

The only physical exertion they did at all was – oh… oh, Dryads.

Felix let out a short breath and then picked up the phone in front of him. He glanced at the TV and the news and back to the phone.

He started tapping in the number for the mayor.

It was time to push on Mr. Johnson and see if he could be part of Felix's plan. Because if he didn't miss his guess, Jordan Johnson didn't want to stop at just being a mayor. Being halted at that point wasn't his end goal.

Felix could use and help him.

I mean, I even have some political experience I can tap into. I wouldn't ever want to run for anything, but I can certainly get him moving.

Letting his eyes move back to the TV after dialing, Felix just listened to the line ring. If he got the timing right, the news station would have something to show off here in a few minutes.

If he was going to get the world to watch his puppet show, he had to set the stage accordingly. He wanted to get everything arranged for the audience to have a seat and simply get invested in what was going on.

"Good afternoon, Mr. Campbell," said the mayor a second after the line picked up. Apparently, he'd plugged in this phone's number.

Hm. I'll have to try and keep this number if possible, I suppose.

"Good afternoon, Mayor Johnson," Felix replied with a smile on his face. He knew it would transmit easily enough to his voice and he wanted this to start on the right foot. "I wanted to reach out to you because I wanted to offer a service, but to also ask a favor that'd be required for that service to happen."

"I see. Well, I can't promise anything, of course, but I'd be more than happy to listen," offered the mayor. It was a standard political statement that Felix had certainly expected to hear.

"I've purchased a farm and I plan on turning it into a non-hazardous landfill. It was a poultry farm once upon a time and was no longer being utilized for anything," Felix explained. "I've purchased the property outright, put up a few buildings, and already excavated a section of the property.

"For now, I'm just inviting those in the surrounding areas to dump non-hazardous materials in the pit that currently exists. I've already explained that I'll dispose of all trash that's brought to the landfill for now.

"Once I get permission to proceed and the zoning rights, I plan on expanding it so it can hold a great deal more.

"My favor is regarding the classification and zoning. My service provided is that I'm more than happy to let Brandonville as a city, or its citizens, utilize it free of charge for any trash disposal needs. As long as you're the mayor, or part of the leadership for our great state.

"At this time, I'm already explaining to citizens that I'm doing this simply because I want to help the city due to your leadership."

Mayor Johnson was silent on the other end of the line.

There was no doubt in Felix's mind that the mayor could make this happen for him. The question was, was it worth it to the mayor to do it.

If Felix had set a hook the last time they

spoke, then it was a foregone conclusion that the mayor would agree. After all, it wasn't every day a seemingly prominent citizen stepped out of nowhere to assist you and then ask you about your political goals.

It was the type of thing that would give any politician a great deal of pause. These were situations that one authored books and made movies about. A chance encounter with someone you're not sure means you good or ill, but is likely to propel you higher.

"Not a problem," Mayor Johnson said suddenly and with conviction. He sounded considerably more excited now. "I'll get it taken care of. That does actually help me a great deal. My current contract for trash collection has become… tiresome.

"Can I start having trucks come today? I have a few neighborhoods that missed a trash pickup or… four."

"Certainly," Felix agreed readily, feeling his heart rate actually climb. It also explained why so many people had already showed up and were tossing trash bags down the pit. "That'd be wonderful. If you can get it zoned today, I'd be more than welcome to take any and all trucks even as the ink dries."

"Trucks will be showing up in an hour. Just write down the truck numbers, as well as how often they visit. I can initiate some emergency payments on this since there's a contract dispute and I need to solve things," added the mayor. He sounded relieved.

"Ah, I'll have that done," Felix murmured. This was turning out far better than he'd expected. "If you don't mind, could I ask you the name of the company handling the trash pickup contract? I have a sneaking suspicion they might try to come visit me. That or give me a call."

"Ah... Adorable Collection Services," the mayor answered without even a second of hesitation. "They have the gall to label themselves that way given how they act with their contracts. I'd stuff them all into their own trucks if I could."

Felix snorted at that and refrained from commentary. It wouldn't be the first time a business like that named themselves to the contrary.

He was fairly certain that someone from that company would reach out to him.

The question becomes do I go full mafia and have Miu pay them a visit after they call, or ignore them outright and wait for them to show up here.

Then bury them.

Even as he thought about it, he realized the answer was obvious.

Ignore them, do nothing, play the good guy role. If they came after him, respond, and make sure there was nothing for them to guess at.

Remain above, beyond, and behind.

Don't get involved unless I must. When I do, nuke it from orbit.

It's the only way to be sure.

"Right. Other than that, I was wondering if I

could perhaps ask for another favor," murmured Felix. This was the point where he wanted to push forward. He needed to set the stage for one of his actors. Someone who would believe they were entirely independent in their actions, yet never truly step away from the spotlight Felix would aim at them.

"I… what is it?" asked the mayor.

"I was wondering if you could tell me where I can put contributions for your upcoming political campaign," Felix stated clearly and directly. Unbelievably, his mind came up with a blank for the title he had just been thinking about. "I was told you were planning on running for a state position. I wanted to contribute to that, as I think you could do a lot of good for us."

Once again, the mayor fell into silence. Felix assumed the man was thinking over everything he'd just said to him. This would be a step that couldn't be undone obviously.

"Yes. I plan on running for the House of Representatives," Mayor Johnson finally said. "I haven't made my intention known, but I think it's about time I did. The problem was the funding to make it happen and only recently was I able to secure that."

Ah, I do love a dance like this.

Now… Goldie said they had already pulled in about four million dollars all told from all the armored cars. A lot of that would go to a house campaign I imagine.

"I can certainly appreciate that. How much was it that you needed if you don't mind me asking?" asked Felix. "As well as what group is running the campaign to see you elected?"

There was a chuckle from the mayor at that. Felix had apparently asked the right question and in the right way.

"On average, it's about three or four million to win. I already have a good part of that. I was only looking for an additional two million or so to finish up and I'm fairly certain I secured that.

"As to where to put the donation, I have an organization that I think you should donate to. They'll take care of the rest," directed the mayor. "I'll have it sent it over to the landfill with the paperwork coming your way."

Alright then. So he only needs two million from me. That's more than I want to spend on something like this, but this is a perfect opportunity.

A chance to really set up my personal "good-guy Hero" puppet. The man to lead the political world on the side of goodie-goodie heroes and their core beliefs.

I just have to set up the Guild of Heroes as well, and get him to step in as a supporter.

That'll solve one side of the equation.

"Makes sense. I'll be looking forward to it," promised Felix. "Be sure to look me up when the contract comes due. I'm sure my landfill and people will be ready to meet whatever the contract is at it stands, then do it for half the cost.

"I'll speak with you again later, Mayor Johnson."

"Until then, Mr. Campbell," said the mayor,

then disconnected the line.

"Perfect," murmured Felix after hanging up the line. Setting the phone down, he looked towards the pit.

A large truck had pulled up and was busily shoving out a large amount of shattered wooden pallets and cardboard. All of it was just being sent to the bottom of the pit.

Felix once more brushed it all away the moment the person dumping it all had turned away.

Smirking to himself, he turned his head back to the TV. He was waiting for Goldie to make her entrance. To truly appear for the first time in a way that no one could ever deny.

"I mean, I gave them a tip to have a helicopter in the vicinity for a reason. I just didn't tell them why," said Felix to himself. He was hoping they'd listened to him.

"Felix," came a voice over one of the radios.

"Yes, my Grove-maiden?" asked Felix, pointedly using the nickname. "May I assist, Maiden of the Grove?"

He knew it was either Alma or Carlota, but there'd been enough static in it that he wasn't sure. His response would get him an answer though.

Any type of flirting would be Carlota, a pause followed by a normal response would be Alma. Their personalities were somewhat night and day.

"I… errm… I'm… yes. You may assist me,

Grove-husband," said the voice that was now clearly Alma by her response. "Carlota just reported that there's a rented moving van heading this way. Should we let that in?"

"Yep, anyone and anything. Don't even question it," Felix stated. "The only thing you need to do is write down a serial number if a garbage truck shows up, then write down how often they show up.

"Anything else, Alma? Are you alright? Feeling better? Should I come charge you up again? Do you need me to relieve you? Something else?"

"I… no, no. No, I'm fine. Thank you for your concern. I'm… well," Alma said hurriedly, there was an obvious smile in her voice, though. "I'm doing very well. Just… just adapting. I'm fine. I can man this position until it's time to switch. Faith trusted this to me and-and I can do it.

"Thank you, grove-husband. I… I appreciate all you've done for me already."

Alma had ended up having some kind of episode in the middle of the night. To the point that she'd blasted out nature magic in every direction.

She had ended up nearly unconscious from overuse.

When she'd finally calmed down and almost passed out, Felix had refilled her with magic but hadn't pushed her for answers.

All he did was comfort her and remain there for her.

He had a suspicion of what it could be but

didn't want to put a voice to it.

If it mattered to her, she'd tell him in time.

Turning his head, he looked to where Faith was sleeping in the cot in the other room. He could just barely see her head and shoulders, the bottom half of her under the covers.

With only three of them and an Andrea, they were working in turns for night watch as well as taking care of everything else.

Miu and Andrea were currently distributing fliers in Hardysburg for the free dumping. They'd be back in an hour or so.

"Alright, just let me know," Felix said and then set the radio down. His eyes moving back to the TV.

Suddenly, the picture switched to something else.

It was an aerial view from a helicopter. The center of the viewer was centered on Goldie. She was just barely coming into focus as she began to dive toward the ground.

She was in her brilliant, shining gold Dragon form.

The camera managed to trail her down to the ground as she slammed into the pavement next to an armored car that'd just stopped at a red light.

Pinning it down with her left clawed hand, she reached over with her right hand. Using a claw, she tore the hood off it and scooped out a chunk of the engine in the same movement.

As she did so, she tilted her head to the side

and opened her mouth.

A masked Andrea rolled out and hit the ground. The fact that her tail was held up behind her made it very obvious.

An SMG came up and pressed into her shoulder. A single second afterward, and eight Others popped out of her. Two went to the front of the armored car, while the rest all ran to the back.

The one with the SMG posted up near a door and waited.

Goldie turned partly and used the same clawed hand that had pulled out the engine to shear off the rear door. The whole thing clattered to the ground with a rattling bang.

Andrea had flicked in what looked like a flash-bang as soon as it happened. There was a bright flash from the back of the vehicle and then Andreas poured in.

In only a few seconds, they came back out, dragging two guards to the ground and disarming them. The two Others at the front of the car were still watching the driver.

Shifting around, Goldie leaned down and peered into the windshield of the car.

Lifting a single claw, she delicately sunk it into the front driver's door of the car and pulled it away. Then she did the same to the passenger side door.

The driver was now exposed on both sides, which left the guard with nothing he could do. Instead of doing anything stupid, he held up his hands.

The Andreas fell on him quickly, pulling him free of the armored car and then stripping him of weapons as well.

As quickly as it started, it was clearly over. The Andreas were all bounding up into the back of the armored car and vanishing from view.

Goldie turned her head and looked straight at the helicopter as the camera zoomed in on her. She tilted her head to one side slowly, then held up a clawed hand and made a finger-wagging motion.

All it needed was an "ah-ah-ah" sound effect to go with it.

Then Goldie let out a soft puff of fire. One that came out from her mouth and rolled up the sides of her jaw, bathing her face and giving her a glittering glow.

As the flame cleared, she gave the camera a wide smile that exposed her fangs, and winked at the camera. Turning to the side, she oriented herself on the vehicle.

Picking up the armored car with her front two hands, Goldie tilted it forward. Putting it so the back of it was at the top. Likely to keep the contents from spilling out.

Getting in a low crouch, Goldie then leapt into the air and began flying away.

The camera of the news chopper followed her, but the helicopter itself made no move to follow her. Apparently, her warning had been received loud and clear.

"We have our heroic mayor who will go into the House. Our villains becoming public knowledge. Next... the organizations," murmured Felix to himself. He looked at the laptop that wasn't far away.

Both websites for the League of Villains and Guild of Heroes were done and up. Their writers and editors were already churning out articles for them and posting them.

With the news today, Felix imagined both websites would get some traffic.

"Especially, if the news actually goes with the way I worded the tip. I did, after all, say that the supervillains known as The Golden One and Myriad would appear in the area. With all the keywords already set-up for the website, it should go well for both."

Felix grinned and leaned back in his chair. Things were working out quite well.

He did regret that it seemed like the news cycle for this world was melting down. With the previous footage of their interaction with the police, and now this, it was going to be a really wild time, he imagined.

Chapter 31 - Plant Food -

Felix couldn't help but chuckle. The number of interested parties who were submitting applications to be tested for superpowers was enormous.

Each and every one of them had supplied him with a great deal of information. They had also all signed and submitted the TOS that came with that from the "Guild of Heroes".

A rather straightforward agreement that any and all lawsuits that might arise would be handled by a mediator. That they forfeited all rights to a class-action lawsuit as well.

It all came down to a simple analogy that Felix had used to explain what he wanted to the lawyers who had written it up.

"It's my bar. If I want someone gone, I want them to have no recourse," muttered Felix, reliving the memory.

The lawyers had certainly provided that.

For the League of Villains, the same was also true, though the website was hosted outside of the country.

One that thought anything going wrong in the country Felix was in, was a good thing. They'd be very unlikely to ever lift a finger to help unmask the Villains league.

It was also behind permission to do a background check, a number of affidavits and TOS acceptances, and a promise that no harm would ever be done.

On top of that, it could only be reached through a different process than regular means. Felix didn't honestly know how it all worked, but Jay had set it up and assured him that all these hoops would be more than enough for the time being.

Surprisingly, there were a great many people who seemed to believe they had superpowers that would line up in an evil direction. Or they simply wanted to network amongst those people.

Someone had also asked him if they had an app that could be downloaded. It'd triggered a series of thoughts he was only barely exploring at the moment, but he liked where they were leading him.

Especially owning such an app.

"Felix," called Faith over the radio. There was no mistaking her voice considering how often he'd spent just talking to her lately. She really was his counselor at this point and his worry rock.

When he thought about it like that, it felt like a lot longer than just two days since he'd spoken with the mayor. The endless amount of things being dumped into his landfill only blew up that belief.

It was a surprise how much trash was being dumped.

He had no idea that there would be so much coming in.

Apparently, Mayor Johnson had told others at his little budget meeting about the situation and there were suddenly a lot of out-of-state garbage trucks dumping loads off. As well as citizens arriving from other cities and towns.

Felix was now charging people a flat rate of five dollars for any non-government vehicle, or those who didn't have an ID listing them as living in Brandonville.

It was cheap enough that no one could fault him for it and while a few grumbled, no one had ever driven away either. They'd all paid and dumped their waste.

"Yes?" Felix asked after picking up the handheld radio.

"I just let in a group of people who I don't trust at all. They had nothing to dispose of, looked like thugs, and didn't have a license plate on the vehicle. Nor did they even try to show me an ID to get in for free or say where they lived," reported the Dryad. "They just asked if this was the new Three Trees landfill."

Raising his eyebrows at that, Felix looked to the ceiling.

The name on the company that owned the landfill and the land deed was "Three Trees". Named for the Dryads, since they were the primary owners as far as the outside world was concerned.

As far as he knew, the donation he'd handed over to the super PAC to be used for the mayor had come from "Felix Campbell" so that ruled them out.

That only left anyone involved in the landfill itself.

That could only mean it was someone who'd managed to get a copy of what the Mayor had set up for him. Which could easily be the opposing trash contract company.

"Okay. Keep the booth stalled and don't let anyone in. We're probably going to have to resolve this before we bring in the next person," decided Felix. "Just tell them we have a city truck with a broken hydraulic system. It's taking a bit to unload by hand but we're doing it."

This has to be the garbage collection and recyclables contract I imagine. I wonder if they're the adorable ones, working for them, or something else entirely.

They're probably handing the recycling center as well as the trash pickup contract. Did they come here to cause me problems? Threaten me?

Is this going to be more like the mob and how they strong-armed the industry once upon a time?

How curious.

And interesting, really.

"Understood," Faith replied.

Standing up from the desk and the long list of interviews for superpowers, Felix went to the backdoor. Exiting the home, he found Andrea working with Alma and Carlota on hand-to-hand combat.

"We're going to have visitors," he said simply. "Good time for some live-battle experience. I have to make sure you two don't die on me though."

Alma and Carlota suddenly both looked excited and very nervous. They'd never been in a fight before as far as he knew. They'd been getting drilled by Faith and Andrea endlessly whenever there was free time.

He knew what that kind of training would do to you first-hand. They also were simply better than him in almost every stat, which meant they probably were already much stronger than someone would suspect.

Felix walked right up to them and laid his hands on their shoulders.

Both Dryads leaned toward him, though Carlota grabbed his wrist with both of her hands. Alma, on the other hand, was staring at his middle, not quite as self-assured.

He fired off a request to empower them and accepted the costs with only a flicker of thought. He'd gotten so used to this, that it was as easy and fast as a thought now.

Both Dryads' eyes flickered to life and then began to glow brilliant crimson. Magic power began to roll off them as he empowered them.

I… wonder. It didn't say they had a latent power.

Though that really does feel like the same magic power from Faith.

Would theirs cost less to bring up to a higher power since they're from this plane? As natives, would the earth-spirit itself assist me?

Felix turned his thoughts toward making these three Dryads far more akin to what he was used to. The monstrously magically powerful version that came from Vince's world.

Dryads who could go toe-to-toe with faith-based magic and magic-honed sorcery and win. How Faith was when he overfilled her and let her run wild.

Then he wondered how much it would cost him to do that while inviting the earth-spirit that the Dryads venerated and worshiped to participate. To assist and come more fully into the world.

There was a sudden gut-wrenching feeling as a presence loomed over him. One that felt eerily familiar to him.

Much like when he'd dealt with Abera and Desh, in fact. Or his Benefactor and Uncle.

Taking in a forced breath, Felix paused in pushing his power. Instead, he held tightly to the Dryads and addressed the presence that'd join them.

"Good afternoon. Is it Gaia? Mother Nature? Earth-spirit? Earth-mother? I'm not sure how to respectfully address you," Felix offered in a polite and conciliatory tone. "But I would very much like to do that."

There was a long pause after he spoke that felt a lot like a mountain shifting. A giant lifting its head to peer at him with slowly opening eyes.

"I… am," said a deep, rumbling female voice. "All."

Okay. In other words, she's all of that and more. Though… err… this was a mistake, wasn't it? I just woke her up. She was still dormant even as the earth fell apart.

Now she isn't.

Damnit.

"Then I'll address you as Aunt, if you don't mind. You're not the world that birthed me, but you'd likely consider her a sister," Felix said with as much friendliness as he could cram into his tone. "I have two of your daughters here. I was planning on granting them power.

"I wanted to invite you to this moment just in case you wished to participate or at least bless it. Or at worst, give you a chance to naysay it."

"No," replied the loud voice. It felt like it was coming from the ground beneath him, in fact. The single word was far sharper than the previous ones had been. The spirit was most certainly waking up. "No, I will not naysay it. I shall bless it. Encourage it."

Felix nodded his head. He imagined that was the case.

After hearing what Faith had said about nature, or the world as a whole here and how it was harmed, he was planning on changing that. He'd need the world to be stabilized and brought to a point where it could continue on indefinitely.

If it died, failed, or simply could no longer support life, he wouldn't have a world to recruit from.

"In fact, I will bring all my daughters to you. Here, in this place. I shall give them enough energy to come to this place. All of them," confirmed the goddess. Her speech had shifted entirely now. As if she were quite literally adapting to the situation by the very second. "They will come here and forge a new grove. A grove that will work toward my goals which is to assist you, Felix Otherworlder.

"I will support you, my nephew. As well as my niece, Faith Otherworlder. I can feel from her a connection to a much stronger spirit such as myself. I shall regain that strength for myself in time.

"I shall send to you the remnants. The cast-offs and forgotten edges of a world long forgotten. Welcome them all for me, Nephew?" asked the goddess.

There was no threat in the goddess's words. It really was just a request for him to assist her. To take in those who she would send his way.

"I shall, Aunt. I'll accept them all into Legion as long as they abide by my decrees," Felix agreed honestly. Then he pushed on his power again. He wanted to bring these two Dryads up to a much higher power level. Open them to their full magic and power.

Name: Alma Campbell	**Condition**: Nervous, excited, falling in love.
If No Action Taken: None	**Action >> Empower Race Power**: Cost 0*

*COST OF 24,103 OFFSET BY YOUR AUNT GAIA.

Name: Carlota Campbell	**Condition**: Nervous,

	excited, falling in love.
If No Action Taken: None	**Action >> Empower Race Power**: Cost 0*

*COST OF 21,784 OFFSET BY YOUR AUNT GAIA.

"I… thank you, Aunt," Felix murmured and then activated the power shift.

Where before, magical power had been rolling off the Dryads, it was now being pulled into them. Condensing, forming, and coalescing into something else.

Distantly, Felix could feel a third such situation. It felt very similar to what was happening with Carlota and Alma.

"I'm also empowering my niece; you don't need to guide my hand this time. I understand what needs to happen. She's not a daughter of mine, but… she feels like it. Feels like a daughter in every way," murmured Gaia. "I'm going to go begin gathering those I shall send to you, Felix Otherworlder.

"Now that I'm awake, I shall not rest. This world has gotten away from me. It's… time to take action. I've awoken from peaceful slumber to a nightmare and I shall not lay my head to sleep again."

Err… yeah.

I fucked up.

Oh, well. At least she's on my side.

Sucks to be everyone else.

Letting his hands fall away from the Dryads,

he peered into their faces. They were gazing at him with wide and very brightly-glowing red eyes. In a way, it was like staring directly at laser beams.

Moving to the side, Felix heard Andrea come up beside him.

"Nn! Good, good. This is all very good," she said, wrapping an arm around Felix's shoulders. "They needed some power. It'll help them grow faster.

"This'll be an opportunity as well because it sounds a lot like someone has come here to try and intimidate us. Live combat is just what they need."

Wondering what she meant by that, Felix tried to pay attention to the world around him. In his fixation on the Dryads, he'd lost all sense of what was happening.

He could hear people calling out now. They sounded like they were at the side of the house. Likely moving around it, toward the rear.

Several seconds passed before a handful of men came into view. They had indeed gone around the long side to pop out over here.

"Ah, there you all are," said the man in front.

He was tall, somewhat attractive, and his hair was pulled back off his face.

Glancing to the side, Felix saw that Alma and Carlota's eyes had returned to normal, though they were eyeing the men now. Alma looked particularly angry at the sight of them, though it didn't look like she recognized them in any way.

"See, we're here to buy your landfill. No

reason for you to operate it the way you are," claimed the man as he walked over. His jacket came up partly as he emphasized his words with his arms. Spreading them out in a near "shrug" like gesture. "It doesn't even make sense. You can just sell it to us at a really good price for you and we'll call it even and done."

Felix had noticed that a pistol was tucked into the waistband of the man. It wasn't in a holster or anything, but just shoved into his jeans.

Hm. I see. So it's a strong-arm tactic.

One that would elevate to them killing everyone here and dumping the bodies, if it didn't work out.

I won't pity their deaths at all.

Legion first, meatbags.

"Plato o plomo, right?" Felix asked with a smile. Next to him, he could feel Andrea shifting toward his right. It likely meant she'd already gotten her hands on her own weapon and was moving around to get a clear line of sight.

"Uh, what?" asked the man, looking confused now.

Apparently "silver or lead" wasn't a thing here.

Before anyone could say anything further, Andrea's hands snapped down, then came up with a pop as she pushed the safety off.

Moving forward quickly, she came within a few feet of the man, the muzzle pointed at his face. Her eyes were flat and empty as she stared at him.

"Listen here, Chadbro," she said in a low

growl. "You're all going to drop your weapons to the ground. Then we're going to have a talk. You may think you're some type of overpowered gift to the masses, but around these parts you're just worm-food that hasn't been planted yet.

"So put the iron on the ground. Do it slow, without making me nervous, and I won't just shoot you in the face. If I have to, I will. Then I'll just dump all your bodies into the shit-pit out there with all the other garbage."

Andrea had lined herself up in such a way that she could easily hose all four men down with one sweep of weapons fire.

"We'll start with you, Chadbro," hissed the Beastkin. "You can disarm first. If anyone else moves, they'll catch some lead. I don't care other than it's a waste of ammo."

Felix reached into his hoodie and unslung the pistol that was in the chest holster there. Pushing the safety, he pulled the slide back and made sure there was a round in the chamber.

Holding it toward the ground, he moved around Andrea to stand in the rear of the group of men. He only lifted his weapon and stuck his finger into the trigger loop after passing by Andrea.

"Perfect timing," Felix said with a smile.

This really was perfect timing. He also had a large number of points to spend and wanted to push Andrea into an even larger role.

He wanted to give her the ability to summon up another ten Others.

Name: Andrea Campbell	**Condition**: In heat. Excited, bloodthirsty.
If No Action Taken: None	**Action >> Alter Power**: Cost 21,831 points

Felix eagerly hit accept on that and then glanced at Andrea. He watched her shudder for a moment, before ten Others simply sprang out of her.

They were likely Eleven through Twenty and hadn't existed up until a moment ago. Standing around Andrea Prime, they looked somewhat confused for only a second or two.

Then they all aligned on the newcomers.

"What the shit?" asked one of the men.

"Eleven, go get their car. Bring it around this way," commanded Felix. "Twelve through nineteen. Collect their weapons as they get laid down. Don't approach until each disarms. Then go arm yourselves accordingly. We're going to get our Dryads some hand-to-hand experience.

"Then we'll let these fools get back to where they came from. After they've gotten to taste the dirt a few times."

Smiling, Felix couldn't help but feel a little bad for lying to the men about the fact that they'd be leaving here.

They most certainly wouldn't.

Alma and Carlota hadn't likely killed anyone yet.

This would be a perfect opportunity for them to get experience in more than one way. To get them blooded and ready for what was coming.

Legion was going to become what it once was again. Just not in the same way or fashion.

A leading organization that controlled many things, yet offered no proof or evidence to that fact. That no one would ever know it.

And after this, I'll need to chat with Jay about the app.

Slowly, the man Andrea had called Chadbro began disarming.

Well. We'll just have to bury the car and the bodies real deep. Good thing I can excavate and fill in holes like a machine.

Felix only continued to smile as the Others got to work with his commands.

By the time they'd been disarmed, Felix had already headed back inside. He didn't need to be there while Alma and Carlota became blooded. He had work to do.

"You, Chadbro," declared Andrea. "Step forward. Alma, you're first. Everyone else gets to watch. Anyone moves, they get dropped. End of story."

Entering the home, Felix went back to the laptop and his cell phone.

He hesitated for a moment, then picked up the radio.

"Good for more customers, we cleared the truck. Going to see if we can't fix it before we send them off," Felix said over the radio. He wasn't sure if there were people right there with her or not, but it'd be best to play as if there were.

"Understood, thanks for the update," Faith replied.

Felix set down the radio and then picked up his phone. He punched in Jay's number and held it up to his ear.

Jay picked up on the second ring.

"Hey, Legate. What... what can I do for you?" asked the man.

Legate.

Well.

I didn't encourage that nickname, but it's spreading. So that's fine. That's who'll be in charge of Legion, after all.

Not a man with a face, but a person with a moniker.

The idea sprung into clarity in that moment for him. What he wanted Legion to actually become.

That's what Legion will be do the same time.

There won't be a good or evil Legion. Just Legion.

A neutral Legion.

I'll just have to make a few movements to get this lined up with the change, but it shouldn't be too hard.

Legion can be a neutral party that walks the line between the heroes and the villains. We'll just force both sides – conveniently controlled by us from the shadows – to accept Legion as an intermediary. As a neutral party.

A peacekeeping force when it came to larger things.

It's one thing for heroes and villains to do what they would, it's another when things get to a level where the really strong powers surface. Where they could theoretically take out a country.

The type that had to be immediately controlled before it went wrong.

Legion will exist to be the entry point and neutral observer force. We'll be the one the government turns to, to help institutionalize it all.

We'll take over all power finding functions once we get that contract. Claiming that we have the tech to not just figure out a power, but activate it for someone.

Not everyone will go active at the same time. Some will likely remain dormant until they die.

I can make things happen.

Then we'll write the contracts such that I own all the data that comes with it. That anyone who signs onto Legion will grant me conservator-ship over their powers. Which I'll phrase as the only way I can activate it.

Then I'll activate it, but do it in such a way that I can deactivate it as I wish. They'll become beholden to me.

Smiling to himself, Felix suddenly realized the final iteration of Legion on this world and how he'd do it.

He needed everyone to willingly get into the first part though. Providing him with data.

"Jay, I need a program. I need you to write one specifically to me. One that I'd own," Felix started.

He could see how he'd do this.

The program would be made with his end

goal in mind. He'd have it put together. An encrypted program that sends data to one point. That stores nothing client-side other than its own encryption key and what it receives that Felix would send to it.

And since I own it, I can change the program's functionality.

I could… theoretically… make it so that it had an encryption that couldn't be broken by any technology available until the year twenty-two-fifteen.

Where I could simply modify the code as I wished to fit my needs, because I owned it. Where I could spend points to facilitate it to happen instantly, while leveraging Jay as the means.

Even as he thought about it, the plan spread out further and further.

A neutral Legion. An encrypted app that sent all information his way. One that could do it without being detected.

Then designing a host of programs and protocols that he could modify, shift, change, and alter as he saw fit.

Proprietary operating systems that wouldn't work without being on the Legion network. Mobile devices that were hard-encrypted.

Being able to pull out every single user that has the application, filter them by their job, and force the program to be able to do it through point usage.

"A number of programs, actually. I'm going to need you to hire an entire team of programmers to help with this as well. Anything and everything. From an Operating System to video-editing software. I also need a basic version of the program as quickly as you can. Even if it's terrible," corrected Felix as he spun in his chair. He was suddenly feeling a lot like a Bond villain again.

Chapter 32 - Writing the Show Program -

Staring up into the clouds, Felix couldn't help himself. He was grinning from ear to ear as Goldie came down toward them.

Clutched in her front paws was a city transit bus. Apparently, somewhere along the line she'd taken it for the simple purpose of tearing the back off it, then using it to hold everything they'd stolen.

Landing with a thump behind the swamp farm, Goldie turned her head and spat Second Andrea out with a flick of her head.

Leaping out of the Dragon's mouth, Andrea came right at Felix. Apparently, she'd been trying to line herself up in such a way as to fly at him.

He could see that Others Three through Ten were with her.

He had about a second to brace himself before she hit the ground, then dove toward him. Almost like a dog leaping for a Frisbee.

Her mouth open, her tail behind her, and her eyes wide and locked on him.

Then he caught her and held onto her.

"FEEEEEEELIX!" squealed Second Andrea. Then she began to pepper him with kisses.

"Yes, hello, everyone. How are you all? I'm glad you're all back," Felix replied. As soon as he could he set Second to the side, Andrea Prime moved up to her.

Something passed between them, and then Second stepped into Prime and vanished. Then she just stood there, staring off into nothing.

She'll be busy for a minute or two as they all catch up.

"Goldie, my dear Dragon, how'd it go? Haven't heard from you since you said you were going to break into a casino," he asked, peering up at the Dragon's head. The golden chains that were strung back and forth between her horns glittered and sparkled as she turned to look at him.

She'd just put down the bus to one side. When it'd been put flat, a number of duffel bags began falling out from the back of it.

A wide grin spread across the Dragon's face, and she chuckled. It was a deep rumbling sound.

"Oh, it was good. Very good," she said with a light shake of her head. "I expect you to add many rings to my bridal gold. Andrea and I worked hard for this.

"As to the count, we've brought you around sixty million in currency. We tried to count it, but it was simply too much."

Blinking, Felix didn't know what to say to that.

They'd already dropped off a small amount of cash previously, so he could donate it to the mayor's campaign fund. If it was all totaled together, they had close to seventy million in cash.

Goldie gave herself a shake and then her body started to shift and morph. Shrinking into itself, she took on her Human form.

In only a couple of seconds, the beautiful and impossible to look away from woman stood before him. The gold in her horns had shifted with her, looking unharmed and perfect.

"It's amazing, isn't it?" she asked, reaching up to run her fingers through the gold chains. "I love it so much. I love what you did. Thank you, Nest-mate.

"Now... as much as I want to steal you away for some personal attention, both for you and I, you didn't call us back for no reason. Something's changed, hasn't it?"

Stepping close to him, Goldie lifted a hand and ran her index finger down from his ear, along his jaw, and finished at his chin.

The touch had been intimate in a way that made him feel like when Faith went "Tree tender" mode on him. Where she'd inspect, sniff, and taste him, leaving him feeling rather tingly and warm.

Goldie just stood there with a smile, waiting for him to speak.

"Sorry," he apologized when his brain eventually turned back on. "Yeah, we got a visit from a group of thugs. Alma and Carlota killed them, and we buried them.

"With you and Andie making waves and pushing the focus of the news onto you, this is a perfect time to really... launch everything."

"Ah, I see. Then I shall go find something to wear and join you in the camp, yes?" asked the gold

Dragon, tilting her head to the side and making her gold lightly clatter together.

"That'd be great. Andie put up a few rooms. I put your clothes away for you rather than just… leaving them… as they were. They looked like they were getting somewhat wrinkly. I just handled them real quick so they'd smooth out," Felix murmured.

He felt weird doing stuff like that, but he wanted to at least try and help her out. She'd spent a great deal of time since they'd arrived in this world repairing, mending, and adjusting all his clothes.

Everything fit him in a way that was incredible, and he appreciated it.

"I know you do, Nest-mate," Goldie purred, her eyes glowing slightly, her smile growing. "I know you do. Thank you for putting my clothes away. I'll see you there."

Goldie gave him a finger-wave and then began moving off. There was a rolling gait to her walk that reminded him of the strut she'd shown off to distract the cops. It had somehow crept into how she carried herself regularly.

"She said you often think about her walking like that," Andrea said in a loud whisper. Certainly loud enough that Goldie would hear it. "She wants you to want her more so she's going to work harder. She even bought a whole bunch of makeup and is gonna ask Faith about it.

"I don't wear any, so I couldn't help her. Makeup gets in my eyes and stuff when I get sweaty or covered in blood. You wouldn't believe how blood makes mascara clump up.

"I'll just keep doing what I've been doing. That works for me and I... honestly... I'm not as much of a girly-girl as Kit or Lily was. Don't wanna be, either."

Goldie had kept walking, not stopping at all. Though he was fairly certain he could see her ears were bright red at the moment.

I do like the walk, Goldie.

Chuckling, Felix turned his head and gave Andrea a quick kiss.

"Uh-huh. You all caught up now with each other?" he asked.

"Nn! We're all good now. Everyone said hi and we're all good," answered Andrea, then she stuck her tongue out between her teeth. There was a mischievous look to her. "You didn't tell me you trapped Third in the truck before they left. Naughty, naughty. You have favorites of us."

Felix would never admit that he did have a soft spot for those who'd been Death Others. The most he'd be willing to admit to was that they all had their individual skill-sets to a degree.

"Of course not. You're all my favorite," he countered. "Come on, let's go talk this plan out. Everyone else is already waiting inside."

"Nnnnn. Good," Andrea said and then slipped her arm through his.

Walking into the one of the rooms the Andrea's had put together, he found everyone sitting around a table.

Alma and Carlota had gotten through their first kills. The latter had done so without too much trouble, though she'd hesitated to kill at first.

Surprisingly, Alma had gotten very into the fight. Beating one of the men to death outright, then gladly executing two by herself.

They were seated on either side of Faith, who'd gotten a power-up as well from Gaia. She now had access to her magic and a great deal of it.

Miu was waiting for him, seated to the position that'd be on his left.

Her eyes jumped to him, stared at him hard for several seconds, then skittered off. Her body trembled for a second afterward.

She was doing far better around him than she'd ever done before, wasn't killing Andreas, and generally seemed almost normal. The only real time she absolutely lost herself was in their lovemaking.

Which honestly didn't bother him in the least. If anything, it was rather interesting to explore the darkness in her, with her.

Sitting down, Felix took her hand in his and squeezed it, his fingers slipping in between her own. He was going to hold onto her during the meeting if only because physical contact with him tended to help her mentality.

So long as he didn't look at her too much.

"We can start without Goldie," Felix said, looking around and meeting the eyes of everyone else. "She'll just pick through my thoughts anyway as well as everyone else here. Goldie can catch herself up even without us helping her."

Faith chuckled at that and looked to Alma and Carlota.

"She's a mind-reading Dragon. Don't worry about any bad thoughts you have. She doesn't really care," Faith explained to the other two Dryads. "Goldie is like a Dragon housewife that's already seen it all. Well, the Dragon part is the big part of that statement, actually. She views things differently."

"Indeed. Well, let's begin," Felix agreed and then coughed, clearing his throat. "Our goal is very simple. We need for the world to fear supers. To be afraid of what they can do.

"But they also need to firmly believe that the only thing that can fight supers, is supers. That there needs to be government-sanctioned supers to fight those who aren't.

"To that end, we're going to make sure we put on an exceptional performance for them. One that's going to make them really view everything through a different lens. A new way to see it."

"I… I have questions," whispered Miu from beside him. She wasn't looking at him, but at their joined hands. Her fingers were holding his firmly, but not too tightly.

"Okay, let's hold on that for now," offered Felix. "Let me roll out my plan first and then we'll answer questions after. That way Goldie can participate."

"Erm, yes. Yes. Thank you, Felix. My… my

Felix," whispered Miu, her shoulders hunching up toward her face and her head scrunching down. It looked like she wanted to crawl into herself.

Felix gave her hand a squeeze to reassure her.

"It's simple. We're going to have 'The Golden One' and 'Myriad' attack their gold repository. It's a fairly well known and iconic location. It's starred in several movies and other things," explained Felix. "Honestly, the name escapes me at the moment, but it's apparently managed by a military force."

Goldie appeared at that moment and came over. In her arms was a coat Felix had bought but hadn't worn yet.

Mostly because Goldie hadn't had a chance to fix it for him yet. Apparently, she'd already gotten that thought from his head and had stolen it from his own wardrobe that was here at the farm.

Goldie sat herself down next to Alma and gave the Dryad a smile.

"Oh, thank you for the compliment," Goldie said, holding the Dryad's eyes. Clearly, she'd stolen a thought from the Dryad's mind. Reaching up, Goldie ran her fingers along the golden chains that draped from horn to horn. "It's bridal gold. Felix gave it to me as his Nest-mate and because he treasures me.

"If you can be as good to him as your thoughts lead me to believe, I'm sure he'll decorate you in gold as well. Faith is going to put some gold bells and charms in her hair and on a choker."

With a nod of her head, Goldie pulled out a sewing kit and set to work on the coat. Her eyes flicked to Felix and she gave him a smile.

"I'm all caught up. Please proceed," she murmured with a smile that showed her bright white teeth.

"Well… Myriad and The Golden One will attack this bullion depository. The Tender, Shadow, and the Elex PMC will show up to counter them," Felix continued. "And before you ask, Myriad will only be around ten or so. The Elex PMC will have more. I'll have to expand your capability again, Andie for that, but I don't think you care. Do you?"

Glancing over to Andrea, he found she was smiling at him, shaking her head and grinning ear to ear.

"Do I get to fight myself!? Fight, fight, fight?" she asked, excitedly.

"Exactly. Since we're fairly certain none of you can actually die, because I can bring you back, this is all just part of the show," Felix explained while nodding his head. "So, the two teams will fight each other to the death or to a standstill. I expect you to go all out on one another.

"Faith will be incredibly overpowered at the start so she can erect a Dryad faith-shield. That way there's no outside sources to hinder our stage production. You can go all out on one another and handle it from there.

"If Goldie ends up being the last one standing, or is going to fall, she needs to gather up all the corpses and get out. So you'll need to develop a code word so that you can fake being injured and break apart. Can't leave bodies behind this time.

"Then we call it done and let the news world burn itself down. They'll all try to figure out what's happening. We'll push our websites harder and try to promote the idea that not only can we identify supers, but we can activate powers in people.

"That we can make people Powereds. Supers. It's actually the truth in a way, because there's no laws about who owns a superpower. Right now, it's a bit of a blind spot."

Everyone paused at that and was now looking at Felix.

"I can easily have them transfer a limited ownership of their powers to me, along with power of attorney. It wouldn't be magically enforced or anything, but that's fine. I can set my own limitations on the person," Felix laid out. "As in, I'll open their powers to them with their acceptance of some limited liability agreements, as well as temporary ownership of their powers so that I can modify it.

"From there… I just put in a caveat that I'll activate their power, but I have the sole discretion to deactivate it and reactivate it as I see fit. They get their power turned on, I get control over them forever forward even after I lose ownership of their power, and that's the end of it.

"We put all of it behind the forward-facing mission statement of the 'neutral Legion' organization and how it supports proper documentation of all Powereds. The same Legion that can work as a neutral party between both the League of Villains and the Guild of Heroes.

"All the while, we collect all information and utilize it for our own ends. Utilizing both sides of the fight to further our own goals, controlling everything. While outside of that view, everyone thinks it's three different entities."

"That's… really convoluted," muttered Andrea. She threw up her left hand and moved it past herself in a weird fluttering motion. "Like… way too complicated. I feel like it's gonna go like… creeeeeak, then bonk, with an ooof, then everyone running away."

As she spoke she'd lifted up her right hand and smacked it into the left. As if they were two opposing pieces from the same whole who couldn't function in concert.

Wait, I think… I just… translated everything she meant.

Either I'm getting worse, or she's getting better.

"We'll be fine, Andie. I just have to make sure that whoever is in control of each side all understand my intentions," he replied with a smile. "That's part of the whole charade. We'll control both sides, act as the neutral observer from the middle as well as the government contact, all while pushing everything around.

"That way, Legion never becomes the focal point. That way, even if someone really went after the Heroes, or the Villains, we could just as easily step back, assist, or stop it as we needed."

"Nn, nn, nn. Okay. Okay, that'll work. Maybe. I don't know. Do I get to shoot people?" asked Andrea, tilting her head to one side.

"Probably," Felix admitted. Then he looked at Miu and squeezed her hand. "Did I answer your questions, Mrs. Campbell?"

"I… uhm… ye… ah… can-can I be in charge of security for the Heroes? It would be nice for us to be in charge of it," she suggested. "If we needed to kill everyone, we could easily do it if we had control of security."

"Sure. Andrea can do security for the Villains as Myriad," Felix said and tossed a thumb at Andrea. "We'll have both of them paying taxes to us, while we provide them with targets, information about either side, lawyers, and a black market. We're going to be busy playing power broker and never get involved in the stupid side of it."

"I like that," Goldie murmured while rapidly sewing stitches in a pant-leg. Apparently, she'd brought in more than just the jacket he saw. "We can sell it all to everyone, control it all from the sidelines, and never put ourselves in anyone's sights.

"That's perfect, Nest-mate. By the way, I spoke briefly with Gaia about my kin. She was very interested in me and the fact that I was, and wasn't, one of her children.

"I reminded her that you could easily resurrect any long dead species given enough bones and points. We may have an inroad there. Apparently the idea of bringing back her children is a very real wish for her."

I… yes. I didn't even consider that.

If she's willing to supply us with things to use… well, hm. Maybe I'll have a wing of Dragons here after all.

"Perfect. Right, then," said Felix with a forced shove at his own thoughts. "That's my plan. It's very simple, if somewhat stupid, but it'll do what we need it to.

"I also have a test case I'm going to utilize later for my plan on powers and how they work. I'm betting I can give people powers so long as I have their permission and can own them, if briefly.

"We'll just have to make sure they never pass legislation against who owns a superpower. Though I'm not sure how long we can fight that. I have no doubt countries will want to own such things as a means to increase their offensive and defensive power."

There was a collective nod of heads at that.

"Alright. Let's tip off all the news stations to expect something big in two days. We'll get ready, set this thing off, and then lean back and let it all roll in.

"In the meantime, I'm going to upgrade some of your powers, confirm we can bring you back from a finger. Then back from the dead from that and go from there."

Felix reached over and into Miu's jacket.

The young woman froze absolutely still as his hand moved across her upper chest and shoulder.

Finding what he wanted, he pulled out the carry knife she had strapped to her shoulder holster. Setting it down on the table, he gave them a grim smile.

"Let's have you all take a moment to lose the tip of a pinky. We'll have our Dryads restore them back afterward. It'll give them a chance to practice their healing magic some more," commanded Felix. "Then I'll see if I can grow a body from it, and bring it back to life. I won't actually do it, mind you. We don't need duplicates of you running around. I wouldn't even want to consider what that'd mean at a spiritual level, either."

Miu snatched up the weapon and flicked it open. Releasing Felix's hand she swapped the knife over to it and promptly severed her pinky at the base. Blood began to squirt out rapidly.

Dropping the knife, she grabbed the pinky and held it up to him, gazing at him with wide, fully-dilated eyes. Her hands were trembling and it was obvious she was very over-stimulated.

"H-he-here, m-my Felix. It's for you," she said in a breathy whisper. "I don't talk about it often, b-but I remember. I remember wh-when I was dead.

"I remember you came for me. You accepted m-me when I was a corpse. Everything hurt all the time. C-constantly. But you were there. W-wanted me. Came for me. Stayed for me. Kept me near even as a corpse. N-never put me down o-or left me behind. Al-always with you.

"For you m-my dearest love… I'll give you

a-anything. Anything, my Felix."

Felix smiled, took her pinky from her, and then gave her a kiss on the brow. Anything more than that would set her off into a frantic mess.

"I did, and yes, I remember. Thank you, my love," he said and set the pinky down in front of himself, the collected the knife again. "Now… tips only please. I don't… need a whole finger."

"I don't want just your tip," Carlota said suddenly. "I want it all."

"I… yes," agreed Alma. "All."

Both Dryad's eyes were glowing that very evil-looking red of theirs now.

To which Faith started laughing, her own eyes starting to glow a bright green.

Nymphs… certainly falling within expectations.

Well, at least they keep it fun.

Chapter 33 - Legion City Shuffle -

Through the camera, Felix watched Andrea push it down into place and then step into the camera frame. She held up a thumb in front of it. She turned it up, then down, and just stared into the camera.

Someone must have responded to her because she then nodded her masked and helmeted head and then left the field of view.

Andrea and Faith were moving around the perimeter of the gold bullion depository and setting up the cameras. This was at Felix's request and they were carrying it out perfectly.

"I don't like it," whined Andrea. "Nnn... there's no real way to know if they'll buy the footage. It's a risk for us, isn't it?"

"Yes and no," replied Felix, not looking up from the footage on the laptop. It was all being fed here through a series of signal repeaters. This was all on a closed network that never even touched a public network or the internet. "They'll most definitely buy the footage. Especially if we tell them we're only going to sell it to one network and one network alone.

"It isn't a risk though because we can control what we send them. On top of that, we'll just have Miu be in charge of making sure it stays untraceable. This'll work out, I'm not concerned."

"I... that... G-Grove-husband?" asked Alma from his left. She had been quietly going through a mass of paperwork. An endless amount of things to sign and fill in for more shell corporations, misleading company names, and bank accounts.

"Yes?" he asked, looking away from the laptop to her.

They were sitting in the back of F-Two a few miles away from the planned puppet show. They needed to be close enough in case something really went sideways. Also, because the signal could only go so far before it'd become worthless and the footage would be unusable.

"Can… can I have some days off? I'd like to have some time to myself," requested Alma. She sounded incredibly unsure and worried as well.

Shit.

I've been running everyone into the ground. They've barely had any time for themselves at all. This is exactly what you always warned against.

Don't burn out the high performers.

"Of course," Felix stated quickly. "I'll also get everyone's salary set up, as well. As soon as we're done with our theater performance, we'll start getting everyone some private time.

"Thank you for asking. It'd honestly slipped my mind entirely. Keep doing that, Grove-maiden Alma. Question, poke, prod. I need people to challenge me."

"Could you poke and prod me again, Grove-husband? I think I need more attention," asked Carlota. She was off to the side of F-Two, wrestling a rather large container around. Getting it upright, she put her hands on her hips and gave it a critical once over. Then she nodded her head and looked at him.

He had no idea what she was doing, but he imagined it had some sort of purpose. She didn't seem keen on wasting time or effort.

At his side, Alma nodded her head rapidly. Where Carlota asked outright, Alma simply tagged along.

Though she would take control from Carlota once they all started.

"Uh… later. Kind of need to focus, you know?" Felix offered. Carlota and Alma needed a lot of attention from him. Faith had assured him that would fade with time as their trees strengthened.

Carlota sighed, gave him a crooked smile, and shrugged her shoulders. There was a faint dull-glow in her eyes regardless of his answer.

"A girl can try. I mean, you can always just say no and it is what it is. That's fine. Unless you tell me to stop, I won't," said the Ironwood Dryad. Looking at the case she seemed to be measuring against it.

Moving off to the side of the road where there were some bushes, she started rooting around in them. Digging through what looked like some type of berry-producing shrub.

"Y-yes. Exactly that. W-won't stop. Ever," Alma added, then held out a paper to him. "You need to sign this. It's the last one."

Andrea whined, then rolled to her other side.

She was inside the cab of the truck and laid out on the bench seat.

"This sucks. I wanna go fight myself, too. I bet the Myriad group wins. That's got my Third in it and she's really tough," complained Andrea. "Like… grrr… roar… punch punch kick, kind of tough. With a crunch and pop when the fists go bamf. Way more like our Feral Friend."

Felix shook his head with a grin and signed the document Alma had given him, then he handed it back to her.

The Andreas were going to actually try to kill one another. Apparently, whoever did the best was supposed to get a reward. Miu and Goldie were going to go against one another and try to kill each other as well.

They could all be resurrected by Felix. Faith, Miu, Andrea, and Goldie were all valid to be brought back to life.

Felix assumed the ability to bring them back to life was because they were all part of the original Legion.

Carlota and Alma, however, couldn't be brought back. If they died, that was the end of the road for them. They might be in a grove with Felix and considered his wives, but they weren't part of the original Legion.

They weren't brought here by Runner.

On the view screen of the laptop, Felix was able to catch the exact moment Goldie and the "Myriad" Andrea group appeared.

Goldie went right up to the front of the building and slammed her claws through it. She tore away massive chunks from the exterior and dislodged the door as well.

"Damn. We could probably actually rob it," muttered Felix. Then he sighed and shook his head. "That'd ruin this country though. This'll be bad enough just with us attacking it and nearly succeeding."

"She's v-very strong," Alma whispered. She was practically on his shoulder now, watching the screen. "It's a shame there aren't any m-more Dragons."

With a grin, Felix nodded his head. He already had a few ideas about that.

He had plans on how to brutalize his power. To force it to work for him and to support his wishes. So long as what he was trying to use it for was realistic, possible, and doable, he could shoe-horn it.

Like… asking Goldie to begin searching for Dragon bones. Keeping a map and notes on where they all are. Use the Dryads to assist her in her search with Gaia's help.

Then spend points to have the map filled out as if she'd done that for a year.

Just like the Fist.

While he'd been lost in his thoughts, Faith, Andrea as the "Elex PMC," and Miu had arrived on scene. They'd already engaged with Goldie and Myriad and we're now in the middle of a full-out war.

Faith was being left alone as she "set the stage" further. They needed a few devices to make things easier for them, as well as to provide them with leverage in the future.

Faith set down a glass case that was filled with LEDs, RGB computer parts set to flash a lot, and lasers that would rise and fall in intensity.

Felix had made sure to fill the damn thing up with power for Faith to tap into as well. Loading it up like a battery in a comparable way that Lily used to.

The case looked like a sci-fi piece of junk up close that wouldn't fool a ten-year-old.

From a distance, it looked considerably more impressive. Especially on a camera that would pick up more of the lights and less of the substance.

Goldie shrieked pitifully as soon as the case hit the ground and shrunk down to a Human-sized version of her Dragon self. Somewhere between the different changes to her power, they'd discovered that she could become a much smaller Dragon.

Faith then slammed her hands into the ground and a giant glowing green dome formed around them. That would keep out anyone trying to get in and interfere with their production.

Like say... the army. Trying to shoot at them with rifles, tanks, or jets from the outside. Can't have that now.

Everything became a mad scramble of fists, feet, bullets, and bodies, along with weapons. The Andreas had all agreed to use firearms and miss until they ran out of ammo.

Then they would engage in hand-to-hand combat with weapons and actually murder one another. The winner would simply absorb all the rest.

Surprisingly, Goldie and Miu looked like they were evenly matched. Battling fist and foot to claw and tail.

Faith was responsible just for monitoring everyone and keeping the dome up. She was there more as a referee of sorts.

Apparently, it was none-too-soon either.

Soldiers were rushing toward the area. Both from the depository as well as from the nearby base.

Armed with firearms, riding in and on vehicles, as well as more than likely scrambling aircraft. Several helicopters zoomed past overhead.

Felix noted the news station designations on the side of them as they went. Converging on the superhero battle.

"Perfect," Felix said, leaning up against the back of the truck bed. Things were moving in the right direction.

"I mean, yeah, it kinda is. It'll fit perfectly, too, so we can take it home," Carlota said, looking at the case in front of her. She'd managed to grow a bush into a nearly life-sized plant version of a Human. It was only as big as the case that it'd been grown next to. "Kind of surprising that I was able to make a plant… golem… though. Didn't think I had that much magic power, but my grandma used to tell me stories of Earth-spirits who could do it."

The plant creature suddenly turned its head toward Felix. It lifted a hand shaped from leaves and branches, and waved at him. There was a very faint glow of red where the eyes would be.

In that moment, he happened to notice it wasn't growing out of the ground either. Its feet had been formed of roots and it looked like it simply stepped right out of the ground.

"Uh… neat," he said, really unsure of what to say to this. He'd never thought that a Dryad could do such a thing.

"Isn't it, though? I bet I can make a bunch of guards like this. They can patrol the farms for us," Carlota said with several nods of her head. "Okay. I've now contributed to Legion again. You should reward me. Oh, Alma came up with the idea by the way

"So you need to reward her, too. Or just both of us at the same time. Whatever works."

Turning her head, Carlota laid her very brightly glowing red eyes on him. There was a smile on her face.

"I'm sure Andrea wouldn't mind giving us the bench seat if she gets to watch," Carlota said boldly.

"I don't mind! It'd be better than this!" chirped Andrea, suddenly sitting up in the front of F-Two. "Though that'd be really—er… What's that noi—"

A jet slashed through the sky above them. It was flying low and moving incredibly fast. Fast enough that it had probably broken the sound barrier.

Slapping his hands over his ears, Felix had only a second or two before the boom smashed through him. It felt like everything was rumbling and jittering around.

Soon as it ended, Felix let his hands fall.

Looking at the cameras that'd been placed, he watched as a number of things slammed into the shimmering green dome. As well as a few actually exploding, as if some type of splintering missile or rocket had struck.

A second or two after that, the jet tore through the area. Flashing across the view screen and leaving quickly.

Faith's dome remained intact and undisturbed.

"That's a hell of a first response," grumbled Felix. He'd expected this to happen, but not at this point. This felt like something that'd occur after someone had already tried to enter the dome or approach on foot.

Looking at the laptop screen, Felix watched as everyone in the dome ignored the jet and what it was doing. There was very little that'd be able to breach Faith's magical shield.

He'd simply given her too much power for it to fall to anything this world could throw at it, short of a nuclear weapon.

Felix was more than willing to bet on the fact that they most certainly wouldn't nuke their own bullion depository. That didn't mean they weren't willing to fire lower yield explosives, however.

Then something unexpected happened.

Something that was far and away outside of Felix's expectations or plans.

In one of the camera feeds, he could see the news helicopters. They were angled and positioned in such a way that they weren't directly over the fight. Nor were they over the airspace above the military.

They were more than likely illegally in the area though, he imagined. Most likely they'd been ordered to leave.

A few had started to turn and move away. A few had lingered, before suddenly spinning away from the situation.

Then a jet that couldn't correct for the helicopter's sudden maneuvers, or hadn't been paying attention perhaps, came through.

One of its wings clipped a helicopter that'd suddenly turned away. The helicopter shattered apart and began spinning wildly as it went down. Straight toward the neighborhood below them.

The jet made a whump noise that Felix could hear even from where they were, then spun sideways. There was a whoosh of air shooting out of the front of the jet that Felix assumed was the ejector seat firing.

Then the jet sailed through the air a bit further and slammed into a commercial building.

Splattering itself across the side of it and

lodging right into the middle of it. A good bit of the jet had broken free and peppered the buildings around it with bits and pieces as well.

There was a high-pitched whine following the thump of the crash. It reached an incredible volume that Felix could hear with his ears as well as on the camera.

As abruptly as it happened, the noise died.

Flames roared to life from the impact point of the building.

"Holy shit," Felix muttered.

His mind dove into what he'd just witnessed and it came back with an unexpected answer. If he could involve himself in this, or Legion more specifically, he could kick-start a part of his plan that wasn't active yet.

To push Legion into this as a neutral party that wanted only to help any situation that Powered people were part of. To help the non-supers and deal with those who had powers.

"Andie, get us back to that hardware supply store," commanded Felix and then looked to Carlota. "Get in quick and grab the briefcase from the passenger seat. We only have a few minutes to buy supplies and then get moving. I need to seriously abuse my powers."

Andrea had already fired the ignition of F-Two over and cranked the transmission into gear. Carlota had a second to get in before the Beastkin jammed the gas pedal.

The plant golem was left in the dust along

with the case Carlota had been toying with. In fact, the passenger side door wasn't even closed yet.

Pulling hard to one side, Andrea drove them off the road and over the median between. Then up into opposing traffic, and across to another field.

Driving in a straight line, it was obvious she was going to get them there as quickly as possible.

"What do we do?" Andrea shouted, her voice carrying through the open rear window.

"Buy up all the steel you can. Anything that could be classified as armor or used in making armor," Felix yelled back. "We'll hit the hardware store. Carlota, Alma, go with Andie! We've got two minutes. We'll divide the briefcase money in half and make it happen.

"After that… well… I'm going to spend a whole shit load of points, I bet. Way too many."

They bumped, bounced, and rattled their way across the open field.

Distantly, Felix could hear sirens.

Damnit.

Even now, the plan is still going perfectly. It'd just be a shame to not capitalize on this situation.

A rather large bump later and Alma had pushed herself up against him. She was bracing her legs against one side of the truck bed and her arm to the other. Felix was held tight against herself.

She was certainly stronger than he was and apparently valued his life over her own. She was trying to keep him safe and secure in the bed of the truck as they bounced along.

"I have you, G-Grove-husband," declared Alma, gazing at him with terrified eyes. Her arms were flexing as she held onto him, even as she gave him a brave smile.

Aw, aren't you a sweetheart?

Such a tender Dryad.

Now… material, point plan, make a… a… suit of armor. Fitting the "Legate" of Legion.

Become a super. A Powered.

Make duplicate suits for the others, then head into the crash site. See what we can do to help. Going to be point heavy.

Really point heavy.

There goes all the gains we made from the trash dump-offs.

Chapter 34 - Legate -

Andrea threw down a bunch of empty ammo canisters into the truck bed. Followed by Alma dumping a whole bunch of what looked like ballistic vests and older styled flak jackets.

"There's an Army surplus store next door. It had a bunch of stuff," Andrea said excitedly while throwing bags and other things into the truck bed. "I also found a RDS I'm really excited to try out and —"

Felix tuned out her excited chattering about gun accessories and focused on all the stuff that was in the truck bed. There was a lot of it. To the point that they'd actually spent the entire thirty grand that'd been in the briefcase.

Focusing on all the contents of the truck bed, he wanted to make a suit of armor. Similar in style to the types he'd worn that Felicia had made for him.

Something that would protect him from small arms fire. That'd take care of anything that'd be man-portable that he might run up on.

Everything else would take too much, he imagined. The point cost would skyrocket.

Then he pitched the whole request as what he'd come up with if he spent a year working on the design. If he started at this moment, and worked on it for a year, with the help of everyone in Legion, what would he come up with?

He felt a shuffling in his power. In the way it

interacted with him and the world. It distinctly reminded him of when he used to use it to try and ascertain the future and how it would change.

A box floated up in front of him.

Type: Armor (Legate 1.03)	**Condition**: New (Materials and work provided)
Owner: Felix Campbell (Legion)	**Construction**: Cost 178,312 points

Felix just about choked on his own tongue.

The value was incredibly high. To the point that he couldn't quite believe it. It'd nearly wipe out the entirety of his account. There'd be almost nothing left.

Grimacing while hating himself for spending so much, only to remind himself he had no other choice if he wanted to do this, he accepted the cost.

Before it could be revealed, he threw a tarp over it. They'd need to get to somewhere that they couldn't be seen before he put it on.

"I felt that," Alma said suddenly.

"Me, too. It was like magic, but not," Carlota agreed.

"Get in the truck. We need to get somewhere I can put it on," stated Felix. "Get your masks on, as well. We're going to move into this area and do what we can to help.

"Andie, how are you with bombs and defusing them?"

"Oh, oh, pretty good!" declared the Beastkin as she practically ripped the driver's side door open to get in. "I used a lot of them when I was doing contract work. It was easier to kill targets that way.

"It just ended up killing a lot of other people, too, so I kind of had to stop. My employers really didn't like it much and I lost a few contracts."

Ah… yes. Andrea was a supervillain.

Right.

Keep forgetting that.

Clambering up into the bed of F-Two, Felix sat down on the tarp. A rounded object shifted out of the way as he did so. This time he braced himself accordingly, as well.

Both Dryads had gotten into the cab with Andrea.

They took off like a shot, racing toward where the jet had smashed into the building. All three women had pulled on their masks at the same time. Apparently, they simply brought them with them everywhere now.

***

Andrea slammed F-Two through a barricade that blocked off a parking structure's entrance and went up the wrong way. Going straight in, she whipped them around a corner and right into a very dark corner.

There were almost no cars nearby and no cameras either.

Practically kicking the driver's door open, Andrea popped out and rushed over to the back of the truck.

"Nn, nn, nnn! Let's seeeeeeeeee iiiiiiiiit!" she said excitedly, bouncing up and down.

Felix now realized what she was so energized about.

The armor.

Getting out of the bed, Felix pulled the tarp down.

What sat there was an inspired-looking piece of body armor. It was several parts that would all hang together nicely when worn at the same time.

It was painted in black and red Legion colors.

A breastplate, armguards, spaulders, armored tasset, leggings, boots, and a helmet that even had a red-bristled stripe down the center. It was very modern-looking though cut, sewn, and put together mimicking armor from the Roman Empire.

Picking up the helmet, Felix was surprised.

From what he saw at first glance, it looked somewhat silly. The front had an actual mask on it. It was shaped in a basic Human face with holes for the eyes only. Those were filled with reflective glass that were more like mirrors.

Up close, it was obvious it was an enclosed helmet. There were a number of rubber gaskets that'd close it up around his head tightly. Even the cheek flaps that came down would hook into the rest and seal it shut.

Err… I hope it has some type of oxygen canister or filter system. Otherwise, that just won't work and I'll be gasping for air fast.

"Ooooh, it's so nice. I can't wait for my own suit. It even has a cape or cloak or whatever it's called. I want one," Andrea said excitedly, clapping her hands together. "Legion is gonna be so cool! So cool. Alright, bucket-up, Felix!"

Andrea snatched the helmet out of his hand and thumped it down over his head. Plunging him into a strange view.

The eye slits felt like they practically rested over his eyes. They barely changed his view of the world at all.

This truly had been tailored to fit him perfectly in every way.

"Get his boots off, Alma," Andrea commanded as she snatched up the breastplate. "We can just put the rest of it on over his clothes."

With only a minute spent being jerked around, they did manage to get Felix completely suited up.

"Okay, yeah, I need one," said Andrea, standing in front of him. "Felix, I want one. I'll do whatever I need to do, for you to give me one. And I —"

There was a muffled boom as it sounded like something blew up.

"Time to go!" Andrea said excitedly with a tilt of her head. A second later, her ears vanished beneath her mask, then her tail retracted and was no more.

She looked perfectly Human.

Turning on her heel, she made a mad dash out of the parking garage.

Chasing after her, Felix found that the armor was incredibly light. It didn't seem to weigh him down at all and practically moved for him, rather than with him. Everything felt perfect on his person.

Just need to upgrade it again later to give it electronics. Like my old armor.

This is a great starting point though.

Storming out of the parking garage, they only had to go a short distance to the building. At the base of it, and blocking the entrance, were a number of soldiers with weapons. They were keeping people out of the burning, smoking, quite possibly collapsing building.

There was even a team of paramedics who looked like they wanted to get inside to do exactly what Felix was there to do.

Andrea ran right up to the soldiers.

"Where's the ordinance!?" she demanded. They looked at her and her masked appearance somewhat shocked. The second it was obvious they were hesitating, she leaned in close to the soldier. "Defusal must occur swiftly before the fire spreads. Where is it!? NOW!"

That somehow broke through the soldier's thoughts.

Felix didn't pause or wait to find out what

would happen next. He ran straight into the building, dashing through a shattered door that was hanging from a single hinge.

Alma and Carlota were right behind him, leaping through after him even as the soldiers behind shouted at them to stop.

Passing into a lobby that looked fairly normal—except for the flashing emergency lights and screaming people—Felix noted that the elevators were clearly not working. Everyone would be trying to get through the stairs then.

Okay. We just need to be present, help guide people out, and go up to make sure people can get down. Take on the role of just a simple superhero from the old timey comics.

Nothing big, no big bad guys yet, just... just disasters that—

There was a rumbling creak from above that made Felix feel like this was a really stupid idea. Going up this inside building was going to be a risk.

Glancing around, he saw a great many people who'd collapsed, been dropped off, or were just milling around here.

For whatever reason, they hadn't left the building, and the soldiers outside didn't seem to want to let anyone in. That'd have to change.

"D-One, D-Two for clarity's sake," Felix said while pointing at Alma, then Carlota. "Establish this as triage. Start putting people back together if they're hurt. If they can walk or be moved, get them the hell out of here. Goal is to clear the lobby completely.

"This building could come down and we're just asking for trouble being here. Got it?"

Both Dryads nodded their masked heads understanding the designations as well as their role.

"I'm heading up, I'll send people here or bring them back," he commanded. Turning, he went to the emergency stairs and then raced up them. He made it to the second floor and then opened the door.

Leaning into the area, he peered down the hall.

"Is there anyone there?" he called at the top of his lungs.

He wasn't quite sure how loud he'd be given that his helmet was sealed, but he had to at least try. Also, there was the distinct possibility of it having a microphone attached to it.

There hadn't been enough time to really test and check out what the armor could do. Right now, Felix couldn't help but feel like he had more questions than answers.

Lifting his hand, he slammed his fist into the door several times.

"Anyone?" he called again. There was no response. Neither verbal, nor someone hitting something in return.

Felix turned and re-entered the stairs, racing up to the next floor.

He repeated the process again, calling out to

anyone inside.

Even as he did so, he could hear someone coming down from above.

Turning as a small group of people came down, he looked them over quickly. They had on emergency reflective vests and were rushing down the stairs.

"Anyone up there?" Felix asked as they came close.

"You, yes! Yes, there is!" said a woman at the front with a clipboard. "There's at least three people on the fifth floor. We couldn't through the rubble, but we could see two people standing and a third on the ground."

Again there was a rumbling and ominous creak from above.

"Anyone else?" he asked.

"Not that we know of, we need to take a roll call but—"

"Go!" commanded Felix, pointing down the stairs.

Moving around the group, Felix got to the third floor and called out while banging on the door. Then he did so again on the fourth.

Both times there was no call or response to him. There was nothing to be heard at all.

When he got to the fifth, he could see why they hadn't been able to do anything.

The remains of the jet was partly here. A large section of the fuselage, part of a wing, and the cockpit was all spread around on this floor.

On top of everything else, large pieces of the ceiling and roof had come down as the fire spread further out of control. The sounds he'd heard were from the ceiling collapsing inward.

"Ah, shit," growled Felix, wondering how bad this was going to be. Looking through the wreckage, he could see how the other group had given up.

There was literally fire.

Everywhere.

Gritting his teeth, and suddenly thankful that the armor had actually had a lining that connected all the pieces together, Felix hoped it was all fireproof. Given the way he'd upgraded it, he imagined it probably was.

Just like how Felicia had put in the teleporter gun, right?

Right… yeah… we'll just… believe in that.

Marching forward, Felix kept his teeth together and went through the fire. He could immediately feel the heat bearing down on him, but it wasn't painful.

It didn't seem to be burning him.

He wasn't going to dilly dally though and traipse through it just to test how far the armor would go.

Getting to the wreckage, Felix saw that there was a passage through. The problem was it was very much on fire and wouldn't be usable.

Maybe by himself in his armor, but not to get people back out. He'd need another option.

Looking over what was all there, Felix saw something that'd probably work. It just wasn't going to be very fun and it would leave him in a position he'd just determined he wanted to avoid.

Marching up to the fire, and more or less standing in it, violating the cardinal rule of gaming from his youth, he started to heave and shove at a fallen column. It looked like it was a thick wooden beam partly faced with stone.

It appeared heavier and more decorative than being of any actual use. Straining with all of his might, pushing with the entirety of his being, Felix struggled to clear the way.

If he could get this single beam moved, or at least just dislodged, there'd be a path to move through. The fire was being fed by the beam, as well as blocking the way through.

This isn't a damn job for me!

I'm not a Powered that just has strength or speed. I'm not a telepath or a psychic. I'm a damn glorified middle manager who spent too long giving VPs reports!

Letting out a guttural yell, Felix put everything he had into trying to move the beam. Pushing with every muscle and fiber of his body.

There was a sharp crack, followed by the beam breaking.

Felix hadn't managed to move it at all, but he'd succeeded in his goal.

It'd broken under a combination of his efforts, the weight of the stones, and because it'd been weakened by the fire. The whole thing broke in half at the midpoint.

Stumbling forward with the sudden change, Felix ended up shoving half of the beam to the other side of the wreckage. The loud boom of it hitting the burnt carpet felt heavy under his feet. The sudden and unexpected lack of exertion made his head swim and his hands tingle.

A sharp breath was all he allowed himself before he went forward again. The other group had said they could see the survivors from where they were.

That meant he had to move straight ahead to the other side. There was nowhere else they could have been seen from.

Marching across the open floorplan, he found all three people. They were huddled up in a corner, the furthest from the fire they could be.

There was a great deal of smoke pouring out past them through the gaping hole in the building. The whole area felt incredibly hot to him but he wasn't sure if that was from the fire he'd been standing in or the area.

All three people were unconscious.

Unmoving, unresponsive, and very much not going anywhere under their own power.

"Shit," Felix said, suddenly realizing just how blatantly foolish this idea had been. While he wanted to push Legion into a neutral position, one that could mitigate situations between supers, this was a damn foolhardy way to get his foot in the door.

"Okay, uh… what—"

Standing there, Felix had a momentary flash of thought.

He'd been able to force-feed power into Carlota and Alma. He'd done so through utilizing his own power and transferring it to them.

Could he turn that power toward himself and give himself a momentary rush?

"Okay, okay, ah… we'll just, yeah, why not," he muttered to himself.

Opening himself up to the power within, Felix began to pool his power. He was going to thrust it into his body and empower himself.

Then get them to the stairs, one at a time. Once all three were there, he could start bringing them down.

After that, it'd be as simple as three trips.

Then I can just—

The ceiling gave way in that moment and the floor beneath him as well. The fifth floor suddenly became the fourth floor, but with vaulted ceilings.

Felix had all of a second of losing his balance before everything collapsed out from under him. He moved forward and fell atop the unconscious trio.

His armor would protect him from any damage better than their own skin would.

Or so he thought as everything fell.

Chapter 35 - Moderated -

Even before everything had finished falling, Felix managed to get partially upright. He found himself standing above the same three individuals he'd been before, only now they were all sprawled out amongst what looked like flooring material.

As well as a crumpled metal beam that'd torn through part of a wall.

"Shit," Felix said and finally got himself to a full standing position.

Staring out through a massive hole in the building, Felix could see all the way to the bullion depository. There was still a green dome present out there.

There were a number of news helicopters hovering around as well. Two were even facing towards Felix now that he looked at them.

No time to stop and smell the roses. Need to go.

Need to move.

Can't stay here.

I'm not a strength super or one that's made for speed. I'm just a damn Human who can change things.

A Mastermind type at best, Production class at worst.

Looking at the biggest of the three people laid out at his feet—an overweight man in a suit—Felix grabbed him first. Flinging the man over his shoulders, he began walking back toward where the stairs should be.

While there was certainly fire here as well, it

was less so than what he'd been dealing with only a short while earlier on the floor above this one.

Shifting past a cracked slab of sheetrock and a bundle of some sort of cabling, Felix made his way through the debris. Thankfully, he didn't actually have to go too far out of his way.

Reaching the stairs, Felix yanked the door open, then stepped into the stairwell. He put the man down and then looked at the door. It was swinging shut and appeared to be a fire door.

Fine, that'll help for now... and it doesn't seem as smoke-filled in here.

One down, two to go.

Nodding, Felix pushed the door open and went back into the ruin of the building. Moving at a quick trot, he made his way back to the other two unconscious victims.

No sooner than he'd reached them, there was a loud grinding noise behind him. Turning his head, he was just in time to watch the bulk of the jet slide down from the floor above and crash down before him.

The cockpit was now right in front of him and he could actually see that the pilot was still inside. The canopy had blown off, but the ejection seat had failed to correctly activate.

Trapped in the seat was a very unconscious pilot.

God damn it.

Back to three. That's just fucking great and—

There was a bang and a large object that

looked like a rocket or missile clattered free from the jet and rolled around on the floor. Right next to a large fire that was burning away merrily.

Okay. You know what? Fuck you, Fate.

You nasty bitch.

Why're you doing this to me?

Haven't I always been fair with you?

Growling, Felix had no idea what to do now. He had no idea if the weapon was a dud, disarmed, active, or would even explode if exposed to fire.

This wasn't his area of expertise in any way, shape, or form.

Shaking his head, Felix grabbed both of the people at his feet by their collars. He didn't have the time or luxury to be kind with them.

Holding tightly to their clothes, Felix began to practically run back toward the stairs. He needed to get them out of here as quickly as possible.

That meant not sparing them indignity and exposing them to actual fire. There were no other options available to him anymore.

Dodging around a larger chunk of broken plane, Felix took a different route to the stairs this time. His previous one wouldn't work with dragging two people along.

Grimacing, he saw that he would indeed have to run them right through a rather large flame. With a shake of his head, he did his best to scare up what energy he had and then muscled forward.

As quickly as he could, he charged through the fire, dragging along his unconscious companions with him. Pulling them into the fire and out the other side.

Coming out and finding himself in an open space, Felix oriented on the door to the stairs and rushed over.

He let go of one person to pull the door open, then dragged the other person to it to wedge it open. In that moment, he realized they were on fire.

"Ah, fuck!" Felix said loudly and quickly worked at patting out the fire that was burning their pants.

Getting it out quickly, he looked at the other person and found they weren't burning, though they were face down on the ground.

"This is so fucked," he grumbled as he grabbed that person and pulled them into the stairwell. He dropped them down atop the first who was actually starting to move a bit.

Grabbing the third, Felix pulled them across the doorway as well and dumped them with the other two. Taking a moment to catch his breath, Felix looked at the man he'd pulled over first.

He looked like he might be coming around.

Unable to wait any longer, Felix instead shut the fire door. He needed to go see if the pilot was alive or dead.

Fuck. This is all your fault, Kit.

Your fault.

If you were here, I could just… do whatever the hell I wanted.

But no, because you're not, it's like you're a damn ghost. Hovering over me and demanding me to do things.

Because if I don't, and I show up in front of you with a bunch of villainous things in my head, you'll look away from me. I have to at least… I have to try.

Growling under his breath, Felix rushed back into the fire.

Dashing through the narrow space where he'd gone previously, Felix worked his way around to the front of the jet. Stepping up onto something that looked a lot like the remains of a watercooler, Felix managed to get up close to the pilot.

The helmet they'd been wearing was pulled partway to the side and the visor had been flipped up. As if they'd been trying to get out of the seat after the ejector failed.

It was a man who looked to be bleeding from his shoulder. The fabric of their uniform from the top of their arm to their elbow was drenched in red.

Examining their straps, Felix had no idea what he was looking at. It looked like a harness that'd be able to quickly disengage, but he truly didn't know. Nor did he have any experience with it, either.

This sucks.

Reaching into the cockpit, Felix immediately realized the man was alive. He shifted around at Felix's hands suddenly touching him. That wasn't much more than a flinch followed by a slump in the seat, but it was something.

Grabbing at the clasps, Felix tried to get the

man out of the harness.

Nothing gave and he couldn't seem to get it to release. It felt like there was something that'd jammed it up and it wasn't going to let go of its catch mechanism.

Looking down toward where it ran, Felix noted some type of loop. The man's hands were hanging quite close to it as if he'd been reaching for it.

Mechanical release of the harness? Maybe.

The partial fail on the ejector seat could have locked it in, right?

Felix grasped the yellow-and-black cord and then jerked on it.

Nothing happened at all. It didn't seem to do anything.

Clambering up onto the jet itself, Felix peered into the cockpit and at the controls. Everything was dead and there was no response from anything. There didn't seem to be any power reaching the controls.

With a grunt, Felix leaned back to look at the seat more closely.

His boot slipped a fraction and he ended up grabbing the top part of the pilot's seat, pulling the whole thing to one side as he did so.

There was a sudden hiss followed by a clank and the pilot was jerked away from Felix. In fact, his entire seat was pulled away from him.

Two rockets shot out of the seat at an angle and propelled the pilot away from Felix for several seconds. A small drag parachute popped out of it at the same time.

The pilot shot away and out of the building. Clearing the burning wreckage, it moved out over the tops of buildings.

Right as it got level in its arc there was a pop from the top of the chair and another, much larger parachute deployed. Then the seat separated from the pilot and vanished out of sight while the pilot slowly fluttered down to the ground.

Still unconscious, the pilot escaped the flaming wreck of the building.

"Oh, that works," Felix said, standing atop the jet, watching the pilot. "Now I just have to get back to—"

There was an abrupt and riotous explosion and the whole world became flame.

Felix was launched backward by the explosive force of the blast. Sent tumbling out of the building entirely. He had a brief view of the street below him before he slammed into it at full force even as the world still rang in his ears.

All he knew was blackness and the ringing that wouldn't stop.

Felix felt the world come back to him sometime later.

His mind was still cranked hard with the adrenaline of the situation he remembered last, and he tried to get up.

Looking around, he blinked several times.

Everything looked like he'd last known it, so

he couldn't have been out for very long, or maybe at all.

Getting to his feet, Felix groaned. His whole body felt like it'd been run over by a steamroller. One of the lenses in his mask had a crack running from one side to the other as well.

Then he noticed there several soldiers with guns all rushing toward him. Quite a few of them had them drawn on him and were clearly ready to hose him down with rounds.

Yeah... let's not get mag-dumped here. No telling how well the armor would stand up to that kind of abuse, given what I've already put it through.

Holding his hands up, Felix just stood there.

Amongst the group of service men, there were officers spread amongst them. A number of them even looked to be of higher ranking, though Felix was unsure of their designations. He hadn't looked into the military of this world.

"And who the fuck are you, god damnit?!" shouted one older man. He was in a uniform and a cap only, though he did have a sidearm at his waist. Other than that, all he had was a handheld radio which was actually in his hand.

The lack of equipment made Felix feel like this man had more rank stuffed up his ass than the others.

"Legate," Felix said, even as the man stormed up to him. Keeping his hands raised was clearly the right answer with so many fingers caressing triggers. "I'm the Legate. I command the

Legion. I came here to help."

"Leg— What? Fuck that. I don't give a shit. You're going to take your fucking helmet off nice and slow, and then I'm going to put your ass in a cell!" screamed the man. There was a constant situational report being given over the radio at the same time.

"—unable to engage. They're moving slowly toward the depository. Quite a few of them are dead," reported a voice.

The man who'd been screaming at Felix looked disturbed by what he heard over the radio.

I... okay. Let's make a play.

Play the Legion card completely.

It's the only one we've got right now. Otherwise, it becomes a lot of fighting my way out and hoping no one dies.

That wouldn't do Legion any favors at all.

"I can stop them," Felix said, using his right hand to point at the walkie-talkie, while still keeping it raised up. "I can mediate this. Make them stop. That was another reason I came here. Legion is neutral in their war but strong enough to get them to agree to a cease-fire.

"If only because I'm here in person this time and it sounds like they have casualties. If I show up, they'll at least stop long enough for you to get people into position."

Staring at Felix intently, the officer was clearly considering his words. As if he might actually go for the idea.

"The Dragon just let out more fire," said the voice on the radio. "It went outside the dome this time and the grass is burning."

Wincing, the senior officer looked like a man who really didn't want to be here or given this situation.

Felix could certainly identify with the man.

Any person who made an executive decision in a situation like this was responsible for it. There would be no one who could save you if you simply made the wrong call.

"I can stop them," promised Felix. "But only if I go right now. The Golden One must be regaining their power if they're able to put out that much fire through the fight.

"There's no telling when Myriad will rise again. You can't really kill them. They just get back up."

"I will find you and kill you myself if you do anything else," threatened the officer. Clearly, he didn't want to make the choice, but it was better than not making it.

Dereliction of duty wasn't a thing that you could just sidestep, Felix imagined. In his own world, one could also get relieved of command, which was more often than not a career killer.

"You won't have an issue. The Legate solves problems," Felix replied. Letting his hands fall to his sides, he hesitated. "There are three people in the stairwell that I pulled from the fire. The pilot was—"

"I'll get them all," promised the officer.

Waiting only a second longer, Felix took off at a run toward the depository. He didn't look back and he didn't hesitate.

This was his chance to escape a promised loss of his freedom and getting cornered into revealing his identity. It'd only create the situation he'd been trying to avoid this whole time.

Dodging between two buildings, Felix managed to get through to the other side. Ahead of him was a street that would run parallel to the freeway leading out of the area.

Turning hard, he kept running, moving right along the sidewalk at a hard pace.

People turned and stared as he went, and more than a few people lifted phones to take video or pictures of him.

Out of nowhere, Alma and Carlota appeared beside him. Falling in on each side as he went as if that was where they belonged.

Alma held up her left hand and a red dome appeared around them. Carlota lifted her right hand and the dome became a wedge and much darker in color.

Both of their eyes were glowing through their masks. A bright, vibrant red that gave them that sinister feeling he always felt when he looked at them.

A postal box was shunted to the side as it connected with the wedge and it was torn off its footings. Knocked into the street, as if it were pushed aside by a giant.

Right, okay.

With a hard pivot to the right, Felix began storming through the street. He did it in a way that he felt the wedge wouldn't cause too many problems or accidents, but he was more than willing to trust in it to protect him.

A single parked car was bumped to the side as he reached the sidewalk, crossed, and ended up reaching the highway.

Behind him he could hear a horn blaring the "shave and a haircut, two bits" call.

Glancing over his shoulder, Felix saw Andrea heading right for him. She was driving a black pickup truck that was raised and had some type of flag hanging off the back of it.

Moving to the side, Felix smiled to himself as he ran on. He was always at his best when surrounded by Legion.

And they were likely at their best with him acting as support.

Andrea pulled up right alongside him and waited, still moving forward.

Grabbing hold of the tailgate, Felix jumped inside.

Snatching up the flag, Felix tossed it out the back as he did so. Then he turned and held his hand out to Alma.

Grasping her by the forearm she'd reached out, he hauled her up partway into the truck. Carlota needed no such assistance and practically flew into the truck bed on her own, having grasped the side and hopped in.

Felix went to the front and grabbed hold of the bar that was there. He didn't spare the light rack and just hung on instead. He was expecting Andrea to floor it.

Alma and Carlota stood on either side of him and the magic wedge reformed itself, jutting ahead of the truck.

Then Andrea dropped the pedal and they took off at full speed. The engine roared as it was pushed to maximum power.

Glancing over his shoulder, Felix looked back at the building where he'd gotten free. It was still very much on fire and looked like it was getting worse.

That was stupid going in there like that. I could have b—

There was an explosion in the building and part of it was engulfed in a fireball.

Ah… the missile went off.

Hm. Oh!

Yes, hello, Hubris. Welcome back.

Indeed. Hello.

That was a… really stupid idea, Felix.

Thanks Hubris, I realize that in retrospect.

I mean, I'm all for getting in there my dude, but damn. Damn, damn.

You could have been vaporized.

I know! I know… shut up.

Looking ahead, he focused on where they

were going. Straight towards the green dome of his people.

He could hear Andrea singing at the top of her lungs inside of the truck cab. It sounded like she'd found some sort of alternative station and had it cranked to full.

Apparently, she was adapting to the culture of this world very quickly.

"—burn in hell to make it all true, but I never loved anyone else in this world but you—" screamed Andrea as the truck bounded off the highway with a rattle and a clank. They smashed through a concrete divider that was blasted apart and scattered in every direction by the red Dryad magical wedge. "I don't give a damn what other people think!"

Felix shook his head as they raced across the field toward a chain link fence.

It lasted about as long as the concrete divider had, blasting apart, and being thrown in every direction.

"I feel so fucking alive!" shouted Carlota, standing next to him. Her hands were holding fast to the bar just as his own were.

"Yes!" agreed Alma in a similar position on Felix's other side. They were both staring ahead even as Andrea continued to scream along with a song only she knew the words to.

Even as Felix and company approached, Goldie, Faith, Miu, and what remained of the Andreas all stopped what they were doing. They were all looking his way and clearly aware of his approach.

Alma and Carlota's red shield struck Faith's at the extreme edge.

There was a sound like a loud explosion a second before the green dome was eaten by the red one. It spread over it and dominated it in one go.

Felix wasn't sure if that was Faith simply accepting the Dryad magic of the others since they were all in the same grove, or if Alma and Carlota were stronger than he knew.

Either way, he didn't know or care.

The cameras are still on and watching.

"Don't let me fall D-One!" Felix called and then jumped up on top of the cab. He felt stupid and like he was about to be flung off, but he was determined to make this look heroic.

Planting one boot down on the hood, the other resting on the top of the cab, Felix braced himself. Racing ever onward, right at Miu and Goldie, Felix felt like this was way over the top.

Except that's how heroics went.

Coming to a stop in front of them, Felix felt the Dryad magic acting on him. Forcing him to physically remain in that spot. A great deal of force in fact. To the point that it sounded like his boots were crumpling the hood.

Thankfully, Andrea had hit the brakes in a way that didn't send him sliding to the side. He was able to use his back foot to keep his footing as well.

Coming to a full stop, Felix hopped off the

truck and walked over to Miu and Goldie.

"Hello, sorry, things happened," he said, putting his hands behind his back. "First off, who won?"

Miu's entire bearing had changed as soon as he started speaking. She was facing him head-on now, her hands fluttering at her sides.

"I was winning, but… but she's very strong," Miu confessed. "I'm not sure I could beat her at her normal size. She's been generous to fight me as she is."

"You were doing fine, Miu. Very well, in fact. Honestly, there isn't a Dragon who could probably beat me in my old world. I could have taken Taylor on if I wished," Goldie said in a secretive way. "I just never really wanted to be with Vince. I didn't care for him much. I wouldn't take it too badly, though."

"—know I'd rather die than to fuck this up. Wouldn't get another try. You're my god and I worship you!" screeched Andrea, who was still quite literally rocking out in the truck cab.

"Oh, I like that song!" said one of the Myriad villains who then rushed over to the truck.

"Nn! Yes, yes!" repeated a number of other Andreas, all running over to the truck. They also absorbed and took in all their fallen sisters.

As soon as they were absorbed, they simply popped right back out. All of the Andreas gathered around the truck.

Apparently, the show was over for them and

they'd rather listen with Andrea Prime.

"Hm," Felix said, watching the Andreas for a moment before looking back to Miu, Goldie, and Faith.

"—promise you could easily go toe-to-toe with Kris. It'd be a coin flip for which of you won," Goldie was saying.

"R-really? Oh. Thank you… thank you, Goldie," murmured Miu. Felix could hear the smile in her voice.

"Alright. This is over. I'm going to make a few dramatic gestures here, then it's time to get this done. You take Myriad and get out of town, Goldie," asked Felix. "Miu, just vanish. "I'll have Prime take everyone in. Faith, Carlota, and Alma can give us a nature screen I imagine.

"You did say you could make things invisible after all, Faith. It'd work here, right?"

"I... yes, it'd work," said the Dryad. She'd apparently taken a few turns battling Goldie as well since there was blood smeared around and over her. There were also visible signs that she'd healed herself. "I fought Goldie as well, you know."

"I see that. Looks like you did well enough to not get killed. Did you try to end her, Goldie?" asked Felix, glancing at the Dragon.

"I did, actually. I almost killed her with a tail-stab. Almost. She was able to slip away by the skin of her teeth, darn it," admitted the Dragon with a dark chuckle. "I wouldn't fear Dryads on a one-on-one basis, but… I would most certainly be unwilling to fight all three that are here at the same time."

"Goldie, my Golden One, you're a beautiful, magnificent beast, you know that? You may not claim to be a very dragon-like Dragon, but I think you're fantastic," Felix complimented her with a laugh. Then he made a chopping motion as if he were done. "Okay. That's it. Everyone leave immediately. Goldie, go 'eat' that device. You can just spit it out later so that people can't find it."

The first televised battle of supers in this world ended just like that.

Epilogue

Felix shook his head back and forth. This was absolutely one of the last things he wanted to see right now.

For perhaps the sixth time since it happened, a news station was showing their helicopter footage. Felix was in his Legate armor rushing out to the injured victims.

Only for the collapse to occur and then the image of him standing over them. As if he'd protected them.

"Yeah, no, no more of that," he said and turned physically away from the television. He put his attention back to the laptop.

At least it's not me shooting the pilot into the air again. That always makes me cringe. I didn't mean to do it!

"But it's so gooooooooooood!" Andrea argued from the couch.

They were in the home on the landfill. It was easier to work out of this location since everything here was legal.

Including the internet, TV service, water, and electricity.

"Nn, nn, nn," cheered Third. "My Felix was so brave!"

"My Felix," Second argued.

"No, mine!" insisted Andrea Prime.

Pressing his fingertips to his brow, he considered leaving the room. Ever since their battle to the death, Second and Third Andrea had been in an argument over everything.

Which really came down to who won the prize in their fight to the death.

"Prime, pick one," Felix said suddenly. It'd been two days of their constant bickering. "You've gone through both of their memories. Who won the fight? This bickering needs to end."

Andrea Prime sighed loudly, then actually growled.

"Third did," she muttered. "I don't want her to win though. You already prefer her over us. She hides her memories from us. You take her to bed often, don't you?"

Felix couldn't deny he did actually bed Third Andrea when he was given the opportunity. He just really had a thing for the Death Others.

They weren't his favorites, but if he had a preference, he'd veer toward them. He was just impressed with them.

Identified with them in a weird way.

Probably why I also was really happy when Myriad and her Others came back.

All Death Others.

But I don't have a favorite.

"I have no favorites amongst you," Felix said with a sigh and then stood up. "She hides memories from you for the same reason you do. You treasure things that make you unique. Otherwise, you wouldn't be Prime, Second, Third, or any other Other.

"She gets no more attention from me, than anyone else. I mean, ask Second where she was this morning. She probably hid that from you and didn't share it.

"Not like you can talk either, Prime. Did you share with them everything that happened while they were off fighting? Or did you save a few things just for you?

"It's normal. You're all Andrea, but you're all… individuals. Otherwise, you wouldn't have numbers. Names. Nor would I recognize you all.

"You're all Andrea, you all want to keep just a piece of yourself to yourself. It's normal. Be happy and loving to one another, just like you always were. It's just a little different now because you're a much better version of yourself, so you're more aware of things.

"I've taken each one of you when you were alone and I was given the chance and opportunity. I know that for a fact."

Having suitably pointed out they were all Andrea, that they all wanted to be unique, they could probably move on from it.

"Are you three good now?" he asked.

"Yes," they said in unison a moment before Prime stuck her hands in the hands of both Second and Third.

"We're okay. We're Andrea Campbell. We're all unique because we all want the same. You," she said with a determined smile. "You're right. We hide bits of you to ourselves. Maybe we should just… share it all with one another and share those special moments."

Second and Third were both nodding their heads now.

I need to be more careful about that. No more cornering Third for a bit. Even if I don't have a favorite, I need to be aware of it for a bit.

Picking up the laptop, Felix left the room. He was trying to read through the news right now and how governments were reacting. There'd been universal acknowledgment that the world wasn't what it seemed anymore, but official statements were "being prepared" for distribution.

Exiting to the back, Felix saw Faith, Alma, and Carlota all standing in front of Goldie. They were apparently practicing their magic work on her.

Her resistance to it was incredibly high.

As demonstrated by the fact that she was currently working on planting what looked like flowers in a garden bed. All their spells just slammed into her and did absolutely nothing.

"Oh, hello, Nest-mate," called the Dragon, giving him a wide smile from where she was kneeling. Her horns were prominent today and the new golden rings he'd put on the gold chains were very visible, as well as two charms and a bell.

"Hello, my Golden One," Felix said with a smile for the beautiful Dragon housewife. He dropped down into a wicker chair. Pulling up a news website, he started to scroll through the headlines.

Felix had just barely managed to not think about how lovely Goldie was in her gardening clothes, or how wonderful the Dryads looked either in their casual clothes.

"Why, thank you! I'm so glad you like them. It was hard to find some red and black that fit and went with the goal in mind, so I'm glad you appreciate it," Goldie said, having apparently gotten the thought out of him anyway. "And yes, I'm most certainly your Dragon housewife.

"Speaking of, make sure you take your shoes off when you go back in. I don't want you trailing in pieces of the yard. We just aerated the grounds this morning and it'll stick to your shoes if you're not careful.

"I just swept up this morning and I don't want to have to sweep again today just because you got distracted thinking about me in these clothes and the 'incredibly beautiful and sexy Dryad girls' as you thought of them."

Three pairs of flashing eyes turned his way, then a fourth as Goldie peered up at him from where she was bent over. Her smile was predatory.

She'd maneuvered him to this moment.

Her whole goal was exactly this.

She wanted to take him away by herself. Away from here and likely back to the trailer where they could be alone.

To "save him" from the Dryads.

Ah... yes. Time to go.

Getting back up, Felix nodded his head and

went around the house. He'd honestly known better than to think he could have sat there without them paying attention to him.

They were predatory, after all.

Dragons hunted anything they wanted and Dryads stalked men.

Moving to the front of the home, he sat down on the porch bench and put the laptop on his lap.

Opening the screen, he once more began to sort through everything that was listed out as news.

Nothing stood out to him and everything was more or less unchanged. No one had officially said anything at all.

Almost every piece of news was about the "battle of the supers" or "Legate's intervention."

To be sure, this was what he'd actually wanted to occur.

The world was heading toward its Awakening with supers and he was on the inside line. A head start that he could fully utilize and maximize for his own ends.

"Felix," whispered a voice from his side.

Turning his head, he found Miu perched at his side on the bench. She'd snuck right up to him and was within biting range.

Before she could act, Felix leaned in and kissed her briefly. With his right hand, he gently patted her cheek and then went back to the laptop.

If he did it just right, that'd short-circuit her and he'd be able to get a little work done. Too much and the bite was coming, not enough and she'd pop and need attention.

"I... I... th-that is... I love you," murmured Miu.

Ah, just right.

"And I love you. Now, what's up, my darling Miu?" Felix replied and closed the website.

Until Jay called him at some point today, he was mostly just doing research or poking around.

"I-I'm your darling," repeated Miu with a strange tone to her voice. "Err, th-that is, they bought the footage. I have the money. I put it in the bedroom. It's in a briefcase. You were right."

"Mm. Figured. Glad to hear it. Good work, Miu," Felix congratulated her. Reaching up with his right hand, he stuck it behind her head, then tugged her head to his shoulder. Wrapping his arm around her, he held her tightly at his side.

With his left hand, he opened up the window to start going through the interview requests for Legion.

Abruptly, his phone began ringing.

Reaching into his pocket with his left hand while still holding Miu with his right, he fished it out.

It was Jay.

Popping the accept button, he held it to his ear.

"Hello, Jay. Is it ready?" Felix asked in his 'Legate' voice.

"I... yeah. It's all ready. Just go to that website and it's there for you. That'd be the production file for the Operating System, phone app, and database. Bunch of programs that make it all work, too.

"They're pretty jank, though. Really jank, actually. You said just to hurry it up, so we did but —"

"That's perfect," Felix stated, interrupting him. "Thank you. I accept the programs in full receivership and will take ownership of them from here."

Hitting the disconnect button, Felix smiled to himself. Setting his phone down next to him, Felix looked at the laptop without seeing it.

He was focusing hard on what he wanted.

The idea that the phone app, the Legionnaire's Call program, was his. His and his alone in its entirety. He owned it and could do whatever he wanted to it.

Which meant modifying the program to fit his needs would be fine.

All he'd have to do is use the programming team he had to make the changes that he wanted. Changes that'd occur naturally over time.

Bending that intent to his desires, Felix called to his power.

First, he needed the Encampment OS to be upgraded. So that it would be completely independent of any other OS and incompatible with them. Everything on it would be proprietary and unable to be used in any other computer system.

There was an entire list of things he'd told

Jay he wanted, which the man happily compiled in a list format. Most of it didn't actually make sense to Felix, but he'd recognized this as one of those situations where it was better to consult others.

Additionally, Felix wanted Legionnaire's Call—the phone app tied to the Legion organization—to be upgraded and modified as well.

With his left hand, Felix navigated to the email Jay had sent him with the requirements Felix had wanted. Everything was listed out, no matter how outlandish.

Slowly, he picked through the whole thing and added those requirements to his intent for the two programs. A tedious mental read out that was more recitation without even seeing the words.

When he got to the last item that simply read "encryption protocol from a decade in the future" Felix pushed it all at his power. He wanted to upgrade those two programs first.

Felix once again felt a whine in his head as his power took all of that and translated it to something else. A demand placed upon the world and what he wanted to happen.

"Okay, seriously, Felix, that's kinda enough, ya know?" demanded a voice.

The entirety of the world had shifted to a gray color and left Felix feeling rather strange.

Looking up from the laptop, he found Uncle standing in front of him.

His brown eyes were flat with his eyebrows drawn in close over them. They were so dark; they were almost black.

His straight black hair was in a bit of a wild disarray at the moment.

"I wouldn't say so. I'm just using my power. It's not like I'll know if it's too much until after the fact," argued Felix.

Uncle stared at him, then snorted loudly with a shake of his head.

"I mean… you're not wrong. It's not like you'd know, I guess. Try to be more careful, would you? One day, I won't be able to make things work again and you'll be wondering why your toes suddenly feel like lime jello," warned the extremely terrifying magician. "Trust me, it isn't an experience you wish to enjoy. It's the kind of thing that sticks with you."

Felix grunted at that, then tried to pull on his power again to do exactly what he wanted to do.

"Oh, my shit. Did you just—I swear to fuck, Felix. I swear to— fine, whatever. Okay? Whatever," said Uncle, sounding incredibly frustrated.

A pop-up window appeared in front of Felix.

He could practically hear Uncle shouting at him through it.

Type: STUPID FUCKING PROGRAMS	**Condition**: New (Work provided)
Owner: Felix Campbell (Legion)	**Construction**: Cost $@#&)%)+! points

"How's that?! You like it!? Did it fit your

needs!?" demanded Uncle in a loud voice.

"No, it's missing points. But I'll accept it," Felix complained and then hit the accept function.

As far as Felix could tell, nothing happened. He looked at Uncle instead.

"Did it work?" he asked.

Staring at him with wide, almost-unseeing eyes, Uncle looked like he was about to lose his mind. Then he twitched once and let out a long slow breath.

Taking in several deep breaths, he looked like someone trying to not start screaming.

"So… it worked then," continued Felix.

Uncle shuddered once from head to toe and then nodded his head. Followed by shaking it.

"I can… I can see now why Runner thinks you're hilarious. I… I can see why. Yes. Yes," grumbled Uncle. "Okay! Okay. Done. Programs upgraded. Woopy dandy doo.

"Now… when the Dryads show up later tomorrow, along with the rest of the earthy things, remember to find out if any of them are single and looking for a wizard. If you're not interested in them, that is. Okay?"

"You got it. Match-maker, match-maker, make me a match," said Felix with a salute of his left hand. He was feeling particularly amused at the moment.

Uncle glanced down to Miu at his side and stared at her for several seconds. As if he were looking at someone else entirely and not Miu.

"T… treasure her. Don't let her get lost in her own head. Hers is a love that is pure and prone to meddling of others," muttered the wizard. "You're fortunate to be aware of it, so… so protect her."

Then he vanished without any sign.

The world returned to color and continued on without any hint of what'd happened.

Smiling to himself, Felix started to run his fingertips back and forth through Miu's hair. With his left hand, he opened the Legion interviews and began to read them over.

"I think I found the other Miu," whispered the psychopath. Causing him to stop before he'd even started. "I want to free her. She's… she's where I would have ended up if I hadn't gotten lucky. If I hadn't escaped."

"That's not an issue, we can do that," Felix agreed as his phone chirped at him.

Glancing to it, he saw it was a new message that'd come in.

The one he'd ignored earlier was still waiting for him.

Both Dave and Zach both want to talk to me. I imagine they want to ask if they're allowed to do something.

Hm, that'll work just fine.

Looking back to the interviews he started to read through all the names.

There were many of them. People who had all signed agreements and bartered away the future of their powers to him.

"Well… it's a veritable super sale on superheroes. I'll buy them all," proclaimed Felix with a wide smile. He flicked through the names of all the people who wanted to be scanned for powers.

Then he stopped on a single name.

One that stood out to him and brought his mind to a horrible, screeching stop.

Georgia Marin.

It was his mother's name.

Thank you, dear reader!

I'm hopeful you enjoyed reading Super Sales on Super Heroes. Please consider leaving a review, commentary, or messages. Feedback is imperative to an author's growth.

That and positive reviews never hurt.

Feel free to drop me a line at:
WilliamDArand@gmail.com

Join my mailing list for book updates: William D. Arand Newsletter

Keep up to date – Facebook: https://www.facebook.com/WilliamDArand
Patreon: https://www.patreon.com/WilliamDArand
Blog: http://williamdarand.blogspot.com/
HaremLit Group: https://www.facebook.com/groups/haremlit/
LitRPG Group: https://www.facebook.com/groups/LitRPGsociety/

If you enjoyed this book, try out the books of some of my close friends. I can heartily recommend them.

Blaise Corvin- A close and dear friend of mine. He's been there for me since I was nothing but a rookie with a single book to my name. He told me from the start that it was clear I had talent and had to keep writing. His background in European martial arts creates an accurate and detail driven action segments as well as his world building. https://www.amazon.com/Blaise-Corvin/e/B01LYK8VG5

John Van Stry- John was an author I read, and re-read, and re-read again, before I was an author. In a world of books written for everything except what I was interested in, I found that not only did I truly enjoy his writing, but his concepts as well.
In discovering he was an indie author, I realized that there was nothing separating me from being just like him. I attribute him as an influence in my own work.
He now has two pen names, and both are great.
https://www.amazon.com/John-Van-Stry/e/B004U7JY8I
Jan Stryvant-
https://www.amazon.com/Jan-Stryvant/e/B06ZY7L62L

Daniel Schinhofen- Daniel was another one of those early adopters of my work who encouraged and pushed me along. He's almost as introverted as I am, so we get along famously. He recently released a new book, and by all accounts including mine, is a well written author with interesting storylines.
https://www.amazon.com/Daniel-

Schinhofen/e/B01LXQWPZA

Made in the USA
Middletown, DE
27 September 2023

39555018R00318